BONES OF CONTENTION

Nino R. Lentini, M.D.

To: Joan, Jacki, Karl, Andrew, Alex, and Gavin.

1

June 28, 1999

Chris Fanning liked to look down. All the instruction he'd ever had in rock climbing, all the books he'd read told him not to look down. But he did it anyway, liked it and did not intend to stop. He was hanging upside down on the lower surface of a promontory, 2,000 feet above the ground. His muscles were pulled taut by the effort, his lungs sucked in the clear mountain air that supplied the oxygen to burn the glucose that powered his activities. He gazed down to ground level 2,000 feet away and saw the terrain fade away like the trough of a giant wave, only the wave was made of basalt and sedimentary rock. He exulted in his own strength, his ability to challenge the heights, come away unscathed and triumphant, reveling in his skill once again to defeat the living rock crags, bluffs, crevices and overhangs. He considered the sandstone heights to be an organic, changing entity, more stable and dependable than most people, but also imbued with a timeless need to change, grow, swell, fold, pleat, split, wear, erode, burst, rise, and then lie seemingly dormant, waiting centuries only to start the process all over again.

He used his skinny body like a spider, holding on to the most flimsy of grips that might not be apparent to anyone else. The times that he spent climbing he considered sacred, a necessary recharging of the batteries, both physical and mental, to renew him for the coming struggle with his graduate studies at the university. He felt reborn at these times of physical struggle and the element of danger added not a little to his pleasure. He also liked the way the exertion made him feel while doing it and the slight achiness the next day.

In this position he felt like a fly on the wall of time, geologic time, silent witness to the endless history waiting to be told by the ancient terrain, the history there for those who knew how to extract it. Fanning liked to challenge the rocks by climbing them, but he also liked to challenge them by digging them. His avocation was rock climbing, but his occupation was Archeologist-Paleontologist in training. He was a graduate student at a large state university in Arizona, close by the open, arid spaces he loved so well. He was a transplanted New Yorker who had moved to the southwest because of his marriage to a native of Arizona.

He looked down again, surveying the vast expanse of buttes, ledges, and fantastic rock formations, far below him, then shifted his gaze to the cloudless, phthalo blue sky above. He always felt insignificant, an intruder, in the midst of all these past eons of geologic time and evolution, culminating in the vista he observed now.

His particular love within the realm of his chosen field was the saber-toothed cat, Smilodon. He would have given his molars to make a significant find of a big cat fossil. He had been more enamored of Smilodon as a child than he was of dinosaurs, unlike most of his boyhood friends back in Queens, New York. He considered the fearsome cats to be more interesting, more mammal-like, which of course, they were. The cat was much more immediately involved in man's prehistory since they became extinct in the late Pleistocene age, some 10,000 years ago. He often imagined or even daydreamed of being one of the animals himself, hunting down and devouring his helpless prey without mercy.

However, at this moment, he started to tire, and he began to search in earnest for a suitable handhold. He used his fingers like a cat uses its whiskers, since he could often feel out a niche when none was visible to the eye.

He remembered the fantastic exhibits back at the Museum of Natural History in New York, which he used to haunt as a child in all his spare moments. How would Smilodon handle this situation? he thought.

He had, however, made one cardinal mistake in not taking a companion with whom to climb. He had difficulty finding other climbers whose schedule coincided with his.

He located a small opening in the rocks. The opening disappeared into a small tunnel-like aperture, and since it was lying in deep shade, he could not see very deeply into it. He was able, however, to gain a solid handhold, but when he peered more closely into the hole he found himself face to face with the biggest western diamondback rattlesnake he had ever seen. He looked directly into the beast's eyes and was transfixed to see the animal coiled in preparation for a strike. He'd not heard the famous rattler warning sound of the vibration of the tail segments, but he heard it now. He tried to retrace his steps, so to speak, but he was not fast enough for what happened next. The startled serpent struck at Fanning's head. The presence of Fanning's body must have obscured the snake's view of the abyss below, and in that instant its ancient brain hadn't comprehended the vast height from which it struck. The beast hit Fanning in the head with its own head, then hurtled down the precipice while Fanning's backward surge left him dangling by one hand. In the hyper-excitement of the moment Fanning had not even felt the hit on his forehead. He started to tire more seriously now, but forced himself by sheer muscle power to stop oscillating, arch his body upwards, secure a toehold, and take a half minute to rest and assess his situation and next moves.

The above events had only taken a few seconds. He was annoyed by a trickle of what he thought was sweat dripping into his eyes. The salty fluid continued on down to his mouth where he could taste it. It was thicker than sweat and more voluminous than he ever remembered sweating. He was thin, muscular and in excellent physical shape. He rarely perspired to the degree where the sweat dripped down his forehead. He licked his lips and tasted what seemed to be blood. He shook his head and was horrified to see a few drops of red splatter down onto his shoulder. Out of the corner of his eye he saw what was unmistakably blood.

He'd seen pictures and even a few people who had suffered snakebite. It wasn't pretty. He had once seen almost an entire leg below the knee of a hiker who had been snakebitten. It turned black, green, and yellow with gangrene and infection. The pain was agonizing. He imagined his forehead starting to change color and the infection extending to his eyes, blinding him. He had to get out of there, but he was really exhausted now. He didn't know if there were more snakes in that hole, but going back the way he had come would take too long, and he would exert himself for too long a period of time, pumping venom into his bloodstream the whole time. He knew that a rattlesnake bite rarely kills an adult, but with one so large and his exertions at a maximum, he thought he'd have a better chance climbing up the ledge and taking his chances on finding no more snakes. Trouble was, now he didn't know if he could force himself up over the ledge. He demanded that his body obey him and scratched himself up an inch at a time. He let the thought of Margie and the kids dominate his consciousness. He suppressed the pain and fear he felt. Struggling, he topped the overhang and with the last ounce of his energy he willed himself to the edge where the rock turned vertical. Then with one more herculean effort he forced his aching muscles to follow his command and pull him over the top.

He breathed a few deep ones and laid his torso on the ground with his legs still hanging over the edge and rested. But he couldn't rest too long. That venom would start to kick in soon. He thought in desperation that maybe he should have just let himself drop down the 2,000 feet and save himself the agonizing death he thought would come now. As he waited and nothing happened he realized the blood came not from the snake's fangs but from the impact of its snout on the vascular skin of his forehead. The beast had started his strike, then seeing where he was headed, had veered slightly and grazed his target. But his large momentum due to his size carried him over the cliff and out into the abyss.

Fanning had to rest a few minutes and as the seconds flew he rubbed the forehead where he bled. The blood flow slowed now and he experienced no pain, no nausea, and no weakness. In fact, he started to feel better, stronger, more confident. He should have felt a stinging or burning, some kind of pain if the snake had actually bitten him. His spirits rose. He started to go over in his mind some of the facts he knew about rattlesnake envenomation. The bite of the western diamondback rattler was rarely fatal to a full sized adult in good physical condition. The venom contained enzymes that lysed or dissolved tissue protein, caused hemorrhage and hemolysis or rupture and breakdown of red blood cells. In those cases which are fatal, circulatory collapse and heart failure are caused by excessive bleeding and pooling of blood at the envenomation site. Obviously this would be more serious in a small child bitten by a big snake because that situation would represent a relatively large dose of venom. Bites around the head are potentially more dangerous than those in the extremities because of the great blood supply of the head and the greater ability to absorb the poison. A bite into fat or a bite deflected by bone may be less serious than a strike directly into a blood vessel, say an artery or vein. The point of entry of the fang into the skin is not the location of the opening in the fang. That is, the small opening through which the venom is injected is not at the tip of the bone so that the bite must penetrate at least some distance into the tissue for envenomation to occur. Virulent bacteria in the snake's mouth or on the skin of the victim can lead rapidly to severe infection, tissue death, and generalized sepsis (infection spread throughout the bloodstream) leading to death or massive tissue necrosis requiring amputation of the part.

Fanning knew all this and he knew that it would take him at least an hour to climb back down the cliff by the route he had already taken. He also knew it would take a half day to go down the cliff the back way, circle around and reach his jeep. Either way, he knew he couldn't make it if he'd really been bitten. And all the activity would surely drive the poison throughout his entire system and make him toxic. However, as the minutes passed he didn't feel faint or weak. He had no pain in his head and he noticed that the bleeding had stopped. For these reasons he began to have some hope that he hadn't even been bitten at all. After 15 or 20 minutes he became elated, because he was now sure he was in the clear and he figured out the likely scenario of what had really occurred. He wondered what had become of the snake. He had no animosity towards the animal. It was only being true to its nature, having felt threatened by Fanning's proximity to its isolated den. How many more snakes were there in the tunnel? How deep into the rock did the tunnel go? Was there a snake pit, a cave under his very feet containing hundreds of the slithery, fanged creatures? He thought he'd like to return some time with a buddy to further explore this area. In any case he was going to keep quiet about what happened because he didn't want those beastly rattlesnake hunters cleaning out the area of the critters for their obscene roundup in which the animals were skinned alive, roasted, decapitated and made into ornaments and trinkets for the entertainment of some redneck ignoramuses and their girlfriends.

He imagined what a confrontation between his favorite fossil, Smilodon, and a big rattler would be like. Perhaps the Smilodon would be smart enough to avoid the serpent. In a showdown he had no doubt the cat would win the fight. However, he might be wounded, or made lame so as to be unable to hunt and would itself become prey, or starve to death. Certainly the two had inhabited these parts at the same time and must have come into conflict on some occasions. He imagined what might happen if the Smilodon was to fall inadvertently into a pit containing several hundred of the vipers. Fanning thought, hell, that could even happen to me here and now. He looked for a stick he could use to test the ground before setting foot on it. He didn't want to fall into a snake pit if one existed under his feet.

He lay on the rock ledge again and extended himself over the rim just enough so he could see the ground below him. He searched for the snake that must have sailed through the air and hit bottom directly 2,000 feet below. Try as he might, he could not find the creature. He looked carefully and thought he could discern a trail in the dust leading to the base of the cliff. He couldn't be sure. He contrasted his likely appearance if he'd fallen that distance, and came away with renewed respect for the hardiness of the creatures of the wild. He wondered what it would have been like to be one of the early men who lived here, when the now extinct Smilodon roamed free. He questioned whether he could survive out here by himself with no food save that which he could catch himself and no shelter except that which he could make himself. He pondered the extensive system of safety nets with which modern man has surrounded himself. That was one reason he liked to push himself physically against the elements, the forces of nature. He abhorred the idea of growing soft, fat, complacent, and comfortable. He planned one day to stay out here for a week or two by himself with minimal supplies and test himself against this land and the weather, the sun, the heat, the variation in temperature from 115 degrees in the daytime to the bitter cold nights, the snakes, scorpions, and the terrible aloneness of the place.

Having had his fill of adventures for the day, Fanning picked himself up and began the walk back to his jeep the long way, down the back side of the cliff then around the base for 6 or so miles. Night fell around him on his walk back to the jeep and he had to be careful of his footfalls lest he step on another rattler or crevice. A broken leg out here alone might just cook his goose.

Luckily there was a bright moon and a sky full of stars that lit his path. He contemplated the universe and the space-time continuum. What was it he read recently? The universe might be anywhere from 8 to 20 billion years old, depending on something called the Hubble constant which related the size and age of the universe to the rate of expansion of the remnants of the big bang. My God, he thought, these were the only questions worth considering. The fundamentals, the basics which had been pondered by the best minds of the world from ancient times to now. But we're coming closer to an answer and one day we should understand all there is to know. These thoughts did not conflict with his deeply felt religious feelings, for he had been raised a good Catholic.

He spied something gleaming white in the red sand. He approached it cautiously, his club at the ready. Drawing near, he recognized a familiar shape and texture. He crouched down on his knees. This looked like a human os calcis or heel bone sticking up out of the sand just as plain as the nose on your face. What was a human heel bone doing here in the desert? What was attached? Was the rest of a human skeleton buried down there under the soil? He remembered a tornado had ripped through here only a few days ago. Fanning had a sudden, creepy feeling as if someone were watching him. As he jogged away from this place he marked it in his memory so that he might return with his friend and fellow grad student, Jake Hamilton. For now, he was glad to reach his jeep where he kept some beef jerky and fruit juice. All at once he was famished and bone dry. Between bites of his snack he used the car's headlights to write down the specific directions to the location of the os calcis so as to find it easily when he returned. His eye caught some movement out beyond the light of the headlights. He had that spooky feeling again that someone's or something's eyeballs were regarding him from out in the dark somewhere. He went to the rearview mirror to assess the damage to his forehead. All he could see was some dry, caked blood on the skin and some on his brown hair. I sure bled like stink for all that's showing now! he thought. He touched the dried blood with his fingers. There was a little soreness but not much.

He'd stayed out here way past the time he'd planned to, and now he hoped he could find his way back to the freeway through these dirt roads that all looked the same at night. He thought of Margie sitting at home with the two kids waiting for him and wondering if he was all right. He vowed never to do such a fool thing again. At the very least he would not go rock climbing again without a buddy. On the other hand he determined to take the children climbing just as soon as they were big enough. Matter of fact he intended to try and get Margie interested. She was wiry, intelligent, athletic, smart, and game. She only stayed home today because their older child had a low grade fever and a sore throat. She pushed him to go anyway but she didn't know he would be alone. She thought he'd be with his friend, fellow grad student Jake Hamilton. She was usually pretty understanding but she might be pissed off tonight and he didn't blame her. He wished he could call her on one of those nifty cellular phones. But that was out of the question on his graduate student's budget. Of course, Margie's parents were as rich as Midas but he didn't like to ask them for anything nor did he like it when they lavished presents or money on Margie or the children. But a cell phone, that would be "way cool."

~~~

When he finally reached home hours later, disheveled with a cut on his forehead, Margie was predictably upset. It took him a lot of explaining to reassure her that he was all right and that he wouldn't pull such a bonehead stunt again. The children were already asleep and he went in to peek at them. "How's Jerry's fever?" he asked. Margie replied that he was better and would probably return to school in the morning.

He ate a late dinner of homemade chicken cordon bleu, corn on the cob, creamed spinach, oven baked dinner rolls, blueberry cobbler and coffee. Chris settled down with his wife in front of their fireplace. He added logs until he had an inferno going and proceeded to tell her about the heel bone he found in the dirt out in the desert. He opined that it appeared as if it had been freshly buried. He told her about the strange feeling he'd had that he was being watched.

"Yeah, you know who was watching you," she exclaimed. "It was the buzzards. They were waiting for you to die so they could pluck your eyeballs out. You know, that's where they start, the eyeballs, most tasty to a buzzard, of course."

"How do you know so much about buzzards?" he asked. "And besides, the feeling was still there after it got dark and buzzards are not known to fly around in the dark."

"Yeah, they must have special night flying buzzards, specially sent to pick your bones clean when you fell off the rock you were climbing."

"My, you are awfully moribund tonight."

"Well, what do you expect? You come home hours late looking like you were run over by a truck. You tell me you were nearly snakebitten, almost fell off a cliff 2,000 feet to your death, and now you say I'm moribund. I thought I was going to be a young widow with two children to care for." She paused. "I'm going to bed."

"OK, good night honey." He picked up the telephone.

"And whom are you calling at this hour, may I ask?"

"I'm going to wake up Jake and tell him what I found. See if he wants to dig it out with me."

"It's awfully late to be calling now isn't it?"

"No, he's a night owl, and besides, how many times has he called me late at night for less important reasons?"

Margie scampered up to bed while Fanning made his phone call. They discussed the events of the day including the find that Fanning had made of a perfectly preserved human heel bone sticking up out of the sand. He also related to Jake the peculiar feeling of being observed by someone or something. Jake chalked it up to an adrenalin rush resulting from his climbing experience, but was definitely interested in the bone find and promised to accompany Chris on the next free day they both had to investigate.

~~~

The following day, the heel bone was all Fanning could think of. He was intrigued by the presence of the find in that unlikely spot, but who was to say what fossil was to be found where. Except he was sure it was not a fossil. Further, he could not shake the idea that someone was watching him out at the remote desert location. All his senses, all his cognitive skills, told him that was foolish, but he could not get over that feeling of having been watched.

Fanning had the type of personality that whenever everything was going relatively well in his life, that's when the feeling of impending doom overcame him. He'd learned not to rejoice too much in his triumphs nor to be too disappointed at inevitable failures that all human beings suffer. He also had the fatalistic outlook that he should pray for things from some inanimate object, say a statue of a horse, or a painting of a tree. That way when he didn't get it, he would not be disappointed. Whoever heard of being granted wishes from a horse statue or a tree picture? Fanning was independent, self-reliant, intelligent, and possessed of a personality that could allow him to become involved in a mission a hundred percent to the exclusion of all else if he cared for it enough.

Since he could not climb every day, he took up running. In an hour he could run 7 or 8 miles and stay in shape. He had been a member of the track team in high school and undergrad school back east, more for the exercise than anything else. As in everything he did, he liked to push himself to the extreme. And so it was with running. Previously, he entered as many marathon runs as he could but the rigors of graduate school put a stop to that. He also found that he had to make certain concessions to his marriage with Margie and the kids, but this he didn't mind at all. He was as devoted to those children as any man could be. He remembered as a child when he would overdo the running and develop leg pains. Luckily that had turned out to be only shin splints. But as an incidental finding on the X-rays it had been discovered that he had a benign bone condition in his left tibia (leg bone) called non ossifying fibroma. More on this later.

~~~

At the first opportunity the two grad students made a trip back to the spot where Fanning first found the bone protruding in the sand. Everything was as Fanning had remembered it. Jake whistled, "Yep, it's human all right, and from its size and the muscle markings on it I'd say it was male."

"I believe you are right," Fanning agreed. "I was so excited and tired the other day I didn't think about whether it was male or female." They set to work in earnest. The day started out as it had the previous time Chris had been out here. But, soon the weather became hotter and just continued to heat up as the day progressed.

The two men became more engrossed and silent as they worked. They had carefully excavated one lower extremity from foot to hip joint. It laid prone, the knee cap pointing directly downward. The other leg was underneath it, but rotated so that the foot was directed medially or inward.

As they paused for a cold drink from their thermoses Jake mused, "Do you think we could be in any danger?"

Chris replied, "Are you referring to the feeling I had when I was last out here, that I was being watched? No, I don't think so, but the next time we come out here maybe we ought to bring a rifle."

"Good idea," Jake agreed.

They worked on, slowly, laboriously, revealing the back of a pelvis and sacrum. The bones were white and clean, glistening in the sun.

"You know Jake, something is peculiar here."

"Yeah I noticed it too but I wanted to see how long it would take for you to pick up on it. There's no soft tissue here, no skin, no hair, no muscle, no ligaments, for as well preserved as these bones are. See here, the joints just kind of fall apart when you move the bones. It doesn't add up."

~~~

After several more brutal hours in the sun, they had the entire skeleton exposed. They stood back, wiped the sweat off, and surveyed their work. A peculiar smile crossed Jake's face. "You know Chris, it kind of reminds me of you. All lanky and long boned."

"Yeah, right," Chris replied, only mildly amused. "Come on, let's get this thing described on paper, photographed, then pack up and get out of here. This heat is killing me."

"OK, OK, I'm drenched too. I need a cool shower and something frosty to drink."

Chris made the notations in a logbook and then snapped the photos. As they packed up to leave, Chris noticed something protruding from the hard soil next to the recently excavated skeleton. They must have uncovered it with their feet while digging. Hamilton was already in the jeep revving up the motor.

"Hey, come on, I thought you wanted to get out of here," Jake yelled. Chris didn't reply. Jake waited another minute then came on over. He looked up at Jake and said, "Uh oh, I think we got another one here."

In spite of their exhaustion, the heat, the dirt, and the vague possibility of danger, they set out once again to excavate the new skeleton carefully, meticulously, avoiding any injury to it. As the work progressed they could tell this was a smaller, more delicate skeleton, with less distinct muscle markings on the bones. It was in a supine position whereas the first one had been prone. "Looks like this one's female," Jake asserted. Chris only grunted and continued working.

As they excavated the female skeleton, it was apparent from the pelvis that she had borne at least one or two children. A disturbing familiarity of the skeletal structure bothered Fanning. He noticed a slightly incongruous protrusion of the mandible, the lower jaw, a slight condition which affected his wife. He was beginning to have a totally different sense of this whole affair, as if somehow he was meant to find these two skeletons. Maybe the sun was getting to him. Maybe he was finally flipping out from too much work. What would Margie think?

Suddenly he jumped back in astonishment knocking his pal backwards head over heels. He broke into a cold sweat in spite of the heat.

"What in hell has got into you?" Jake demanded, checking his limbs for injury.

Chris sat down and regained his composure. "When Margie was pregnant with our last baby, Josie, there was a question as to whether she could deliver the baby through the birth canal. Apparently sometimes the baby can be too big to pass through. Well, what they do is X-ray the mother's pelvis, then measure the largest dimension of the baby which is the head. Then they compare the dimensions of the bony pelvis to see whether there is room enough for delivery. Jake, I saw those X-rays and I can tell you there are identical markings on these pubic bones in the exact same places as on her X-rays. I'm telling you they are identical."

"Now wait a minute. Just what are you saying? Are you saying this is a duplicate of Margie's skeleton? It can't be hers because we both know you left her home with the kids, alive, and inside her skin. And just what the hell else could it be but a coincidence?"

"Look, Jake, remember when you remarked that the other set of bones could very well be my twin or something to that effect? Well, I laughed it off at first, but the more I think about it the more I think you're right. That male skeleton is so much like mine it could be a twin. I mean there must be millions or at least thousands of people who have the same bone structure, size, shape, muscle attachment markings. But now with this find, this female roughly the same size as Margie, and with those pelvic markings the same, well, that's getting too damn close for coincidence. Don't you think?"

Jake mulled it over a moment or two. "Look Chris, all we really have here are two skeletons. The fact that there is a superficial resemblance to you and Margie is probably totally insignificant. I mean how could that possibly be? What could that possibly mean? I admit it's spooky, but I think you're making too much of it."

That seemed to pacify Chris for the time being. They continued to work, carefully excavating with trowel, spatula, and brush. At regular intervals they snapped photos for the file and recorded in the logbook all the pertinent details of position, orientation of the bones, soil type and pH; in short, all the pertinent details to allow another observer who had not visited the site to understand as much as they did about the find. They loaded the skeletons into their vehicle, careful to wrap each bone with cloth.

~~~

On the way home the two young scientists were quiet for a time. Chris broke the silence.

"Nuts," he said. "I'm jumping to conclusions. We'll reconstruct the skeletons, we'll study the histology, we'll carbon date the material and we'll likely come up with some stupendous scientific discovery. We'll probably become very famous. Think we might be able to retrieve some DNA and identify these two birds, Jake?"

"Yeah, in their excellent state of preservation we should be able to do a DNA analysis, but something puzzles me. If these bones are so fresh, so recent, what happened to all the soft tissue? I mean, there's not even a shred of rotten skin, or muscle, no fascia, no decomposing viscera, no trace of eyeballs, no heart, no lungs. What happened to them? And there's no stench. Every dead body I've ever seen has a stink to it you had to wear nose plugs. So what's happening here?"

They pondered that for a while and then agreed they must be on to something new, something unique, a discovery for Christ's sake.

"Do me a favor, Jake," Chris said. "Don't mention any of this to Margie before I do, OK? I'd like to have this pinned down more firmly before letting her know anything."

Jake agreed, although he repeated his opinion that there was really nothing to tell.

Jake continued, "Since you were the first to find the bones you ought to have the first say in letting anyone else in on it. We can't very well do all the studies ourselves. We'll need genetic studies, electron microscopy, dental chart analysis and carbon dating. Who are you prepared to call in on this?"

Chris replied, "I hadn't thought about that but I think the fewer who know the better off we'll be, at least at first. Don't ask me why, I still think there's an outside possibility we could be sticking our necks out. There may be some danger here. We may have discovered a double murder."

"Want to tell the cops?"

"No. Not yet anyway. Let's wait until we have more to go on, one way or the other."

~~~

18

At the university the next day, the two started out early to study the bodies represented only by their bones. Who were these two unfortunates? How had they come to be buried so superficially and what could account for the beautiful state of preservation? What had happened to all traces of soft tissue if the specimens were so fresh? Oh well, they thought. That's what they were here to find out. So let's get started.

First they laid the bones out on the shiny stainless steel dissecting table and gently washed them off, cleaning off the residuals of dirt and sand with a little waterpik-like spray. Then they carefully dried the individual bones with a warm air blower which was actually a hair dryer. Next they laid the bones out in the supine position as if the bodies were flat on their backs. At this point they made measurements to estimate the life-sized height of each skeleton. The two young scientists noticed the absence of any articular cartilage in the joints as well as the absence of the intervertebral disc material.

Jake mused, "This guy measures out to about five feet ten and a half inches. That would translate to a height of about six feet when he was alive."

Chris absorbed that information in silence. He was just six feet tall himself.

"OK, what do you get on the female?" asked Chris.

"Let's see, about, no exactly, five feet five inches."

"You know Jake, nothing we've done so far has given me any reason to relax. The more we do, the more we find out, the more spooky this business becomes. Margie is five feet six and a half inches. That skeleton could be her sister, except for that irregularity around the skull and mandible."

"Or twin," Jake muttered.

"What?" asked Chris.

"Nothing, nothing," Jake replied a little sheepishly.

"OK, let's add up what we have so far. Skeleton number one is male by virtue of the larger size, by the more distinct and heavier muscle attachment marks, and by the generally bulkier heft of the bones. The pelvis also confirms that. The male pelvis is a more elongated, narrowed shape, while the female pelvis is more broad, with a wider pelvic outlet below for the obvious reasons. The female skeleton is in general smaller, lighter, with more delicate bones, less severe muscle attachment marks. More like the infantile skeleton, which is not to say more infantile."

"Now, where do you want to take a little block of bone for a biopsy?"

"May as well take it from the upper inner aspect of the arm bone, the humerus, so as to do as little damage as possible."

"OK."

With care, Fanning used a surgical bone biopsy needle to extract a core of bone measuring 2 millimeters in diameter by 1/2 centimeter in length. Imbedding the sample in paraffin, then soaking it in an acid bath, it would take two or three days to decalcify the specimens. That is, render the bone soft enough so that it could be cut into thin slices accurately and cleanly with a minimal of distortion. The slices then could be stained with pigments to highlight the structure and contrast the different components for study under the microscope.

~~~

"The formula confirms the fact of maleness for number one and femaleness for number two," Jake said. He referred to a forensic formula used to characterize skeletons as most probably male or female in police work where only bones of a victim are available. Males come out with numbers in one range and females with numbers in another range. At the middle the numbers overlap but a rough idea can be secured as to maleness or femaleness of a skeleton. In addition the bit of information gleaned is only one part of the total in identifying an unknown skeleton.

"Jake."

"Yeah, Chris?"

"I'm going to the obstetrician who delivered my first child. I'm going to make him get out those pelvic X-rays of Margie's and go over them with him."

"So?"

"So what do you think?"

"I still think you're barking up the wrong tree, or swimming up the wrong Fallopian tube, so to speak."

"But I'm gonna do it anyway," Chris insisted.

"Yeah, yeah, go ahead and satisfy yourself, but tell me in the meantime, why don't you decide who you are going to get to do a DNA analysis on these two dudes?"

"Well, the obvious choice would be the Dean of DNA, old Professor Karahsha. Boy, but I hate to include him on this until we know a little more what we're into. He's such a strange duck."

"But who else knows as much about DNA identification as him? Christ, he knows as much or more than old Victor McKusick at Hopkins."

"Yeah I know Jake, but he really gives me the creeps. But we really ought to get his advice before the DNA left in these dudes completely rots away. Hell that may already have happened. Look Jake, I never got along well with that weirdo. I had to take one of his classes and he is the strangest human being I have ever come across. What say you talk to him and make the DNA analysis arrangements and I'll cut you in as full partner if this turns out to be anything significant. OK? But first let's see what DNA studies we can do with the help of his post doc fellow, his name escapes me right now."

"OK," Jake agreed. "You know Chris, a panel of so-called scientific experts including Victor McKusick just handed down a recommendation that DNA ID not be allowed in court cases for the purpose of convicting suspects from blood or semen, or other tissue DNA analysis."

"But that was for criminal cases and the panel's beef was the lack of quality control. It in no way invalidates the use of properly collected and processed DNA for purposes of identification," Chris replied.

2

Fanning went over the skeletons carefully and repeatedly. He and Jake didn't want to let anyone else in on their find just yet. The two weren't sure what they were dealing with and they wanted to avoid a lot of explanations about the skeletons. Given their specialty interest in paleontology, they decided to work on them right out in the open. They figured that would be perfectly natural and if anyone asked they could make up a plausible story to cover themselves for a while anyway.

As he worked, Fanning noticed something that at once interested him and added further to his unease. There was a visible lesion on the male skeleton's left distal tibia, the region near the ankle on the inner surface of the bone. This irregularity on the surface of the bone reminded him of something he'd seen somewhere once before. As he thought about it he remembered his own bone problem when as a child of around fifteen he had sprained his ankle severely jumping out of a tree. It was so severe that his mother had taken him to the ER for an X-ray. No fracture was found but an incidental lesion of a fibrous cortical defect was discovered in the cortex near the end of his leg bone, or tibia. He was assured by the doctors at the time that this represented a harmless condition called a benign cortical defect, also called non-ossifying fibroma. It never gave him any symptoms and he was encouraged to ignore it and continue with his normal teenage sports activities, except for jumping out of trees, of course. The bony lesion in the skeleton he'd discovered in the desert was in the left leg in the same location in the bone, and even on the identical side of the bone cortex, that is, toward the inner side of his ankle adjacent to his other leg. As he examined the bone it reminded him of the X-ray of his own leg since he had pretty well memorized it being the intelligent, curious youngster that he was. The more he pored over the bone lesion and the tibia itself, the more he had the feeling that he was looking at his own bone. But damn it, how could that be?

He knew that the condition was not very common, so what were the chances of finding a skeleton, not a fossil, with the same bone lesion, in the same location of the same left leg as his? He thought it peculiar but couldn't explain it. He wondered whether the owner, while living, had been aware of the lesion he carried, whether it was ever X-rayed while he was alive, and in general who this might have been in life. He felt a certain kinship with the unfortunate corpse due to the similarity of the lesions they both carried in their tibias, but at the same time he felt a certain unease. How had the body gotten there? Was it buried deeply by its murderer and then exposed by the recent tornado? But who? And why? Was this just a fortuitous coincidence or was this a beginning to some mystery that he might be better off without? Well, he knew one thing. He planned to dig up the old X-ray of his leg and compare it with this one. He hoped his mother had not thrown it away. He was glad he'd insisted on having a copy of his own, since most hospitals held onto them for only about five years due to lack of storage space, then discarded them.

~~~

Back at home, Chris called his mom in New York and asked for her to dig up his old X-ray films of the leg lesion. Of course the first thing his mom wanted to know was whether he was having any trouble with his leg. The second thing she wanted to know was when she would see him next. After reassuring her that he wanted the films for academic reasons only, he went to the X-ray Department of the university hospital and had the newly found skeleton's tibia X-rayed. After that, he conferred with the staff radiologist most expert in the radiology of bone tumors. He was reassured that the lesion on the films was a garden variety lesion commonly known as non-ossifying fibroma, or if confined to the cortex, the outer hard shell of bone, it was called a fibrous cortical defect.

~~~

When the old X-ray arrived from New York, Fanning returned to the radiologist and had him study the lesion on Chris' films and the ones of the newly found skeleton. Dr. Henry Vivian contemplated the two sets of films quietly for several minutes.

"Damn if I can tell these apart. You are telling me that these films here in my right hand were taken some fifteen years ago? Yes, yes, the date confirms that even though it is hard to read. And these in my left hand were shot just a few days ago, taken from bones you found out in the desert? Well, they are identical except for the age difference in the bones. That is, the ones from your fossil find come from an adult skeleton. The ones of your own leg bone, the fifteen year old films, are representative of a teenager, I'd say fourteen or fifteen years old. But the skeleton's owner would appear to be one and the same person. The lesions are identical in location, size, shape, and orientation. See here, the fibroma is sort of oval shaped with a bit of a pointed top end. The rounded lower end is in the identical spot on both sets of films. The part that comes to a point like the upper part of a rain drop is likewise at the top of the lesion in both sets of pictures. The sizes are just about identical. Adjusting for the different X-ray techniques used ten years ago and the slight differences in magnification I would say the two films represent the same fibrous cortical defect in the same bone. I don't know how to explain it but it looks to me the films are of the same person."

"But how could that be, Dr. Vivian? I found this one here in your left hand in the desert, buried under several inches of sand. This tibia belonged to someone who is now dead. The other one in your right hand is mine, taken of my left leg when I was a kid. I still have the bone in my leg and I'm still alive, damn it."

"Take it easy, my boy. I have an idea. Let's X-ray your leg now and see what it looks like. We can compare it with your old film and the one made from your fossil."

"I keep telling you, Dr. Vivian, it is not a fossil. The bone I found is bone. It is a recently deceased human being. It is not a fossil, which takes thousands or millions of years to develop as the bone matrix is leached out by running water and replaced by mineral content so as to turn the specimen into stone. This is not the case with my find. This one is still made out of bone."

"All right, all right, don't get so technical, I'm not a paleontologist like you. I'm just a radiologist."

Fanning looked away from the films he was holding. "OK, I'm sorry. I didn't mean to jump on you like that."

"It's OK, kid. I learned something. Come on, let's take that X-ray of your leg."

The films were snapped in a jiffy, three views: AP, lateral, and oblique. It seemed, to Chris, an eternity before they were developed even though it took only a minute and a half. When the films came out the two men quickly hung them all up in sequence on the X-ray view box.

"Now, this is your old film from fifteen years ago on the left. In the middle we have the new find from the dig site, not a fossil, and on the right your own leg roentgenogram that we just took."

"Why do you call it a roentgenogram?"

"Because Roentgen is the man who discovered X-rays. Now let's compare these films."

He mused over the three sets of films for a few minutes while Fanning looked on.

"Well, what do you think?" Fanning asked after what seemed an interminable time.

"I don't know how to explain it but these are all the same. The location in the bone, the size, the shape, the orientation of the lesion is identical. I know I said it but I don't understand it."

"So what does it mean, Dr. Vivian? I don't understand it either. Is it just chance? Accident? Fortuitous? What?"

"I simply don't know, Mr. Fanning, but I wouldn't make too much of it."

"Easy for you to say. It's not your bones showing up in the desert while I still have use for them in my own leg. How could it be? Don't make too much of it you say? Well I have news for you Doc."

"Oh, what news? What is it, son?"

Fanning was annoyed by this attitude he considered condescending. "I have another one."

"Another one what?"

"Another skeleton."

"Well, what of it? You dug up another skeleton, so what?"

"This one has markings on it that I think correspond to markings on my wife's skeleton."

"How do you know? What part of the skeleton is similar? Do you have radiological training? Why don't you bring it in so we can X-ray it like we did your leg and compare it?"

"It's the pelvis," Fanning replied. "And no, I don't have radiological training." Fanning was becoming more annoyed at the guy's attitude. "Right after she had our first child I had an opportunity to inspect her pelvic films. The OB doctor did a study on her called pelvimetry to determine the size of the birth canal in comparison to the baby's head."

"Yes, I'm familiar with pelvimetry," the radiologist said dryly with a touch of annoyance appearing in his voice now.

Ignoring the sarcasm, Fanning went on. "Well, when they took the films of her pelvis I had a chance to go over them with the obstetrician. He showed me the measurements and all. Turns out there was enough room for passage. But the really interesting thing was the markings on the superior pubic rami, near the midline. They were so distinctive the OB pointed them out to me. They are not unusual in themselves but the second skeleton I found yesterday has the exact same markings in the same places, the same size and exactly the same shape."

"Oh surely you exaggerate. Look, when did your wife give birth?"

"My oldest is 6 years old."

"I believe we may have those films in storage if they were taken here. Were they taken at this hospital?"

"Yes, yes they were."

"OK, good. I'll get a technician to pull them up out of storage for us." Dr. Vivian lifted the telephone receiver and asked his chief technician to search out the films from storage in the basement.

While they waited, Fanning couldn't help but betray his anxiety. "What do you think it means, Dr. Vivian?"

"I really don't know. But in the meantime why don't you go get that female pelvis so we can examine it firsthand, and then snap some X-rays of it for a basis of comparison."

After Fanning left to collect the pelvis, Dr. Vivian scratched his head in thought while he stared into space. When the technician brought Margie's film jacket to him he pulled out the pelvimetry film and hung them up on his X-ray view box. He had several minutes to study them since Fanning went to the archeology lab to retrieve the pelvis. When Chris returned the radiologist was still sitting there studying 6 year old films of Margie's pelvis, chin cupped in his hand and a distracted, thoughtful look on his face. He appeared to be daydreaming. Fanning had to interrupt his reverie by clearing his throat and announcing he was back with the pelvis.

Dr. Vivian regarded it with suspicion. "Looks like real bone, not some fossil all replaced with mineral matter." Fanning didn't know if this was another dig or not and he elected to overlook it. "The area in question certainly seems similar to the one on the X-ray. This lesion is not so common. What is strange is the very close resemblance it has to the old X-rays in regards to size, location, shape and orientation. For academic purposes, let's go ahead and X-ray the pelvis and see what it looks like on film since we can't see into it with our naked eyes."

The pelvis was filmed and the two men anxiously hung the new pictures up on the view box alongside the old ones. Neither one said anything for a few moments.

"There we go again." Fanning could restrain himself no more. He looked to the other man as if to say, are you satisfied? They were identical, they both agreed.

3

The puzzle vexed him, the more he thought about it. How could adult human bones, or what appeared to be adult human bones, be so young, so recently dead that they are not carbon datable, yet are so perfect, so well preserved with no evidence of any soft tissue present in any degree of decay? Why would these, obviously not fossils, be found in an area in which real fossils had been found? They had rested just under the surface of the soil, most of which had been blown away by the recent tornado. Was it meant for him to find the bones by someone or something? Could they have been picked clean by animals? But then they would have had to be subsequently buried and who would do that? What if ants or worms had gotten to them after the bones were buried? Chris was not aware that ants or worms could pick a body so clean of its soft tissues so as to remove every trace. These were like prepared laboratory produced skeletons commercially sold to medical schools. They were in an excellent state of preservation, white, gleaming in the bright laboratory light. The ridges and grooves for muscular attachment were readily visible and there were no extraneous marks such as those that would be made by animal teeth, claws, or blunt instruments.

X-rays of the skulls and other bones showed no flaws. There was no evidence of growth arrest, trauma, no sign of infection such as osteomyelitis or tuberculosis. Of course Fanning was at a loss to explain the fibrous cortical defect or the similarities to the pelvic skeleton in Margie's films. And in spite of himself he was beginning to feel a certain kinship with the former owner of the male bones due to the similarity of the tibial cortical defect. It was not so much that the condition of fibrous cortical defect was very serious, but his mother refused to give him permission to engage in any organized sports at school. She was afraid of him injuring his leg in spite of the doctor's reassurance that he could do anything he wanted. But this early frustration gave him a fierce determination to succeed at anything he tried, a determination he might not otherwise have had. In high school much to his mother's distress he pushed himself to be a cross country runner and even won some local meets. Thereby he satisfied himself with his ability, and when he was thus reassured he turned his efforts to other endeavors, mainly academic. Later, he marshaled his talents to win Margie over. This was no mean feat since the two were from completely different social classes. Margie's father was the richest man Fanning had ever known, having made several fortunes in real estate and the stock market.

Fanning was aware of a member of the Department of Anthropology who had made a rather impressive reputation for himself in the art of clay modeling restoration of human faces starting with a skull as a point of departure. He had developed the technique first with prehistoric fossils, in which it was desirable to estimate what a naked Cro-Magnon or Neanderthal skull might look like if the muscle, fascia, skin, appendages, eyes, and hair could be restored.

Having succeeded in that endeavor he had turned his talent to forensic restorations. Mostly the procedure was adapted for criminal investigations in cases of missing people whose bones, when finally located, could not be positively identified. In recent years the technique had been applied to skulls found in mass graves where there was suspicion of political murders as in Argentina, Chile, Nicaragua, and El Salvador. The process had proven valuable in reconstructing faces of peasant people who had never had any dental work and so did not have any dental records on file. He had become so good at it that on several occasions he had taken photographs of the finished products, suitably embellished by draping them in a shirt and jacket. He had then sent the photos back to relatives in the above mentioned countries. He had been surprised to learn that the relatives had thought their loved ones had been found alive because of the startling resemblance. He'd had to disappoint them by revealing that they were only restorations built on the basis of the original skulls by applying modeling clay to simulate the facial muscles of expression, the nasal cartilages, the flesh of the lips, the skin creases, the mouth, the eyes, the forehead wrinkles, and even the ridges of the supraorbital eminences supporting the eyebrows. Of course, all of these features could not approach the lifelike without the reality of the eyes. The eyes were the key. The eyes brought expression to the face making it eerily alive and creating the illusion of a sentient, living brain behind the orbits. His name was Gaspare, Augie Gaspare, and he had taken the dry scientific process to a new level of artistic expression. Gaspare liked to think he presented a sort of a new life for the poor murdered wretches. And in a way he was establishing a memorial where there would otherwise have been none. His work was exacting, precise, and time consuming. The artistic component was by far the most important element in his success. After making an old fashioned plaster of paris cast of the male skull and then using that as a mold to create an accurate replica, Chris Fanning brought the two, the original and the copy, to Gaspare's studio-lab.

"Oh I'm pretty busy, Chris, I'll get to it when I can."

As Gaspare worked on his current project, his knife molded, shaped, formed, and sculpted the clay, bringing dimension and structure to the work. The facial form took on a presence even as Fanning watched. He knew he was watching a master at work.

"What are you working on?" he asked.

"This is one of those unfortunate desaparecidos from Argentina, you know, one of the disappeared ones. His body was found in a mass grave with a couple dozen others. The families of some of these people, parents, brothers, sisters are interested in a positive ID. Most of those missing were killed as young radicals, or so they were perceived by the military government at the time. They were mostly picked up at night and their families told they were being taken for routine questioning, nothing to be worried about, they'd be released in a few days. Of course, they were never seen again. Most were subjected to torture to get them to divulge their accomplices in any plot against the government. Then they were killed. Most were shot in the head by pistol. See here, this wound of entrance in the original skull."

He opened the lower jaw or mandible, which was wired to the skull at the temporo-mandibular joints on both sides. He pointed to a small hole in the hard palate. "Entrance wound."

Then turning the skull he showed a huge jagged hole in the back of the skull. "Wound of exit," he said dryly. Chris felt a frisson of horror jump up and down his spine.

"This meant the poor devil was killed by holding a gun in his mouth and blowing a hole in his brain."

Fanning wondered what manner of man could do that even if it was in a service that one believed in 100 percent.

"Well look here, Augie, I have a mystery just as intriguing as the one you're working on. And besides, it looks as if you're almost finished with that one."

"OK, OK, what is it Chris? Let's have the details."

"I found this skull out near Hang Man's Gulch. As you know some valuable fossils have been discovered out there from time to time. These bones, however, are not fossils. There have been no reports of anyone missing around here, according to the police. I checked with them. As you can see, the skull, as well as the rest of the bones, is perfectly preserved. No bullet holes or other flaws. You can help identify its owner and possibly what happened to him."

Chris did not give him any more information.

"Why do you care?" Gaspare asked.

"I'm naturally curious. It's part of my character."

"Don't get yourself in an uproar. I was just being curious myself."

"So, when can you get to it?" Chris asked.

"I'll have to work on it between these others here, but I'll start today."

"You won't need the original will you?"

"No, I'll just need to refer to it from time to time. This plaster of paris copy you made will do just fine. You did a good job copying it."

The work proceeded at a slow pace as far as Chris was concerned. He was able to drop in on Gaspare every two or three days to check on the degree of completion of the work. Gaspare suggested he take the skull to Dr. Calvin Hughes, Chief of the Department of Dentistry at the university and a locally known dental forensic specialist. He could at least check on the dental pattern and match it with any listed in the FBI's list of missing persons dental records. Fanning took it under advisement but decided to make his own studies first.

4

Radiocarbon dating is a means of estimating the age of an organic material, plant, or animal based on the proportion of carbon-14 to carbon-12 which it contains. Carbon-14 is the radioactive form of the element and decays at a steady state, with a half-life of 5,730 years. Thus at the end of that period of time a given sample of plant material or bones will have half the amount of carbon-14 in it compared with the amount it started with. Using these facts, samples of organic materials can be dated, the age estimated to a reasonable degree of accuracy, say to within a few hundred years depending on the extent of contamination of the sample. Radioactive carbon-14 is formed in the atmosphere by the bombardment of nitrogen by free neutrons. This carbon-14 becomes incorporated into CO_2 and then into plant life by photosynthesis and into animal life by the organisms which live on plant life. The amount of carbon-14 remaining in the specimen can be used as a rough guestimate of its age with a degree of accuracy suitable for most scientific work. By using a sample of bone of sufficient size, less than an ounce, and processing it through an instrument called a mass spectrometer connected to a computer, a read-out of the age of the sample material is produced. This method has been used to date human and animal fossil bones as well as plant fossils.

Chris sat at his desk checking and rechecking his results. He was stumped. The sample of bone from the adult male skeleton would not compute. That is, he could not establish a radiocarbon age by any means he tried. The result came out the same on every attempt. The bone was too recent in origin even to be on the scale. So it's not a fossil, not even a couple of hundred years old. What does that mean? He answered himself. It means that whoever owned these bones died maybe last year or the year before or ten years ago or maybe yesterday. If that is true then where are the soft parts? Some trace of hair or fingernail should be left. It's as if it had been picked clean by buzzards. Well, OK, that's a viable scenario. I've seen enough of those African safari programs to know those big birds could do a really efficient job of picking bones clean. I guess their American cousins could do an equally complete job. OK, Fanning, what does this mean? It means radiocarbon dating isn't going to give me any useful information. Right? Right! We already know the age of the skeleton at death to be about thirty years old by osteon counting.

Here he referred to a count of remodeled bone cells in the cross section of a long bone such as the thigh bone or arm bone. By a technique called regression analysis, the age at death can be estimated. He had used the fibula because he was reluctant to cut the femur, the big thigh bone. He wanted to keep that intact. Moreover the size of the femoral heads, the shape of the pelvis, and the length of the sternum pointed to a male aged around thirty-two at the time of death. Study of the skull, jaw, and spine confirmed this finding. He was also able to discern that the deceased was a Caucasian male.

The next in order of study was the teeth. The teeth are probably the most important item in the identification of skeletal remains. They are particularly resistant to high temperature and often survive cremation. With an accurate dental chart, including X-rays, comparison with post mortem dental structure, crowns, root canals, and other details, frequently a positive ID can be made of the deceased. Chris thought, well I'm not getting too far with what I've done up to now, guess it's time to try some dental forensics. In his training, up to now, somehow there was a gap in the technique of dental identification. Oh, they'd had passing reference to that discipline but the real experts were the dental boys, and particularly the forensic odontologists. These guys could distinguish between the choppers of identical twins even in the absence of any dental work. Who was it that Gaspare had mentioned? Oh yes, Dr. Calvin Hughes, Chief of the Department of Dentistry at the university and a locally celebrated dental forensic specialist. While it was perfectly normal to lug fossils and bone fragments around in the archeology building, it was less acceptable to do so around the campus. So, he packed the skull up in an old cardboard box that was lying around and went to see the good dentist.

When he arrived at the office of Dr. Hughes he was disappointed to learn that the dental professor was out of the country. What the hell, he thought, I'll give old Dr. Barnes a call. Dr. Barnes had been his local dentist ever since he'd arrived from New York. He'd not seen him in the last year or so and he expected to catch hell from the dentist on that account. While he knew that he was also going to be chewed out for dropping in without an appointment, he knew that Dr. Barnes was generous to a fault and would not refuse to see him. Dr. Barnes was also interested in paleontology and that mutual interest was the basis for their friendship. He would jump at the chance to vary the tedium of looking in people's mouths for a change.

~~~

Fanning wasn't wrong. The nurse-receptionist, Gloria Pemberton, was glad to see him. He sat and waited the requisite time dutifully waiting his turn and was finally ushered into one of the examining rooms and seated in a dental chair. Gloria tried to take the box out of his lap but he would have none of it.

The dentist came in and gave Chris the expected talking to, but he was just going through the motions. His enthusiasm had started to wane. He was suffering from dental burnout. His feet hurt, his back ached, and he was tired of looking in people's mouths especially with the dangers of AIDS, hepatitis, and what all else might come along. He resented having to wear a mask and gloves with every patient and yearned for the day when he could give it all up and move to Key West or Key Largo to fish all the time. Only one more kid to put through school. Unfortunately his youngest, a daughter, had decided to attend dental school so he'd be looking into more damned mouths for several years. Oh well, if he could make it through the next four years he could retire.

"OK now young Chris, open up there."

Chris dutifully complied and while the dentist was delicately examining his teeth he did what all dentists do, he started asking questions.

"How do you like graduate school, Chris?"

Chris tried to answer by nodding his head. He wasn't sure Doc got the message. He could never understand why dentists did that. Maybe they liked that you were unable to answer with your mouth wide open and they did it on purpose. He continued the examination and continued asking questions.

"When will you finish your master's degree? Will you go on to a PhD? Been on any interesting digs lately? Have you made any fossil discoveries that are going to make you famous? How's the old professor, Calvin Hughes doing?"

Chris managed to answer, "Aut a ouwn."

Surprisingly the dentist understood. "Out of town, eh?"

Chris thought it must be from the long years of practice, listening to people talk with their mouths open. The old doc wasn't a bad sort.

"OK, there you go, no cavities, no gingival disease, no inflammation, no problems. In spite of your absence for three years your teeth are as good as new. Here, we'll give them a cleaning and you can be on your way."

After the cleaning, Chris didn't move out of the chair.

"I said you can go now. Make an appointment for a checkup in about six months."

Chris didn't move.

"Look Doc, I'm tickled pink about the state of my teeth but that's not really why I came today."

"Oh no?"

"No."

"Well then what is it, Chris?"

"See this box in my lap here?"

"Yes."

"Well, I'd like you to look at it."

"What for, what is it?"

"I'd like to see if you can identify it for me or at least give me some information on how to go about it."

"What is it?"

"It's a skull I found out in the desert. There are some features that don't make sense about it."

"Just let me get my charting done on your dental record here and I'll be right with you."

Chris opened the box and carefully removed the skull. The Dentist completed his paperwork and laid it down. He turned to Chris and the skull.

"Why, it looks like an anatomical specimen, like one of those that you can buy from an anatomical supply lab."

"Look at the teeth," Chris urged.

The dentist carefully opened the mouth.

"A full set of clean choppers all white and shiny. They look as if they'd just been cleaned by a dentist. The occlusion is perfect. They're as nice as your teeth, Chris. Matter of fact they look a lot like your teeth. Here, let me make a dental chart."

He inserted a special marking paper between the open jaws, gently clamped the jaws together and ground them together to produce a mark on the paper for the upper, maxillary, teeth occlusal surface. Then he withdrew it, turned it over and did the same for the mandibular teeth, the lower teeth. He studied the patterns with a skilled eye.

"Look here. These patterns are the same. Matter of fact the teeth, the jaws, the mandibles, and maxillae are identical to the ones we have been looking at just now. That's strange," he said.

Chris asked, "What's strange?"

"Well, I swear I have just seen this very pattern not five minutes ago. Wait a minute."

He placed the bite patterns down alongside those that belonged to Chris, those he'd just finished his notes on. "Well would you look at this. These two are identical. But how can that be? Dental bite charts are sufficiently individual to be used like fingerprints. How could these match yours to the last detail? I don't understand it. Where did you say you got this skull?" He examined the skull again making sure it was real bone and not some clever ceramic or plastic imitation. "No, that's real bone all right." The two men sat staring at each other for a minute. "This is the weirdest thing I have seen yet.

Are you sure you never had an identical twin? Even if you did there should be some slight differences, some subtle variation. Do you mind if I X-ray these teeth? I'd like to see if they are as alike on the inside as they are on the outside."

Dr. Barnes was now captivated by the mystery and was having a marvelous time. He was having so much fun that he almost forgot about his other patients. He set about X-raying the teeth as if they belonged to some live person. They had a cup of coffee while waiting for the images to develop. Gloria popped in to remind Dr. Barnes he had other patients waiting. He brushed her off with a terse but friendly, "So? Let them wait."

When the films were ready, they eagerly hung them up side by side with the corresponding films from Chris' file. The pictures were identical in every detail. "Is this some kind of fluke?" Chris asked. "How can that be? Who is this, my brother or twin?" As Fanning eyed the skull, he had the impression it was looking back at him.

"Why don't you tell me who you are you dumb bag of bones."

The old dentist was just as puzzled. "My, my this is becoming a real mystery isn't it? I have a suggestion. Why don't you see if you can run some DNA studies on the skeleton, namely the teeth. It is well known that the DNA is best preserved in the teeth."

"Ah, that's where I'm ahead of you. I already thought of that."

"Good. You may be able to compare the DNA with other patterns to get a hint about where it came from. Identification by DNA typing will soon replace fingerprinting, you know. Fingerprinting requires that a person has five fingers, while DNA can be taken from any cell in the body except the red blood cells."

~~~

Every few days, Chris Fanning dropped in on Gaspare to check on the degree of completion of the work. Fanning was frustrated that it was slow going but he was also impressed that it was done with exceeding skill. He had to admire the growing similarity to a human face as layers of reality were added, bit by bit, muscle by muscle, layer by layer. He learned about the small and filmy muscles as well as broad, long and firmly anchored muscles responsible for the various facial expressions. There were muscles that produced voluntary facial movements as in raising the forehead, frowning, opening the eyes widely, winking one eye, blinking both eyes, smiling, laughing, grimacing, chewing, opening and closing the mouth, moving the jaw from side to side, pursing the lips, blowing as on a musical instrument, whistling, sucking, dilating the nostrils, and tightly shutting the eyelids. These muscles, all attached to specific bones or fascia, were simulated by the careful applications of different layers of clay. Overlying the muscles, a layer of fascia thick or thin changed the contour of the emerging face. The trick was to know all the vagaries in detail and to reproduce them with accuracy on the model so as to produce a lifelike result. And this Gaspare could do better than anyone else in the field. Fanning decided to stop the visits since he was wasting too much time watching the master work.

Finally, after two and a half weeks of waiting, Chris had a call informing him that the production was finished and he could come over to Gaspare's studio to look it over. When he did, he was not prepared for what was waiting for him. Sitting on Gaspare's workbench, appearing to mock him, was a perfect facsimile of himself. His face, his head were reproduced so exactly that the resemblance could not have been more striking had he posed for it himself.

"My God, how'd you do that, Gaspare? That looks more like me than I do myself."

Indeed, the reproduction was perfect down to the brown wavy hair, with its widow's peak at the forehead, the cleft chin, the dark brown penetrating eyes, the straight nose. The skin tones, the slightly protruding ears and the early crinkles at the corners of the eyes were reproduced to perfection.

"How in the hell did you do that Gaspare? I mean you must have been scrutinizing my hair and eye color on the sneak to get it down so exactly correct. You son of a bitch. What am I supposed to make of this? The skeleton I found belongs to my twin? I don't even have a brother, that I know of. You're not being helpful here, Augie. It's not funny either. It's downright eerie. What's the big idea?"

"Now calm yourself, Chris Fanning. This is simply how it came out. I did not set out to make a replica of your face with any purposeful design. That's just how it came out."

"But how could that be? It's an exact replica of me, to the last detail."

"I don't know how it can be. It just is. I assure you, I didn't do it on purpose. Well, yes the hair color and haircut and yes the eye color, but that's it. I swear I didn't do it to play a joke on you. Why would I? To what purpose?"

"To shock me out of my socks, that's why."

"Well, you are wrong, my friend. I am a professional and I am starting to resent your insinuations. What could I possibly have to gain by playing such a trick on you?"

"OK, I'm sorry, Gaspare, but you have to admit, it's grotesque. What can it mean? How could some dead guy look exactly like me? Is someone sending me a message? Is it coincidence? It's just too fantastically, perfectly like me to be an accident. So where does that leave me? Someone murdered my exact double and maybe buried him where I'd likely find him. There are no signs of trauma, no bullet holes. Of course that may mean he was shot in the soft tissues only, say the heart. He could have been poisoned or he could have died of natural causes. Or, if he was choked, asphyxiated, or frozen to death you would be left with an intact skeleton. If he was burned to death you would expect some charring of bone, especially subcutaneous bones like tibia or ulna. There were none in this skeleton. So what's going on Gaspare? You are an expert in forensics. Do you have any bright ideas?"

"No, I don't have any bright ideas. And I'm busy enough to not have any time for another mystery, interesting as it may be. I must say, it has some intriguing aspects to it. But I will give you some advice. First take your bones, especially the skull, to a good forensic dentist. I believe we have one of the best here at the university in Dr. Hughes, head of the Department of Dentistry. Get a line on your mystery skull by having the dental charts identified. You may come up with something valuable that way. You may even be able to ID the poor galoot if perchance his dental charts are in the FBI's missing persons file. The next thing you should do is run a DNA analysis of the bone. In well preserved bone specimens there often is a technique which allows retrieval of the DNA especially from the long bones or teeth. If the DNA is recoverable it can be compared with numerous others, and if you get lucky you might get your ID that way. And who do you think I'd recommend to do DNA studies? Why none other than our own Dr. Joseph Karahsha, renowned forensic pathologist, researcher, humanitarian, and outdoorsman.

Fanning asked, "Oh, that nut?"

"I know he has a reputation of being, ah, eccentric, but he's the best damned molecular biologist and biochemist in this part of the country and maybe the best bar none. I've seen him at work. He is a demon of a researcher, he's indefatigable, and he is very much underrated by his peers around the country."

"Two things, I have started on the DNA identification process already. I have a friend at the lab who has agreed to do the studies you mentioned. The other thing is, I already tried to see Dr. Hughes but he's out of the country. Instead I went to see my old dentist. He made dental charts from the skull and compared them with my own charts. You might be interested to know they are identical."

At this Fanning thought he heard a gasp from Gaspare. "Oh my, you really have a mystery on your hands, don't you?" Gaspare said. "Good luck to you, Chris Fanning."

5

Chris and Margie lived in a medium-sized, rented, yellow frame house in the better section of the city's middle class residential area. Just a quarter mile away was the prestigious Willow Wood development, one of the premier neighborhoods in town. Although they could afford it if Margie accepted financial help from her dad, they preferred to pay their own way, at least for now. This was Chris' idea mostly but Margie was content to go along in the spirit of adventure. Margie knew her dad would pay for a vacation, clothes, private school for the kids if she wanted. Hell, they'd had to refuse many an offer of financial help in the past from their parents. They loved their independence. Still, they were secure in the knowledge that they could call on Papa Martin, Margie's dad, in an emergency.

Margie liked the Catholic Church that was just down the block. She had made several friends in the church and had enrolled the children in religious instruction as well as the regular school. She had even wheedled Chris into attending church again on a regular basis just as he did as a child back in Queens, New York. Fanning had a strict Catholic upbringing. He'd even been an altar boy as a child. Later in college and especially in graduate school the daily pressure of his new demanding life gradually pushed him away from the church. He maintained an abiding belief in the religion however, never doubting God as Creator and the value of the moral teachings of the church of his youth and of his mother.

He was, however, put off by the ritual, the rigidity of the church, the constant demand for monetary contributions especially when he was an impecunious student. He liked to say if asked though that the reason he stopped going was that he could never understand why he had to change from sitting to kneeling, kneeling to standing, then back to sitting in Mass.

He'd just get himself comfortable then he'd have to change position again. This he would say in jest. But Margie did a good job of coaxing him to return on a regular basis.

She had a best friend from grade school, Tina Meyer, who was very active in church matters. This friend had a sister who was a nun at the local church. She was a young, modern nun who did not wear the habit, as had become the practice among the modern sisters of the cloth. She possessed so-called modern ideas, believing that women should be ordained as priests. Chris, Margie, and the nun, Sister Angela, along with Tina, would occasionally get together on weekends for dinner and for animated discussion of all the pertinent issues of the day.

Inevitably the discourse would come around to religious matters and that is where the four would part company. Sister Angela, in spite of her outwardly modern appearance took a decidedly rigid traditional view of her religion and the church. Her sib, Tina, was more liberal in her outlook but Chris and his wife Margie often espoused the opposite point of view as much for the sake of argument as for any deep-seated humanistic feelings. For instance, the argument kept cropping up, how could a merciful, just God allow the tragedies to happen that were befalling mankind all the time all over the world, especially to innocent children? How could a benevolent Deity allow certain things to exist as child abuse, congenital malformations, juvenile diabetes, floods, earthquakes, and hurricanes that kill and maim children by the thousands? Chris and Margie agreed there must be a flaw in the system or their understanding of the system to allow such things. Sister Angela was always on the opposite side taking the view that it all fit a master plan and that those who lost out on earth were always rewarded in heaven by an everlasting life. As for those who did enough evil on earth, eventually they got what they deserved, hellfire for eternity, sulfur fumes up their nose, and brimstone cinders down their backs forever and ever. Besides that, Sister Angela would say, the time allotted to us on earth was such a small fraction of the totality of our existence that it was essentially negligible.

Fanning would always take the devil's advocate position and would ask "Why? To what end?"

The nun replied, "What do you mean, to what end? So the good can live forever with their loved ones and the evildoers can be punished for their sins."

Chris would egg her on. "But suppose one is good all his life, I mean good to the max with a capital G, so good that he has no problem gaining entrance to heaven, bypasses purgatory, and is admitted to heaven the very day of his death."

"Yeah, so?"

"Well, suppose this person has a loved one who has been a real stinker all his life. Murdered, cheated, stole, did all those things we all agree are egregious sins. But the good one still loves him. Suppose that a prerequisite to the good person's happiness is that the bad one be with him in heaven. But the bad one can never be with the good one because he has lived a lifetime of total evil. Then you have a conflict, a paradox, a contradiction. The good one can't be happy even though he is in heaven because he is not accompanied by the loved evil one. And the evil one can't go to heaven due to his lifetime of rottenness. How do you reconcile the two? Don't you see that your reasoning is faulty? The whole system of good, evil, reward and punishment is flawed."

"No, no, there are mysteries which are not given to us to know. We have to believe on faith."

"But it defies logic," Fanning persisted. "It is not reasonable, and most of all it doesn't make sense. Don't you see there are a whole set of contradictions that don't make sense? And they don't go away by saying we have to have faith. That kind of blind faith is what led people down the primrose path to all kinds of false beliefs. Take Aristotle. He said that spontaneous generation of life was possible and it took thousands of years to disprove that notion. The point is that the history of man has shown that the world is knowable. The mysteries we don't understand, we don't understand because we haven't yet been smart enough to figure them out. But obviously that doesn't mean that we've solved everything because solving one mystery causes two or three more to pop up. So it's not a matter of belief or faith, it's a matter of figuring out what is going on."

Sister Angela countered by saying that just because we have figured out a lot of the physical world doesn't mean we have the spiritual one figured out too. The wisest sages throughout history have attested to the insolvability of the great unknowns which are not given to man to understand. How could the parting of the Red Sea be anything else but a miracle? How could the Virgin birth, the crucifixion, and the resurrection be explained except by happenings unknowable to men? "Even today, with all your precious science, nobody knows how to restore life once a person has died. The fact that each new discovery just pushes the envelope a little further reinforces the point because that is the way it has always been and that is the way it will always be. That is to say, unraveling one mystery will always reveal two more. Solving these two will produce four more unknowns, and so it will be forever."

"Boy, what a pair of pessimists you two are," Chris said as Margie kept the coffee coming. "Now what if I told you that scientists are on the verge of doing that very thing that you just said is impossible? That is to create a living person where there is only a dead body. Or create a human being from the fundamental chemical bases of life?" Even Fanning didn't believe this. He was just using the argument for argument's sake. The reaction of all three women was a sneer followed by a guffaw of disbelief.

"What do you think, that human beings are as simple as viruses or bacteria? Your vaunted scientists haven't even done that with species lower down on the food chain let alone human beings. The idea that you could build something as complicated as a person from chemicals is simply ridiculous. It can't be done."

Chris replied, without a lot of conviction, "Maybe it can't be done today but the technology is fast developing to the point it will be possible much sooner than you think."

Predictably the women, especially the nun, scoffed at him, scoffed good-naturedly, but it was obvious they didn't believe him, not even Margie.

It was during one of these late dinner conversations with Tina and Sister Angela that Jake Hamilton and Chris Fanning were bemoaning the lack of time they'd recently had due to their graduate studies and the extra work they'd taken upon themselves with their adventure of the bones.

After they had all polished off dessert, and Margie had put the children to sleep, Chris offered the opinion that they would all have to get together more often. Margie thought she noticed a spark of interest between Jake Hamilton and her friend, Tina.

"Hey, I'd like that," Jake said. After the small talk tapered off, the conversation drifted towards what had been on Fanning's mind all the while. He described the events regarding the dental charts that had been definitely matched with his own and how the reconstruction of the facial features made by Gaspare bore such a marked resemblance to himself.

Margie was still inclined to treat it much less seriously than the boys, offering the opinion that the similarity was more likely to be a result of an elaborate practical joke perpetrated on him by the dentist and especially Gaspare whose reputation as an eccentric was well known on campus. "In spite of the peculiarities you describe, don't you archeology-paleontology types constantly dig up finds that raise more questions than they answer? Isn't that just the nature of the beast?"

That's what Chris loved so much about her. She was so practical, so down to earth.

"Look, honey," Chris said. "Sure we've raised questions. But these are, ah, a little different. These bones are very recent, maybe their owners died within the last year or in the last few months. With a find that recent there ought not to be total obliteration of the soft parts like the clothes and hair. This is a special situation. These are not really fossils in the way we know fossils. These are too recent."

"Then why not call the police?" She wanted to know.

"Well, there is really no evidence of any foul play. It's almost as if someone put those bones out there for us to find. On the other hand had it not been for the tornado blowing off the top layer of soil we wouldn't have a clue that they were there."

"Yeah, that was lucky," Jake said, pouring himself another cup of coffee, a trace of irony in his voice.

The sisters were silent on this subject so Chris decided to draw them into the conversation with the simple question, "Where did the universe come from?"

"Oh Chris, will you give it a rest!" Margie almost shouted. "Do you have to bait my friends every time they come over for a simple visit?"

Sister Angela replied that it was OK, she enjoyed the religious discussions and didn't mind the challenge. In fact she said Chris' constant questioning of the faith kept her sharp and able to debate with the best of them.

Encouraged, Fanning continued. "If the universe came about by the hand of God, then what was there before? If nothing, then that meant that there was also no God by definition. But how did God himself come about? To say that He invented Himself was no explanation at all since how could something cause itself to exist? It is hard enough to imagine a being created from nothing, but one which actually creates itself is too much to imagine. And if God did not create himself, then He was either always present or He was created by someone or something else, two equally untenable choices." He tried to approach the problem with logic, Margie did so with resignation, and the two sisters, one a nun, the other a religious lay person, approached it with faith arguing again that there are certain truths unknowable to human beings while on earth and that these truths would be revealed once they arrived in heaven.

Chris scoffed at this idea as illogical, then remembered that he had read an article in a physics journal which said that matter could be made from nothing at all as long as there was enough energy available! It could get confusing. How could you have energy in the absence of matter? And just how does energy transmute into matter anyhow? Oh sure, everybody knows the famous Einstein equation, $E=MC^2$, where E stands for energy, M stands for mass and C^2 is the speed of light squared. But what is the mechanism on a fundamental level? That was as much a mystery as the other questions, but the inexorable progress of science had provided answers to previously unanswerable questions. The trouble was that for each previously unsolvable riddle that science explained more came up that were themselves inexplicable. Even so, the solution to each problem widened the envelope of knowledge and moved the unknowns to a more fundamental level. If ignorance steadily gave way to the scientific method to reveal ever more basic levels of truth, then why couldn't the holy unknowables of the church one day yield to the same methodology? They kicked this one around a lot in their late night discussions maintaining a respect of the other's point of view even while continuing to disagree.

They discussed the pomp and ritual of the church, the evolution from a ragged beginning of faithful rebels willing to die for their God to the present area of liberalism, dissension, permissiveness, the newly popular liberation theology, political activism, celibacy, and the considerable wealth of the Catholic Church today. A particularly recurring sore point was the behavior of the Catholic Church during the Spanish Inquisition and the inordinate political power in the past of the popes who had rivaled kings and emperors. Chris frequently teased the females about the change in the Mass from strict Latin to English, the guitar playing, the speaking from the altar by lay parishioners, the newly introduced ritual of turning to one's neighbor in the pew to shake hands and wish him well, the abandonment of the traditional garb by the nuns. He felt these all conspired to cheapen the church, to debase its foundations for the expediency of catering to the lowest common denominator in order to increase attendance and thus financial contributions.

And what about the delicate issue of celibacy for priests? Was this a concern that would lead eventually to the dilution of the influence of the church by the scarcity of priests? Already the Pentecostal movement was making great strides in South America, taking millions of the faithful away from the church because of the issue of celibacy and others. What about the insidious but persistent rumors of homosexuality in the priesthood? Worse, there were recent revelations of sexual abuse by priests against those who gave their unquestioned loyalty such as nuns in training or even children. What about the subsequent unsuccessful efforts at a cover up by the church bureaucracy? Would these factors all come together to shake the very foundations of the greatest religion the world has ever seen?

Why for instance have there been no recorded confirmed miracles in the last several hundred years? Oh sure, there were the sightings at Fatima, at Lourdes, and at Medjugorje. There were reports of wondrous events at various other places. But none of these are available for the vast majority of people to see even if they made the long journey to these far off locations.

Where are the miracles of old? The three loaves of bread that fed multitudes? The miracles on a scale of the parting of the Red Sea (even though this was strictly speaking a miracle belonging to the Hebrews)? The miracle of sight to the blind, the healing of the lame and crippled, the sick and the mad? Clearly, the time had come for some sign, some re-affirmation of the faith, some new demonstration of the church's authenticity, its resurgence to the forefront of consciousness of the masses to divert the modern obsession with materialism, money, power and amusement. The church was in almost as much trouble as it was in the beginning. As its survival was in doubt then, so its propagation was in doubt now. Already some parishes were forced to share priests because there were not enough to go around. Some churches were being consolidated because of the relative paucity of adherents in some jurisdictions. The church was drawing fewer and fewer acolytes to the seminaries, forcing it to depend more and more on older, retired and widowed men to take up the priesthood to fill up the ranks.

The three women refused to concede that the mother church was in any kind of serious trouble such as Fanning had suggested. They thought rather that all institutions go through a natural ebb and flow, a cyclic waxing and waning of power and influence that in the long run serves to strengthen them. Yes, the church was in one of its more difficult periods but not nearly in the kind of trouble as say the time of the Spanish Inquisition. They thought the potential for serious harm to the church was infinitely more probable at that juncture, that its integrity had rebounded in a renewed, reinvigorated form to spread over the New World, inspiring converts to Christianity by the millions.

Chris said, "Yeah right, at the point of a sword. You know how all those converts were made. They were for the most part given a choice of converting to Catholicism or being ignominiously killed. And when they were converted what happened to them? They were put to work, involuntarily, as slaves for the Spanish, digging up as much gold as they could find to be shipped back to Spain for the enrichment of the king and the Spanish court."

The give and take was animated but not mean spirited. After this, the discussion turned to the question of the bones and the various interpretations of the findings.

The nun, her sister Tina, and Margie didn't think too much of the bones except to acknowledge that there might be a potential find worth pursuing. But they didn't see any significance beyond that. The two graduate students however resolved to pursue the mystery with as much vigor as they could muster and still do justice to their graduate studies. For the purpose of the greatest efficiency they decided to stagger their times at the dig site, as they had started to refer to the location of the bone find. Hamilton was to take the next opportunity to search at the desert location and Fanning was to do whatever lab work he could. Then they planned to switch tasks.

6

Back at the lab, Chris took some time between classes to work on bone identification. He prepared slides from small dowel-shaped sections cut from the fibula. According to the method of Kerley, a procedure has been devised for the determination of the age of a body at the time of death by measurement of the osteons, the bone cells, their numbers, sizes, shapes, arrangement, and remodeling and certain other characteristics. These, used in the aggregate, enable one to determine with a reasonable degree of accuracy the age at death of the owner of the bones.

As he studied the slides, Fanning became more uneasy. From these studies, it was becoming obvious that the ages of the respective skeletons at death coincided rather closely with his and Margie's present ages. This was becoming downright spooky. He could not explain, nor could Jake, the fact that no soft tissue in any stage of decay could be found. No hair, skin, fingernails, muscle, ligament, cartilage, tendon, liver, stomach, eyeball, brain, nerve tissue at all.

As he pondered the puzzle, he drifted off into his favorite reverie of the great saber-toothed cat, Smilodon. He was fascinated by the big cat and at times imagined himself transformed into the animal during the period it lived and in its own ambience. He knew he might be ridiculed by Jake and his wife, not to mention his teachers, so he kept this little fantasy to himself. If only it were possible to find a live one somewhere, or even one frozen in ice as in a glacier somewhere up north. He wanted a frozen sample that could be restored back to life as was possible with some fish and frogs. He imagined he would be a solitary animal like today's modern tiger, only much bigger, coming together with the female only once a year for mating. Chris delighted in picturing himself as the great terror, the monster feline, showing no mercy to any competitor such as bears, sloths, or prey animals like camels or horses. He would rule a territory stretching for miles and would be the undisputed beast whose very spoor would create fear among all other animals of his domain. He would be magnanimous, leaving the little creatures alone such as the squirrels, ground hogs, prairie dogs, and rabbits unless he felt particularly vicious or hungry. But the others, the deer, the antelope, moose, wild horses, pigs, and camels could count on being terrorized every few days as his appetite dictated. Indeed Fanning sometimes felt a viciousness in himself that was hard for him to understand. It went beyond the necessity of killing what he considered inferior animals for food. It was a glorification he imagined the cat to feel in the use of his finely tuned skills, his agility, his cunning, his power, his intelligence, his ability to outflank and outwit his adversary. Then the inevitable final struggle, the gripping, the tearing, the sinking of his stiletto-like claws into the live yielding flesh from which there was no escape gave him an exhilaration beyond the merely alimentary. He relished the smell of fresh meat covered with blood, the feeling and sound of bone cracking under his teeth and yielding the sweet, fatty marrow in which he imagined the soul of the animal to reside.

Fanning did not know why he had such a fascination with this extinct beast. He thought it might be some long forgotten memory buried deep in the genetic murk of all predatory animals. For are we not the end result of evolutionary refinement over the millions of years during which most of our genetic material remains as it is, only made latent by the more recent changes in our way of life? Are we not, as human beings, some of the most ferocious predators ever to appear on the evolutionary scene? In point of fact there is no other species known that massacres its own kind in the way we human beings do and for the reasons we do. There have been some scholars who would like to change the scientific name of Homo sapiens to Homo sanguineous to reflect more accurately the nature of the human animal based on our murderous behavior over the course of recorded history. Is there not a special fascination among the public in the life activities of predatory animals from insects like the praying mantis, to arachnids like spiders, to the sharks of the sea, the polar bears, the Kodiak bears of the north countries, the lions of the veld, and the raptors of the air? Are not the television shows and movies that depict this kind of hunting activity some of the most popular, not only with children but also with adults? How fascinated we are by wars over territory, by accounts in books, newspapers, and other media of the struggle of people to enlarge their areas of dominance and control, by struggles whose motive is territoriality and power over other groups of humans. Even the powerless, which include most of us, are fascinated by the struggles of the powerful whether on a one-to-one basis or in the aggregate. The more ruthless, the more brutal, the more bloody the process, the more we are fascinated. Thus, the name Homo sanguineous would seem a fitting substitute for Homo sapiens (knowing, wise, intelligent) because the latter applies to a very small percentage of people.

For whatever reason, Fanning was obsessed by Smilodon and sometimes fantasized himself to be one. He had become enthralled with this particular killer way back in grade school when he saw a movie purporting to depict prehistoric man and his struggles to survive the predations of the hunting animals of the time. He knew even then that the dinosaurs were not coexistent in time with man. He couldn't really get too excited about a large cold-blooded lizard with a brain the size of a walnut. He felt much more akin to the warm-blooded, giant-toothed, intelligent hunting cat. Insinuating himself in the body of the cat gave him an imaginary power that was denied him in his own world. He therefore determined at an early age to study the beast as a career specialty and become the world's most authoritative scholar on the subject. He recognized he was not a natural genius but in place of that he made up for it by working like a demon possessed. His upbringing gave him another reason to excel. His family was on the poor side due to his father's chronic illness which finally killed him at the age of fifty. Several times the family came close to public relief, but thanks to his mother's industrious laboring in a factory they avoided that. They did, however, have to live in public housing for a period of two years and he hated this loss of control over his life. He found a measure of escape in the fantasy of Smilodon.

The saber-toothed tiger was the most perfectly adapted land killer of the era. The massive head was supported by an equally massive neck and shoulder muscles. The broad chest flanked by the great muscular forelegs gave origin to the large pectoralis muscles which attached to the upper arms

53

and contributed to the awesome power of those mighty limbs. The chest tapered sharply to the tight hard belly which looked a little loose and paunchy because of the heavy protective hair. The rather smaller hindquarters ended in a stubby tail whose function was problematic but did give the animal a distinctive appearance. The most fearsome attributes, however, were the giant canine teeth growing to a full eight inches and deeply anchored in the heavy maxilla or upper jaw. These were weapons which enabled it to fear no other creatures, to attack even the seemingly invulnerable mastodon with success when hunger drove it to that extreme. The senses of sight, hearing, and smell were likewise highly developed for a hunting existence as was the animal's intelligence. In cunning, stealth, and strength he was second to none. The tawny haired beast weighed up to 500 pounds and could run at speeds surpassing 30 miles per hour on short spurts. He could climb trees but preferred not to. He could swim and like most modern tigers even liked a dip in the cool waters during the punishing heat of the semi-tropical summers.

And now Smilodon was hungry. He moved with the grace of a much smaller animal directing his aim for the high ground where he could survey the countryside below for miles. Fifteen minutes of steady climbing brought him to the crest of a plateau that ran west to east for several hundred miles. He stopped to drink at a shallow rainwater pool, the ears flat against his head, pausing often to listen and shift position so as to view the entire 360 degrees around him. His thirst satisfied, he resumed an easy pace along the crest, scanning the horizon for the telltale dust clouds that would signal big game. After an hour he had covered four miles. Now he picked up the pace feeling a more insistent grumbling deep in his gut. He did not remember nor did he care that he had not eaten more than a mouthful in the last 3 days. He stopped again and urinated, more as a scent marker than a need to empty his bladder. He began moving again when a small cloud of dust far in the distance on the plain below caught his eye. He focused on the movement within the dust and his appetite quickened as he made out a large group of mastodons moving slowly on a course parallel to his. He sniffed the air noting the direction of the wind, for while stalking he would be careful to stay downwind of his prey. He calculated he would have to overtake the group then double back so as to remain downwind. Since they were several miles distant he would have to make good time. He took advantage of the huge beasts' rambling locomotion, gaining on them when they stopped to browse or drink. Since he was a solitary hunter, he had to rely on his own skills and athletic prowess to approach close enough to make a charge. He took every advantage of the terrain to hide himself, the brownish yellow color of his coat adding further camouflage.

Finally he was only a quarter of a mile from the herd. There were around thirty-five in number. Among them were several massive bulls but these were much too big for him to attack. There were a half dozen immature bulls and cows still too risky to take on because of their size. The remainder of the herd was comprised of females, about half of which had calves of varying size. These were the ones on which he concentrated. Careful to remain downwind, he searched for any immature animal that might stray ever so slightly from the herd or lollygagged behind. His killing technique was per force which adapted to the size and strength of the prey. He knew that mastodons were highly protective of their young and one goring by an enraged parent could prove lethal over time. If one of the bulls stepped on him even once or fell on him he could be fatally crushed. So he watched and waited, his hunger contractions forcing him to persist. After all he was smaller, quicker, much more agile and desperately famished. Patiently he waited, searching for an opportunity, inching closer until he was only yards away. He systematically assessed all the immature animals for any sign of weakness or inattention that would make it an easier target. He searched for a limp, a lack of alertness, a tendency to separate itself from the herd, a wound, any obvious sign of malnutrition or any difficulty in keeping up. Finally, after being unable to find any animal with an obvious problem, he settled on one of the smaller calves that appeared to be vulnerable but who might supply him a week's worth of meat. He made himself as flat as he could, bulging muscles straining in a tight coil ready to pounce. He positioned himself in the path of the oncoming group but slightly off to one side. Taking cover behind a slight rise in the ground, a stroke of luck came his way. A flock of pheasants disturbed by the lumbering mass of mastodons took flight, alarming and distracting the herd for a moment. The giant cat recognized his opportunity. Springing from his crouch with furious speed, he covered the forty or so feet in two or three bounds catching up with the hapless chosen victim. The mastodon calf was instinctively seized by a massive panic and at first could not make up its mind which way to run. That was a fatal mistake. Instantly Smilodon was on him from the side, leaping onto his flank and holding on by the fearsome fangs that gave it his name. The cat sank his front claws in the flesh of the shoulder and arched his body so his hind legs came under the calf's middle. He used his powerful rear claws to tear at the soft underbelly while the mastodon ran terror-stricken in no particular direction. If the bleating, panicked animal had fallen down and rolled over onto the smaller cat, Smilodon would have been crushed under him and would have had to let go to save his own life. But the calf continued to run totally overcome and continued to have its belly clawed until the cat achieved its purpose which was to open the abdominal cavity and spill the contents. At this point the feline sprang off knowing that he had succeeded. By this time the mastodon was several hundred feet from the rest of the herd. With the cat no longer tormenting it the doomed animal slowed down, stopped, and stood on wobbly legs trying to recover. The cat beat a hasty retreat while the rest of the herd caught up and tried to help the injured one. Of course there was nothing they could do to save the youngster. The wounded baby soon collapsed to its knees then flopped over panting frantically for breath. The herd milled about for some hours then started slowly to move off. The calf's mother, however, lingered for several more hours while the smaller animal succumbed to blood loss and shock. After many futile attempts to push it to its feet the mother, with reluctance, slowly turned to walk away and catch up with the rest of the herd. When she was out of sight the cat fed. Instinctively tearing into the exposed bowel he ripped out and devoured the entrails, the liver, the spleen, the pancreas, and lungs. He used the powerful incisors, fangs, claws and the molars to tear and slash contentedly. Then, tilting the massive head, he used the scissor-like molars to gnaw off bite sized chunks of meat. When he was finally sated he clamped his massive jaws on the carcass and dragged it a quarter mile to a more secluded location in a copse of poplar trees for storage. He covered the carcass with leaves, grass, branches, and other debris he found. He now searched for water which he found in a nearby ravine, filled with melt water from the high country. Drinking his fill with swishes of the spongy bristly tongue, he maintained where he had hidden the kill. Feeling an overwhelming drowsiness consume him, the predator settled in for a long peaceful rest.

~~~

"Hey sleep meister, hey wake up. What have you been doing, staying awake nights doing your homework?"

Fanning slowly became aware that someone was gently shaking him by the shoulder. For a moment he thought he was being shaken by the mother mastodon whose baby he had just eaten. He awoke, dazed and in a sweat, disoriented, ready to fight.

"Hey, take it easy there Chris, it's only me, your friend Jake, Jake Hamilton, remember?" Chris realized where he was and what had happened. "Are you all right, pal?"

"Uh, yeah, I'm OK, Jake. I was just having a weird daydream. I'm OK, I'm wide awake now. What's up? Find anything out there worth talking about?"

Now Jake turned serious. "Well, er, I did find something of interest as a matter of fact. Out at the dig site."

"Well, what is it, man, what did you find? Spill it will you, before I stroke out with curiosity?"

From his appearance Jake had just returned from the field. Mud covered his work boots, his shirt was stained in sweat, and he looked as if he hadn't showered in days. Jake hesitated, then said, "I don't know how to tell you this, Chris, but I just found two more skeletons, this time two children's skeletons, but a little more primitive than the other two."

"What do you mean, Jake?"

"Well, mainly the skulls. The skulls are more like Cro-Magnon and the younger one is more primitive in appearance than the older."

"Where did you find them?"

"Same place."

"Are the specimens old? What state of preservation? Males, females, what? What age at death? How long are they dead? What, what? Give, Jake, tell me more."

"Hold it," Jake said, "I'll tell you one thing at a time. They are two perfectly preserved children's skeletons, one appears to be male, the other female. The male appears to be around eight years old, the female around six, but I just found them and I haven't had time to do bone ages on them yet. They are in the same condition, that is, perfectly preserved. Found both in the supine position, no evidence of trauma, complete to the last phalanx, and get this, just like the other two adults there's no sign of soft tissue, no trace of decaying skin, muscle, hair, fat, etc. It's just the weirdest thing you ever saw. No odor either."

"Christ," Fanning blurted. "Next thing you'll tell me they correspond to my own children's skeletons in size and shape. Those estimated ages you just gave me are close."

The two men looked at each other intently, not sure if they should be concerned, perplexed, amused, worried, or scared.

"Confound it, let's just keep our heads about us and proceed like the rational, scientific beings we know we are," said Chris.

"All right, we'll do all the studies by the book. We're onto something. I don't know what, but I think it's significant."

They both agreed to continue their investigations into the affair of the bones while at the same time working toward their advanced academic degrees. Fanning even thought it might make a good grad school thesis. Jake agreed there was enough material for them both.

~~~

At the next opportunity to work on the bones Hamilton took his regular rotation out in the field and Fanning remained at the lab to carry out more diagnostic studies.

As part of the investigation Fanning had brought some of the material from the first skeleton to Marty Greenspan in the genetic lab. Greenspan was another transplanted New Yorker who was a crackerjack in the laboratory. He was one of those brilliant scientific types who went into medicine strictly for the academic thrill of it and not necessarily to save anyone's life. He really didn't think very highly of the human race and he figured that only about one in a million people was worth getting excited about. His heroes were geniuses like Newton, or Einstein, or Professor Karahsha who was the head of his department and whom he was sure would win a Nobel Prize one day. "Well, we isolated some material from the teeth which looks promising. I will have to do the enzyme splitting and PCR studies before I'll have anything to identify, but it shouldn't take too long." Here he referred to the technique, recently developed, that allowed small snippets of DNA to be reproduced rapidly in almost any quantity necessary.

"Basically I think you know the principle is that more than 20% of the genes in the human body, of which there are roughly 100,000, are polymorphic. That is they are different in different individuals. The others are essentially smaller, that is to say, the 80% of the genes we have in common make us all recognizable as part of the human race. The fact that we each have a backbone, two arms, two legs, the fact that we stand and walk on our hind legs, bipedalism, the way our circulatory system is laid out with the heart in the chest and the arterial, capillary and venous systems, these are determined by the genes we all have in common. Get the picture? But the other 20% of the genetic material is uniquely characteristic to that individual so that this fraction of the DNA can be used in identification, the so-called DNA fingerprint. Which is, by the way, not used anymore in polite company. It is not politically correct to say that people are better or worse, more or less valuable, possessed of greater or inferior talent or God forbid are genetically predisposed to alcoholism say, or to criminality. But I digress. It then becomes a matter of cutting up the DNA with enzymes, locating the polymorphic or variable proteins, isolating them, reproducing them by polymerase chain reaction and then plating them out on a gel by applying an electric current. This latter process is called electrophoresis. Once you have that you can compare it with DNA from any other source and make your identification.

"Here, we have the electrophoresis patterns of a DNA fragment from a child. This is from a polymorphic portion of DNA. Now here is the same segment of DNA from a putative father. See how the blobs line up in this critical area? This means that to a certainty of 99.99% the putative father is indeed the real father, very handy for establishing paternity. On the other hand, it could aid in proving that someone could not be a father of a specific child to a reasonable certainty. So it is very useful in 'ID-ing' blood found at the scene of a crime in implicating or clearing an accused. This type of evidence is assuming more and more importance in legal identifications and is being viewed more and more favorably by the courts. It can be applied in animal studies as well as human and has given us a handle on why the African cheetah, for example, may be on its way to extinction. We find the gene pool in these animals very similar and they just go under from inbreeding and lack of new genetic stock to vary the bloodline. Over here, we have a very interesting electrophoretic pattern. Recognize it?"

While showing the pattern to Fanning, Marty covered the name label with his thumb.

"It doesn't mean anything special to me," Fanning said studying it with an amateur eye.

Marty moved his thumb, uncovering the name label. Fanning was surprised to see it belonged to him. "Hey, that's got my name on it. Where'd that come from?"

"Oh, we sometimes use excess blood from marriage tests or routine blood tests and the like to let the students practice and for purposes of demonstration."

Fanning studied the gel pattern. "Hmmm, interesting. See anything unusual about it?" he asked.

"No, nothing at all. OK, here come the preliminary plates on your skull find. We took some DNA from the teeth. You know, the genetic material is most often well preserved in the teeth. Take a look. I haven't seen it yet myself."

"Doesn't mean a lot to me," Fanning admitted. "Here you take a look."

Marty studied the plate. A frown crossed his face.

"What? What is it, Marty?"

"I don't know, but let's compare this one with yours."

"Mine? What do you mean?"

"Well, I'm not sure, but I do believe I noted a certain similarity between this one and yours."

"Really? But how can that be?"

"I don't know but let's take a look."

As they both studied the plates side by side it was apparent even to Fanning that the two were identical.

"I don't understand," he murmured. "I don't get it."

"I don't understand it either," Marty replied.

"How could these two be genetically identical?" Fanning continued. "Could there be some mistake?" he pressed.

"Well, of course there is always that chance. We'll check it over and repeat the tests, but I ran them myself. I don't see how there could be so gross an error or so close a similarity on a chance basis. Just look at them. They are identical."

"What the hell does it mean? Could it be chance? How can you explain it, Marty?"

"I don't know what the hell it means. There is no way in hell it could be due to chance and I don't know how to explain it. You and your skeleton find are genetically identical. Have you ever had an identical twin you didn't know about? I mean it's pretty unlikely, but have you forgotten you ever had an identical twin? Could you forget such a thing, and why would he turn up on a skeleton in just the location you were climbing in? The coincidence is too unlikely."

"No, I don't remember a twin, identical or otherwise. I mean, I don't remember forgetting about an identical twin if you know what I mean. This is really too much. You know about the tibias?"

"No."

Fanning told him about the fibrous cortical defect in his and the skeleton's tibia. He told Marty about the dental identification and the reproduction of the face based on the skull reconstruction. He told him of the skeletal findings on Margie's pubic bones.

"Hey," Marty said, "I had a DNA identification run on Margie, just like we did on yours. Can we have her skull for dental DNA studies? I mean the skull you found, of course."

"Yeah, OK, I'll bring it in first thing tomorrow. But what the hell is going on, Marty? I'm becoming concerned here. At least I think I should be concerned, don't you? I'm not really sure what to think. Is this some kind of joke? How in the hell can I find a dead skeleton buried in the wilds of Arizona and then find out the skeleton is related to me by having the identical genetic makeup? And what if, just what if the second skeleton comes out to have the same DNA as Margie? This is just too weird."

"Well, Chris, it looks like you have a bona fide mystery on your hands. Just consider it a challenge, a puzzle, a riddle. One thing I know there has to be a rational answer."

"Yeah, I guess you're right." Fanning hadn't even mentioned the most recent finding. "We found two other skeletons."

"You did?"

"Yes, we, that is, Jake Hamilton found them."

"Anything significant about them, Chris?"

"I'll say they are significant. They are children's skeletons and they roughly coincide with the ages and sizes of my own children. One is a boy and one is a girl."

"Where were they found?"

"In the same place as the other two, out in the desert."

"Tell you what, Fanning, why don't you bring the skeletons in here. We can run some DNA tests on them and see what we can see. Actually we already have some samples from your kids, we can see if they match up like you and Margie's do."

"What? You have DNA samples from my kids? How do you do that? Where the hell do you get DNA samples from my kids?"

"Take it easy Chris. It's just a preserved blood sample. We always save them. Everyone has a blood test at one time or another."

Fanning was pacified by that explanation.

~~~

The next day, after cleaning the small skeletons, Fanning brought in sample bones from each of them. Marty Greenspan isolated some samples of the

DNA from each and ran an electrophoresis on them. After the patterns were ready he called Fanning in to witness the comparison between the newly found bones and the DNA from Fanning's offspring. Disturbingly these also proved to be identical.

At this point Fanning made a decision. He decided to obtain assistance from the only source he thought could help. It was time to consult with Professor Karahsha.

7

Professor Karahsha was known to be eccentric. But what was not known about him was more significant. As a small child he was precocious, small for his age, and insatiably curious. He grew up on an Indian reservation, son of a drunkard father and a dissolute mother who showed minimal interest in him. The main relationship he had with his parents was to keep out of their way especially when they had been drinking. He was scrawny, even to the point of appearing emaciated. His determination and endurance, however, belied his physiognomy. He had a first rate mind and a deceptively wiry body. He reveled in being by himself, loved to study, and even more loved to challenge himself both physically and mentally. He was an expert outdoorsman, a hunter, and tracker who learned these skills by self-instruction. He tested himself from time to time by going without eating and drinking for two or three days at a time. He stayed out in the woods overnight by himself in different weather, learning to survive by sleeping in a hollowed out log and wrapping himself in leaves and small branches for warmth. He tried to inure himself to pain and discomfort by deliberately subjecting himself to fatigue, cold and hunger, ignoring the effects on his sinewy body and thus toughening himself for he knew not what. He naturally was viewed by his peers as somewhat of an outsider and was therefore sometimes picked on. If that happened he carefully kept a mental note of anyone whom he considered might have done him an injustice. He kept it buried alive but in the back of his mind and when the opportunity presented itself he would exact a just revenge. Sometimes he had to create the circumstances for that vendetta, as we shall see. As he grew older he was fond of thinking that he couldn't have any respect for anyone who did not hold a grudge.

At thirteen, he was, for a time, bedeviled by three bullies led by the most malignant 14-year old he had ever known. They picked on him because of his size and his superior intellect. The leader of the bullies was named Carlos, a beefy 220 lb. tub of a boy. They would often ambush him as he walked to school, his school books in hand. They didn't carry any school books. They would take his lunch money and taunt him about his chicken legs and skinny arms. There wasn't much he could do to avoid them except take a different route to school each day. But if he could get a good running start on them he inevitably would leave them behind. This went on for six or eight months. Then the three bullies took to some other diversion and eventually let him alone. But he did not forget.

Two years later he befriended the two older boys who were by now seventeen and were moving past the bullying stage. He aroused their interest by showing them his collection of Indian artifacts that he had dug up in the fields: arrowheads, old bones of animals he'd found, and his collection of spiders and scorpions both dead and alive that he kept in a small pen behind his house. He had dried rattlesnake heads, fangs, rattles, and skins that had been shed in molting and were the remains of long deceased serpents. The boys became friends, or so the ex-bullies thought.

One day after school, on a particularly hot day in July, as the sun burned out of a brilliant clear blue sky, he convinced the two boys that he knew the location of a dead body. He told them he had found the body on one of his many lonesome solitary wanderings in the arid countryside. Their interest piqued, they were happy to follow him to the barren desolate outskirts of their reservation where nobody ever ventured.

They walked for what seemed like hours. The older boys quickly grew hot and thirsty. They wanted to rest. They had no hint of any impending disaster. Karahsha became more aloof and maintained a coolness about him that did not betray his intentions. Finally, when the two older boys began to surmise all was not well, it was already too late. Karahsha had made sure that they had taken off on their little sojourn without telling anyone. As they looked at each other with a vague rising apprehension they tried to catch up with Karahsha to grab him and force him to tell them what was going on. Each time they tried he just sprinted away, with ease, just out of their reach.

With each lunge the younger boy simply put on a burst of speed and eluded them. Their concern and fatigue grew until it was apparent that they were actually lost in the brush country and totally dependent on Karahsha to get them out. Their desperation increased with each unsuccessful grab at the younger boy. They took off again and again determined to catch Karahsha who by now was showing his pleasure at their distress. He ran off at a rapid trot, widening the distance between them. He began to run in an "S" shaped pattern, thereby covering nearly twice the distance they did. His running was effortless while theirs was labored. They began to follow him in the "S" shaped zig-zag but tired rapidly of that. They perceived that they could gain ground on him by running in a straight line down the middle of the "S" he was making. And that is just what he wanted them to do. And that was their fatal mistake. As they ran at top speed, they seemed to be flying. They flailed in the air, arms and legs pumping mightily. Without warning, they were falling, falling down into a deep pit with sheer vertical walls that had obviously been made by someone's handiwork. There was not a niche or handgrip in sight. They fell into what appeared to them to be a hole from hell. Hundreds of agitated, angry rattlesnakes hissed and struck out, biting, rattling, re-biting, re-striking and envenoming with a vengeance until they had spent their fury and the boys were still. Karahsha watched the gruesome proceedings with a detached, scientific curiosity, rather than a spirit of revenge. He had attempted this more as a test of himself than as a vendetta and he was now rather satisfied with his achievement.

Such was the nature of the man Chris Fanning was prepared to consult.

8

Chris Fanning was ushered into the professor's inner sanctum. He was flattered because few were ever invited into this most elite of sanctuaries. The room was small, dimly lit, and clinically arrayed in white. Along the walls, on the three sides opposite the door were little stacks of storage compartments from floor to ceiling. They reminded Fanning of his compact disk storage bins. There was a desk and a work bench upon which were three microscopes, all frequently used. One, on the near table, was arranged so that a teacher and student could sit opposite each other and look through different eyepieces at 180 degrees to one another and study the same slide. The room was warm and uncomfortably humid even though a ventilation pump kicked on and off automatically in a duct that Fanning vaguely felt under his feet.

Fanning's curiosity level at all the little storage bins was hard to contain. He forced himself to remain outwardly calm. The professor was thinner than Fanning remembered but he'd only seen him dressed in his baggy white professor's coat in the past. He wore a faded but clean polo shirt, nondescript casual slacks, which had long lost any hint of a crease, and old, comfortable loafers which had also seen better days. His hair, however, was neatly brushed, even styled fashionably white around the ears and jet black on top. Without even a greeting or a smile of welcome, the professor behaved as if he had expected Fanning's visit.

Squinting in the dim light, Fanning was able to determine that each small compartment was individually labelled but he was too far away and the light was too weak to allow him to read any of them. He turned around scanning the bins behind him, but just at that moment the professor asked him to sit down on the bench opposite to where he took a seat. These were the first words the professor had spoken. He switched the light on to activate the microscope, pushed a slide onto the viewing table, centered it and gestured to Fanning to look down the eyepiece. Chris' stomach tightened and he became apprehensive without knowing why. Adjusting his eye to the microscope and focusing on the image he was first startled, then shaken, then horrified by what he saw. Inside the slide slowly floating around in a kind of miniature nightmare were all sorts of fantastic shapes and caricatures in three dimensions of grossly formed and misproportioned human beings swimming around in the drop of water. They performed rollovers, dives, twists, summersaults. Some swam like fish, some even had tails and some cavorted with gill slits plainly visible on the place where their necks should be.

Fanning was at once fascinated and repelled by the sight. Slowly floating into his view from one edge of the slide now came, in a kind of grotesque ballet, gently turning over and rotating on itself, a totally misshapen bizarre caricature of a deformed and dwarfed human being. The thing that made it so horrible to look at was the fact that it had no visible skin anywhere. Bare muscle was exposed over the skull. Tiny but recognizable tendons of the arms and legs were out in the open. The head was about twice the normal size of an adult head in proportion to the body, which was all jumbled together with no distinction between torso and abdomen. The arms and legs were tiny, misshapen and sort of flipper-like, as seen in a thalidomide baby, especially the legs. But the most riveting, the most dreadful sight was the eyes. Covered by no lids, no lashes, no folds of protective skin, the eyes were like a fish's eyes. As the thing, for Chris didn't know what else to call it, gently bumped into a glass wall and rebounded, the eyes switched their direction of gaze with a jerky motion like a fish moves its eyes. The eyeballs jumped from one position to another without any smooth drift in between. He wasn't sure the thing wasn't looking at him.

"What's that?" Chris asked as he withdrew from the sight. "Is it alive? What in the hell is it?" The professor replied that yes, it was alive. "And what is it?"

"What it is my young friend is you, or to be more exact, your clone. But unfortunately it didn't turn out exactly as I had hoped."

As Fanning gaped at the thing, it appeared as if it were grinning up at him with its skinless lips. He was filled with revulsion beyond description. "What do you mean, my clone?" The visible arteries throbbed in tune to the creature's heartbeat, and he could even see the bluish veins in the neck pulsating though with less amplitude.

"But this is horrible," Chris spat out. "You can't do this."

"Oh, but I can, and I did, and I will," the professor replied. "All these clones were, shall we say, conceived with DNA taken from routine blood tests you had when you were planning marriage. It's not illegal. There's no law against it. It's not even regulated. I've just had a hell of a time in perfecting the process. And I'm not completely there yet, although I now know how to fix it. Human beings are not frogs, you know. They are orders of magnitude more complicated. These specimens represent varying degrees of success, each slide more advanced than the last one, each slide teaching me some new fact, some new methodology on my path towards final achievement of my goal."

Fanning was appalled. As he perused the slides he gazed on specimens of various stages of development towards the adult human form. There were half-sized and three quarter-sized dwarfs whose body parts looked almost normal. The dimensions were of course only relative since they were microscopic and only visible through the scope. Some had body parts which were barely recognizable as fingers, feet, ears, and even hair. Chris felt his own hair stand up on the back of his neck. He screamed at the professor.

"What the hell are these things? Are they human or half human? Do they have feelings? Can they live outside these slides? How long have you been doing this, you nutcake? Why, why are you trying to create these abominations? Are you playing God? Who gives you the right? How nice of you to introduce me to all my relatives that I didn't even know I had."

"Hold on now. Slow down. When you calm down I'll explain," the professor soothed.

Chris ignored him and kept on inspecting the slides. He inserted slide after slide into the scope, watching all manner of grotesque microscopic creatures float around in the fluid. He was transfixed by one particular slide which contained a tiny beast that looked like a tadpole. It was comma shaped, with a tail, and gill slits. It had a face that was capable of change of expression and as it appeared to look back up at him through the mirrors of the microscope Fanning almost swore that it grimaced at him like an expectant dog begging for a morsel.

"What the hell, have you crossed me with a frog?" he demanded. "What, or who are these creatures? And what gives you the right to create them from my DNA and then keep them in a tiny droplet of water? Don't they have some rights too? After all, they are related to me, in a manner of speaking."

"All right, sit down and relax." The professor went over to the small refrigerator in the corner of the room, took out two soft drinks, opened them and offered one to Fanning, who gratefully took one of the colas and took a long hard pull.

He began, "Whether you participate or not, whether you like it or not, whether you consent or not, genetic manipulation is here to stay. It's the future and I for one intend to be an active player, even a leader. If I had not done this with your genes someone else would with someone else's genes. When you think about it in a rational way, you'll be glad you had an opportunity to be in on the ground floor. This is downright history making and you are an active contributor. It's very like Columbus' discovery of America. Sure, there are those who carp about the enslavement of the Indians, hell, I'm Indian myself. The diseases brought here by the Europeans, the destruction of native culture, the fact that Columbus may not even have been the first to see the new world, all that is irrelevant. When all is said and done he changed the world irrevocably. But if it had not been him it would have been someone else. This is just the same. There are people working on gene technology all over the world. It's just a question of who gets there first, not whether it will be done. But who does it first? I believe I will. There is no turning back, no holding up progress, for better or for worse these developments are irrevocable. And they are mostly overwhelmingly positive developments for the benefit of mankind and womankind and even animal kind. Think for a moment of the possibility of eliminating the genetically transmitted diseases like hemophilia, Parkinson's, muscular dystrophy, Tay-Sachs, Hurler's syndrome, Gaucher's disease, asthma, cystic fibrosis, osteoarthritis, scoliosis, and the list goes on and on. Say you had your leg amputated in an accident, why we'll grow you a new one. There will be no question of rejection because they will all be your own cells. No tissue typing. No immune system attack. No need for steroids or cyclosporine or other drugs to prevent rejection. No need to wait for organ donors. No one need be blind or deaf anymore. To change the subject, imagine the insights into history that will be available."

Fanning had followed him up to now with interest. "You lost me, Prof."

"Have you ever heard of the project that is now underway to determine from his remains if Abraham Lincoln had Marfan syndrome? His blood-stained shirt was preserved from his assassination. The DNA taken from his blood cells is even now being studied for that purpose. Imagine the possibility that scientists will be able to use the DNA from endangered species to clone new specimens. The possibility exists that long extinct species, if we can get hold of their DNA in sufficiently preserved condition, can actually be brought back from extinction."

This caught Fanning's imagination as he thought immediately of Smilodon.

"Once we know the exact molecular chemistry of the DNA from any organism we won't even need the preserved DNA. We can build it ourselves. It may interest you to know that the entire genome of a common bacteria has recently been elucidated. Every last triplet in the genome of Haemophilus influenzae has been identified. This has also been done for the common yeast and a simple worm. We now know exactly what part of the DNA programs for all the proteins, all the enzymes, all the chemicals that that organism makes. Imagine restoring life to Pithecanthropus erectus, Neanderthal man, Cro-Magnon man, Australopithecus. What if we could resurrect the dodo bird, the extinct homing pigeon, the vast range of animals and plants that have become extinct through man's folly or nature's ravages? Man, we could bring back the pterodactyl, the dinosaurs, Eohippus. We could even retro evolve species with computer-generated programs and study the very beginnings of life on this planet back to the one-celled animals that first originated from the primordial zone. We could gain control over our own destiny at last."

He was warming to his subject. His eyes took on a feverish intensity and he spoke now with a conspiratorial intimacy. "I wonder if you can guess, though, what my ultimate objective is? All those marvels I just enumerated by comparison to my real purpose are minor league. Do you have an iota of an inkling of what I am getting at? Can you cut through the flotsam and jetsam of genetics and perceive the final grand design? I've been watching you, Christopher Fanning. Are you the visionary I think you are?"

In spite of himself, Fanning's revulsion was starting to give way to an intense curiosity. Surely this lunatic was mad, but what if he wasn't? And even if he was mad couldn't a crazy man be responsible for positive scientific ideas? Weren't all scientific breakthroughs first greeted with hoots of unbelieving skepticism from the establishment? Fanning did not consider himself part of the establishment. Now his curiosity was tickled. What, after all, had the old crackpot done that was so bad? Maybe his cheese had fallen off his cracker a long time ago but did that necessarily void the reality of his achievement? Fanning had never heard of anyone who had done what the professor had done. He must be breaking new ground here by himself without government money or major grants that he was aware of. Fanning was now much calmer, more receptive than before. The level of disbelief had ebbed to be replaced by a grudging but growing admiration for this lone researcher who had, with modest resources, apparently vastly outpaced all the other high-powered scientists in the world at this one particular discipline. He had to give it to this "nutcake." He was far and away ahead of all the others even if he had not published his work. Fanning was not strictly speaking of the subject of research biology, but if anyone had made such an important contribution as the professor's he was sure he would know about it. After all he did read the more important science periodicals. The professor told him that it was largely due to his fascination with the Human Genome Project that he had become interested in this line of investigation.

Chris volunteered, "I know I've heard some about the Human Genome Project but I don't know any details. What is it exactly?"

"It has been likened to the Manhattan Project during the Second World War. Whereas the Manhattan Project was carried out in secret by the U.S. alone in Chicago to develop the atomic bomb before anyone else, the H.G.

Project is being developed among a dozen premier research centers throughout the world. What it is, is nothing more or less than the elucidation of the blueprint for the human species. It is really much more than the Manhattan Project to which it has been compared. It is constructive rather than destructive like the atomic bomb. The human informational code is transmitted to offspring by means of the chromosomes of which there are twenty-three pairs. Surely, you know the rudiments of human heredity and evolution are governed by the genes located on specific sites on those chromosomes. The genes in turn are themselves made of the famous double coiled helix of Watson and Crick who won a Nobel Prize for their work. The Human Genome Project used their work as a foundation and built on it, and now that it is complete every last arrangement of the helical strand is known and mapped out in a systemic way. The specific molecules, the proteins, the types of chemical bonding and the exact arrangement of every last cytosine, thymidine, guanine, etc. are known for the human species. Now, this information fills volumes, but to those who know how to read it the entire basis for building a human being is available. The gene or combination of genes that cause cancer, the genes for eye color, height, intelligence, memory, musical ability, mental retardation, and a whole host of others are there to be manipulated for the betterment of mankind or even one specific individual. But the possibilities go much farther than that. With completion of this knowledge it is possible to build a human being to a precise specification. We could, for instance, grow a race of super athletes, runners, weight lifters, musicians, composers, scientists, mathematicians. We could even look further into the future evolution of the human race by dialing in the DNA into a computer, for example, and then programming various atmospheric and geological conditions. Then we could fast forward to a million or two million years from now to see what the effect will be. As for your concerns about all your little relatives in the microscopes, they don't even qualify as human."

"How do you figure that?" Fanning asked.

"The definition of a human life has been put at conception by the Catholic Church, to which I happen to subscribe. Others describe it as the time when the blastula, the single-celled hollow sphere of early gestation, becomes imbedded in the uterine mucosa. Still others would say it is a viable human being when it is 32 weeks into gestation and has a chance of survival out of the uterus. These microscopic slide creatures have none of these characteristics. It would be a long stretch of the imagination to call them beings who have rights and privileges, let alone call them human beings. All they are, are combinations of DNA, messenger RNA and various proteins, sugars, lipids, amino acids and vitamins that I put together and caused to grow; an experiment, nothing more, nothing less."

Chris had no challenge to that statement because as a good Catholic himself he had a very good idea of the church's definition of the conception of human life.

"Now come on, Chris, you have to admit the possibilities are staggering and endless. Why, think of what is happening to our very fragile planet Earth. When it comes time to escape to some other planet because we've befouled our own do you really think we will be sending human beings to Mars or somewhere else? We'll more likely be sending packets of freeze-dried DNA. And when that DNA lands on some suitable host environment it will grow into a human being just as surely as it did on Earth. It may lay dormant for hundreds or thousands of years until conditions are right. Can you not see the potential of this technology? And I have not even told you my ultimate aim. That which will be my crowning achievement to stand the world on its ear. It will be a feat so fundamental and inconceivable that it cuts to the very heart of creation itself."

Chris blinked and said, "What are you going to do, recreate the Big Bang?"

The professor replied, "No, I intend to recreate the Creator of the Big Bang."

Mystified, Chris gulped. "What do you mean by that?"

"Think about it. According to your own Catholic Church, the living connection between the Creator and the created was actually here on earth in human form at one time. A Messiah who was a living God, a being who incorporated features of both the Creator and the created. He was an animated, breathing embodiment of the force behind all forces, the spark of all fires that ever were, the intelligence behind the Big Bang itself."

"Whoa, wait a minute, who in the hell are you talking about, Jesus Christ himself?"

The professor replied, "Yes, yes of course Jesus Christ, who else?"

"But you must be nuts. How can you possibly recreate Jesus Christ?" Chris asked incredulously.

"By cloning of course. You have already seen what I have done with your own DNA and I have progressed way beyond that in the last several weeks." His eyes burned with an intensity Fanning had rarely seen.

"But how do you know you can perfect the process? And even if you do where in God's sweet earth are you going to get your hands on Christ's DNA? Besides you are an American Indian, you are not supposed to believe in Christ or God. You believe in clouds and rivers and mountains, eagles, bears, storms and such. Man, with all due respect, you are really off your rocker and I say that in the most respectful way."

The professor relaxed and sat back waiting for Fanning to finish sputtering objections. When Fanning stopped for breath the professor began again.

"Yes, it is true I am an American Indian, Navajo, to be precise. I believe in the air, the water, the animals and the earth itself as spiritual entities. But I have made an exhaustive study of all the great religions of the world in an objective, scientific method, and I have come to believe in a profound way that the story of Christ as Son of God, the birth, life, death, resurrection and ascension to heaven really did happen. I believe it so firmly, with so much faith that I am willing to stake my future on it, career, life and all. There is also a body of very firm archeological and historical evidence that confirms the fact that Jesus Christ actually lived and was indeed the Son of God. As for the DNA, did you ever hear of the Shroud of Turin? That is the death cloth that was used to wrap the dead body of Christ. But supposedly it has been shown by modern scientific analysis to have dated from the Middle Ages, not biblical times. I know one of the physicists who worked on that most recent study of the Shroud. He was an undergraduate classmate of mine back at Princeton University. He is brilliant and honest to a fault. I have information from him and other sources that indicate the studies were done with less than the strict scientific vigor that the world was led to believe.

For example, the Vatican allowed tiny fragments to be cut from the Shroud but only from the margins. Now, we know there were certain sections of the Shroud destroyed by fire and that it was restored by some nuns after the fire. It is entirely possible that the Vatican allowed the very portions which were restored to be taken as samples. In that case the result would certainly indicate that the Shroud dated from the Middle Ages, since the fragments analyzed were indeed from the Middle Ages. There is other information, not widely known, that findings from that study that would tend to verify that it dates from biblical times was suppressed by the church. The information released to the public is therefore flawed and is the precise opposite of the truth."

Fanning was skeptical. "Why would the church misrepresent their findings to the public? What would be their reason? I'd think it would be the other way around, that they would be anxious to have it known that tangible physical evidence exists from biblical times that is scientifically proven to be tied to the resurrection. That would constitute incontrovertible proof that Jesus Christ lived and died according to the biblical account. That would in turn constitute almost proof positive that the Catholic Church is the one true church tied to the Almighty by a chain no other religion could claim. So wouldn't it be to their advantage to have the truth known? To invoke this incontrovertible proof in any discussion with Buddhism, Judaism, Baptism, Protestantism, Lutheranism, and all the other religions including Islam, Hinduism, Shintoism, Confucianism or any other would serve to discredit them in a striking way."

"Not necessarily so," the professor replied. "In the first place the present day Catholic Church is so bureaucratically hidebound and fossilized that any disturbance in the status quo would rattle them to the very foundations. They, the central power elite of the church, would not want nor would they know how to handle a Second Coming. Why, they would quake in their ecclesiastic boots at the prospect of a modern Christ proselytizing the masses to avoid the trappings of wealth, give away their possessions, lead a life of poverty, charity and penance, as well as avoiding pomp and ritual. How do you think the pope might react to being kicked out of his palatial digs and told to live like a pauper? No more first class seat on the Alitalia Airline. No more Popemobile, fine clothes, servants, meetings with heads of states, vacations in Gardenia. Do you think he would want to hear that? Then, of course, the other possibility might be that we, you and I, have been chosen through some divine godly plan to perform this service against all odds in the fulfillment of the Second Coming. Maybe we are the chosen. How do you think the church establishment would react to that?

"Look, Chris Fanning, I know this all sounds fantastic to you, something out of my deranged imagination, but believe me, I have thought it all through and I know I can be successful."

He gave Fanning a moment to digest these last words. Chris was intrigued in spite of his skepticism. The professor went on. "Another scenario might be that the being we create is Christ-like in somatic form but turns out to be a weak-minded retard or worse, just a regular guy who happened to be a good Samaritan. A person who had an entire mythology grow up around him while in reality he was just some simple fellow who will be totally out of his element on modern day planet Earth. Don't you think those fellows in the Vatican have thought of all this? Don't you think the Shroud is as protected as if it were housed in Fort Knox for the reasons I have outlined?"

"OK, OK, for the sake of argument, let's say your assumptions are all true. How do you know it will work? How do you know the Shroud contains enough DNA in a preserved, useable form to allow you to replicate enough so you could grow or build a human body in His likeness? Mere possession of DNA, even if you knew all the base units and their exact combinations, that doesn't mean you can grow a body from it. It's a totally different question to be able to take that DNA and make a human body out of it. You need a supportive environment like a mother's uterus. You need maternal hormones, the proper pH, oxygen tension, growth hormone and a thousand other ingredients. I'm not a molecular biologist . . ."

"Ah, but I am," interrupted the professor. "All those considerations you have mentioned, I have long ago thought of them and worked them out."

Startled, and a little unnerved, Chris asked, "You mean you have a new Virgin Mary already picked out who's willing to bear the child?"

"I'm sure we could get one if we needed but we don't."

Fanning silently noted the "we" in the professor's speech.

"All of your concerns, Chris Fanning, are mere physical parameters like standard temperature and pressure, and in any case I have worked them out so that we would only have to provide the initial stimulus and then the process becomes self-sustaining. Once the DNA is organized into a cellular structure it will control reproduction on its own so long as the ambient conditions remain optimum."

"Whoa," Chris yelled. "What cell? You don't go from naked DNA to a cell already formed. Where does that one cell come from?"

The professor's face twisted into a sneer. "Can't you guess, Chris Fanning, graduate student? Have you never heard of a test tube baby?"

"Well, yes," Chris replied. "But that involves putting a sperm and an ovum together in a test tube under the proper conditions." Slowly it dawned on him. "Jesus, you mean you would use a human ovum? Where would you get it?"

"Come on now, Chris," the professor was almost condescending. "I am Chief of Pathology at a university hospital. Almost every day pathological specimens come to my department from living, breathing patients, many of them perfectly healthy or at least have healthy ova. Often, total hysterectomies are carried out on perfectly healthy young women for such benign reasons as uterine fibroids. A total hysterectomy includes the ovaries and oops what do the ovaries contain? Why, that's where the ova are. Now, it's simple today to plagiarize a viable ovum, conduct microscopic surgery to remove the nucleus and its DNA, then substitute the DNA from the Shroud and give it a gentle push in the right environment. You have the diploid number of chromosomes, you have egg penetration, you have eliminated the troublesome problem of the mother's DNA. What more could a bodybuilder want?" The look of triumph on the professor's face was scary.

"But isn't that illegal?" Chris asked.

The professor gave him a look and a shrug that said "what of it."

Chris was torn by this turn of events. On the one hand he was thoroughly impressed by the professor's thoughtful scholarship, his triumph over obstacles that still perplexed the other major researchers in the field and his major command of the subject. He had been able to rise to each difficulty in his path, and had effectively countered all the negative arguments of a technical nature that he could think of. Of course, Fanning was no molecular biochemist so maybe there were other objections he had not even thought about.

"OK professor, now I have a different question for you," and Fanning went on to tell him about the mystery of the bones. He'd almost forgotten this with all the fantastic science the professor had been describing. Somehow he was not surprised when Karahsha confessed that he had been responsible for the bones. He had simply used DNA extracted from blood cells taken from Fanning and his family. Then using PCR, or polymerase chain reaction, to reproduce as much DNA as he needed he went ahead and tried to clone Fanning and his family. The professor admitted that he'd run into problems in that he couldn't get the process to go past the bone stage. He'd had to discard the skeletons and never intended that anyone find them. By chance, the tornado exposed them and by an even greater coincidence Fanning found them. The professor confessed that he was the guilty party when Fanning felt he was being watched out in the desert.

Fanning felt a great relief, rather than any animosity toward Karahsha. A relief that nothing more sinister was responsible for those confounded bones and he could wrap up that puzzle and put it to bed.

"I have one last question, no make that two. Number one, how do you know you can retrieve suitable DNA from the Shroud, and how are you so sure it will work?"

"I'll take those one at a time, Chris," he answered. "First you know that intact DNA has already been recovered from a kind of bug, a weevil, to be precise. This weevil was determined to be 120 million years old. This little bug was trapped in a tree's solidified resin which covered him, hardened and became solid amber, preserving that little bug for 120 million years. Think of it! If DNA can be preserved and recovered from 120 million years ago how much easier must it be to recover DNA not yet 2,000 years old! As to the integrity of the material to be recovered from the Shroud, you see, I believe that the facial and somatic images are real. I believe it is an actual transfer of the very material from Christ's body onto the cloth of the Shroud. I don't know how it was done, but I am sure there was an energy transfer, a physical basis, or electromagnetic searing of the cloth at the time of the rebirth. Remember the dead body of Christ was buried in this cloth and later it came back to life. I believe that was the result of a real miracle. But even miracles have to have a mechanism, a process based in the real world through which they are accomplished. What makes it a miracle is only that we don't know how it is done. It's like a magic trick, only on a scale which is orders of magnitude more impenetrable. Once you know how the trick is done it's not magic anymore. It's the same with miracles, only we haven't learned how it's done yet. But give us time, give us time.

"Therefore, if the very essence of the physical body was etched into the cloth by some type of energy, say electromagnetic, or thermonuclear, or electric, or chemical or whatever, some residue should still exist imbedded in the fiber. This Christly trace or remnant should be recoverable and should be amenable to study. In addition, there must have been some bleeding onto the cloth or some seepage of body fluids like sweat or tears or edema fluid. The Shroud should be literally saturated with His DNA. We are not dealing here with minute snippets that don't represent the entire organism like those found in some 60 million year old bug fossilized in amber. This is barely 2,000 years old, preserved from biblical times carefully, lovingly by Mary herself, then by the priests of the religion. Preserved, in a dry constant temperature environment with weather exposure, humidity, and human contact kept to a minimum. I believe it is in a pristine state ready to be used by those who are prepared. To paraphrase Louis Pasteur, scientific discoveries are made by those with a prepared mind. And, my boy, I have been preparing for this all my life. So, I am giving you an opportunity to be in on the greatest scientific project ever. It's up to you whether you participate or not. But you should know it will go forward with you or without you. The groundwork has been laid. There remains only the execution of the scheme. For that I need the Shroud or a piece thereof and that is where you come in."

Chris' eyes widened. He was curious and a little scared about what he might be about to let himself in for. He still felt the professor to be out in left field but now his interest level was at its height. "Me," he said. "What do you mean me?" he asked.

"All in good time," replied the older man, "but first I have something to show you that will dispel any remaining doubts you may be harboring. I am sure you are aware of the approach my surgical colleagues are taking in the problem of degenerative joint disease for example. Well, they have devised an extremely unphysiological solution to the problem. It involves implanting metal and polyethylene into the human knee joint and cementing it all in with another unphysiological material called bone cement, or methyl methacrylate. Oh, the implants work pretty well for a time in the knee and hip, less well in the shoulders, elbows, ankles, and wrists. The problem is it's a big operation. Infection can lead to loosening of the components and failure requiring re-operation or even amputation. Eventually, even without infection, the components can come loose leading to failure anyway. I should mention that re-operation always leads to a less satisfactory result than in the first surgery. At first surgeons only did this type of operation in very elderly patients but with experience and refinements of technique they gradually started operating on younger people. Although the surgeons have become better in their methods and vast strides have been made in the instrumentation and implants, the fact still remains that it is an unphysiological approach to the problem. Now, what if you looked at it from another point of view? What if one were able to isolate the genes that were responsible for growing your knee, for instance? Well, I've done that. I'm talking about a living human being with a degenerate, painful knee. There is a patient I want you to meet with this very problem. I've already isolated the genes for growing the bone, ligament, cartilage, connective tissue marrow, in short, all the tissues responsible for reproduction of his knee and now I'm going to show you what it can do."

He motioned Chris to follow him into a small treatment room where an elderly, white-haired gentleman waited. He greeted the professor with a grin and handshake that showed complete confidence.

"Chris Fanning, this is Homer Armstrong. Mr. Armstrong is suffering from degenerative joint disease in his knees. He can barely walk due to the pain, the deformity, and restriction of motion." The professor helped the old man to rise out of his chair. He was wearing one of those short hospital gowns that barely cover the knees. Armstrong was able to stand and take only a few painful steps with the aid of a walker he kept with him at all times.

"You see how miserable this poor man is. If it weren't for his knees he might enjoy his remaining years." The professor switched on the X-ray view box on the wall. Hanging upon it was Mr. Armstrong's knee pictures. "I know you're not a medical person, so I'll explain these to you. See here, the narrowed joint spaces indicating the articular cartilage is almost gone. The articular cartilage is the white shiny smooth material like you see on the ends of a chicken bone. There are multiple giant osteophytes, bone spurs, where the body has tried to make repairs but has succeeded in only producing these shapeless masses of useless bone. There is a bow leg deformity indicating more wear on the inner portions of the joints than the outer. The patella or knee cap is completely degenerated on its articular surface, which is the inner surface that should be smooth and even is now rough, uneven, with pits and ulcers that interfere with motion and cause pain. Also, notice the enlarged, knobby appearance of the knees due to the disease."

The professor turned away from the X-rays to Mr. Armstrong's knees.

"See how any movement is restricted and painful." Armstrong winced as Karahsha moved the joints. "It's a wonder he can even stand up."

Chris began to wonder where all this was leading.

The professor went on. "Again, because you are not a medical professional Chris, I'm going to explain to you in detail just what is going to take place here. Mr. Armstrong is not willing to undergo the risk of major surgery to replace his knees in the conventional way. I have talked to him at length and he agrees to be my first test patient in an experiment that has never been attempted before in humans, or any other animal for that matter. In the worst scenario he won't be helped at all, but will be no worse off. In the best possible scenario, which I expect to occur, he will soon have new pain-free knee joints that will be his without risk or cost. I propose to inject into one of his knees a preparation I have made by isolating the genes responsible for growing a knee. To mention only a few of the constituents besides the genes themselves, there is the interleukin 8, the multiple proteins for structure, the messenger RNA, and genetically engineered human growth hormone or HGH. I expect the growth factors to begin a cascade of reactions, at first only a kind of chemical communications system. Then a chain reaction will ensue that will produce a new, functioning, fully integrated knee joint in the proper orientation, not sitting sideways or upside down or backwards, but appropriately aligned, made of his own tissue and identical in every way to the knee joint he had, in say his mid-twenties. The growth of the new tissues will be infinitesimally tiny at first, but then will take on a significant bulk in his own degenerated joint. The diseased, non-functional tissue will be absorbed and disappear partially by the mechanical pressure of the new growth, a benign tumor, if you will, and partially by the elaboration of enzymes whose function will be to digest the old worn out tissues. The energy for all these mechanisms will come at first from nutrients in the synovial fluid of the joint itself. Then, at the next stage of development, from Mr. Armstrong's own blood supply. In fact, all of the substances, oxygen, glucose, proteins, etc., that are needed, aside from what I inject, will come from his own body. The final fully formed structure will fuse to his own tissues like a bone graft, only there is no possibility of rejection in this case."

Karahsha then went on to prepare the old man's knee with an iodine solution. Normally, this would be done by a nurse or an assistant, but in the interest of secrecy, he did it himself. He finished the prep in six minutes. He went to a refrigerated cabinet and removed a stainless steel container. Inside this was a sterile needle and syringe assembled together and containing a 12 cc quantity of a yellow viscous fluid, vaguely reminiscent of clear motor oil, along with another sterile syringe containing a small amount of a local anesthetic. He injected the area just lateral to the upper pole of the knee cap. When he judged the area to be numb he took the larger syringe and gently probed between the patella and femur to find the cavity of the knee joint. Then he injected the entire contents of the syringe into the joint with no discomfort at all to his patient. The 12 cc of fluid produced a gentle bulge in the knee just above the superior pole of the patella. He encouraged the older man to be up and around with his walker until he tired.

"Come on over here," he said. He motioned Chris and Mr. Armstrong over to a large impressive looking piece of machinery. "We have here a cine MRI machine. Simply put, it subjects the living tissues to a strong magnetic field for a fraction of a second. This in turn forces the molecules to orient themselves in line with the magnetic field, positive poles north, negative poles south. When the magnetic field is shut off the body's molecules jump immediately back to their previous random alignment. This reversal to normal orientation produces a surge of energy that can be detected and turned into a picture much like the picture formed from tiny multiple pixels on your television set. The cine part of this device allows one to observe the tissues as they are now in real time with movement of the joint visible on the screen. We can also snap hard copies at any point in time. I hate that expression but that is what it's called. By the way this technology has nothing to do with X-rays. Mr. Armstrong, if you would please take a seat here."

The old man sat as still as possible in the machine. A bluish-green image came into focus on the monitor when the professor flipped the on switch. This was accompanied by a low hum of electric motors. Chris was now able to make out the old knee on the screen. It was somehow different than the X-ray picture but still showed the same basic structure, something like the difference between the quality of a moving picture as opposed to a video camera.

"I added in a generous dose of growth hormone and other stimulatory factors to speed the development. There are some risks to that but I wanted to have a result as soon as possible."

As they both watched the image on the monitor, Chris was transfixed by the changes that were rapidly starting to take place. Almost like a flower blossoming in stop motion photography there were stirrings starting to take place in the tissues under surveillance. Difficult to detect at first but definite, the atmosphere became charged with excitement.

The knee itself was stimulated to a gentle erythema by the extra blood supply drawn to the area by the demands of the new growth. In response to questions, Mr. Armstrong denied any sense of discomfort or pain. The softly humming MRI machine gave an interrupted picture of the events occurring within the joint. A tiny amorphous mass now appeared to float in the joint fluid or more precisely in the fluid the professor had instilled into the knee. As they watched, the nondescript mass grew in size and began to take on a discrete form suggestive more and more of a structure with specific parts arranged in a definite order. As the structure grew past a certain point it was apparent that it had ceased to rotate and float about aimlessly. There was now a front and back, a left and a right side, and an up and down. From this point onward the orientation did not change. The thing seemed to imbed itself in the host tissue. At the same time the host's own structure surrounding the new mass could be seen to assume a fuzzy appearance as if it were dissolving at points where the new growth touched it. And in fact that was exactly what was taking place as explained by the professor. The MRI pictures were imaged on a video screen and at critical points the professor's rapture was evident in his face and in the animation of his demeanor. He made no attempt to conceal it.

Chris however was filled with a quiet awe and wonder. He began to realize that he was witness to a feat never before performed ever in the history of man, a feat which had limitless potential to help mankind. He asked, "How can this process take place so fast? I'm no physician or biologist but I would think this should take months or years."

Karahsha explained that it was all controlled by the various growth hormones and other stimulatory factors that set off the genetic DNA and messenger RNA regulators of growth.

The two continued to watch in fascination as the new structure or neoplasm gradually assumed the shape of a miniature knee and the degenerated, defective tissue gradually faded away to be replaced by the new tissue at the margins.

"At this rate the process will be complete by morning," Chris offered.

"No Chris, it will be full grown by midnight tonight. The new joint will take its place properly oriented as to up, down, left, right, front, back, and will be anchored in place firmly attached to the parent structure and stably incorporated into the host."

"Since there is DNA identical to the patient's own in the new growth no possibility of rejection is possible. What could be more perfect? We have captured the ability of the tadpole and salamander to regenerate an amputated or injured part. Think what this will mean for humanity! Think of the technical achievement we have created all by ourselves before anyone else."

Fanning thought the professor had worked alone too long and needed someone from the outside, namely himself, with whom to be conspiratorial.

The tiny structure on the screen became more and more recognizable for what it was. The growth was almost visible to the eye. When Chris looked away from the screen, then let his gaze fall on it again he was able to notice a definite increase in size and definition. In the meantime Mr. Armstrong lay in the contraption perfectly comfortable without any pain or discomfort, barely conscious of the momentous changes taking place in his body.

Professor Karahsha continued, "At the end of its growth this knee will be fully flexible from 180 degrees of extension to about 140 degrees of flexion. It will be in pristine condition unmarked by the scourge of time and disease. By the way, the propensity to acquire the disease of degenerative osteoarthritis has recently been found to be inherited. Up to now there wasn't much the victims of this disease could do but wait and watch as they became progressively disabled. Oh, the Medical-Pharmaceutical establishment makes lots of noise about how they can control the disease with their arthritis medicines, the so-called nonsteroidal anti-inflammatories or injections of cortisone into the damaged joint. Then, when all else fails and the patient doesn't respond anymore, the surgeons, master craftsmen that they are, enter and put a chunk of metal and plastic in through a risky major surgical procedure. In contrast, Mr. Armstrong's new knee will be at the relative stage of young adulthood when its growth ends. It will last way past his expected lifetime. It will carry no risk, least of all, that of rejection and his other knee can be done anytime."

Even as he spoke the new structure continued to enlarge visibly on screen. In the midst of his awe Chris had a thought.

"What makes it stop growing? I mean how does it know when it has achieved the correct size and shut off the growth?"

"That depends on the amount and type of growth hormone used and the volume and type of nutrients injected. Also, in part, the size is mandated by the genetic determinants. There are specific genes that program for a cascade of controlled and monitored hormonal reactions that determine the point of growth cessation."

~~~

As midnight approached, the process was complete. Mr. Armstrong was removed from the magnetic resonance imager. He was allowed to sit up, regain his bearings and take a deep breath in preparation to testing the new knee. When he was ready, he was encouraged to rise and begin slowly to ambulate using a cane on account of the pain in the untreated knee. Mr. Armstrong became quickly ecstatic. The years of misery, of constant pain in his right knee were gone. Even though his other weight bearing joints were still painful he felt as if he had been freed from a prison. The old man practically leapt across the room with joy.

"Hey Doc," Mr. Armstrong wanted to know, "When will you do the other knee? This is just great. I'll be doing the Irish Jig when my other knee's done."

The professor sounded a bit of caution, "Now hold on Mr. Armstrong, this is the first time this has been done, ever, in the history of man. We need to make sure there are no side effects over a period of time. Here let's examine the knee."

He proceeded to check out his achievement.

"See here Chris, even the skin looks younger. He now has a full range of motion, the ligaments are stable, swelling and inflammation are all gone. I do believe we have a successful result. Come on Mr. Armstrong, let's see how it stands up to a walk around the block."

The three co-conspirators jauntily walked several blocks. Filled with the happiness of their newfound accomplishment the three ducked into the first bar they encountered and spent the next several hours celebrating. When it was time to go home the two triumphant scientists drove Homer Armstrong home and parted company. The professor made Fanning understand that he was not to breathe a word of what had transpired to anyone. Fanning, in the glow of all he had seen and heard this night and with the added fortification of the recent alcohol intake, agreed to keep all he had seen to himself. When he returned home at 3AM, he was greeted by an irate Margie, who once again had been forced to fear that she might be left a young widow. In his defense, he told her of the fantastic events he'd been a part of this night and swore her to secrecy as he'd been sworn. Margie didn't know whether to believe him or not.

~~~

The next night after dinner, Margie was still peeved at Fanning, so she declared that she needed a night out. She made Fanning babysit the children, and went to spend the evening with the Sisters of the Order. Fanning cautioned her not to stay out too late since this was a city with all its inherent dangers. She replied, "Oh don't worry Chris, if someone grabs me tonight, surely they will turn me loose by morning."

9

Some days later Chris Fanning sat in the professor's office discussing Mr. Armstrong and his knee.

"So how is he doing?" Fanning asked.

"Couldn't be better," the professor replied.

"OK. I admit you have convinced me there is a possibility of succeeding. But I have another question, in fact several."

"Go ahead, shoot," the professor said.

"Does this project of yours have anything to do with the finding of the bones that had been driving me to distraction?"

"Of course, I thought I explained all that the other day."

"And you used my wife's and children's DNA to grow the bones?"

"Yes, yes I told you I could only get to the stage where the bones would grow, then I got hung up in the physiology and couldn't proceed any further. But now I have that worked out, I know how to get past the bone stage and get the rest of the job done."

"But why did you discard the bones in that particular area? Did you mean for me to find them?"

"No, I didn't deliberately mean for you to find the bones. That was fortuitous. But when you found them I realized that was a way I could raise your interest. I needed someone intelligent, someone who could recognize the importance of what I am doing. I think I judged you correctly. I knew that at some point you would come to me with your mystery."

"OK, but why my bones, why my family?"

"Because you were the ideal combination of subjects, one adult male, one adult female, one male child, one female child. This combination gave me

89

the most to work with, and with each one of you I learned something, something important, so that now I am poised to begin the most important experiment man has ever devised. The fact you found the bones yourself as well as those of your family was entirely fortuitous and would not have happened save for the tornado that lifted the top soil and exposed them."

Chris continued, "I have another question, why? What is your ultimate purpose? What if you have a perfectly cloned body of Christ, live, walking, breathing? How do you know what He will be, how He will act, what will He say? His brain will be just a blank slate with no imprinted memory of who He really is. I mean the brain works by synapses, dendrites, axons, chemical and electric processes, ions flowing across cell membranes. It doesn't work at the genetic level. That much I remember from my college biology."

"How do you know?" the professor asked.

"That's what I learned in neurobiology."

"What you learned in neurobiology is the received wisdom from the establishment. What I am doing is on the cutting edge of the state of the art. The envelope expanded to another, higher level, heretofore unconceived. If what you say is true and we produce an innocent, why then it will be up to us to teach Him who He is. If we do the science correctly He will have to be intelligent, maybe the most intelligent, perceptive, incredibly capable person and able to learn to pick up quickly where He left off so long ago. If you are wrong and He instantly knows who He is and what He is, well then we have no worries, do we?"

"OK, suppose it works, then what are your plans for Him?"

"Oh that's easy, the same as the last time He was here. Can you imagine the potential for good that would bring to humanity? Can you fathom the depth of religious re-awakening that would follow a Second Coming? Can't you see the entire future of the world changing because of what we will have done? Doesn't it fill you full of wonder, awe, and anticipation? Haven't you seen the power some of the phonies have had, the James Joneses, the David Koreshes? Can you begin to imagine the level of gratitude the world will have when we give them the real thing?"

At this point Karahsha's eyes glowed like black fire. He took on an enraptured, messianic appearance. The temporal arteries in his head throbbed with a life of their own. Fanning almost became alarmed.

"Can you live with the fact that no matter whatever happens in the world, we, you and I, will be the ones who will go down in history as the resurrectors, the restorers of the Christian faith? We will be responsible for a resurgence in religious fever the world has not seen since the start of Christianity."

Fanning sat down heavily. In spite of himself, he began to catch the enthusiasm. Still some doubts continued to nag.

"Suppose nobody believes in Him? Suppose people take it as a joke and refuse to believe in His authenticity? Suppose He doesn't cooperate? What if our creature doesn't or cannot act the prophet? We could be horse laughed off the academic scene. Remember cold fusion?"

"It will be up to us to make certain that doesn't happen, won't it?"

"OK, I have another concern," Fanning continued. "How in the world are we going to prevent the flood of demands to clone everyone's dead loved one? Once people know we have the technology won't there be an overwhelming unstoppable demand that we clone old Uncle Joe or Aunt Mary who just died? One of the most powerful human desires is to bring back poor old mother or father or son or any other loved one who is deceased. It won't even be limited to humans. Once it is generally known that we can do our little trick people will want us to clone their dead pet dogs, cats, birds ad infinitum. Where will we put all these people and pets? History shows that if the technology exists and there is enough of a demand then it will be done. What are you going to do, charge $10,000 a head to bring back old departed mother? And then when the clone itself dies there will be an incentive to do it all over again. The world will even more quickly become overcrowded and we'll be like a bacterial colony on a Petri dish that dies out because of a shortage of food and inability to get rid of its own waste."

"But wait, it gets better or worse depending on your point of view," the professor warned.

"How so?" Chris asked.

The professor considered ducking the question. "Well, for one thing, due to genetic engineering we will be able to create all kinds of combinations of people. By using the techniques of gene isolation, reproduction, splicing, localization and recombination, in short genetic engineering, we will be able to make a clone of you or your brother if you had one with different colored eyes. We will be able to make a clone of you but in a female form. We will be able to insert genes for longevity, tallness, thinness, athletic or intellectual prowess, genes to prevent baldness, genes that will resist or protect against cancer, stroke, heart disease, diabetes, arthritis, ugliness, acne, obesity, flat feet, bow legs, asthma, cystic fibrosis, Alzheimer's disease, muscular dystrophy, multiple sclerosis, and the list is not even one tenth over. This technology already exists in a fundamental way. We are already using it to produce enzymes, proteins like insulin, growth hormone, vaccines, hormones that make cows produce more milk, bacteria that will eat waste products, as in oil spills either in the ocean or on land. It is just a question of time. We will be able to create new species, say a spider that produces silk that can be used for clothing or structural materials. We will be able to genetically engineer sting-less bees that will produce more and better honey. These are just a few of the possibilities. Use your imagination to think of all kinds of different, new, useful, bizarre, grotesque, dangerous combinations. We could for instance program people to become smaller over generations so as to use less of the mineral and foodstuffs we now use wastefully. Smaller people would use less water and less fossil fuel, extending the life of those resources and cutting the degradation of our environment. Truly, it boggles the mind.

"As with all new technology it has the possibility of good or evil, progress or regression, and will raise more ethical dilemmas than you ever thought possible. It will pose problems that would give Einstein a headache. These capabilities will make possible, in the next 50 to 100 years, changes more profound than what we have seen in the last 1,000 years. When you then combine molecular biology with the power of computers we will be able to predict the course of human evolution. By placing different gene pools in varying environments, in computer simulation, we will be able to predict the likely future course of humanity and whether we will become extinct or not. In the case that the future holds extinction for us we will be able to predict the animal most likely to replace us in the domination of the earth. And I don't think that human extinction is in any way incompatible with theology. The possibilities positively astound the thinking observer.

"For instance, there is already a project in the planning stage to colonize Mars with human beings. Now what do you suppose is the major snag in such a project aside from the problems in transportation? The major obstacle is that 96.5% of the Martian atmosphere consists of carbon dioxide. This is of course not user-friendly to human beings. The atmosphere is so thin that the sun's radiant energy heats it up intolerably in the daytime and the planet radiates its heat off so efficiently at night that it becomes impossibly cold for most things, like people. But therein lies an opportunity. What if we could genetically engineer an organism, a plant say, or an algae that could withstand a long interplanetary trip to Mars? Further, what if we could land it in a location on Mars where there is an abundance of water? It is known that the polar caps on Mars are made primarily of water ice. So this would be the logical landing place. Once there, the transplanted genetically engineered organisms, be they algae or bacteria, any green plant capable of photosynthesis will set up housekeeping. Using the abundant carbon dioxide in the atmosphere and the available water the plants can make the sugar they need for respiration and lo and behold what else? Why, oxygen of course. Think of it. An oxygen producing machine introduced to a planet that has very little oxygen in its atmosphere! No one knows how long it would take to create a viable oxygen atmosphere but hell, what's the rush? Once enough oxygen is produced we could send a shipment of rats or canaries or whatever you like to test it out. Also, we could send probes to relay back to Earth the oxygen content of the atmosphere. When it becomes sufficiently life supporting, we could begin to send astronauts to form colonies and start to explore the place. Of course, the atmosphere would have to be deep enough to absorb radiant energy and dampen the loss of heat at night and offset the high temperatures in the daytime. Needless to say, all this will be extremely expensive but suppose we have mucked up our planet by that time and our survival is in danger? We will have no place to go. Certainly we will always be faced with the crybabies who say we should use all our resources to feed and house all the poor, non-productive people in the world. But if we do that we will simply have even more poor, non-productive people."

"Whoa, wait a minute, you just threw a curve and I'm not going to let you get away with it," Chris interrupted. "If you help poor people you get more of them? What kind of medieval thinking is that?"

"Oh come on, I don't want to get into that kind of a discussion with you. You know we will always have the poor among us. You also know we could pour all the resources we want at the problem and it won't go away. Look at Lyndon Johnson's famous war on poverty. What good did that do? But look, I really don't want to get into that. We have enough to handle without getting into sociology and economics."

Chris did not persist, but the professor's attitude disturbed him, good Christian that he was.

"OK," Chris said, "let's not get into sociology, but what about other scientific projects that demand government money? Say, for instance, what about the Superconducting Super Collider? Don't you think we should spend the big bucks on that? After all, that gets us down to the basic building blocks of the universe."

"Oh sure, I think we should spend on that but we are getting away from the point here. And that is that the future is in molecular biology and its related fields. If I were you I'd switch my major field to that. For myself, I've had to learn it all on my own while continuing in my regular field of forensic pathology during the day. Granted that they are related, but I have come to the point now where I would like to give 100% of my time and efforts to that discipline because as living, thinking human beings, that is where our ultimate truth is. Oh, we can identify the quarks and the muons and the gluons and we can ultimately find out whether the universe will expand forever or collapse on itself to a destructive end in a giant black hole. But what will we be able to do with that knowledge? Will we be able to create new universes? Hell, we will never be able to see over 99% of the one we have now, let alone go to its extremes. So I believe our future is in the life sciences and that we are rapidly getting a handle on them. When I say our future I mean man's future. We have almost come to the point where we can control our destiny, control that which we will become. We don't have to depend on blind chance and take what is dished out to us. We are uniquely positioned to take charge of our own evolution for God's sake."

"Isn't that coming awfully close to playing God?" Chris asked.

"I suppose the answer to that one is yes, it does come awfully close to playing God. But if we don't do it someone next year or the year after will. With the state of the technology as it is today that is inevitable. So why shouldn't it be us, you and me? We have it in our power to influence the future course of human evolution or the evolution of any animal or plant species we choose. We have the power to create new species. Your favorite pet Smilodon, we could introduce human genes into an embryo grown from its genes if we could get our hands on them, genes that could give it a more human brain. Think of it. No one has ever done that before. No one's even ever thought of it before."

"What good will that do?" Chris asked.

"It's not a question of what good it will do. No one thought the space project would produce anything of practical use but look how it spawned the development of new materials, new technology, new methods unheard of before that now have application in our everyday lives."

"But what about a new genetically engineered virus or bacteria that can cause human disease that we have no immunity for? Suppose somebody inadvertently produces another virus like the AIDS virus. Suppose someone produces a hundred different diseases as bad as AIDS or smallpox and we have no treatment or antibiotics that are effective?"

"Chris, you're thinking unscientifically again. In the first place that condition already exists. We are seeing viruses and bacteria which do not now respond to the drugs we already have. AIDS is one of them. TB is another one. There are antibiotic resistant staph, Pseudomonas, and strep whose only cure depends on new drugs created by genetic engineering. On the other hand if one were able to genetically engineer a new virus doesn't that mean that the creator of that virus would know all the capabilities it has in all its permutations and combinations? Don't you think that the means of its destruction could be built in and knowable to the creator?"

"Yes, but what if it mutates, what if it changes its skin or its core, what if the maker purposely builds it so that it is invulnerable to any attack by humans, then what?"

"Why Chris, we have had such viruses with us all the time and they have scarcely threatened humanity's survival. Think of the flu virus. Even in its worst years in the early 1920s, when millions across the world died, it hardly made a dent in the human population. Consider the worst scourge ever to effect mankind, the bubonic plague. It only destroyed one third of the population and that was limited to Europe. As for AIDS, far more people die of cancer, stroke, and heart disease than AIDS could kill in any given year in this country. No, in spite of all your objections and playing the part of devil's advocate, it will be done. It will be done by us, you and me or it will be done by others. I would prefer it to be us.

"The cloning of bovine embryos to produce more stock of selected animals with specific properties is already old news. There is no scientific reason the same cannot be done with human beings. Of course, the bioethics committees and the institutional peer review councils of most large universities, no correct that, all the universities are scared to death of antagonizing one interest group or another, so the easiest thing for them to do is just to sit on it. That is to say, anything new that happens in the field of genetic engineering, recombinant DNA, the Human Genome Project, anything that deals with human beings, their gut inclination is to discourage, disapprove, reject, and deny everything so they won't have to deal with it.

"There is a report for instance of a researcher in Washington, D.C. who cloned human embryos. He took some defective embryos, the report didn't say what the defect was, and using microsurgical techniques separated the cells, then extracted the nuclear material as in DNA. Then he put the DNA from the embryos into a denucleated ovum. The embryos were allowed to grow up to six days. It is not clear if they stopped growing on their own or the researchers discontinued the project. The point is this could have been done by many researchers, including fertility experts around the country. But they are all scared to death. You see even these guys stopped their project after only six days. They are all afraid of what the ethicists will say. Now, in the main, the ethicists are people whose creative lives if they ever had any are over. They have run out of juice, out of ideas, energy, and creativity, but are still tenured into university and academic positions of power where they spew out their overwhelmingly negative influence on anything that threatens the status quo. They have much to say about where research money goes and would rather not give their approval to anything that promises to rock the boat or create new situations which the scientific community has not faced before. They do all this out of fear. Fear of the unknown, fear of what people will say, fear of what the government will say, fear of change. Then again, your point is well taken. Just because you are able to clone somebody doesn't mean that he is going to be what or whom you expect physically, emotionally, intellectually, philosophically or any other way. That is why I plan to take no chances. I plan a program of education, training, indoctrination to begin just as soon as our little prodigy is able to understand. Considering who He will be I expect that to be relatively early. This being we create, you and I, will need to be coached in English, history, politics, and yes, even religion. We cannot expect Him to be familiar with all that's happened in the last 2,000 years. Or, who knows, maybe He will know everything and will be able to educate us. He may be fully conscious of who He is from the beginning. He may be aware of His identity, His capabilities, His relationship to us. And that's one of the things that makes this so much fun. In that case our job will be easy. Or more correctly our job will be done and we will find ourselves working for Him or at least we may be His new followers, His disciples, if you will, or then again He may bring down the wrath of heaven on our heads. But that is part of the delicious unknown of not being sure what is going to happen. Don't you feel the same, don't you agree?"

Chris could not deny the thrill of expectation he felt, the pioneering feeling with a conspiratorial edge to it of secretly being in on something no one had ever done before, no one had even thought of before.

"How about Hebrew? Are we going to teach Him Hebrew?"

Chris was now caught up in the excitement. "Where will we get someone to teach Him Hebrew in this cultural wasteland of Arizona? Anyway the Modern Hebrew language has to be different from the ancient classical variety. Wait a minute, it wasn't Hebrew they spoke in biblical times, it was Aramaic, the language of the Prophets, wasn't it?"

"Yes, yes it was Aramaic, but think what a surprise the 20th century is going to be to Him! Airplanes, atomic energy, modern communications, computers, modern health care, surgery that we take for granted, submarines, television, records, CDs. Think of the changes in the world since His time. He will be astounded at the sheer number of people in the world, at the size of the world. In His time the only known world was a little part of the Middle East, North Africa, and parts of Europe. He is going to be surprised out of his socks."

Karahsha paused thoughtfully, "And yet given who He is, maybe we are just being childish here, maybe He will have heard of all these things before we have a chance to educate Him. After all, if He is really the Son of God there shouldn't be anything unknown to Him. Well, that remains to be seen, doesn't it? That is one of the many unknown ramifications of this project. Even if we fail, and I do not intend to fail, we will have raised some pertinent questions of philosophy, theology, and history that can be tackled by those who come after us presuming they have the advantage of better technology. But if we succeed think of what we might be able to learn from the Son Himself if He is willing to teach us. He could direct us to the location of the remains of Mary, of Joseph, of John the Baptist, of all the disciples. He could identify the ossuaries, the repositories of the bones of all the principal players in the crucifixion and any other biblical characters He cared to. He could shed new light on the meaning of the Dead Sea Scrolls and clarify the Hebrew origins of Christianity. He could explain to us how the miracle of the parting of the Red Sea was carried out, for example. He could describe how His image came to be seared on the Shroud of Turin, and He could elucidate why, when He was crucified, why He did not save Himself from that terrible agony, smite down the guilty Romans and Jews and start Christianity that way. He could shed light on whether He is the one and only Son of God and even whether there are any daughters of God. He could tell us if He wanted the actual physical location of heaven, hell and purgatory, if they exist. If they don't exist in the literal sense He might be able to give us a clue as to what really awaits us humans after death. The possibilities of what He can teach us are limitless. We could, for instance, learn what the Deity thinks of abortion and birth control, instead of relying on the pope's interpretation of the Bible. We could get it from the horse's mouth so to speak. We could learn what He has to say on race relations, whether He meant for the various races to live apart forever or to comingle into one big happy family at some point in our evolution. He could if He wanted give us a hint as to whether there are other forms of life in the universe, created by God, of course. We might learn whether it is in the cards for us to discover them or them us. We might ask for His guidance on what to do about the environment, global warming, the ozone layer, the rain forests, atomic energy. We could ask Him to resolve the dispute between creationism and evolution. For instance, if you believe in evolution and all the implications of that belief, that the earth is 5 billion years old instead of a few thousand years, that most of the creatures that have ever lived have already become extinct, that we are the result of millions of years of genetic mutations, adaptation and change, if you believe all that, then why is it necessary to exclude the hand of God from the equation? Why can that not be consistent with the belief that all these things are real but that they are mediated by God and are not inconsistent with a belief in God? He could explain that to us. He could stop the counterproductive war that goes on between creationists and evolutionists. He could even give us His guidance on how to proceed with the Human Genome Project and the ultimate use to make of it. I'll bet He could give us some good advice on that one, after His education, of course. He could advise on human cloning and lay out some rules governing that whole field. I'll tell you, if there is anyone whose advice I'd be willing to heed you can bet it would be His, not those mealy-mouthed university ethics committee types or worse the arrogant know-it-all liberals of the federal government's regulatory bureaucracies like the FDA.

"Of course, I believe He will have as difficult a time in getting people to believe in Him as He did originally. There will be a thousand doubting Thomases for each one in the biblical account. There will be people who think He is a nut, a phony, a fake, an imposter. He will need bodyguards, something like the Popemobile when He travels among the crowds. His close visitors will have to be searched, screened and carefully chosen lest they try to harm Him, and then presuming He will live out His life to the proverbial four score, He may want to marry and have a family, thereby setting a precedent for the Catholic clergy. If that happened He would shake the bureaucracy to its very foundation and open the door to the ultimate salvation of the Catholic Church by affirming that marriage and the priesthood are not mutually exclusive. How can fatherhood for priests be looked upon as abnormal if the Father of the Church is also a father Himself?"

"But what if He doesn't want to be Christ?" Chris asked. "I mean what if He doesn't want to be a prophet? Suppose He doesn't want anything to do with the clerical life? Suppose by some unknown cause He is unable to be what or who He really is? Suppose you put in too much potassium, or not enough growth hormone, or too little oxygen or some other inappropriate ingredient. What if He comes out with a perfectly normal intelligence but in no way is willing to believe He is of divine descent? What then, eh?"

"Well, how could He explain His existence? How could He explain not having an earthly father, mother, hometown, schoolmates, et cetera? He might think He suffers from amnesia or some other memory robbing condition. He could even believe all of what we tell Him but still not want any part of a missionary life. Maybe, He will just want to marry, settle down and raise a few kids, work at the local factory, enjoy bowling with the boys, and die of old age. Ah, but that will not be possible. He will be who He will be. He will have been created from divine ingredients and it will not be possible for Him to take any course, save the divine one. On the other hand He is the Son of the Father and as such will do as He wants."

"You mean to tell me that we may have His progeny running around playing basketball for God's sake? The sons of the Son could not do such a thing because there will be no progeny. My point professor is that you will be unleashing forces that beyond a certain point you won't be able to control. Don't you see?"

"I see you still have your doubts, my young collaborator. I encourage you to do that. But you see that just as I will have created this new Messiah I reserve the right to pronounce judgment on Him if He turns out not to be what I have worked towards all these years."

"And what the hell does that mean, professor, with all due respect, of course?"

"It means that as a worst case scenario I can terminate the experiment at any time."

"You mean you would kill Him if something went wrong? You would be no better than a murderer. It is one thing to rebuild Him, bring Him into the world, but you would be no better than the Roman executioners if you did that. You would be worse. At least they were ignorant, superstitious, and thought they were protecting their empire. Why, you would be the new Nero, Judas, and Herod all rolled into one. On the other hand, if you lose control and can't manage or kill Him and if He chooses to have sons and daughters, then all by yourself you will have produced a new royalty which is really descended from a divine progenitor. You will have recreated the divinely descended Japanese emperors, or the European royalty, or the Egyptian Pharaohs. Congratulations."

Fanning went on, "Maybe the DNA is not Christ's at all. Maybe it came from a demonic criminal, a serial killer, who will then turn out to be the Anti-Christ, rather than what you planned. Then when He starts to evil things up it will be too late. You will have created the real life Frankenstein's monster, only infinitely more potent than Mary Shelley's. Or suppose the DNA did belong to Christ but it gets twisted horribly in the reproduction. What if He is a truly evil being with supernatural powers that would be a colossal force for evil even to the point of threatening our civilization, mankind itself, a kind of living Satan on earth? Are you willing to accept that responsibility? Suppose further that He is indestructible and that He recruits legions of evil followers to commit baby sacrifice or some such objectionable ritual. Suppose He embraces Voodoo or Santeria or some other cult that relies on spells, black magic, curses or zombies?"

"All of that is very alarming and amusing, my friend, but you see, I am prepared to take those chances. The odds of anything remotely similar to what you describe are slim to none. The likely benefits are so overwhelmingly positive that the risk-benefit ratio is favorable."

"What are the putative benefits here, professor?"

"We have been through some of it before, but briefly, it is to re-dedicate, to reaffirm by His presence the absolute value of a positive religion to halt the decline in morals and all manner of evil propagating over the world today. It is the restoration of that which has been considered sacred in the last 2,000 years and which has been lost in the past 50 years in a slow ethical rot that has taken over in this country and is responsible for the third worldization of the greatest civilization the world has seen. I'll spell it out for you. When a civilization reaches the point where everything goes, it is usually the civilization that goes. And we have reached that point, my boy. We have reached it in spades. I don't want to sound preachy or like a politician but we are approaching the point where fifty percent of the births in this country are to unmarried teenagers. Can we continue to subsidize that? We are allowing an underclass to develop that can neither provide for its own needs nor compete in the world market. Already sizable portions of our major cities have been changed to the status of a third world country. There are places in New York City, for instance, where you cannot go into a store, say a drug store, pick an item off the shelf and give it to the cashier to ring it up. Everything is behind plexiglass so the locals don't steal it. I call it the third worldization of the United States. The public schools are a scandalous joke, dangerous, dirty, and in a shameful state of disrepair. The teachers are afraid of the students. It is not even accurate to call them students. For the most part, especially in the inner cities, they are gun-toting thugs who would just as soon gun down another 'student' or a teacher as blow their nose. The criminal justice system is a disaster. If you have money you can buy an acquittal from almost any crime. There is no end of slimy lawyers, only too happy to use the system to sleaze their clients out of a tight situation for a price, while the hardened career criminal is yo yo'ed into and out of prison so that in most cities it is not safe to walk the streets, let alone be secure in your own home. This is not original with me but it is still true that if you subsidize something or someone you get more of it. If you tax something you get less of it. The so-called war on poverty of President Johnson was a total failure. Poor people don't need a handout. They need education and sometimes a boot in the ass."

"That can be considered biased and racist by some."

"It is true in spite of that and you know it. It is just not politically correct to say so. I haven't even mentioned the drug problem, the issue of product liability in this country, the problem of illegal immigration, the selective dismantling of the American medical care system, the finest the world has ever seen, by the government, the lawyers, the HMOs, the insurance companies, and the oxymoron called managed care."

"Aren't you being overly pessimistic?" Fanning interjected.

"Not at all. You see the degradation of this country everywhere. The exportation of American manufacturing jobs, the impotence of the U.S. in foreign policy, the precipitous decline in this country's contribution to basic science, all are symptoms of the third worldization of this country. The list goes on and on, all caused by the moral rot and abandonment of the values which made us great in the first place. You see it in the streets, in the work place, in the university where students enter unqualified and are then passed by teachers who have abdicated their responsibility to flunk, yes flunk, a fair number of students because they just don't measure up. Higher education used to be for the elite, the cream of the cream. Nowadays, everyone who wants to goes to college does so, but that doesn't necessarily mean they learn anything. And what about the role of the press in all of this? The way the media manipulates, perverts, and flimflams the news to suit their own purposes is an ongoing scandal which no one cares to confront lest they become the subject of excessive reportorial attention, as did Gary Hart, although he did bring it on himself. In short, the land of the free and the home of the brave is fast going to hell. There is a crisis of morality. The family is shot and that is probably the biggest threat to our way of life. A stable family life is the very linchpin of a flourishing society. You know it and I know it. But you see what is happening now. Radical feminism coupled with economic constraints are decimating the American family. Kids are conceived, born and in effect rejected by their progenitors who take minimal responsibility for their nurturing and rearing. One way that is done is by treating them as adults as soon as they can. This is worse than a pack of wild dogs. At least the dogs raise their young, teach them how to hunt, what to eat, how to avoid danger et cetera, the equivalent of a human education to a pup. Because the human youth takes so long to achieve maturity it needs to be taught, cared for, educated over a relatively long period of time. In many cases this is just not happening. The entire fabric is coming undone and no one seems to care. Well, I do. But I can't change the world by myself. With His help however we might have a chance to return to sanity. Maybe this time for ten or twenty years, maybe for the next two thousand years. It is worth the effort on that basis and it is also worth doing for the pure science of it. I have come to understand the nuts and bolts of the process but I need the raw materials and that is where you come in."

Fanning thought at last he would find out why the professor needed him.

"I have it within my power to reproduce the most significant, the most important force for good the world has ever seen. I didn't come by this ability by totally ethical means. That phone call I had, from the controller, was about misappropriated funds. Well, I admit to it. But the use to which they would have put it, that I call misappropriation. The importance of this Project so vastly overwhelms any impropriety on my part that when the time comes I will be willing to fess up to what I have done and take the consequences. But the Project has to be successful. I suspect that when the magnitude of our accomplishment becomes known, there will be such a volume of support for us that no one will dare to try and punish us, no matter how much university money we will have misappropriated."

Fanning was impressed by the older man's frankness in admitting what he did. He felt himself drawn into a confidence he would not easily betray and he admired the professor's candor and his willingness to bring him up to speed as to how he was able to fund his research. He felt more and more committed to help this brilliant, solitary researcher, eccentric though he might be. He was also drawn to a conspiracy that would result or could result in such a spectacular ending that no one else could have possibly anticipated. But at this particular moment, Chris was disappointed the professor hadn't yet told him what his role in the "Project" was to be, or why his help was so indispensable.

"I'll make a deal with you," Fanning said. "I'll help you. I'll devote the next two years or whatever it takes to the Project. I'll keep my mouth shut about it. But I reserve the right to object, to argue, to dispute what you are doing. And if I get the idea we are in over our heads I reserve the right to pull out and even to cancel the Project by making it public, if necessary."

As soon as the words were out, Fanning knew he was only blustering. He was already so convinced, so totally hooked by this time that he couldn't pull out even if he wanted to. And as for canceling the Project, they both knew that was a bluff because Fanning didn't have that kind of power.

The professor only chuckled and said, "You won't be sorry. Now come on, let's study these little microscopic relatives of yours a little more."

Fanning was drawn by a kind of morbid curiosity to the little creatures on the slides. He was attracted and repulsed at the same time as he settled his gaze over the eyepiece, focused the coarse adjustment knob to bring the tiny curiosities into sharp view. He was shocked, amazed, disgusted, and fascinated all over again by what he saw.

"You see," the professor explained, "these guys are so tiny that they can absorb nutrients and excrete waste by the simple process of osmosis. All I have to do is to provide some glucose, some proteins, vitamins and minerals and these little critters eat them right up. Maintaining a constant temperature and making sure there is enough oxygen pumped into their water baths are the only other parameters necessary to keep them alive."

"How long do these little creatures live?"

"It all depends on how accurately the genetic material is reproduced and in turn how accurately they reproduce the amino acids, polypeptides, and all the other requirements for life. Some died right away after birth like a microscopic miscarriage. Others are alive after months."

"So do they have consciousness, are they aware of the environment, or of themselves?"

"Oh yes. Just watch for a while. You will see them turn over, swim, avoid debris, settle down and rest awhile. If you introduce a dilute acid or hit one end of the slide with a penlight, they will react in general to avoid extremes of heat, cold, acidity or other noxious stimuli."

"How big will they grow?"

"It depends on the amount of food and space you give them. I haven't been willing to grow them bigger than their present size for the time being. I don't want to create a bunch of haploid, genetic, full-sized freaks just yet."

"Are you saving that for later?" Fanning said with a touch of sarcasm.

The professor ignored the crack. "You could consider these experimental cousins of yours who didn't make it to adulthood a sort of man-made genetic sidetrack."

"Have you tried putting more than one creature on a slide?"

"I admire your curiosity but now who is being ghoulish? What do you want them to do, reproduce? I told you they are haploid and as such are incapable of reproduction."

Fanning continued to study these strange little relatives of his until late that night, entranced by their beauty and grace. On the way home Fanning pondered the best way to tell Margie of his new involvement. He also thought he might have to make some arrangements in his schedule to be able to help the professor effectively. Oh well, he thought, he was young and could afford to drag out his degree for another semester. Happily enough, Margie did not oppose his plans. The only request he made of her was one of secrecy. She agreed, but Fanning thought there was something strange in her demeanor.

~~~

The next day he was back at the professor's lab asking about something the old prof had mentioned in passing. "Tell me about the experiment in Boston you started to describe last night."

"Sure, sure, delighted to," the professor replied. "Seems there were about nine or ten surgeons, four or five internists, one anesthesiologist and one real scientist, you know, like me. Also a bunch of nurses, technicians and a few visitors. What they had was a man who had two failed arterial bypasses in his lower extremity. In other words, attempts at bypass grafting of an obstruction in the main artery of his leg failed, partly because the patient continued to smoke and eat indiscriminately. These were contributing factors and who knows, the bypasses might have failed anyway. In any case, the plan was to introduce DNA that would program for the growth of new arteries to bypass the blockage. They thought it would take two hours to do the job but of course all their previous work had been done on rabbits, so everything was smaller and simpler with rabbits. Now, with this, their first human being, it wound up taking upwards of five hours, but that was OK since it was either succeed in this attempt to revascularize the leg or amputate. The first problem they ran into was the fact that the ideal place to deposit the genetic material was not reachable by catheter because it was closed off by plaque or cholesterol deposit. They had to thread an ultrasound probe into a groin artery first. Needless to say, the man was under heavy sedation with morphine and Versed, a new kind of Valium. The image intensifier had to be used to keep track of the location of the probe. This is a machine like the fluoroscopes of old, used when I was a kid in the shoe stores. You'd try on a pair of shoes and stick your feet under the fluoroscope to see how your toes or more correctly the bones of your toes fit in the new shoes. The shoe store fluoroscope is not in use any more because it exposed people to excessive radiation. Anyway, today we wear lead aprons and lead tinted glasses to protect against excessive radiation. The modern fluoroscope, or as it's called today, the image intensifier, is a very indispensable tool in medicine and in this case is used to keep track of the location of the catheter probe at all times. Otherwise, by probing blindly you could puncture through an artery and get into a whole lot of bleeding. This could really mess things up and even lead to the death of your patient.

"OK, so when they discovered that the ideal place to deposit the genes was unavailable, they had to look for another artery. They found one all right, but it was less satisfactory because it was much smaller and therefore more easily damaged. The inside layer of arteries is lined with a tissue called endothelium, which if damaged, immediately starts to initiate the clotting mechanism. In order to prevent this, the patient had to be anticoagulated with a drug called heparin. Anyway, it took much longer to find and catheterize a vessel they could work with. By the way, the catheter had a probe on the tip which emitted sound waves. The echo of these sound waves was analyzed by a computer to tell the exact diameter of the vessel. It was much smaller than they wanted, but it had to do. It has been known for some time now that a tumor, or a fetus, will elaborate a substance that will induce new blood vessels to grow. These are obviously necessary for nutrition and growth. This substance has been identified as vascular endothelial growth factor. The word endothelial refers to the inner wall lining of the blood vessels. Further, it was recently found that there is a specific gene that controls the programming of this material. That gene has been found, identified, and isolated. It occurred to one of the researchers to try the experiment on rabbits, and when it worked out successfully, to try it on a human being. The man was going to lose his leg anyway. He had nothing to lose. Regardless of the result in this particular experiment, the mechanics represented the future and they felt it would be successful at some point.

"This obviously has great application and implications for the future. It will be possible I believe to regrow a failing heart, liver, brain, kidney, spinal cord, arm, leg, finger, whatever, by isolating the genes responsible for that organ's growth and implanting it or them in the right place. But that's the hard part, implanting it in the right place. It takes a lot of sophisticated equipment and a highly skilled team of specialists to do it. It's almost easier to start from scratch, so to speak, and build an entire human being from the genetic material and that's what the Human Genome Project is all about. That is precisely what I have been doing with the polymerase chain reaction. That process allows one to reproduce, from a fragment of DNA, unlimited copies with which to work, study, play with, examine in detail, and put together in any way that suits one's fancy. This is not fiction. This is real. It is available now and demands to be considered. Those who don't want to think about it, use it, experiment with it will be bypassed. I think it was Max Planck who said that bad ideas in science die only when their owners die. Well, this is a now idea, a happening idea. Those who refuse to recognize it will be swept away with the tide."

Fanning was duly impressed.

In a sudden change of subject Karahsha asked, "You are a climber, yes?"

Fanning wondered what climbing had to do with anything. "Yes, I like to climb for exercise and for the challenge of it."

"Are you very good at it?"

"Well yes, even if I do say so myself."

"Could you climb up the side of a building if you wanted to?"

Fanning wondered where this was going. "Yes, I suppose I could climb up the side of a building."

"A building with a dome?"

"A dome would make it easier. What are you getting at professor?"

"The church in Turin which houses the Shroud of Turin has a dome. It will be necessary to climb the dome and drop down into the church in order to get a piece of the Shroud."

"So that's why you need me for your Project. I have been mystified. Why me? What special property do I possess to make you interested in me with relation to the Project?"

"That's right. Now you know. I can't very well go to Turin myself and climb up the wall of the dome of the church to get hold of the raw materials."

That little mystery out of the way, Fanning turned to the slides again and pondered this new wrinkle while he studied the little denizens of the slides. He could not get over the fact that he was looking at the product of manipulation of his own genes, his own software so to speak. He could not pull himself away from the microscope. He was fascinated anew by the array of variegated creatures he found floating, swimming, bobbing in the watery milieu of the slides. He realized that what he observed was the gamut of anatomical forms represented by various segments of his own DNA, as the professor was able to isolate and clone different segments and various combinations of the double helix. My God, he thought, this could very well represent the entire range of animal forms tried by nature. Most would have been rejected by evolution and rendered extinct. Others would become successful and might be akin to the earliest missing links between the one-celled organisms and the great succession of invertebrates and vertebrates that came later. Only the former were entirely soft bodied so they would have left no fossils. This madman, as he'd begun to refer to Karahsha, had been able to produce in less than a lifetime what it had taken natural selection millions, maybe billions, of years to do. Well, not quite. But give the rascal enough time and he might do it.

He studied some more slides and was transfixed at what he saw. He saw little beasts that looked like normal mammalian embryos but with a leg growing out of a head. He saw beautiful thread-like corkscrew shaped organisms with no difference in the head or tail end, except that they undulated in one direction only, one end leading, one end trailing. Based on the variability of forms he noted, he wondered whether the human genome contained the program for every living being, every form of life now extant, and every form that ever was. Plants? He didn't know. Could it be that human beings, which start out as fertilized ova, have the capability to develop into say, an elephant, but don't because the program for elephant is somehow repressed? Would it be possible to take the entirety of human DNA and by preferential repression of some aspects and preferential stimulation of others produce an elephant? Fanning knew some biology but was not versed enough in the details of molecular genetics to answer these questions or even formulate proper questions. He had to depend on the professor for the answers and even most of the questions.

He continued to scrutinize the animals on the slides while pondering these questions. Giant heads relative to the size of the attached bodies floated by. He saw forms in which the cardiovascular system was exaggerated at the expense of the other body structures. He studied forms in which the organism looked like a fish but had a tail like a monkey. He saw organisms in which there were no eyes and others which were almost entirely two big bugged out eyes and very little else.

Suddenly there was a frantic pounding on the outer laboratory door. The sound was somewhat muffled due to the barriers the professor had erected for privacy, but it was persistent. There was no phone in Karahsha's inner sanctum.

After allowing the pounding to go on for several minutes the professor asked Fanning if he would mind going to see what all the commotion was about. Fanning went out to the outer office and opened the door. The department secretary burst in. She had tears in her eyes, her face was flushed, and she was shaking uncontrollably.

"Take it easy," Chris tried to console the woman. "What's happened? What is it?"

"Oh Chris, it's terrible. It's Jake, Jake Hamilton, he's been shot."

"Oh my God," Fanning exclaimed. "Is he alive? What happened?"

"I don't know, but it sounds pretty bad," she blurted and ran out of the room.

"Oh Jesus, my best friend, my buddy," Fanning could only repeat. "What the hell happened?"

He ran out of the room too. He ran out of the lab forgetting about the professor and the creatures on the slide. The only thing he could think to do was to go to the nearest police station and try to find out if his friend was still alive and if so how badly he was hurt. He drove in a daze to the first station house he could find and inquired about Jake. He was referred to another precinct where he was told the body was in the City Morgue. Fanning felt his knees give out from underneath him. The dingy police room spun around him in a sickly green whirl. He paled and had to sit. The policeman behind the desk asked if he was OK a few times before he could answer that the dead man was his best friend. After pulling himself together, in a manner of speaking, he drove to the morgue and tried to determine exactly what had happened. The medical examiner was able to provide some sketchy details. From what they could tell, Jake was at the dig site when someone on a ridge a half a mile away started shooting at him. It was apparent that the shooter was just trying to scare him since at that distance, using a telephoto lens, it would have been a simple matter to knock him off at any time. It seemed that a bullet had ricocheted off the nearby parked jeep and hit him in the head. There had been an anonymous call to 911. The police believed the sniper had placed the call. The police were totally in the dark about motive.

Now Fanning was afraid he'd have to tell his story about the bones to the cops. He dreaded having to deal with the police. He was told that by the time the ambulance arrived Jake Hamilton was already dead. Fanning felt responsible. Jake had no family, no brothers, no sisters, no living parents, no cousins that Fanning was aware of, and now he was dead. A promising academic career in the sciences wasted. And for what? Fanning felt a terrible guilt that he had involved Jake in this enterprise and thereby subjected him to this danger. He knew he was not responsible but he couldn't shake the feeling of remorse he felt. His best friend, dead, because of his, Fanning's activity.

If only he had decided to remain in the field at the dig site and let Jake stay in the lab, maybe things would have been different. He requested to see the body for purposes of identification. Again his knees gave out and he had to sit. It took him several minutes before he could gather himself up and leave.

He went home, broke the news to Margie, and vowed to do all he could to get to the bottom of Jake's murder. He turned it over in his mind again and again. Why would anyone want to scare them away from the dig site?

Was the killing related to the skeleton find? What should be his next step? Was he now in danger? Was his family in danger?

The next day Fanning went about making funeral arrangements for his friend. He couldn't, however, get out of his head the events which had transpired at the professor's laboratory. He made an effort to find any family Hamilton might have, though Fanning knew he had none. A painful aspect of the next day's chores was talking to the uniformed police. At first they were reluctant to talk to him, but when they found out Hamilton had no known kin they grudgingly allowed Fanning to become privy to some of their information. In fact, they wanted to question him about what the two of them were doing out there in the desert anyway. Fanning didn't let on that they had found any skeletons because he didn't think he should divulge that information until he'd figured out what it meant. He knew the police would be interested but he wasn't ready to share that information with them just yet.

He discovered that Hamilton had died instantly after being hit by a bullet which bounced off the roll bar of the truck he drove. The missile had entered the back of his head and essentially exploded his brain, something like Fanning had seen in Gaspare's studio. At least he could be consoled by the fact that there had been no suffering. Poor guy. He didn't even know what hit him. But why? The police had determined that a shooter with a .30-06 rifle fitted with a telephoto lens could easily pick someone off from any one of dozens of vantage points. But they could not locate footprints, nor empty cartridges, or any other definite evidence pointing to where the perpetrator had shot from, or even any tire marks going into or out of the area, aside from those that Hamilton's vehicle had made.

There was a pathetically small turnout for the funeral and this made Fanning feel even worse than before. After the funeral he drove out to the desert again for no particular reason. He pondered the death of his friend while driving aimlessly through the open country. In a way it was easier that Hamilton had no family because Fanning could not imagine how he'd have faced them if he had to be the one to break the news of his death. As he drove he noticed he was approaching the area of the bone find. Whether this was subconscious or deliberate he could not say. All he knew was that he had an unexplained need to be out here again, out where it had all started. God, he thought, how did things get so out of control? What now? Should he just forget about the bones and turn the whole thing over to the police? He knew he was on shaky ground in not telling the cops about the skeletons but for the life of him he couldn't see how that would help find Hamilton's killer.

And now what about this new turn of events? What was Karahsha really up to? How could he presume to even think he could be successful in his harebrained scheme to restore Jesus Christ to life? Still, he'd managed to do some tricks with DNA that Fanning was not aware had been done or even tried by anyone else.

As he gazed at the beautiful countryside anew he couldn't help but be entranced again by the spectacle of colors, shapes, and dimensions of the place. He stopped the vehicle and surveyed the vista before him. There was the cliff side he'd climbed that day. It seemed so long ago. There was the area where he'd made the find of the bones, and there was the spot where Jake had met his end.

He continued to watch as the sun began to decline behind the craggy mountain peaks. As the last bit of the circumference of the scarlet ball, magnified by the atmosphere, dipped behind the rocky protuberance, he was astonished to see an unnatural formation of light and cloud take place. As if in slow-motion, a vertical shaft of light extended itself like a long, bony finger from the distant mountaintop to the desert floor. The thing was so bright and appeared palpable, so that had he been closer he felt he could touch it. He decided to drive as close as possible. However, as he did so another shaft of light came shooting across the first one, forming a perfect cross. Fanning was transfixed. He'd never seen anything like it before. He watched for a full ten minutes while the apparition became brighter and appeared more solid than ethereal. At the end of ten minutes, he watched as the vision disappeared almost instantaneously. It left a dark, vertical cross shape in the sky for another two or three minutes before vanishing altogether. Fanning was not a superstitious person, but he had a feeling that this was an omen he should not ignore.

When he arrived home well after dark he found Police Detective Frank O'Hara waiting for him.

10

Detective O'Hara was another transplanted New Yorker. He'd put in the requisite number of years in the NYPD and then thought he would reap the benefits of retirement in the land of the sun and the deserts. He quickly found that his two children didn't share the same worship of the warmth of the southwest. One, his daughter, went off to Chicago to attend law school. The other, his boy, couldn't adjust to what he called the cultural deprivation of Arizona and took off to Los Angeles to try his luck at acting. When his wife died, young and unexpectedly, he was left with a cavernous void in his life, so when the opportunity to return to work with the local police department opened up he jumped at the chance.

He was overweight, intelligent, cagey, and believed that most men weren't worth the powder to blow them to hell. He'd come by his cynicism from long years of observation of the human condition mostly in its seedier form from his perspective. He greeted Fanning and his wife with condolences from himself and from the uniformed officer who accompanied him. "I'm sorry for your recent loss Mr. Fanning, these situations are always difficult."

"Please call me Chris," Fanning said.

"OK then, Mr. Fanning," he ignored Fanning's invitation. "I suppose you understand I have to ask you some questions. You seem to be the closest to the deceased, and might be able to shed some light on the recent tragic events."

"I don't know how I can do that but I'll be happy to cooperate any way I can."

"Fine. Let me ask you what you and the deceased were doing out there in the desert."

"Well, we are both graduate students in archaeology and paleontology at Arizona State University, and that area, called Hang Man's Gulch, is where we went to look for fossils. There have been significant bone finds in that area in the past and we were hoping to make some more finds. One of my areas of special interest is Smilodon, the saber-toothed cat, which became extinct around ten thousand--"

"Excuse me Mr. Fanning, but I am not really interested in extinct big cats. My purpose is to try and shed some light on the unfortunate murder of Jake Hamilton."

"Oh, right," Fanning said.

"How long have you known the deceased?"

"We met in undergraduate school, back at the University of Pennsylvania. We had the same interests, the same backgrounds to an extent, and we just hit it off. When we both wound up here in graduate school in the same program we naturally became close."

"I see. Did Hamilton have a girlfriend that you knew of?"

"No, no, he was too wrapped up in his school work. He came over here for dinner frequently though, and I must say, Margie, my wife here, was not above trying to fix him up with some of her friends from time to time. But he was just too busy."

"You say you were in the same program with Hamilton yet you manage to fit in a wife and family and graduate studies pretty easily."

"What can I tell you? Different strokes for different folks."

"OK, Mr. Fanning, did you notice anything out in the desert that might shed some light on this mystery? Did you find anything of value or anything suspicious or anything in any way that can be construed to have a bearing on this case?"

"Well, we found some bones."

"Oh, did you? What kind of bones?"

"Human bones."

"Human bones?"

"Yes. Human bones."

"And did you report them to the police?"

"No, we did not."

"And why not?"

"We didn't think the police would be interested. That is an area where human bones have been found in the past and the police have never been interested in them before."

"Where are these bones now Mr. Fanning?"

"They are at the university in the Department of Paleontology. They are being studied to try and identify them as to age at death, the civilization they represent, whether they have any diseases or signs of trauma, the usual thing."

O'Hara did not miss the quick look that passed between Fanning and his wife.

"You will make these bones available if the department would like to examine them, I mean the Police Department?"

"Well, they belong to the university now but I'm sure there would not be any problem."

"How about you Mrs. Fanning? Is there anything you can add or suggest that would be of some possible help in solving this murder?"

"No, I really can't think of a thing that would help, Detective."

"OK, but if you think of anything please let me know. Here's my card. Call me any time." He turned to Chris again, "Mr. Fanning, do you have any enemies or are you aware that Jake Hamilton had any?"

"No to each of those questions."

"Did Hamilton have any outstanding debts like gambling debts for instance?"

"I don't think so. He didn't have money enough to gamble. He was in hock to the hilt with student loans. I am much better off in that respect."

"Mr. Fanning, I am going to give you some friendly advice. Please don't take it the wrong way. And that is that withholding evidence in the investigation of a murder is a serious offense. I hope that if anything comes up, anything at all that could help in the resolution of this case you will feel free to get in touch with me."

"Sure, I'll be sure to do that."

"One more thing. Do you have any suggestions as to who we can talk to next, anyone, neighbors, friends, school associates, faculty, anyone who could have a bearing on this case?"

"No, I'm sorry I can't think of anyone."

"Well, OK folks, we won't be taking up any more of your time. Let's go Johnny," he nodded at the uniform and the two policemen were on their way.

When they had gone Margie questioned Fanning as to whether he'd been as honest with the policemen as he could. Fanning said that he told them all he knew and didn't believe he'd held anything of significance back. Margie was not reassured, and Chris could tell her level of anxiety was up. Margie was very sensible and down to earth but she had an exaggerated sense of possible trouble and didn't want anything to rock her boat. He tried to change the subject. "Come on, say w-i-n-d-o-w for me," spelling it out. He always teased her because she said "winda". Margie wasn't having any of it, so Fanning left her alone and went to bed early.

11

The ornate chamber in another part of the world 6,000 miles away waited in an expectant hush. The two ranking officials, who operated at the highest levels of the organization and as such were privy to the most important of its deliberations and decisions, waited as well. The square outside could be seen from the open window. Throngs of the faithful milled about as was usually the case in the pleasant summer balm. They waited patiently for the appearance of their leader at the balcony. Without fanfare or ritual, His Eminence entered the room. He behaved in a businesslike manner with a determination that precluded small talk.

Without delay he began. "You both know the purpose of this meeting?"

They rose to greet him but he waved them back to their chairs. They nodded in agreement.

"Good, we won't spend a lot of time on it." His manner was like one who had many of the cares of the world in his heart. He moved in a slow, almost painful manner across the room and gazed out at the crowd, being careful to keep himself just out of the view of anyone in the square.

"This project, this cloning experiment being attempted in America by the Indian, Karahsha, I want it stopped and I want it stopped now. You have authorization from me to do whatever it takes to accomplish that goal. I understand there has been an unfortunate accident in which a young graduate student was killed. That is very regrettable and I will pray for his soul. However, the very idea of reincarnating the Son by the hand of man borders on heresy. It has the potential of making a laughing stock of Christianity, let alone the church."

He spoke in a learned but pained voice as if it caused him grief to have to address this issue at all. "Suppose this, this creature was actually successfully cloned. Suppose He was retarded or had no memory of whom He really was? Suppose He was perceived by the masses as the real Son come to earth by some miracle and suppose He decided to use the power He had to go about changing everything we now take as gospel? The possibilities for mischief are too great and I will not tolerate it."

"Your Eminence," one of the others spoke for the first time. "Do you really believe this, ah, project has any chance of success? Do you actually think the American madman can successfully clone a human being from 2,000 year old DNA? As you very well know it has not even been done with mammals at all before. Suppose it is just a big bluff. Suppose the whole thing is a scam to fool the people."

"Yes, I have considered that. In the first place I do not think it will actually work. If ever there is any chance that it could work in the future then of course it will have to be done under the aegis of the mother church. But even if it is a ruse I am not willing to take the chance that it will be credible for the reasons I already stated. You will redouble your security precautions as regards to the Shroud, both the relic itself and the results of our recent studies on the subject. The public must never know of the real origins of that most holy of icons because of this very type of possibility. Do you understand?" There was a pause. The kindly face became impatient. "Well?" he persisted, a hint of irritation in his voice.

"How far are we to go in putting a stop to this? What means are permissible, Eminence? We want to break no laws, moral or legal, in carrying out this, ah, mission."

"And neither do I want you to. I want no more deaths. You will begin with persuasion, using perfectly legal methods at first in hopes of dissuading them. You are to escalate the means incrementally to get the job done. I do not want to know the details. But get the job done you must. The fixture of the church may depend on it."

"With your permission, Eminence, how so?"

"The church has experienced many challenges in the recent past. For the immediate future I do not expect that to change. Even now we may not have enough priests to serve the faithful in South America. Evangelicalism is mounting a powerful attack against the church. Admittedly we have picked up a large following from the fall of the Soviet Empire and recently in Africa. But can you imagine the jolt it would give the one true church if it was shown that a mere mortal was responsible for resurrecting the second of the Holy Trinity? Even if this creature were not genuine I do not believe it can do us, the church, any good to have the multitudes believe in Him. Suppose He is formed in the image of what we believe to be the Son. Suppose He convinces the faithful that He is the Son reincarnated. Suppose He has only a superficial resemblance to the one true Christ in His heart, in His mind, in His teachings. He could turn the church on its ear. He could deny the very validity of our modern mother church. He could be a force for disruption, revolution, dissension, and confusion, and could set in motion forces that might change or even destroy the church and its hierarchy as we know it. Gentlemen, are you willing to risk such a catastrophe? The most important aspect of any martyr is his remoteness, his mysticism, his connection to the past. A new Jesus Christ on the face of the earth would be the most disruptive force the church could face at a time when she is least capable of defending herself. For all these reasons, my friends, I believe this should not happen."

The two officials glanced at each other and the same thought went through their minds at the same time. That is why he is the Eminence and we will never be. As the two took their leave to begin work on their assignment, the Eminence turned to the window and basked in the adoration of the multitudes waiting below. He scanned the horizon and the hills of the city. The one shining truth in this world of deception, materialism, and moral rot must not be sullied by doubt. The product of 2,000 years of evolution and refinement could not be challenged by some madman Indian on the American continent. The faith that was instrumental in bringing down the blasphemy of godless communism would not be subjected to the ridicule of a false prophet. No, the great mother church to which he had devoted his life would be safe in his hands to be passed on to the next Vicar of Christ intact and inviolate.

12

The professor disdained automobiles, motorcycles and even bicycles. On those rare occasions when he found it necessary to vary his routine and travel about the city he walked or most times jogged about the city. He believed the exercise was not only good for his body but that it also kept his brain in tune and helped to wash out the cobwebs that tended to accumulate therein. Accordingly, late one night as he made his way home from some nameless errand, maybe to the library, maybe not, he became aware of a presence in his vicinity of a force watching him, observing his progress in the background. There was neither moon nor stars to light his way, but he knew the path and could have made his way home had he been sightless.

Aware that no good could come of a late night encounter, he walked in the center of the street away from the buildings, wondering what they wanted, who they were. Were they some street hoods looking for what they perceived as an easy mark or was it something more sinister? Suddenly two punks in a pickup were almost on top of him, forcing him toward the curb on his right. Quickly the first puke, the one on the passenger side, was upon him. The attackers were so confident, they carried no weapons. Two big young goons against a frail old bookworm of a man shouldn't be a problem. The first puke wrestled him to the ground trying to throttle him and cutting off his air. He could make out only words to the effect, "So you won't stop. A warning's not enough? Well how do you like this pop?"

Suddenly a cry of anguish from the first puke cut the night as two bony but steely fingers dug deeply into his eyeballs. Painful flashes of white light exploded in his sockets, then darkness. The victim and his attacker rose from the street. The would-be attacker reeled unsteadily in agony unable to see. He cried out like a whipped pup for help. The truck idled now with headlights cutting through the darkness silently spearing the black of the night. The second puke was on him now as he tried to sprint away. The younger man, his second attacker, punched at his head but the agile professor weaved and the blow fell glancingly on his temple. No problem. But now Karahsha was angry. He realized at this point they had no weapons. He was almost exultant. Did they think he would be such an easy mark, these two pukes in a pickup? The struggle brought back old feelings of combat in him, stirred emotions he had not known in a long time. He allowed the bigger man in close, then with one hand firmly in back of his neck, gripped the sissy ponytail that appeared to be there for his convenience. He jerked the handful of hair backwards forcing the chin up. While vulnerably exposed, he slammed his fist again and again into the soft throat making it softer with a sickening, crunching sound of breaking cartilage.

The bigger man, surprised, tried to back off but found his breath difficult to sustain. He released his hold on the professor, staggered, clutched his throat, and gagged. His feelings were hurt. He didn't realize the trouble he was in now. He didn't come to really hurt anyone, just to throw a scare into him. He gasped, tried to inhale, but his crushed trachea simply collapsed under the suction. He became worried. He couldn't breathe. He looked to his intended victim for help. His face turned dusky gray. He had trouble with his vision. He collapsed in a gurgling, dyspneic heap. If he could he would ask "Why me?"

The professor was on his feet now running at a deliberate pace, aware that there would soon be others attracted by the ruckus. He ran at a steady, slow to moderate lope trying to appear an innocent jogger, which after all he really was.

The puke with the injured eyes climbed behind the wheel of the pickup realizing his quarry was escaping. With a determination borne of malice, he was intent on carrying out his job. He saw the jogger only as a bouncing blur in front of him. He was using only a part of one eye whose vision remained. He gunned the engine, attempting to run down the jogger.

The professor realized what was happening but was unable to outrun a motor vehicle. He ran close to the building line, hoping to make it hard for the pickup to follow. The pickup jumped the sidewalk, careening and almost flipping over.

The pain in his eyes was maddening but the puke continued to gain on the running figure.

At last, the professor found a doorway indented enough from the level of the building to provide him a cubbyhole the vehicle could not fit in. He was panting and grateful for the momentary respite. The pickup turned in a wobbly circle. The headlights framed him in the doorway. Now, bearing down fast, the vehicle picked up speed. Now he understood. The driver meant to ram him, squash him into the door like a rolling pin on a lump of dough. But he still had his wits and his speed. The little respite was all he needed. He jumped out of his little refuge that had become a trap. The vehicle slammed into the doorway with a crash, broken glass exploding in all directions. The professor heaved a sigh of relief and began to walk away. The vehicle however jerked into reverse, whether out of control or deliberately, he did not know. He tried to avoid it but the rear end caught him off balance and sent him fifteen feet in the air. He landed with a sickening thunk. The vehicle slammed into a corner of a building and came to an abrupt halt.

The professor was on his back motionless trying to regain his senses. There was no pain, only anger. He felt somehow incomplete. He tried to raise himself off the pavement. He could only elevate his head, his neck, his arms, and torso. The bottom half didn't move, didn't feel, didn't respond. He raised his head and looked down. He saw the feet, the legs, and the knees with which he was so familiar and which have served him well as long as he could remember. Only they felt like they belonged to someone else. They were not his. They did not bring him to his feet on command. They were numb, lifeless and weighing him down. Struggling to turn, he felt a dull nagging pain in his back. He wondered why the pain didn't radiate into his legs.

Then in one horrible instant of understanding, he knew that he had a broken goddamned back. He was paralyzed from the waist down. He didn't delude himself. He was a realist. He knew this disaster, this calamity that took a second to happen will be with him forever. His mind fast-forwarded to the next likely scenario. There will be those among his doctors who will want to operate and those who will not. There will be those who say his injury is stable and will not progress, and those who will argue that the injury is an unstable one and will need to be internally fixed in order to prevent further deterioration of the spinal cord. Internal fixation meant rods, plates, or screws. Then there will be disagreements as to the most efficient way to stabilize the spine. There will be further disagreements as to when to mobilize him, how soon to move him from bed to wheelchair, or when to start therapy and what the goals of therapy should be. He'd seen it all a thousand times before. He winced at the thought that now he would be on the other end of the doctor-patient relationship.

Even though his experience in medicine did not involve much patient contact he shuddered to think of the loss of independence this would cause him. He did not want to be at the mercy of a bunch of patronizing nurses with their "And how are we doing today?" Even worse, to be at the mercy of some pompous neurosurgeon with his fresh-faced gang of trainees who would all think they knew what was best for him. He, Dr. Joseph Karahsha, knew what was best for him and he alone would continue to take responsibility for his life and his future. Damn the accident. Damn the attackers whoever they were. At least the police would be able to question one of them and get a handle on who put them up to it. Maybe the death of Chris' friend was somehow connected. In any case he was sure it was related to the Project. The Project, my God. A delay. But how much of a delay? He had to talk to Chris Fanning as soon as possible. Now he would have to depend totally on the youth for a time. Surely this was only a temporary setback. Now what's this? Blood from behind his left ear. Might be just a laceration.

He didn't feel any pain in his head. Again, he tried to pull himself up to his feet. This time the street started to spin. He was lightheaded. His strength drained from him as he fell into a syncope. Consciousness ebbed and he was unfeeling, uncaring, and pain free.

~~~

Sirens now, police, ambulance, onlookers. The street brightened with the pulsing police dome lights. Paramedics jumped out of their vehicles to assess the situation then tried to assist the injured. Cardiopulmonary resuscitation didn't work because the air pipe was collapsed. What was needed was tracheal intubation, itself a tricky procedure for an experienced anesthesiologist given this amount of trauma. Utterly impossible for the neophyte paramedics who knocked out a couple of teeth in their haste while trying futilely to intubate. The attacker with the crushed throat was dead.

The first attacker writhed on the ground in pain, blinded, his eyes gouged with the fingers as it was done in the Middle Ages. He would be lucky to regain any sight at all. A quick shot of morphine helped to quiet him down and he was loaded into the ambulance for the trip to the local hospital.

Policemen completed the obligatory chalk outline on the sidewalk. A couple of Polaroids were snapped and the body hefted and taken to the hospital. The other live body was taken to the same hospital, different department, the one for treatment, the other for autopsy.

"Any ID?" the cop in charge asked. He did not wait for an answer. "So what the hell happened here? No gunshots were fired, so how come we got one dead and one near blinded? Any witnesses? Anybody see anything? Who are these guys? Pretty big bruisers. Whoever did this to them must be one hell of a tiger. Christ, this is starting to remind me of New York. This is why I left."

Detective Frank O'Hara was on the scene.

"Hey Detective, we got one witness here, was looking out his window and saw the whole thing. Says a pickup truck pulled up to this skinny dude and two guys jumped out and attacked him but they didn't bargain for the way the skinny guy reacted. He says the two bruisers were no match for the little guy. He just cleaned their clocks for them. They didn't know what hit them."

"OK, so did you get a description? Where'd he go? The skinny little guy, where'd he go?"

It was another ten minutes before the broken, comatose body of the professor was located.

13

He awoke early the next morning, strangely calm, the new day bringing with it a fresh start. Morning is the time of singing birds, an assurance of new hope, the optimistic potential of a new day, opportunities unlimited. He was encouraged. He was even elated. It had all been a mistake. The horror of the night before has paled. Surely he would overcome his nighttime doubts, his midnight fears. He moved his eyes slowly, deliberately upward. His gaze fell on the IV tubing running from the plastic bottle labeled Ringer's Lactate down to the catheter impaling his arm vein fixed in place with those clever new transparent tapes. He looked a little further and saw the piggybacked plastic container. With a little craning of the neck he could read the label. It said dexamethasone, a steroid, the kind used to lower brain swelling after a severe head injury. He knew he had no significant head injury. He had a Band-Aid in back of his left ear but his head didn't hurt and his mind was clear. He knew who he was, he knew where he was. He was aware of the day of the week, the date, even the hospital room number having been in it many times before. But why was the steroid solution piggybacked into his IV tubing? Steroids are used to reduce edema, swelling, injury of the spinal cord.

He turned his head, looked out the window. The sky was blue, no clouds. The birds were flitting about and singing happily at their breakfast. He lifted his hands out from under the bed covers, looked at them, inspected them, palms and backs. He clenched his fists as though to test them. The familiar network of veins was there on the back of his hands, reassuring. The hair, the skin markings were there just like always. He shrugged his shoulders, took a big, deep breath of air and watched his chest rise then fall. He felt no pain. He looked down at his feet under the sheets. They looked the same as ever. He pulled at the sheets dislodging them from where they were tightly tucked under the corners of the mattress. Now he could see his feet, bare and looking as they always do. He stared at them for a long time. He lifted himself up at the shoulders using the steel triangle hanging from the overhead bar attached to the bed frame. He stared at his feet again, commanding them to move, to feel, to lift him out of this alien bed and take him home. His feet did not respond. He marshaled all of his strength to impel his feet to move, to turn his body, slap his soles to the floor and propel him upright. He needed to remove himself from this human warehouse and get back to his work, to his laboratory, to the Project. The lower extremities again failed to respond. A temporary aberration he thought. This cannot be. He refused to consider the possibility that his senses were accurately telling him the reality of the situation.

He struggled to lift himself using the overhead bar and trapeze. The body responded, but only to the level of the umbilicus, the belly button. He slapped at his lower abdomen, below the umbilicus. Nothing. No sensation. He seized a thick wedge of skin in his groin and squeezed it as hard as he could, digging in the fingernails. Nothing. The abused skin reddened, began to swell, turned blue as he watched but still there was no pain, no sensation at all. Not a twinge, no sensation whatsoever. He was angry now. Still unwilling to accept what his intellect and experience told him, he lifted himself mightily on the trapeze and swung over the edge of the bed. He hit the floor with a heavy thump. The Foley catheter anchored in his bladder jerked loose and went slithering across the room with its attached urine collection bag like a balloon uncorked. Blood now started to ooze onto the floor from the injury to his urethra. He watched in detached amazement as if observing someone else's body. Still there was no pain, no feeling whatever from the waist down to the disobedient feet. Though he appreciated no pain, he now was aware of an uncomfortable sensation in his lower thoracic spine. Exhausted by his recent efforts, he could only lie face down on the floor gasping to regain his breath.

A nurse walked in to investigate the commotion. She scolded him and checked to see that he hadn't hurt himself any further. She noticed the blood on the floor and became a bit unnerved. She ran out of the room for help.

All the professor could do was mutter curses and deny to himself the fix he was in. By the time the nurse returned with reinforcements he had crawled up on the side of the bed and was now leaning over it on his face. He would have made it too if not for their premature return. The slender nurse and two stocky nurse's aides helped him back into bed and proceeded to dress him down. Didn't he know how severely injured he was? Didn't he know he could hurt himself worse, what with him being a doctor himself?

They were starting it already: talking to him as if he were a child. He wouldn't have it. He summoned up his most evil mannerisms, his ugliest face, his most intimidating voice, and fairly bellowed at them. They were not to treat him as a patient for God's sake. He was who he was, and up to now, no one of any authority has come in to tell him how injured he was. And anyway he felt no pain so how could it be that he was seriously injured?

"Well," the nurse replied, "you can't move your legs can you?" Even as she uttered the words she regretted having said them. "Here, Dr. Karahsha," she clucked, "now you just lie back and relax. Here, here's a little orange juice." She poured from the bedside pitcher into a paper cup.

He drank it down. It tasted good, wet his gullet, but did not make him feel any better. The Project, he thought, the Project was now endangered by this turn of events. He would have to depend more heavily on his assistant, Chris Fanning from now on. This put a whole new urgency on the matter until he was better. The possibility of his never improving did not occur to him. He would have to accelerate the whole process. He would have to pretend to cooperate with his doctors, the bozos, so as to gain their confidence and impress upon them how fast he could recover. Then he would be free again to pursue his dream.

He announced to the nurse that he was now ready to talk to the physician in charge and she was to go get him forthwith. The nurse informed him that the neurosurgeon in charge of his case was very likely in surgery but that she would get his message to him. He lifted himself up again on the trapeze.

Nurse Jennette couldn't help thinking he looked like a monkey hanging from a tree.

"Now you listen to me, Nancy Nurse, you go tell your Doctor Krigston that I demand to see him right now or by God I will walk, crawl, fly, or roll out of here and go to another hospital for my treatment." He made as if to throw himself from the bed onto the floor again. At that precise moment Dr. Krigston entered, followed by an entourage of residents, interns, fellows and one medical student.

The neurosurgeon was an imposing figure, tall, lean, stately and possessed of matinee idol good looks on the order of a Caesar Romero. He had a large handsome head crowned by a full mane of hair so white it appeared to emanate light instead of reflecting it. He had not lost one strand of hair with age. In fact, his hairline seemed to have metastasized further down onto his forehead, compared to when he was young to those who knew him. He had on a new shirt and tie. His white coat was so stiff with starch it appeared to be a coat of armor with pockets. His shoes were black and polished to a lustrous sheen like the old army spit shine. He looked the caricature of the natty professional, and his entourage held him in awe.

"Ah, Dr. Karahsha, I'm sorry to have heard of your unfortunate accident." When he spoke his perfectly aligned teeth gleamed. They were a white that competed with the white of his hair.

"I have just had a look at your X-rays and I'm afraid to tell you that you have a T10 thoracic lesion, that is, your spinal cord is injured at that level and you are paraplegic as of now. The injury to the bone is a stable one and the cord is in the shock phase, after which some recovery is possible. I'm sure you are aware of the concept of spinal shock and the subsequent possibility of partial recovery. In cases such as yours there is a chance of eventual ambulation with long leg braces and crutches depending on the amount of recovery. Your age is against you but your excellent health and physical condition are in your favor."

"Oh nonsense," the professor exploded. "You know damned well I'll recover, so don't come in here with your portents of doom and disaster."

Dr. Krigston seemed saddened but was not offended. He was used to this type of reaction from victims of spine injury who cannot accept the finality of paralysis.

In general, this type of injury happens to young, healthy men in their prime who are injured in auto or motorcycle accidents, less often in horse related or swimming injuries. The first reaction is a complete denial and inability to accept the devastation of paralysis. Usually the notion is bolstered by family and friends that the doctors telling him he is forever paralyzed are just so many quacks who need to return to school. No one is willing to believe that little Johnny is never going to walk again. The sad phase of denial takes weeks or months to elapse.

"Look, Dr. Karahsha, I have gone over your physical exam, done last night by my chief resident, Dr. Marko here. We reviewed the X-rays and went over the spinal MRI. There is nothing more to do in the way of diagnosis. Your bone injury is stable so you need no internal fixation surgery but the injury to your spinal cord is severe and likely to be permanent. As you know, many patients like you undergo some degree of neurological return but that is variable and unpredictable. Only the future will tell us how much if any recovery will occur."

"But, Dr. Krigston, I have my work, my research, which is in a critical phase right now. I have to return to it as soon as possible."

The professor was much calmer now. He realized that difficult behavior on his part was counterproductive.

"If and when the time comes you can carry on with your work from a wheelchair until you don't need it anymore. You can still do your pathology, still work on your slides, still do your autopsies with help, and still do your research. After all, you still have your residents and fellows."

Dr. Krigston gave him the opportunity of privacy for his physical exam. He would shoo all the residents and other trainees from the room if the professor desired. The professor, used as he was to teaching, declined and allowed all the underlings to stay.

After a thorough physical exam and neurological testing, the neurosurgeon established the level of injury by gentle pin prick. By this means he was able to confirm the lesion to be at the level of T10, which is at the level of the umbilicus. Testing for sensation below that level was negative, no feeling below the belly button. There was also no motor function below T10, that is, the muscles below that level were paralyzed as were the deep tendon reflexes like the knee and ankle jerks.

"And now to add indignity to injury the 'anal wink' reflex and perianal sensation are to be tested," Krigston explained to the group. They helped the professor to turn to the prone position and tested those reflexes. There were none. The test, carried out by light pin prick to the anal area, would cause the anal sphincter to contract producing the so-called wink reflex. A positive wink would indicate that the corresponding portion of the spinal cord was still intact. However, in the presence of spinal shock this reflex is absent until the shock wears off. The significance of this test is that if the reflex is present after the shock has worn off that indicates partial cord injury. A completely absent reflex would mean a complete spinal cord injury. In the case of Professor Karahsha the cord was non-functional, indicating a complete spinal cord injury with very little likelihood of recovery.

14

Two suits and one uniform approached the nurse's station on the surgical floor at County Hospital. Detective Frank O'Hara knocked loudly and objectionably on the desk. His beefy face and air of authority brought the ward clerk, now euphemistically called the unit secretary in most hospitals, to her feet. He flashed his shield and in a matter-of-fact manner asked the location of one Mike Melone, alleged victim of a mugging tonight. The young girl behind the desk had trouble finding the room number. She was new to the job. O'Hara leaned over the desk and in his most intimidating voice asked, "What the hell, how many mugging victims do you have here at a time? Hey girly, this is official police business, what's taking so long?"

"Uh," she fumbled, "room 410, bed 2. Go right in." She pointed the way, glad to get rid of him.

Without knocking, the trio entered the room. The attending ophthalmologist was in the midst of his examination and the policemen waited until he finished. When he had completed his assessment he turned to the waiting men as if to ask who they were. Before he could say anything the detective identified himself and said, "Now you aren't going to give me any of that stuff about how I can only have a few minutes to interview the victim because he needs his rest, are you?"

"No, no, he just needs his eyes bandaged, immobilized, and protected from the light."

"Well, thanks Doc."

He turned to the patient lying in the bed, somewhat sedated from the pain shot he'd recently had. His eyes were covered in white patches and wrap-around dressings. He was so big his feet protruded from the end of the bed.

"It says here your name is Mike Melone. Care to tell me what happened? I'm Detective Frank O'Hara of the fourth precinct up the street. I'm here to investigate a ruckus tonight in which your partner was killed."

"Geez!" The big man in the bed gulped. "I didn't know he was killed. Olson was my best friend. I sure hope you find that maggot that did this to us Detective."

The three policemen looked at each other.

"If you answer my questions, you know, cooperate, there's a very good chance we can track him down. How about answering a few questions?"

"Sure, sure. I'll be glad to help. We were riding around minding our own business when we noticed this skinny, er, ah, wiry guy in the street, looked like he was having some trouble, stumbling like, you know? So we pulled up alongside of him to see if he needed any help. My buddy, Chuck Olson, got out and approached him to ask if we could help. Well, the little turd musta been playing possum because next thing I know Chuck's lying in the street, can't get his breath, and turns blue right in front of me. I tried to help him, you know, loosen his clothing when all the sudden there's these hot pokers in my peepers and I got a pain in my head like I never had before. From then on everything goes black and I can't see. Next thing I know I'm in the ambulance and then the hospital. Geez Doc, will I be able to see again?"

The eye doctor told him one eye was irreparably damaged and he had a good chance to regain complete sight in the other, but he must take it easy, lie around, avoid shocks, and take his antibiotics to try and ward off infection.

"Can you describe him?" the policeman persisted.

"Well yeah, he was wiry and scrawny but lightning fast."

"How tall?"

"Oh, about five feet ten, six feet, kind of swarthy complexion."

"How old?"

"Well, that's the funny thing. He coulda been twenty-nine or forty-nine. It's just hard to tell. He moved like a young man, an athlete. No, like a cat, but I'm sure he had some grey, y'know, around the ears. He coulda been Indian or Mexican or something."

"Can you estimate his weight?"

"Maybe one sixty-five, one seventy."

"So you mean to tell me that a skinny balink older man, maybe fifty years old, weighing no more than one hundred seventy pounds took down two big galoots like you and your friend?"

Sheepishly, Melone replied, "I told you he was fast."

"How much do you weigh Mike?"

"Two twenty, two twenty-five."

"How tall are you?"

"About six one."

"And Chuck Olson, your late friend?"

"He's about the same, maybe an inch or so taller than me. I don't know how much he weighs. Geez, it don't seem right him being dead, it don't seem real. What am I going to tell his mother? We been friends ever since we was kids."

"What do you think was in his mind, Mike? I mean, why did he attack you? Was it robbery? Did he get any of your money?"

"Nah, he didn't rob us. What the hell do I know what he wanted? Maybe he was rabid. I read in the papers there's rabies going around in raccoons and bats. Maybe something bit him."

"Mike, you ever been in trouble with the law?"

"I've had a few scrapes in my time but nothing recent. I'm strictly legit now, a regular Honest Abe."

"What do you do for a living, Mike?"

"I work in construction and sometimes I'm a carpenter. Geez, I'll probably have to go on welfare now if my eyesight don't come back. I'd like to get my mitts on that little rat."

"Have you ever met him before?"

"No way man."

"Did you have a good look at him?"

"Yeah, I got a good look at him before he put my lights out."

"Mike, when your vision returns do you think you could ID him for us?"

"You mean if my vision returns, don't you? Yeah, I could pick him out of a lineup if that's what you mean, the little bastard. Hey, you bet your buttons I want to press charges. He's maybe ruined me for life. I wanna sue the maggot too. He thinks he's gonna get away with this. No way, man."

"OK Mike, when you get released from the hospital I'd like you to stick around town. I may have some more questions to ask you."

"And just where do you think I'm gonna go without my eyeballs working, huh?"

"For your information, Mike, the man you tangled with last night was Professor Joseph Karahsha, a well-known pathologist at the university hospital. He was hit by your van, sustained a broken back, and is now paralyzed from the waist down. As I hear it, I haven't interviewed him myself, but his story is completely different from yours. He says he was attacked by two big hoodlums intent on doing him harm. Now whose story do you think is more credible Mike, his or yours? You have a police record going back many years. He is a well respected member of society, a pathologist, and research hotshot. Think about it Mike. You may want to change your story."

As the policemen left the room one of the uniforms said, "Give me a break. This guy is acting as if he was Mother Theresa. We all know he's a hood and a thug. But one thing bothers me. How could a guy twice their age and maybe one third their weight get the drop on them? Think they tried to mug him and got the surprise of their lives when he wouldn't roll over and play dead for them?"

Detective O'Hara said, "That's very likely the way it was. I think they attacked him and he blew some sunshine up their skirts by taking them out. I wish Mike Melone regains his sight sooner rather than later so we can confront the two together and see what comes of it. Look, I want you men to go out to the crime scene. Knock on doors, talk to people, try to find out if anyone saw anything that we didn't. We don't have anything else to go on. At this point it's one's word against the other."

"Say boss," the first uniform piped in, "do you get the idea he was trying to hide something? Not give away his true feelings or something? I mean I obviously can't call him shifty eyed, but I get the impression there's more here than what's visible on the surface. It doesn't fit. Why would some skinny guy attack two big monkeys like that? And then it turns out the scrawny guy is some big time head job of a professor at the university. It just doesn't make sense. Maybe the mugging's a smoke screen. Maybe they were put up to it by a third party for some reason. But what reason? I don't make a connection."

O'Hara agreed. He could not see any connection either. "But," he said, "that guy Fanning is sure some kind of a jinx isn't he?"

"Why? What do you mean, boss?"

"Well, first Fanning's best friend, Jake Hamilton, gets creamed out in the desert, then his professor is attacked by two hoodlums. Don't you suppose there is a connection? Something funny is going on here and I mean to find out what."

"How'd you know Fanning had anything in common with the professor, boss?"

"Simple. I asked."

~~~

Mike Melone, though genuinely worried about his vision, was more worried about the holes the police had punched in his story already. He was a two time loser and he didn't relish the idea of going to prison in his wounded condition. Any time before when he'd had to spend time in the joint he'd been respected by the other inmates and even by the guards by virtue of his size and reputation. But if he had to do hard time in a blinded condition he didn't know how he'd handle it. He did not feel proud of being pummeled by a middle-aged geek of a professor, and he now worried about his reputation among the rabble who frequented his world. He did not want to lose the extra money that came with these special "assignments".

Moreover, he wondered why he got this special assignment in the first place. He had found a message on his answering machine. The message was in a vaguely unfamiliar accent. He didn't think about it much at the time. He was to go to a specific location in a city park, leave a short note signifying his interest, and if he wanted the job he was to write a simple "yes" on a piece of yellow note paper, wrap it in aluminum foil and toss it into a garbage can near a phone booth. If his reply was affirmative he would receive another phone call with further instructions. Intrigued by the offer of easy money and the prospect of bashing some unfortunate to get it, he had followed through. Subsequent phone calls had led him to a substantial cash advance and a description of his victim along with the victim's usual late night jogging route. He had followed through, collected the advance, which was mailed to him, and at the suggestion of the anonymous caller picked himself out an accomplice to forestall the possibility of any slip-up. Now it had come to this. Melone didn't know the nature of the man who had hired him, nor of the proposed victim.

15

When Chris came into the lab the next day, there was a message for him to go to the university hospital, room 1267. Fanning was shocked to see the professor in the fix he was in.

"Sit down my boy, I have some disturbing news to tell you." He related the events of the night before. "Chris, I believe we are in a certain amount of danger. Last night I was attacked by what I can only describe as hired goons. They were going to work me over or even kill me as a warning but they didn't get the chance. It was only through a fluke that they did as much damage as they did." In spite of his condition he chuckled at the surprise he had given those two birds. He told Chris that he thought he might have killed one of them.

During all this Chris' eyes bulged with shock and apprehension. "Why is it you don't think it was a random mugging?"

"Because you just don't have two big gorillas chase after someone with a pickup truck as if they were after that one person if it was a routine mugging. Those two guys were not typical muggers. They were well dressed, driving an expensive souped up buggy, you know the kind with wheels the size of dirigibles. They appeared to spot me, make a positive identification, then move in, all very deliberately, very purposeful."

"And what's the purpose," Chris asked in astonishment.

"I think there is someone out to prevent the completion of our Project."

They had all taken to calling their experiment The Project.

"Who might that be?"

"Remember when you first became involved in this Chris? Remember the discussion we had? I believe there is any number of groups with a vested interest in our failure."

"You mean they would go so far as attempted murder to stop us, to stop the Project?"

"Yes, I believe they would, the stakes are that high. All the other religions of the world have a stake in stopping us because once we have a new Jesus Christ on the scene and we reveal how we recreated him, the validity, the connection between their icons, their prophets, and God will be called into question. Now you are going to hear the news on TV or the radio that these two hoods were attacked by a crazed lunatic, me. I'm sure they or the survivor will accuse me of starting the fight. But they sure got a surprise didn't they?"

"What did you do, scalp him? You don't carry a gun or any weapons that I've ever seen. How could you overpower two bigger, younger guys who should have it all over you in strength, speed and just plain viciousness?"

The professor leaned back in his bed and admitted, "Well, I did have some pretty vigorous training when I was young and I guess it just stuck with me. And in case you hadn't noticed I can be pretty vicious myself. Be that as it may. That aspect of it is not important now. Those two boys won't bother us any more. But now we have a two-fold problem. One: There is someone or some group out there that wants to stop our Project. And Two: we can't go to the police about it because what we are doing must remain secret from the authorities until it is completed."

"It looks like our secrecy has been breached already. And who would want to stop us so badly they would do a thing like that?"

"We have been over that once before but I can see any religion other than the Catholic Church wanting to stop us for the reason that reincarnating the one true Savior puts all the other faiths to shame and calls into question their legitimacy. For that matter the present day Catholic Church itself may be the one responsible for the reasons already discussed."

"But how are you going to carry on in the condition you're in?"

"Don't worry about me. I'll be OK. If we succeed I may be able to ask for a miracle cure. In any case we must press on. I'll have to depend on you more

139

heavily now and if the police come sniffing around I intend to deny everything. Also, you'll need to get your family out of this area. Do you or your family or your wife's family have any out of town vacation spots or any place at all where you can send Margie and the kids until this is over?"

"Oh for Pete's sake, I really don't believe this is necessary. No one is going to threaten me or my family. Don't you think that is a bit far-fetched?"

"Not only is it not far-fetched but I think you ought to stop your jogging alone in the streets, you see what happened to me. You ought to vary the routes you take, to and from school and buy a gun for protection. I don't mean to imply you can't handle yourself but the level of violence may escalate and you may as well be ready for it. That is if you want to continue."

"Oh come on Prof, don't you think you are going overboard with this security danger stuff?"

"Do you think I'm faking paralysis?"

"No."

"All right then. I believe we may be dealing with fanatics and the level of their attempts to stop us may escalate to the point of deadliness. If it involves only myself I can face it. But I won't have you or your family endangered. Please listen to me and take this seriously. I need your help to complete the Project and I really don't want you or your family to get hurt. I also don't think I have the time, inclination, or patience to break in another graduate student of your caliber."

"By the way," Chris asked, "what do you mean you are going to deny it all? And why can't you cooperate with the police? I don't see how our security could be breached by filing a complaint against those two guys."

"Look Chris, I have a lot of work to do before this Project becomes a reality. I can't afford to be distracted by getting involved with the police. I will be polite, I'll answer their questions. But I cannot afford to give away any of the details of our work. If the university found out before I was ready for them to all my funding would dry up and that will be that. Even though the cops have no inkling of what we are doing the people who set the thugs on me do. I don't want to take even the remotest chance that our Project will be exposed to the authorities. Do you realize how the so-called moral medical ethicists would react if they got a whiff of what we are up to? We could be put right out of business. The other aspect of this is that if that one fellow was really killed the police have an unsolved homicide on their hands and in a worst case scenario they may accuse me. In that case it's my word against the survivor's. Now, granted, I'm a pillar of the community type professional man, professor, physician, pathologist and all that. But filing a complaint puts me in the limelight and that's exactly where I don't want to be. I'd be willing to bet the surviving thug is blaming me for attacking them. He's not going to own up to his part in this attack because that throws the focus on him. He's already probably got a criminal record. Now, do you know if you can whisk your wife and the kids off for the duration to some out of the way, remote place, where they can be protected?"

"Oh sure, my in-laws have more homes around the country than OJ has lawyers. That's the easy part. The hard part is going to be explaining it to Margie and the kids and the in-laws. How long is this going to take? I don't like the idea of being separated from them for more than a weekend. God! This is getting complicated."

"Well, I guess you must make a choice, Chris. I think it is mandatory that you get your family out of any potential danger. Or you have to consider seriously whether you want to continue in this Project of ours. I certainly don't want to influence you to do the wrong thing but you know I need your help. By the way, how soon could you get ready to go to Turin, Italy?"

"Turin, Italy, where they make the Fiats?"

16

Fanning jogged home in spite of the professor's warning. When he arrived at home he noticed the mailbox was full. He pulled out the usual mail, a bunch of utility bills, a couple of pesky flyers advertising this and that and a copy of yesterday's New York Times. Intermingled with all of that he found a wrinkled envelope addressed to him in a strange handwritten script. He opened it up and in the same foreign looking handwriting was the most vicious threat he had ever seen.

It read: "Chris Fanning, you are playing with something you do not understand. Your association with the heretic and barbarian Joseph Karahsha must end immediately. What he is doing is blasphemous and criminal. You will not be warned again. Instead, if you persist in this outrage, you will not see your children or your wife alive again. You will see them in little pieces at a time. We will send them to you in a plastic bag, a finger at a time, an eyeball at a time until they are all dead. Heed this warning Chris Fanning. This is the only one you will receive."

Fanning found himself in a sweat. He fairly catapulted himself into the house and started to search for his family. He almost panicked when they weren't there. He ran through the house yelling and searching until he remembered that Margie and the kids were over visiting their grandparents and were not scheduled to return home until that night. He called his in-laws and confirmed that all was well. Then he decided to move the children and Margie to a country house his in-laws had until this danger was over.

17

The house was a split level ranch house at the top of a steep hill with a commanding view of the surrounding countryside. Margie's dad had bought it as a kind of rustic retreat and as a hunting lodge though he had not hunted in over twenty years. The rear of the house faced south and the main floor was some eighteen feet above the ground. The southern walls were mostly composed of double paned storm windows. In the summer the sun shone almost directly from above so that the rays did not enter the house directly. If it became too hot in spite of this the blinds could be drawn. The east wall was likewise all enclosed by glass windows with a wooden deck that could be used as a patio for grilling steaks and such. The front of the house faced north and it too was enclosed by glass. The only part of the north wall that was not glass was the two car garage to the east side of the front door.

The garage door could be opened by a button at the doorway into the home or by a portable garage door opener Margie kept in the Toyota parked in the garage. The only wall without windows was the west wall and this was at the top of a steep cliff. The basement had been made into a separate apartment with a small living room and fireplace, two small bedrooms, and a large unfinished storage room. There were bookcases at the foot of the stairs and a gun rack over the fireplace.

Margie kept her dad's hunting rifles locked up in the gun rack and the ammo under lock and key in a separate cabinet upstairs. The latter was a safety precaution due to the presence of the children. Margie was not squeamish when it came to guns. She was just careful.

She had been there with the kids a week, feeling kind of foolish. She was settling herself and the kids down to a routine although they all missed their daddy. The children were early risers and usually went out back to start their play and wait for mom to fix breakfast. The two children were out back this morning as usual. They did not notice anything unusual this particular morning. Margie arose from bed, checked out the back window to make sure the kids were all right, showered and dressed. Then she went to the kitchen to start breakfast. Her plans were to go into town today twenty-five miles up the road and meet an old high school chum for lunch. She planned a shopping trip after that to stock up on some summer clothes for herself and the children. Chris didn't like it but she usually had extra money from her parents for these shopping trips.

She had the two fed and cleaned up by 8:30 a.m. She threw a load of wash in the machine, turned the automatic bread maker on, and headed for the garage. She opened the garage door by flipping the switch on the wall just outside the door connecting the TV room to the garage. She kept the Toyota sedan in the garage and the Blazer out back in the yard. She did that just in case of a malfunction of the garage door opener even though the garage could accommodate both vehicles.

She hit the switch on the wall and the big garage door jerked to a start. As it rose she saw something discordant and unexpected, but its meaning didn't register in her mind at first. Two pairs of dirty men's running shoes seemed to be just sitting there right outside the garage door. The door creaked higher and she remembered she'd meant to spray the runner tracks with graphite to smooth the doors' glide. The door had been sticking. The door continued to jerk upwards revealing a pair of men's jeans attached to the shoes. She realized at last what was going on now. She wheeled around, hit the button again and the door stopped in its tracks. The sneakered feet hesitated. Quickly she punched the switch again. The door gave a jerk and started downwards again. Feet shuffled in confusion. One set of legs squatted. A man's hand reached under the door, then a shoulder, then a muffled curse. A torso came rolling in under the dropping door. The torso, panicking, now attempted to crawl under the door. Too late. The door slammed shut on the mid thoracic area of a large, beefy man dressed in a flannel shirt. The head jerked up with pain. Two eyes fixed on Margie and called out in silence for help. Another curse is heard from the other side of the garage door. Then muffled yells. The torso's head turned from one side to the other as if to shake himself loose, one arm in the garage, one outside, invisible. The door pressed down squeezing, crushing the breath out of the lungs, and making inhalation impossible.

Margie was panicked. She didn't want to be responsible for a death. She ran to the door, tried to lift it, bent down and was startled to see a second man's face inches from hers, peering under the door. She recoiled horrified, jumped back on her heels and ran into the house. The children. Must find the children.

She ran through the house, glanced out the window to the backyard. She ran out back nearly in a panic. She grabbed the children roughly, one by the shirt, the other by the arm. The children were not sure of what was going on. Thinking it was a game they squealed but then they saw the expression on her face and turned scared. She shoved them roughly into the Blazer. The children berated her for omitting the seatbelt routine. Normally she went through a ritual with them, fastening their belts before taking her own seat. She screamed at them to be quiet and behave. She had the key in the ignition now. She started up the engine and threw it into gear, speeding around the circular driveway. A man stood in the drive blocking the way with his body. She determined to hit him if necessary and bore down. He dove out of the way at the last second. She aimed the car down the driveway toward the gravel road towards town. She glanced out the rearview mirror. Two legs still protruded from under the garage door. Another man rose from the bushes dusting himself off. She zoomed past their car which was parked off to the side of the road. It was a red Dodge Shadow with Phoenix tags. Should she stop and disable the Dodge? She slowed down, thought better of it, and gunned her own vehicle. They must have left their car off the road in order to avoid alarming her with its sound. Then they skulked up to the garage door and were standing there figuring out what to do when she raised the door.

She sped down the road checking the rear view mirror as she drove. It was twenty-five miles to town and the police station. The two children enjoyed the new style of mom's driving thinking it a game except for mom's demeanor. Twenty-five short miles to go. She revved it up to eighty miles per hour. Not too many hills or curves. Shouldn't be a problem. Wonder who the creep was stuck under the garage door. What do these guys want anyway? She was up to eighty-five miles per hour. The car handled well at this speed. Uh oh, the rearview picked up a speck a mile or two back, doing at least ninety mph. Of course she couldn't tell their speed. All she knew was that they seemed to be gaining on her. Damn! Well he's not going to get me or the kids. She was up to ninety mph.

"Faster, Mom, faster, he's gaining on us."

"Hey you two, this is not a game. Those guys are up to no good. A little prayer here couldn't do any harm."

One hundred miles per hour! The car started to shake.

"Can't push it much more than this. Hope the tires hold up."

She had never driven this fast before. Maybe she should play it cute here, turn off at one of the small country lanes and give them the slip. But then she'd have to slow down and maybe give them a chance to catch up. The dirt roads would kick up a lot of dust giving her position way. Scratch that idea. Oh, she wished Chris were here. She'd just have to barrel on through to town on her own to the police station. Maybe the cops could catch the two creeps and she could find out what this was all about anyway. The shaking worsened now and the red Dodge continued to gain on them. In spite of the shaking she floored it but the Blazer could only squeeze out one hundred three miles per hour. It felt like the body would shake itself right off the frame. "Bastards," she thought. The Dodge was only a quarter mile away now and still gaining. Speedy little devil, she heard herself thinking. The kids, over their fright, started pointing their fingers and going bang, bang. Margie in a voice subject to no misinterpretation said, "Those two guys are trying to kill us," she yelled. "I want you two to get down on the floor and stay there."

"But Mom--"

"Dammit, do as I say," she screamed at the top of her voice. The two kids, shocked, had never heard this tone of voice from her. They looked at each other and dove for the floor. The Dodge was almost within three car lengths now. "Oh God, another eight miles to go."

Not enough. The Dodge caught up to her, forced her off the road onto the shoulder. Out of fear for the two children she brought the vehicle to a bouncing screeching stop. They sat in the car quietly, wide eyes waiting. The two men approached on foot a bit perturbed. Doors and windows were locked. The children started to be scared. The Dodge was parked in front of the Blazer impeding its forward progress but not its backward motion. The two men were now rapping on the windows, one on either side motioning to roll down the windows. She saw no obvious weapons. She jammed the gearshift into reverse and hit the accelerator savagely. The two children were catapulted into the back rests of the front seats. She hadn't the presence of mind to get them to fasten their seat belts. Except for the shock and fright they were not harmed but both started bawling. She backed up onto the road and jammed the car into forward gear. Foot on the gas savagely she peeled out sending the kids reeling backwards this time. The two would-be attackers were back in their car again taking up the pursuit.

This time she covered the short eight miles before they had a chance to force her off the road again. Her heart threatened to burst out of her chest. She allowed herself to hope they might escape. At all costs she must keep the children from harm. Oh, if only Chris were here to help. She felt no resentment for his absence only fear for the children. She hadn't given a thought to her own safety.

The two pursuers were not so sure of themselves now. They knew they were approaching town and with that the danger to them increased. They were confused and began to argue between themselves. The victim of the garage door wanted to give up the chase and get himself to a doctor. He was sure he had broken ribs at the very least. The other, who was now driving, wanted to continue the pursuit while acknowledging the fact that they had already bungled the job and the more they chased at this point the better their chances of being caught.

Margie gained confidence that they would get away from these creeps. She usually didn't wish any misfortune on anyone, but these guys, well she wished she'd caught them both under the garage door. She felt a frisson of relief up her back as they approached the city limits of the small town of Jasper, Arizona.

~~~

147

Meanwhile the two defeated perpetrators looked at each other dejectedly and wondered why their prey ran away as if their lives were in danger.

"Geez, we only wanted to talk to them."

"Yeah, but I guess they didn't know that. What would you do if you seen two big goons, like us, trying to climb under your garage door and you were a young mother with two little kids alone in the country?"

"OK, so what were we supposed to do, send them an invitation in the mail, an invitation that could be traced through handwriting and God only knows what else right to our front door? Anyway we tried to warn them with threatening letters already and it didn't work. Come to think of it I guess we're pretty lucky she only attacked us with the garage door. She coulda come out blazing with a shotgun."

"Nah, women don't have the hormones for aggression. I was reading about it in a magazine. Aggression is caused by a male hormone called testosterone. And women just don't have it because it's what makes a man a man. Anybody with hormones can be aggressive like a male cow, which is a bull, or a billy goat. But the female of the species will rather run away than have a confrontation. Or, a female will get aggressive if she is defending cubs, say a mamma bear with cubs, or a mother fox with babies."

"What the hell do you think this woman was, a female with babies, so how come she was not aggressive?"

"Because even in spite of her being a mother with children she would still rather avoid confrontation where she or her children might get hurt. I'm telling you I read it in a magazine. It was written by a professor or something."

"What kind of a magazine?"

"It was one of those Field and Hunting magazines or Stream and Trap or one of those kinds of mags. See, the trouble with you is that you don't read enough. You're ignorant, you lack education. Oh sure, you can hot wire a car or forge a check adequately but you lack learning, you lack sophistication, you don't read enough like I do."

"Enough already with the ignoramus bit."

"Whoa, now. I didn't say you're an ignoramus. I said you're ignorant. There's a difference."

"Which is?"

"Well, an ignoramus is dumb, incapable of learning. But to be ignorant means you really don't need to go to school to get an education. You could read like I do. I read lots of things in magazines. Some of your finest brains in America were self-taught geniuses who never went to college, like Einstein or Edison or Henry Ford."

"You know for a fact that Henry Ford never went to college?"

"Oh yeah, it was in a magazine I read. I told you, there's a whole lot of stuff you could learn just by reading. Like Yogi Berra said, 'When you come to that fork in the road, take it.' That means when opportunity knocks once you should open the door because you never know who it might be. Anyway, we better take the opportunity to get the hell out of here just in case she's gone to the police station. They might be out looking for us before too long. I hope she didn't get our license plate number or we're a couple of dead ducks."

~~~

Margie and the kids arrived at the Police Station about the same time the above conversation was taking place. After the stress and excitement of escaping the pursuers her iron self-control began to falter. She felt a terrible weakness in her knees. Her hands trembled. The children, however, took it all in stride and were even starting to lose interest in the recent adventure. Jerry complained of being hungry while little Josie complained of a stomach ache and a dizzy head. Margie vowed then and there that her next stop would be the mall, and her very first purchase would be a car phone. The next stop would be Kenny's gun shop where she would buy a pistol. Well, maybe not the pistol, she'd have to think about that.

She parked the car crazily, jumped out and found her legs would barely hold her. She checked to see if the pursuers were anywhere to be seen and took both children in tow straight to the precinct. She spilled her guts to the policeman at the desk then phoned Chris to tell him what had happened.

18

Fanning was at once shaken and furious. He'd have to make better arrangements to ensure their safety. He asked her to stay at the police station and wait for him. He'd make the two and one half hour trip as soon as possible. Damn, he thought, what if those goons had got to her and the kids? No telling what might have happened. Bless that girl for being so resourceful and knowing how to drive fast without killing herself. He quickly excused himself from his responsibilities at the university and jumped into his car.

He used his old college technique to drive well above the speed limit and avoid the police. He was proud of never having a speeding ticket after having figured out his own system of avoiding the cops. He had devised his system after careful study and observation because he had been nabbed several times while commuting from college to home and back again on holidays. It became a game to keep from being bored and falling asleep on those long lonely trips. He never used a radar detector because he figured the mere presence of such a device would tip a wavering policeman into giving him the ticket. His technique was to avoid speeding when there were vehicles behind or in front of him which he could not definitely rule out as police cars. This included the oncoming lane of traffic on the other side of the median. When he was in the presence of vehicles he could not identify positively as not being state police or county sheriff's cars, he drove near the limit. When he saw only pickup trucks or semis ahead or to the rear he'd pick up the pace until he could see another group of unidentified vehicles in the distance or until the terrain became ideal for the smokies to hide in, say a curve in the road with high shoulders or rock cliffs or a rise in the road where he could not see above the crest of a hill as he approached it. He learned to be extra vigilant when he was in the vicinity of cars he deemed suspicious. Unmarked police cars have a certain aura about them. They are usually bristling with antennas. There are multiple lights in the rear window. The vehicle is always an American made car, clean, with a solitary white male driver. Fanning considered himself a law-abiding, taxpaying citizen and he felt that what some of the police did on the highways was akin to harassment and that everyone would be better off if the cops went after criminals instead of people like him. He'd had a couple of close calls though. Twice it happened that he was tooling along southbound in his little red Miata when he noticed a state police car going north across the median divider. In his rear view mirror he saw the vehicle cross the grassy median divider and begin to come after him. He had the presence of mind on both occasions to pull off the road, taking advantage of a curve in the highway. Once he turned into a housing development and watched the cop go by from the parking lot. The other time he pulled into a factory and watched the police vehicle go by under cover of the factory building. On those occasions he couldn't help but chuckle to himself at the poor trooper who must have wondered where in hell he'd disappeared to.

Now he had an important reason to avoid the fuzz and reach his destination as soon as possible. He felt guilty and vulnerable. He was enraged at what Margie and the kids had just been through. To think, the two creeps got away. His thinking drifted to the hypothetical. He had found over the years that he did some of his best thinking while driving alone. What if we could identify a gene or genes for criminality, for the perpetration of criminal behavior? He knew he'd read somewhere that certain chromosome abnormalities were associated with a higher propensity towards criminal behavior. What if we could remove those "bad" genes or neutralize them and replace them with other "good" genes? Here he knew he was bordering on the politically sensitive issue of the genetic determinant of behavior. To isolate a specific group of people, predominantly males, who had a "bad" gene or set of genes was to come close to the thinking of the Nazi Germans who instituted a system of first sequestering, then killing those whom they considered to be defective or as they described it themselves, life that did not deserve to live. But, he thought, this was different. He wouldn't advocate killing anyone, only the genetic alteration of some people who had demonstrated anti-social tendencies and who carried the "criminal" genes.

It would be a boon for society but it would be a tremendous plus for the criminal himself who would not have to contend with his anti-social, criminal tendencies anymore. He'd bring it up with the professor just as soon as he returned to the university.

He was thus deeply engrossed in thought as he drove. He was in that curious state of withdrawal when the mind is occupied with its own devices and the outside world is put on automatic pilot so to speak. His thoughts turned to Margie and the kids. When he'd first met her and they started to become serious about each other she was only eighteen. He used to be uncomfortable with the difference in their ages but Margie used to say she was perfectly content with the age differential. She'd say, "You could raise me to suit you." And he thought that was so special and was one of the many things that made him fall for her so hard.

He therefore was taken completely by surprise at the flashing dome light that now insisted he pull over for speeding. He thought, "Oh no, not again." He'd allowed his preoccupation to distract him enough into another speeding ticket.

The officer asked for his driver's license and vehicle registration, the usual. Then he asked Fanning to get out of the car and walk a straight line in tandem. Over Chris' mild objections he took a breathalyzer test.

"Just how fast did you clock me, officer?" He really had lost awareness of his speed.

"I clocked you at eighty-two miles per hour," the policeman replied. "This is a fifty-five mile per hour zone, sir," he said icily. "The good news is that you passed the breathalyzer test."

"I could have told you that," Chris shot back, annoyance in his voice. Of course he realized everyone stopped for speeding maintains his innocence. He was sorry as soon as he said it. As he sat in his car waiting for the officer to run the computer check on his vehicle and his driving record he mused on the value of telling the cop why he was hurrying to get back home and whether the cop would believe him.

Who the hell were these people that they could threaten him in his most vulnerable area, his family? They must have a source of information that went right into his bedroom if they could locate the country house and know when his wife and kids were actually going to be there. He strained his brain trying to figure out where the leak might be. Who could have learned about the venture in which he was involved? Was he being set up? By whom? Why? He could face anything himself, any danger, any adversary, but to have his family threatened, that was not part of the bargain. In spite of the danger he was determined to go ahead with the Project. He vowed however to protect Margie and the kids better. He would go to Italy like the professor wanted him to and he would take Margie and the kids as well where he could keep an eye on them. He would move them somewhere temporarily, somewhere that his talkative in-laws didn't know about although he had no reason to suspect them for the leak.

The policeman returned from his computer search in the cruiser and Chris Fanning braced for a costly ticket. The officer was smiling broadly. "I understand you were speeding because your wife and kids were attacked by two thugs. I can't condone your speeding but under the circumstances I would have done the same. Sorry for the delay. You can be on your way, Mr. Fanning. Just watch the speed limit, OK?" He gave a small salute and turned to walk away.

"I'll be damned. What good luck," Fanning murmured. "That's the first time anything like that has happened to me." Even as he exulted at having beaten the ticket he remained uneasy at what had happened. What if this was only a first fumbling attempt to get him or his family? He was concerned that whoever was behind the attack would try again with more sophisticated methods and smarter perpetrators. But the why of the thing kept eluding him. Why would anyone take these kinds of extraordinary means to put a stop to the Project? Was it related at all? Was the death of Jake related, and if so, how? Who could be so threatened as to resort to this kind of behavior? If it really was the church why couldn't they just destroy the Shroud or at least hide it to make the DNA contained therein unavailable? It wouldn't be the first time the Vatican acted in an unethical, if not downright criminal, fashion in order to safeguard its own interests, he thought. Take the behavior of Pope Pius XII during the Second World War. Didn't the pope act scandalously regarding the Jewish question, never once speaking out against the Nazis and their final solution?

Thinking these issues out in his mind, he again became self-absorbed and didn't notice his speed inching up again, up to, then past the posted speed limit.

The thoughts continued. Didn't the present pope recently confer a knighthood, the Order of Pius IX, on Kurt Waldheim, a purported Nazi sympathizer and conspirator? So even though he was a devoted lifelong Catholic and took his religion seriously Fanning didn't put it past the church hierarchy to do whatever they thought to be in their best interests, just like anybody else. History was there to evidence that what with the Spanish Inquisition, the burning of heretics, the enslavement of whole Indian civilizations in the name of Christianity in the new world. While these considerations prompted him that it might really be the church which was attacking him he had difficulty accepting the idea on an emotional basis. But if not the church, then who? Who could be responsible? Whose interest could be served by preventing this "process" to go to completion? The favorite villains in many scenarios he could think of was the government, the CIA, the military, or big business. He couldn't think for the life of him what any of these groups had to gain from harassing him and the professor.

Fanning was in the habit of using his brain to solve his problems, but try as he might he couldn't come up with a satisfactory answer. Nor could he figure out where the other side, as he was beginning to refer to it, could have obtained their information. After all he and the professor had been careful not to go blabbing around campus. But somehow they had tipped their hand. Or someone had tipped it for them.

His thoughts drifted back to Margie. He had teased her at times telling her she looked like Elvis Presley. When she denied any such resemblance he'd tell her he meant it as a compliment. He was aware now how empty his life was without her and how he missed her. He vowed to redouble his efforts to protect her and the kids.

19

Fanning hadn't expected the storm of protest from Margie's family when he proposed to take her and the children to Italy. They presented cogent arguments to show how they would be safer in the care of the in-laws compared to a strange foreign land where they were ignorant of the customs. His father-in law even made arrangements to hire a bodyguard for Margie and the children during the time Chris would be away. As far as the nature of his trip he could only make up a story that it was graduate work related to his study program and that it represented a major career opportunity for him. Margie, as always, was supportive and encouraged him to go for it though she knew full well what the "it" was.

Chris settled into his seat in coach on the 747, safety belt fastened, tray secured, seat rest in the upright position. The Alitalia jumbo jet taxied to take off speed and left the ground at New York's Kennedy International Airport, headed east over Long Island Sound and out over the North Atlantic.

"Remember, the portion of the Shroud you bring back must have blood on it." Chris mulled over the words the professor last said to him as he was about to leave Arizona. If he didn't bring back a small swatch of linen with real blood stains on it the whole trip would be wasted and the Project could not go forward. Hell, I don't even know where the church is, he thought, but it's a tourist magnet so it shouldn't be too hard to locate. The hard part was going to be getting into the church and stealing a small piece without getting caught. At this point the entire Project depended on him. No wonder the professor was so careful who he trusted. What he risked, if he were to be caught, he was not sure: fines, imprisonment, expulsion from the country or worse. He might be stripped of his undergraduate degree and prohibited from enrolling in any graduate schools. What a bummer that would be. Oh well, he could always join his father-in-law's company and go into real estate. Ugh, he frowned at such a possibility.

He had never read about anyone trying to break into the vault where the Shroud was stored. There had been an occasional deranged person who attacked a famous statue like Michelangelo's David but these were usually nut cases who needed psychiatric care more than punishment. From his reading on the subject he could not find a single case of attempted forcible access to the icon. Well, as long as they don't start shooting if I get caught, I'll survive. Might destroy my academic career, but what the hell, it's in a good cause.

"First time flying, huh?"

"What?"

"It's your first time flying, right? I can tell."

"Oh hell no, I've flown before."

"Well, I coulda sworn you were a first time flier, the way you were grinding your teeth and clenching your hands. Hi, my name's Charlie Martin. I'm on vacation. How about you?"

Oh boy, one of those friendly types, Chris thought. Well, I may as well make the best of it.

"Made our reservations at the last minute and I couldn't get seated near my girlfriend. She's back there in a window seat. Say, I couldn't get you to change seats with her could I? So's we could sit together, you know, for the flight. Hey, it's OK if you don't want to."

"No, no that's all right. As soon as the pilot shuts off the seat belt sign I'll move over there and she can come over here. I don't mind a window seat."

"Hey man, thanks, that's really good of you."

"Think nothing of it pal, I'm happy to oblige."

Fanning found himself wishing he too were on vacation and that Margie and the kids were close by. Well, their time would come, business first. He realized with a small jolt that he'd never done anything illegal or even unethical before. After changing seats with Charlie Martin's girlfriend he settled in and tried to doze for the rest of the trip. He did not take the head sets, did not watch the movie, nor listen to the piped music channels serving canned classical, popular and rock music along with the usual mix of stand-up comedians. He drifted into a troubled sleep and was awakened an hour and a half before landing when the cabin attendants started serving a continental breakfast of juice, coffee, rolls, and yogurt. They also gently aroused the passengers and alerted them to the imminent arrival.

~~~

After landing at Milan he had to switch to a smaller two engine job that was cramped and much less luxurious than the 747 in which he'd crossed the ocean. The short flight from Milan to Turin was over almost as soon as he settled in. Now he had to deplane and retrieve his baggage, pass through customs, and find the rental car office. He wondered again what the hell he was getting himself into. He spoke no Italian, was alone in a foreign country on a mission which at best could only be described as criminal and at worst as a disaster.

He was in a half trance while waiting for passport clearance. He noticed the paramilitary carabinieri with their sharp uniforms and snub-nosed machine guns. He also noticed the menacing police dogs wandering around at will sniffing for drugs. Wonder if they could sniff out old linen he thought.

Passing through customs was another ordeal. Why couldn't these Italians do something to speed up the process? He was sure the whole process, in reverse, when he returned to the States would be streamlined from baggage retrieval to passport check to customs. Did he have a surprise in store for him! This was his first trip outside the U.S. so he didn't have any experience with American airports when returning to the country.

He was elated when the whole ritual of checking into a country was over. He drove his rented Lancia onto the autostrada leading to the city of Turin. This was a bit of a chore, driving a stick shift in a strange country where all the road signs were in Italian. He found that in Europe it was nearly impossible to find a rental car with automatic transmission. This had to do with the higher price of gasoline in the European countries because of much higher rates of taxation by the government. After a few jerky starts he threw it into third gear, reached 80 kilometers per hour, eased into fourth and then fifth gear and cruised at speed to the Turin city exit. After a few wrong turns and several stops for directions he finally found his hotel, parked the car, checked in, went to his room and fell asleep.

Rising early the next day, Fanning shaved, showered, and dressed as much as he could to appear like a native. He failed to realize that his shoes and gait gave him away as a foreigner even before he opened his mouth to speak. He breakfasted on a hard roll with butter and a tiny cup of strong coffee that made him more alert than he had been in a while this early in the morning. He noticed how it appeared as if everyone smoked cigarettes. He almost felt conspicuous drinking his coffee without a cigarette. Breakfast was strangely satisfying even though he was immediately recognized as a foreigner by the locals. He could tell by their furtive looks and the way they looked away when he caught their eyes.

He walked to his rented car, fired up the engine, and followed the route he had prepared on his street map of the city, a map he had obtained from the Italian consulate in New York, courtesy of his mother. He took his time approaching the church of his interest, memorizing landmarks and possible escape routes. He took notice of the location of stop signs, one-way streets, bus routes, squares, piazzas, and anything else he could. After a while, he turned slowly and unobtrusively onto the street in which was located the Cathedral of Turin, in the Square of St. John the Divine, famed home of the Holy Shroud of Turin. The Shroud of Turin is one of the most unusual of religious relics to be found in any religion.

He was lucky enough to find a tiny parking space. Many streets remain as narrow as when they were built in the Middle Ages. In general, main thoroughfares in European cities are wide and spacious, however, once the driver wanders off the beaten path he may sometimes encounter passageways so narrow that he enters with a vehicle at his own risk. Many is the foreign motorist who has negotiated himself into a winding street only to find that the only way out is to back out. With the path to the rear crowded with mopeds, motorcycles, and tiny cars sometimes even that route may not be available.

He went into the church and looked around. There were no other visitors. It did not look like anything special. The eyes had to get used to the subdued light. The scent of burning candles floated on the air. The sounds he made with his feet seemed accentuated, loud, and somehow inappropriate. The walls between the naves contained descriptions of the Shroud in English, German, Italian, French, and Spanish. No surprises there. What they did not say, that was the important thing. Was the Shroud real? Did the areas already tested for age and authenticity represent the real Shroud or were these just peripheral disposables submitted by the church to confound the public and discourage more serious study? He was determined to find out.

On the way to the hotel, he tried to map out a plan for his coming invasion of the church. But thoughts of Margie and the kids kept invading his consciousness. He remembered small disagreements he'd had with her in the past, a past that now seemed a long time ago. One of the continuing silly differences he'd had with her concerned the color of her eyes. He always referred to them as green and she would insist they were hazel. No big thing, but he couldn't get her out of his mind. He had fears that he would never see her again. He hoped this insane scheme would be over in a hurry whatever the outcome so he could return home where he belonged. He thought of how good she was as a homemaker, her ability to mend and hem the kids' clothes, in spite of her upbringing in a wealthy family where she never had to do such things. She had somehow acquired the interest and skills to sew and cook and enjoyed them even though these talents were not pressed on her by either parent.

20

The Shroud of Turin, a linen cloth 14 feet 5 inches long by 3 feet 7 inches wide, is perhaps the most monumentally important relic in all of Catholicism. However, the Catholic Church has never acknowledged it as such. It is kept under lock and key in the church of St. John the Baptist, Turin, Italy. The storage vault is fireproof, waterproof, earthquake proof and is designed to be burglar proof.

The linen cloth contains two images of a bearded long haired man 5 feet 11 inches in height. The anterior surface contains the front view of a man extending from the bottom to the middle longitudinally and in the middle of the cloth the image changes to show the back of the head of the same man and extends down to the feet showing on this, the back surface, the back of the man. It is as if a body were placed on a long, thin strip of linen from one end and the other half were then folded over the front of the man all the way down to the feet. The front image reveals a body lying on its back with hands crossed at groin level. The left hand covers the right so that only the image of a nail hole in the left wrist is visible. The feet show evidence of a nail or spike hole in each. Those areas where there were open wounds in the body correspond to blood spatters on the Shroud. These are at the hands, the feet, the right anterior rib cage, and the head, where a crown of thorns was supposed to produce numerous puncture wounds around the scalp. The right orbit shows evidence of a black eye. The nose bears an abrasion. The right knee has an abrasion as if from a fall. The rear image shows evidence of a particularly vicious whipping or scourging produced by a Roman flagellum. This was an especially brutal type of whip used by the Romans on runaway or rebellious slaves, army deserters, foreigners, and on those who challenged Roman authority. It was not used on ordinary Roman citizens for the punishment of common crime because it was considered too cruel. It consisted of two or three leather thongs attached to a handle. The thongs had small dumbbell shaped metal balls imbedded in the tips. Sometimes they were made of small bits of sharp animal bone. They were meant to produce open, bleeding wounds, to tear the skin and shred the underlying muscle. They were used to provide maximum punishment in preparation for death by crucifixion. The image of the man's back contained these marks from the shoulders down to the legs. The angles were different on left compared to right, probably indicating that two Roman soldiers of different height delivered the blows. The shoulders and upper back, at the base of the neck, contained smudges and bruises where the scourge marks had been made indistinct as by carrying the heavy cross member of a wooden cross for a distance, as we know Christ was forced to do.

The origin of the Shroud is nevertheless fogged in mystery. It only made its appearance in France for the first time in the year 1389. Many mysteries surround the Shroud. No one knows how the image of the tortured man came to be there. There are many linen cloths which have been found in Egypt and other parts of the Middle East used as burial shrouds but not one has the image of a human body seared into it. The church allows the Shroud to be exhibited for a short time, perhaps three or four times in a hundred years for the purpose of study and only to a select few scholars and clergy, usually out of view of the public. Many photographs, X-rays, and ultraviolet films have been taken, but actual samples from the Shroud itself have been limited to a few fibers from the edges or the edges of holes in the fabric. More commonly the church allows samples to be lifted off the cloth using sticky tape.

The church closely guards the integrity of the Shroud even as it denies it official recognition as a bona fide relic. Its authenticity has been roundly debated for centuries ever since it first surfaced in France under the ownership of the de Charny family. This late emergence has been one argument used to deny its authenticity. The reasoning being, that if it was the true burial cloth of Jesus Christ then why did it surface only at this late date of 1389? Another argument used against its veracity as the true burial shroud of Christ has been the paucity of references to it in the Holy Bible.

There is, however, another icon which has been described as a burial shroud dating from the early first century A.D. and possessive of mystical powers. It remains to be shown whether the two are one and the same. The early one was captured by Muslims and held in Edessa for years. Edessa is now in Eastern Turkey. It has been speculated that the original came into the possession of the mysterious Knights Templar, who by virtue of their secrecy and power kept it hidden for centuries until it surfaced in Lirey, France. In any case, there has been ample discourse, debate, argument, and rancor concerning the object that on several occasions, notably, a scientific inquiry has been made by specialists in physics, chemistry, analytical chemistry, spectrophotography, computer experts, optics specialists, archaeologists, paint, pigment, and art history experts. The result is that one thing is clear: the Shroud could not have been done by an artist because the technique of rendering a painting in a negative mode would have been beyond the capabilities of an artist of medieval times.

The image on the Shroud is very faint and is a negative like a negative of a photograph. That is to say that those areas, where for example the eye sockets are, should be dark, are in fact light, and those areas that should be lighter in tone, like the tip of the nose, are instead dark. Only by photographing it and studying the negatives do the proper relationships become restored. That is, it is only on the photographic negatives that the darker eye sockets are actually darker and the lighter more prominent body areas are actually lighter. The ability to do that on a linen cloth by a painter painting in a negative mode was simply beyond the scope of any artist's know-how of that period. There was no concept of a negative mode since that is a result of modern photography. Brush marks have not been found or identified. There is great controversy as to whether the iron formed in the linen, in what appear to be blood stains, is really present because it comes from the heme in human hemoglobin or from iron oxide found in artists' pigments. It has been discovered that the retting process in which linen is made involves iron oxide, which attaches to the linen at the very earliest stages in the formation of the linen. There are other studies which purport to show incontrovertibly what appear to be blood stains on the Shroud actually containing chemicals such as porphyrins which are breakdown products of human blood. The heme, iron, and hemoglobin are contained within the red cells or erythrocytes. These cells are not important in the study of DNA since the red cells contain no nucleus and the nucleus is where the DNA resides. The blood cells important for DNA studies are the white blood cells, or leukocytes, since these are the ones with nuclei, wherein reside the genes and the DNA. Using modern techniques it is possible to reproduce as much DNA as is needed for study from a small sample. This then brings the issue down to the state of preservation of the artifact. Moisture is known to promote disintegration. High temperature and high oxygen content are also known to promote degeneration by oxygenation, the higher the temperature and oxygen content the higher the rate of disintegration.

If the mechanism of production of the Shroud is enveloped in mystery the mechanism of death by crucifixion is not. Probably death by crucifixion started out in Persia, which is present day Iran. It was spread by Alexander the Great to Egypt, and then Carthage and the Romans apparently learned of it from the latter. It might have started by simply tying the victim to a tree but gradually evolved into the practice as it was known in Rome. It was used only in the case of foreigners or prisoners of war who challenged Roman authority and was considered too cruel for Roman citizens. It was also used on army deserters.

The death by crucifixion was usually preceded by severe scourging as by a flagellum described above and was meant to produce debilitation, shock, dehydration, and a kind of pre-execution delirium. Then the victim was forced to carry the heavy transverse cross piece of the cross on his shoulders for a varying distance. The weight of the cross piece varied from 75-125 pounds and varied from 5 to 6 feet in length. At the site of the crucifixion the heavy vertical piece was already in place. The victim was offered a drink of vinegar mixed with a mild analgesic. Then he was forced down on his back, the cross bar under his shoulders. The nails were driven through the wrists, through the carpal bones and into the wood. It is likely that if the nails were driven through the hands as depicted popularly the weight of a heavy body would tear through the hand ligaments and the victim would fall off the cross. Depending on where exactly the nails were driven one or the other of the major nerves to the hand might be damaged. This could produce lancinating electric-like bursts of pain radiating up the arms. The nails were usually placed in the center of the wrist and so avoided lacerating the major radial or ulnar arteries. The victim was then hoisted up to the vertical member, the cross bar seated and secured, and the feet nailed to the lower vertical member. The ordeal could be drawn out up to two days or could be made to terminate in death in as little as three or four hours. Jesus Christ is known to have died in three hours. Sometimes a small rough wooden ledge was affixed to the upright as a sort of a seat. This was important since it took off some of the weight from the upper extremities and allowed the process to drag on for many hours.

The mechanism of death in crucifixion is, besides the shock due to blood loss, asphyxia secondary to exhaustion. The traction on the arms produced by the weight of the body pulling down forces the thorax to expand. This means that inhalation is easy passively but exhalation requires that the traction be relieved. Instead of exhalation being passive which it normally is, under these circumstances, exhalation requires a conscious effort on the part of the victim. But the only way for him to do this is to lift himself up by standing on his feet which are nailed to the upright. In turn this act produces unbearable pain so that it can only be sustained for the shortest time. As weakness increases lack of oxygen also increases. In those cases in which the executioners wanted to shorten the whole dying process they would break the lower legs of the victim by sharp blows to the areas between knees and ankles. This effectively made it impossible for the victim to raise himself for exhalation thus speeding his death by asphyxia. In this way the process could be over in as little as a few hours, or could be dragged out for one or two days. In the case of Jesus the biblical and archeological records show that He lived only three hours on the cross. The lower legs were not broken but due to the severity of the flogging He had been rendered so fragile that He could only hold out for three hours. The Shroud confirms this, showing no evidence of fractures of the lower extremities. Jesus is said to have spoken three times while on the cross. The expenditure of breath needed for vocalization could only have come with the greatest amount of effort in light of what we know now of the physiology of crucifixion. Another torment to which the victim was susceptible, although not known to have occurred in Jesus' case, was attracted by biting insects, flies, and mosquitoes attracted by the open flow of blood.

21

For the tenth time Fanning went into the church and looked around. Four p.m. and no one else was there except he and a civilian who offered to explain the details of the Shroud. Fanning suspected the man was really a guard who wore a weapon under his suit jacket, ready to let anyone have it who so much as looked at the Shroud with a jaundiced eye. On the walls of a little alcove to the left of the altar was a room which contained reproductions and facsimiles of the Shroud with televised descriptions that repeated over and over in English, German, Italian, French, and Spanish. No surprises there. He had read all that stuff in his researches prior to coming here. What they did not say, that was the important thing. Where was the real one kept? Was it in the metal box behind the altar as the church would have the public believe? Or was that just some more of the disinformation the church put out to obfuscate the public and keep the real Shroud hidden? He wasn't sure how to find out.

Over the next few days he returned to the church several times. His intention was to be as discreet as possible while trying to pin down the location of the relic for certain. After a time he gave that up. He started going to the university library as much to become familiar with the language as to hunt information of the Shroud's whereabouts. In Italy, the universities are the repositories of most of the reference books available to the citizens. However, one must have a pass to be admitted. He knew this and had taken the precaution of bringing proof of his status as a graduate student with interest in paleontology and archeology especially as it pertained to biblical studies. His open-faced good looks helped him get past most of the librarians who were 95% women. In fact they couldn't do enough for him when he made the attempt to speak their language. In this respect the Italians are unlike the French who, especially in Paris, will pretend not to understand when an American tries to speak their language and does not have 100% precise pronunciation, intonation, and accent. After a few weeks he found he had a natural flair for the Italian language and he began to feel much more comfortable with it. He learned such obscure facts as the word quarantine comes from the Italian quarantena, the 40 days of isolation forced upon those who were suspected of carrying a communicable disease before they were allowed to enter the USA at Ellis Island. He learned the origin of the word "video" which comes through the Italian from the original Latin and means, "I see". He was able to delve into old musty volumes that looked as if no one had ever read them. On the sly, he pulled out books and documents having to do with the history of the Shroud, its origin, its previous travels and its modern history including its present whereabouts and the condition under which it was being held.

After a few weeks he fell into a routine of rising late, around 9:30 or 10 a.m., going out for a newspaper, usually the International Herald Tribune, and then having a light lunch. Once in a while, he picked up an Italian paper or a French paper and tried plowing through them but he wasn't able to read them with any degree of understanding. By six weeks he found that he was comfortable in the Italian of everyday necessities. He was able to go into a restaurant and order a dinner with the accompanying wine. He was able to use public transportation such as buses, trains, and taxis if necessary without appearing to be a foreigner. He'd given up the rented car after the first week as unnecessary and expensive while at the same time realizing this might take longer than he'd thought. He found himself gravitating bit by bit to the nightlife of the city, such as it was. Turin is fundamentally a working class, industrial city and the bistros, saloons, restaurants and nightclubs respond to that by coming alive on Friday and Saturday nights. He did not have unlimited funds but what the professor provided made him comfortably self-sufficient for the time being. He missed Margie and the kids but consoled himself with the importance of the Project. He enjoyed walking the streets of the old city. (There are no new cities in Europe). The food, the wine, the music and the lifestyle were all starting to get to him. He thought, boy I sure could get used to this. And the women. He could appreciate the young women and their trendy clothes, but alas, that was as far as it could go.

He had checked out of his original hotel after a few days and checked into a room at a pensione. His weekly rent included a continental breakfast but he was on his own for lunch and for supper. He began to skip lunch or have just a small tart or sweet and he started to favor certain places for supper. He was surprised to find how different this Northern Italian cuisine was from the Italian food he was used to back home in Arizona and New York. He developed a real taste for the skinny, crusty loaves of fresh bread, baked daily and discarded or fed to the cats and pigeons if it was left over to the next day. No self-respecting restaurant owner would be caught dead serving day old bread. He marveled at the variety of white sauces in which pasta was served. He was only used to the red spicy tomato sauce from the USA predominantly favored by the Southern Italian immigrant population who had migrated to America. What with the wine, the music, the culture, the language, and the leisurely style of life he could easily fall into a rhythm and forget why he came here in the first place. The contrast in lifestyle was nowhere more marked than the work schedule the citizens kept. He was at first astounded to find every commercial enterprise closed at noon until three in the afternoon. It happened once when he was in a bank trying to exchange American Express traveler's checks for lire. When his turn came up, the teller shut the window at noon sharp and told him he'd have to return at 3:30 p.m. He was outraged but there was no arguing about it since the window was shut and there was no one to complain to. He'd had to cool his heels and wait until the designated time to return. He had only a few lire in his pocket and he had to go hungry seeking an open restaurant, trattoria, or coffee shop until they reopened. Even the gasoline stations were closed during the rest period so that if travelers ran out of gas during the siesta time they might as well settle down for an afternoon rest themselves.

During his travels about the city he took the opportunity to buy certain items he'd need in his forthcoming break-in. He made sure not to buy the related items all in one store. He bought a black ski mask on one side of town, a length of stout rope somewhere else, a Swiss Army knife elsewhere, and a six foot length of 3/4 inch pipe in yet another part of town. He secreted these items under his bed in his room so as to keep them away from any prying eyes.

He paid repeated visits to the church in question. He was gratified to see that there had been some construction started on the dome and there was now a hole or entranceway at the top of the dome used by the workmen to gain entrance to the top of the structure. He planned to use that opening to his advantage when the time came.

Fanning was struck by the number of bicycles, mopeds, motor bikes, motorcycles, and scooters driven by all sorts of people: young, old, girls, boys, middle-aged people, priests, nuns, and even policemen. And they were not used only for recreational purposes. They were used for shopping, commuting, socializing as on dates, errands, and deliveries of packages and messages. No doubt the high cost of gasoline was the incentive for the proliferation of these types of vehicles. The effect on the automobiles was quite noticeable as well for they were on average made smaller than American cars and not driven at nearly the same frequency as American cars. He noticed there was rarely a teenager behind the wheel of an automobile due to the excessive cost of the vehicle, the cost of gasoline which was heavily taxed by the government, and the high price of insurance. The charge for registration of a vehicle also climbs sharply as the weight of the vehicle increases. The result was an almost constant roar of two-wheeled vehicles at all hours of the night and day. Many a night he was tempted to open a window and throw something at those defilers of the night's quiet. And it is not as if the Italian drivers drove very responsibly either. He was amazed at some of the things he saw. Back when he still had his rented car he was at a corner awaiting the change of a red light. All the other drivers appeared to tire of waiting and en masse took off right through the red light as if it wasn't even there. Another time he was at a street corner again waiting for a red light to change when a taxicab behind him became impatient and drove right up onto the sidewalk, ran ahead of waiting cars through the red light and on into the night.

~~~

One day, as he was visiting the church yet one more time, he learned by listening to the guide that the work on the dome was proceeding ahead of schedule and that it would soon be finished. This would mean the opening in the top of the dome might be sealed up. He could not find any evidence to suggest that the real Shroud was not kept exactly where it was supposed to be, that is, in the metal vault back of the altar in plain view. He decided to cut short his visit to Turin, burglarize the church, steal a part of the Shroud and get the hell out of there before he was stopped. The year was moving on into late October and there were shorter days with more rain and overcast skies, the perfect conditions for his dirty deed.

He completed his purchases of a black cap and a black running suit for the important night. He bought some tools such as a straight razor, a pair of dark gloves, a pair of pliers, some white surgical tape and climbing shoes, making sure to scatter his purchases well. Then he waited for the blackest, most moon free night he could afford to wait for. As he bided his time he revisited the church time and time again so as to learn every possible detail that could help him be successful without being caught. He made sure he varied the hours of his visits and tried to disguise his appearance so as not to be recognized. He realized the burglar would have to cut off the electrical supply to the church some time after closing hours. Obviously he couldn't do any burglarizing while the church was open for visitors. Fanning was sure that the thin metal tubes leading away from the Shroud's enclosure contained electric wires attached to temperature controls and sensors, humidity sensors, and burglar alarms. He would have to cut the power off in the building for at least 20 minutes. He would need to make sure the power stayed off all that time. He hoped there was no negative feedback mechanism to a nearby police station, the kind that would sense a power cut off and raise an alarm. He considered it would be much easier to do if he had an accomplice but he couldn't afford the time to enlist a trusted assistant and he didn't want to leave behind anyone with knowledge of the plot. My God, he thought, what if I am apprehended committing a crime in a foreign land, and against a religious icon like the Shroud. He hoped he would in that case be caught by the police instead of a crazy mob. He knew this would not be a capital offense, and anyway Italy did not have the death penalty. Still he didn't relish the idea of languishing in a foreign cell for the next X number of years.

He scrutinized the area thoroughly, meandering through like any tourist. There was no chance to get in the front door after closing. Like most churches in Italy the doors were massive, at least ten feet high locked from the inside with a dead bolt type of lock, impossible to open from the outside without a battering ram. He went out the front doors and down the steps, walking around the perimeter of the building looking for another, maybe easier way in, a window or some less imposing doors. Or barring those he searched for the most likely place to scale the walls in order to reach the top and the opening in the dome. He gauged the height of the pinnacle and decided one slip from up there and he wouldn't have to worry about spending any time in jail. On the right side of the church as one faced the big front doors across a narrow street was some kind of official appearing building with the national semi-military police, the carabinieri, coming and going all the time. Probably it would be wise to avoid that side of the building.

He planned to make his assault around midnight so he could lose himself in the gloom of the nighttime black sky. Fanning was grateful for his rock climbing experience back in the States. He was young, strong, wiry and agile and this would be an interesting challenge but he was confident he could handle it. He began then to consider his escape plans. Train? Car? Plane? Which direction would offer the most direct, safe, sure route back to Arizona? Which way would guarantee that he would be able to return his precious cargo to the professor? Well, he thought, nothing could insure his escape would be without risk. The best he could do was the best he could do, then it was out of his hands.

~~~

The next night was moonless, starless and overcast to the point that visibility was minimal. Well, he thought, here goes. Forget about bringing Margie and the kids here for Christmas vacation. He had also discarded the idea of using an accomplice as too risky. He didn't want to depend on the tender mercies of some semi-stranger, should the going get tough and the accomplice be arrested. He was sure anyone in that position would spill his guts to the police in order to gain a better deal for himself if such a thing as plea bargaining existed in this country.

The night was dark as a sheet of carbon paper. The pleasant scent of something burning permeated the air. There was an occasional lightning flash that lit up the sky to show a black lining of cloud cover like the murky inside of a man's gut. Fanning was reminded of the final scene from the opera Rigoletto in which a raging storm produces a perfect milieu for a murder. He didn't know if what he was about to do was worse than a murder or not but he didn't like the way the wind was kicking up. Suppose he somehow damaged the Shroud in trying to cut off a small fragment? He was not an accomplished thief but he knew anything could go wrong. He neared the square on foot and turned the corner. There it was looming up in front of him like some animate evil giant daring him. He thought, this is the most dangerous, wildly illegal thing I've ever done, but now he believed in the Project more than ever. He was obsessed even as was the professor.

He hiked up his backpack and adjusted it for comfort. On the far corner of the building, so that the church itself was between him and the carabinieri headquarters, he began his climb. He wished the wind would quiet down. He felt it was strong enough to blow him off the building if he didn't hold on tightly. He noted with satisfaction that not many people were out at this time, one in the morning, he surmised partly due to the weather. The threat of rain was strong. He could smell the moisture in the air. He was dressed all in black down to his climbing shoes. He carried a small knapsack on his back containing all the tools he thought he might need. He had a length of rope coiled about his waist and at its end was a small steel anchor with four sharp barbs like a group of fish hooks. These were for anchoring the rope from which he would dangle. Using only the slimmest of finger and toe holds he was able to climb undetected up the vertically inclined face of the building. Every time a lightning flash lit the slate black sky he froze, flattening himself up against the building, unmoving, and hoped no one was looking. He inched up the wall toward the gently sloping surface of the cupola. The gradual incline away from the vertical made his climbing a little easier. At the apex he paused for a moment to catch his breath and connect his thoughts. Whoa, he thought, it looks a lot higher from up here than from the floor of the church. After securing the rope tightly on the metal pipe he carried he laid it across the opening after gouging out a bit of the mortar with a small metal tool he carried. He did this on both sides of the opening so as to have a kind of rut to lay the pipe in to prevent rolling. Then he dropped the rope down to the church floor. He had taken the precaution of tying knots in the rope at intervals of every three or four feet for extra secure handholds. When he was sure about the rope's stability he began to descend. In a slow and careful way he dropped, taking time to look around from his perch to be sure no one was in the church. He touched ground softly.

The church looked brightly lit compared to the murkiness outside. Carefully he crept around behind the altar where the Shroud stood. He needed to find the main fuse box and electric circuit breakers before he could break into the Shroud's container. He proceeded slowly but deliberately, finding a door that led to a basement staircase. He tried the doorknob. It was unlocked. Suddenly he heard a kind of shuffling coming from the dark recesses opposite his own location. He froze in terror, barely breathing, waiting and listening. The shuffling became louder and he began to discern the rough outline of a figure, dark, small and hunched over. As it continued to approach his location he recognized the shape of an elderly nun he'd seen before. She carried a long taper and proceeded to approach the altar. Her back was bent with the ravages of old age so that she walked with her gaze fixed on the ground. My God, Fanning thought, what if she happens to gaze up and see the rope dangling from the ceiling? He held his breath while she forced the candle into the holder and laboriously fished for a match in the folds of her habit. With the taper lit, a flicker of extra light fluttered around the church front bouncing off the altar and illuminating the church more than Fanning liked. Don't look up, he prayed, don't look up and see the rope. She moved to a front pew, sat down and began to meditate. Fanning dared not move nor take in a deep breath. He had to stand there not more than thirty feet away and wait he knew not how long without making a sound, hoping the old nun didn't shift her gaze upward and spy his rope dangling in plain sight. After what seemed like a century of waiting, the old woman stirred. She moved in her seat and became still again. He thought she'd fallen asleep or died in place. Again an interminable wait and then she finally left with that slow shuffle with which she had entered. Fanning waited several minutes after she left on the possibility she or someone else might return.

He returned to the door and opened it. The darkness down the stairs rivaled the blackness outside. He used his small penlight to guide himself down the stairs. As he crept down the stairs he had the distinct sensation that there were small scurrying things just out of reach of the beam of his light. He flashed his light on the walls searching for a fuse box. He didn't have too far to look. He pulled the doors to the fuse box open and removed all the fuses. He opened all the switches then shut the doors again. Using his penlight he slowly climbed the stairs. He did not want to run into any more nuns or other unexpected visitors. He played his small light on the altar and the Shroud's protective metal container. All of a sudden he felt inadequate to the task. He was no thief. Could he really pull it off? Well, one thing was sure, the more he delayed the more chance he would be caught.

He rummaged in the dark searching his backpack for his glass cutter. He knew now there was a lot more planning and organization he could have done to make the job go more quickly and more smoothly. He continued to rummage in his backpack which was on the floor in front of him. He felt a sharp intrusion into his index finger. The pain shot all the way up to his shoulder. He jerked his hand out of the bag and saw a welling up of blood coming from his index finger. "Oh goddamn," he muttered under his breath. Must have found the glass cutter. He searched in his pocket for the roll of adhesive tape and wrapped it around his finger to stem the flow of blood. Dammit, he thought, now I have to climb back up the rope with an injury. Suppose I get my blood mixed with the blood on the Shroud? I could totally screw up this Project. He wrapped more tape around the finger, making it tighter until it was bulbous, but at least it wasn't bleeding anymore. He used the glass cutter to open a window in one of the panes of glass enclosing the icon. The brass case proved much heavier than he had anticipated and he had to extend the opening in the glass to another surface to get a grip on it. He regretted not having an assistant. After a lot of pulling and maneuvering and more noise than he liked he was able to slide it off the shelf and wrestle it to the floor. He undid the peculiar maroon ribbon-like wrappings from the metal casing and lifted the cover off. A faint musty odor emanated from the depths of the metal box. The contents were buried in the blackness of the night. And then, there it was, the object of his past eight months of scheming, lying there rolled up at his fingertips. He was filled with a strange feeling of impending doom, like he didn't belong here, like he was intruding on something holy. He hesitated, overwhelmed by the enormity of what he was doing.

Using a gentle touch, expecting to be smitten by the wrath of heaven, he eased the linen out of its protective casing. With reverence he unfurled the Shroud on the floor, carefully and with awe. He stood back and observed the linen oblivious of the passing of time. He surveyed the faded image and tried to determine the best place to take his sample with minimal damage to the whole. He settled on a one inch square section where the blood color was particularly dense and with a razor cut it out of the linen. As fast as possible, he folded up the Shroud trying to make it look like it did before. He replaced the folded linen in the box, replaced the lid, and with difficulty replaced the entire thing in the glass case. He didn't really know why he was being so careful to replace everything since it would be obvious what had occurred here. Still, he was a believer and in order to show the utmost respect he wanted to be as minimally destructive as possible. With care, he packed away the square inch of the precious cloth in an envelope and placed the latter in a "secret" compartment in his wallet.

He surveyed the place again before leaving, making sure he did not leave anything that could identify him. He donned a pair of gloves for the climb back out. He started to become warm in his black sweater and pants. Then he turned to go to the rope for the climb up. He adjusted the backpack onto his shoulders, satisfied he wasn't leaving anything that could be connected to him. He grabbed the rope with both hands and immediately felt a searing pain in his lacerated finger. He tried to climb but found it a very different matter to climb up with his finger throbbing so, compared to dropping down with no pain. He climbed only a few feet then slid down again abandoning any plan to wriggle up the rope. He was on the verge of panic. He tore off a length of white adhesive tape, adjusted it on the front of his shirt to simulate a priest's collar, stuffed his gloves in his back pocket, and slung the backpack under his arm. He thought that even if the front door was locked to keep the public out he should be able to open it from the inside and make his exit. He undid the bolt, turned the big doorknob unlatching the lock, and pushed the door open. He eased himself out as naturally as he could manage, and his heart stopped momentarily at what he saw. Coming directly at him were a group of four priests. Making up his mind on how to handle this situation was easy since he had no time to think about it. He closed the big door, acting as if he were locking it from the outside, blocking the fumbling of his hands with his body. Damn, he thought, now I might be identifiable by these priests as a best-case scenario. At worst they might actually stop me and demand to know what I was doing. Finished with the door he turned and smiled at the group. He used his most polished buona sera. He was greeted by a chorus of buenas tardes. Whew, what luck. These guys were Spaniards and not likely to grab him and demand to know what he was doing in the church. Probably, in this murky light of early morning and given the rapidity of the encounter they wouldn't be able to identify him either.

So far he was in luck. His luck held for exactly 45 seconds. He was walking straight towards a group of six carabinieri. Hell, he thought, if the priests didn't give him a second look then why should these guys? His crime couldn't have been discovered so soon, or could it? Could the electricity have been restored so soon? As they approached he could detect no sign of interest from the carabinieri. Or were they going to wait until he was in their midst then jump on him? Or maybe they were going to let him pass, then follow him so he could lead them to a gang. Fanning steeled himself as he came abreast and forced himself to look straight ahead. He wished he had hidden the section of Shroud in a better location instead of in his wallet. The policemen continued to ignore him much to Fanning's relief. When they had passed, he turned and took a furtive glance at them out of the corner of his eye. They continued to show not the least interest in him.

He kept going at a brisk pace determined to send off the precious patch of linen first thing in the morning by air express priority transport. It was his nature to worry most when things seemed to be going well. And now, after these two close calls he was greatly relieved but also greatly concerned. After all, someone would discover the church had been burglarized before too long. Then suppose the government stopped all outgoing mail? He didn't really think that was a possibility. Suppose all exits to the city were closed off? Would the authorities take this church robbery so seriously as to pull out all the stops? They'd catch up to him for sure in that case, but Fanning doubted it. He was sure of one thing though. He had to get rid of the hot item he carried and get out of the country as soon as possible. He was so absorbed in his thoughts he almost let himself be run over by an electric streetcar on the narrow road leading away from the church. He scrutinized every face that came toward him. He continued to look back over his shoulder from time to time. So far as he could tell no one followed yet. He was glad the night remained dark and impenetrable so that no one was recognizable unless they were close by. He tried to lose himself in the blackness. After a mile or two he became confident enough to realize that his stomach was growling with hunger. He was out of luck. He could not find an open restaurant or trattoria anywhere. In spite of the precious cargo he carried he was secure in walking through Turin's downtown because although there is certainly a strong criminal presence in Italy, street muggings, in which the victim sustains injury, is relatively rare as compared to say, New York.

He returned to his apartment and went to bed hungry even though he had food in his fridge. He wondered if the United States had an extradition treaty with Italy, for if they did he might even be accused back in the States if the Project were a success and he might be made to return to Italy to stand trial. He wondered how the professor would react to that. Would he admit his full complicity, indeed his leading role or would he let Fanning take the rap for the whole thing? Oh well, too late for those kinds of regrets now. As always things appeared bleakest in the middle of the night.

~~~

When the morning came he was in much better spirits. He attended to his morning shower and other rituals, dressed, and left the house early to send his precious package on its way. He felt a lot more relaxed than the previous night. He noticed that the radio and TV in the store windows made no mention of his previous evening's escapade. It was too early for the newspapers to carry the break-in even if they were aware of it by now, which he was sure they were not. He went into a stationary store and bought a medium sized manila envelope. He sealed the swatch of Shroud in a previously purchased water proof pouch, placed that in turn in the manila envelope, sealed it, and went to the nearest Federal Express office. He carefully addressed it to the professor back home and entrusted it to the transport company. Having done that a strange craving came over him. He felt an almost irresistible urge to return to the scene of the crime. The silence of the media in regard to the burglary was starting to unnerve him although it was still early. Maybe his crime had already been discovered but for some unfathomable reason was being kept from the public. He wondered how a career criminal could subdue his conscience to the point where he could live off the results of his criminal activities when he, Fanning, was having such trouble engendered by what he had done. At least he could satisfy himself of the triviality of the burglary in view of the immense nobility of the Project and his hopes for its benefits to mankind.

He resisted the urge to return to the church and went instead to the closest American Express office where he bought an airline ticket back to the USA. He then wandered somewhat aimlessly, replaying in his mind the various moral implications of what he had done. He also thought he was going to miss this country of contradictions, this chiaroscuro of a nation that combined some of the best of western civilization with some of its worst. He stopped at a small cafe, bought a cappuccino and a sweet roll, sat down at one of the outdoor tables to sip and watch the people pass by. On the other hand, he looked forward with a keen enthusiasm to getting back to the States and the final completion of the Project. He was now tired of all the preliminaries and was anxious to get on with it. He finished his roll and coffee. Annoyed by the smell of cigarette smoke wafting his way, he rose and left to walk back to his apartment. His spirits rose as he reached his block but when he turned the corner a frisson of fear shot up his spine. His neck hairs stood straight out from the skin and his mouth went cotton-dry. He froze in place and watched the armed carabinieri van parked in the street, blue domed light flashing and blocking traffic. Could it be they were on to him? Was he being followed even now? Were the police ready to pounce on him at any moment? He kept calm avoiding any sudden move that would create suspicion. With as much stealth and caution as he could manage, he backed up, turned and headed away from his neighborhood. This development put a whole new light on the situation. He had planned to fly out from the local airport but he thought in his newfound paranoia that the airport would certainly be watched, and of course he was right. There was no other way to cross the Atlantic today. The era of the ocean crossing ships for passengers was over but he didn't have to use the local airport.

He wandered around a bit looking casual. Finding himself in the region of the main train station, he walked into the depot and made for the Europcar rental station where he had returned the original vehicle he had rented at the airport. Could the clerk be aware of his identity and further know that the police were after him? At least, he thought, the police were after him. He was relieved to see that the rental clerk was different than the original one. He quickly made arrangements to rent an auto and drove out of the station towards Via Vittorio Emanuele II. He wasn't sure about the best way to lose himself but he was sure that the more people, the bigger the city, the more noise and confusion, the better for him. He had left all his maps and other paraphernalia in his room but luckily he had his money in the form of traveler's checks. He had his credit cards and his passport with him. It wasn't so much by luck because he carried them at all times on his person.

He quickly discovered that he couldn't find the easiest route out of town on his own so he took a chance and asked an elderly man in the street the way to Rome. With his directions memorized he headed for the A21 autostrada entrance ramp, thinking if they didn't pick him up on the road, once he arrived in Rome he could lose himself. He drove the rented Lancia southeast to Alessandria, veered due south on A26, then along the coast past Rapallo, La Spezia, and by Pisa to Livorno. Here, he had to decide whether to stay on the autostrada, a limited access toll road where he could make good time, or take a smaller local route where his speed would be limited and he could not make it to Rome as fast. He decided to stay on the autostrada. He'd not seen any police, nor was the speed limit enforced very well, so he made up his mind to stay on the super highway all the way to Rome. He arrived there some 10 hours later but didn't really know where to start looking for a place to stay. He drove along the Tiber River for a while until he became exhausted. Then he stopped and took a rest by the side of the river. Ever aware of the sounds of language he waited until he heard English spoken by some young people who were passing. He asked about local lodging for students and was directed towards a small hotel on a side street off Corso Vittorio Emanuele II. The hotel was called the Hotel Arenula, on Via Arenula. He checked into the hotel, parked his car in the street, and went up to his room. He collapsed into a semi-coma and slept for 12 hours, the sleep of the overdosed although he took no drugs.

He was in a good mood, his disposition brightened by the sleep and by the possibility that he might actually get away with what he had done. He showered, combed his hair as best as he could with his hands, then went to the desk to inquire about the location of the nearest McDonald's. He was told there was one near the Tiber, on the Garibaldi Bridge to the Piazza Sonnino. After a 15 minute walk he found a typical McDonald's just like in the States. There he had an American style hamburger with French fries and a shake, the first he'd had in three months. He picked up a free map of Rome from the dispenser near the utensils and sat down to study it and wolf down the burger. He was pleasantly surprised to find he was centrally located in the city within walking distance of some of the most famous tourist attractions. Well, he thought, why not check out the sights while I decide whether it is safe to board my flight for the States. He thought he could blend in with all the other Americans in Rome and when the time was right return to Arizona.

He'd left his razor and other toiletries in Turin so he decided to let the facial hair grow as part of his effort at a disguise. As soon as he could he went out and bought different clothes and shoes. He didn't know what good this would do but it enhanced his feeling of security. He did not enjoy being on the run but he thought he could outfox the police with a little luck.

Still no mention of the break-in on TV, or radio, or the newspapers. Fanning was sure the burglary had been discovered and a search for the perpetrator was in progress. Why didn't the media report it? He didn't know how far the authorities would go in trying to locate the culprit. They must have their own reasons for keeping the investigation secret. He was sure of one thing. If they watched all the roads, the airports, the borders, and the seaports they would surely catch up with him. If they just didn't want to expend too many resources in the search he felt he could squeak through. In the meantime he would just act like a tourist or student and use the opportunity to take advantage of what the city had to offer. Since he was interested in archeology and paleontology he could find enough to do in the city until he thought it safe to leave.

After returning the rented car he placed a transatlantic telephone call to the professor asking for some more money. He also advised the professor that his adventure had been successful and that he should be in receipt of the package shortly. He described his status and told the older man he would leave Italy as soon as he thought it safe to do so.

He left his hotel, walked to Corso Vittorio Emanuele II, took a right turn and leisurely strolled onto Via del Plebiscito past the Piazza Venezia with its statue of King Victor Emanuele on to the Via dei Fori Imperiale, and thence to the Colosseum. The ancient arena of animal fights, gladiator contests, and the infamous lion. Christian tragedies were awe-inspiring to Fanning although the swarms of tourists did detract from his enjoyment. One of the unfortunate aspects of the area surrounding the Colosseum and the train station across the street was the presence of small gangs of gypsy children who terrorize the tourists. In predatory packs they victimize the unwary and naive tourists making off with their valuables. A favorite technique of theirs is for three or four urchins to gang up on a hapless tourist. One of the thieves will take a piece of cardboard or newspaper and push it up against the victim so he can't see below his waist. Then another child criminal will quickly remove the fanny pack cutting the straps if necessary. They are vicious, ruthless, and so fast that the prey simply has no chance to defend himself. And they are not above roughing up their victim if it meets their purpose or facilitates their escape. Fanning was witness to one of these episodes when a Japanese tourist who lagged behind his group was set upon by a group of ruffians who pushed him into a wall and took his money and camera. The man was dazed by the experience but the little criminals were gone by the time the man's fellow tourists were aware of what had happened. The police came but as is usual in these situations the culprits were on the other side of town by now. Not that the police were unaware of the identity of the scoundrels, but if they were ever lucky enough to arrest them they were back on the street in the wink of an eye because they were underage and the magistrate had no recourse but to let them go. There are only a few places of such danger in Italy and unfortunately the Colosseum area is one of them. When the police follow the little crooks to their lairs they find the older leaders of the group who are careful to keep their hands clean so that they themselves could not be arrested. Fanning was determined not to fall victim to these little gypsy bands of thugs and carried himself in an aggressive anti-victim swagger. But for good measure he hid his wallet, his credit cards, and his passport in his sock. He was young, vigorous, and muscular and did not give the appearance of an easy victim.

Next he walked southwest on the Via di San Gregorio and headed to the Roman Forum. He spent a couple hours there among the old temples, built on top of more ancient temples, themselves built atop older pagan temples. He admired the triumphant arches the Caesars built to themselves, the columns, the arcades, the tiled floors, the marble swimming pools hewn out of the northern mountain quarries by how many men he knew not, nor how long ago. The thought came to him that somewhere in this maze of antiquities he might be treading on a floor or gazing at a column that might have been erected at the very time of Jesus' birth. Might the old ruin of a bath or wall he looked upon at this moment have been erected at the very time that Jesus of Nazareth was alive and preaching? He walked past the temple of the vestal virgins and contemplated the fate of any of those poor souls who was not true to her oath to remain a virgin. They lived a privileged, aristocratic life. But from time to time one of them would succumb to the temptations of the flesh with a Roman general or senator and then their punishment was to be buried alive if they were unlucky enough to be discovered. Fanning thought how far we have come and how things have changed.

From a lofty vantage point on the Roman Forum he gazed on the old Circus Maximus where the chariot races were held and where he imagined the Caesars watched while the nobles made bets on their favorites. He laughed at his previous ignorance of old Rome and its landmarks. Until recently he couldn't tell the Colosseum from the Vatican.

~~~

He used the next few days to further acquaint himself with the Eternal City while waiting for news of the burglary, his burglary, to appear in the media. Still it did not happen. He visited the Spanish Steps, the Villa Borghese, the Pantheon with its ancient marble columns and perfectly constructed dome, and the famous original huge stone doors. The arched dome with its central opening at the pinnacle seemed to Fanning to allow the heavens themselves to enter the world of the visitor. He found the shaft of light resplendent with sunshine cutting through the gloom of the interior mystically inspiring. But the sight that made the biggest impression on him was the Basilica of San Clemente. Since he was an archeology student he took naturally to ancient ruins, but this one really grabbed him because it represented a church built on another more ancient church which was itself built upon a more ancient pagan temple. The excavated lower levels had been cleaned out and made suitable for tourist traffic. There was even an underground stream that ran under the place. The rush of water could be heard from several yards away and turned into a roar as the visitor approached and leaned over a railing to see the water rush under a grating. There were still workmen excavating the place and some of the walls were still yielding up artifacts such as bones and relics of previous civilizations. At one point a workman opened a door between two corridors to show a fully articulated human skeleton stuck in the wall. Fanning suspected this was a plant to surprise the tourists.

That night in his hotel room he collapsed in bed completely exhausted from the day's exertions. When he awoke he was drenched in sweat, shivering with a temperature of 104 degrees Fahrenheit. He wasn't directly aware of the fever, being semi-delirious, but he was unable to drag himself out of bed. Each attempt at arising produced a vicious whirling in his head, a constellation of lights and stars and a vertigo that forced him back to bed in a state of collapse. Each attempt required him to be still for at least ten minutes to recover back to the point where he could see and think with any clarity. In his muddled state of mind he considered the dream he'd had and wondered if it was the result of his feelings of guilt, mixed with vague memories of the church subterraneum from the previous day. His thoughts were confused by his fever and he lost cognizance of the time frame involved.

He imagined himself in a penal colony as punishment for his crime, a penal colony in the blazing tropics where there was no relief from the heat of the sun, or was it this hell? He trembled with the fever of the damned in his brain while his body shook with the fever of influenza in his bed. His eyes sank in his sockets from dehydration. His urine output diminished to almost nothing since he could take in no fluids and his high body temperature burned away the hot sweat of his pyrexia. He called out in a muddled way to Margie a few times then settled into a fitful troubled sleep. He slept the sleep of the guilty fearing he was descending straight to hell. And then he had the dream again, the dream that began:

The Stygian depths fell away from my feet, an unfathomable abyss before me. In one hand my alabaster soul and in the other my unflinching Toledo. I contemplated that which I was about to embark. The night, air thick and cold as an ice floe, filled me with foreboding and brought the sweat to my axilla. Few had attempted this autocidal descent into nothingness. Fewer still had returned. And those that did were blinded, maddened by I knew not what. Many implored me not to go. The artist wrote that I would never again taste the blood of my enemies. The poet painted my portrait but I was not in it. Even my bravest critic, my steely limbed companion Luthor, refused to go and could not, even if he would.

As I descended below the IRT, the BMT and the IND, I could hear the rumbling above me and the electric clang of steel doors, which sealed off any retreat, slammed shut. What madness had possessed me to enter this land of the abandoned? As I continued downward into the jejunum of the place the ebony ashen floors took on a life of their own. The ground hissed and smoke-steam vented from invisible fissures in the subterraneum. What manner of evil habitat was this, where flame burned black emitting neither light nor heat and the very ground beneath my feet was made of the leftovers of unfortunates who wandered here? A frisson of fear flirted on my flank as I saw the first inhuman soul in this godless crypt. In the distance, obscured by smoke and my own doubts, was a sight so horrible I cannot describe it. A crucifix arose from the misty hole before me, and impaled on this cross was a charred, seared body, almost a cinder, with a stink like burned meat and glaring, unseeing eyeballs that extended to the back of the head. I could see this was the source of the sound because the lips moved silently, repeating tautologically . . . "Tell them, tell them."

I turned to flee, but instead of my recent path there was nothing but a sheer vertical wall of black ice impenetrable except to the most cowardly. I therefore moved down, down a spiral sort of staircase, made of hate, envy, and villainy. The scorched path coiled down around crisscrossing on itself and seemed to end at its beginning at another dimension. At last I reached the nadir, I could descend no more. The way ahead was blocked by an enormous iron door that glowed white heat, illuminated the walls, and burned into my meninges. How could I go? How could I stay? What choice would save my hide? Then from deep within the walls a sound so evil came. The denizen of the deep approached, the beast with no name. It was then I found inspiration to flee this awful site.

I plunged head first right through that viscous burning door and to my surprise found I was intact on a grass green garden floor. I looked and there before my startled eyes a party was in progress complete with gals and guys. Dressed to kill in their Easter best they sparkled when they moved. A rose of coronary crimson in each dandy's lapel helped to put behind me my recent trip to hell. An orchestra played by request, guests danced in silent delight. Inside a flowered enclosure framed by contoured hedges, ribboned gowns flashed by in the bright sunlight. A scent of honeysuckle filled the air reminding me of a youthful time, I wished I were there. Then a chill went through my gut, a boney hand brushed my chin. As one dancer whirled past me I saw she wore my grandma's skin. When other dancers came close enough to see they were all pale images of myself, and grinning, beckoning me to join their grisly game. I almost wished I hadn't left the tunnel I'd been in. This new horror was even worse than the other. Were these really ghosts, so elegantly arrayed? Or were they merely visions of my hyper fevered brain? I declined their invitation, refused to join their fun, and with one sweep of my Toledo, cleared an exit, and made a run. Like walking under water my progress was impaired. I stole a glance behind, was chilled by what I saw. They had all peeled their costumes, and naked as newborn babes they had also dropped their pretense, pursuing with vile purpose, their wrinkled skin a-flopping, knobby fingers reaching for my throat. Could I outrun these phantoms or was my fate already sealed? Was I destined to roam the underground condemned to join this cursed group forever?

The night hung in dry clots like coagulated blood. You could scrape it off the sky like cuts of meat. There was something palpable about the dark. A presence behind each whisper erected the hair of my scalp preparing my soul for fight or flight, conflict or retreat. The salty scent of spilled viscera permeated my hippocampal gyrus and left a foreboding of evil deep in my gut. I could not shake the thought that I had been here before, fought this fight in another time, another dimension. The ground swelled and ebbed like a living thing. This must be what happens when the mourners leave and the body is put to its final test, the one that really counts. On one side of the chasm the bare bones of the initiates, on the other, the recently separated flesh, each calling to each other in vain. Did you think, paladin, that you could rescue mankind from itself? Did you imagine you could melt the stalactites of malevolence impaling the hearts and spleens of the damned? Does your arrogance impel you to challenge the very gods of the ages, the ones responsible for your life? For your death? Don't you know you are as a virus daring a cosmos? And yet . . . the sounds I heard were not of this world, nor were the visions of this time. It was as if I had stepped into a nightmare not of my making, someone else's nightmare. The screams of the tormented were as living things that pierced my brain, but the worst were the silent screams of the newly damned searching for comprehension, and finding none screamed without solace, without palliation, and without sound. This melancholy place was causing an ineffable change in my resolve, but I swore to the god Odin that I would not be dissuaded. Then as suddenly as an embolus I saw it again. That specter, that phantasmagoric vision replayed in front of me again. "Tell them . . . Tell them . . . Tell them . . ." The silent scream repeated as the victim was again impaled on the cross, and once again the flames devoured and consumed him until the stink came again and there was nothing left but ebony cinders in what once had the form of a man repeating, "Tell them . . . Tell them . . . Tell them . . ."

Again, Fanning feared he was descending straight to hell and that burned out skeleton on the cross was his own. Was this worth the pain? The possibility of sacrilege and eternal damnation? Would he ever see his family again? In being true to the professor and the Project was he tampering with matters that were best left alone by men? Was this the epitome of human arrogance, to think that the two of them with their so-called superior intelligence, education, and technical expertise could hope to resurrect a being so far above them in every way and expect to get away with it unscathed? Were they, he and the professor, really so special? Were they inviting disaster? Some of the old doubts came back to haunt him. Suddenly he knew that whatever the risk he had to get out of this country, back to Arizona, the professor, and his family.

He settled down again into a deep, black sleep, exhausted but resolved to return to the States as soon as he could. He slept this time with no dreams or guilt. He was as one in a comatose state. He did not hear the muffled sounds of boots furtively approaching his door. He did not hear the tentative jiggling of his doorknob or the whispering voices. He did not know of the danger approaching. He did not see the slow rotation of the doorknob first clockwise then counterclockwise as the unknown hands tried the door, first gently then with more determination to force open the door.

22

Professor Karahsha shifted his weight in his wheelchair using his hands. He vaguely remembered that he'd not slept for three days. Even so he was not sleepy. He was tired but not sleepy. His brain was fired up with the significance of his efforts and the earthshaking importance of his research. He had two regrets at this point. One of them was the unfortunate episode that had rendered him paralyzed and necessitated his confinement in a wheelchair, and the other was the unexplained absence of his protege' Chris Fanning. Fanning had FedExed him the appropriate sample of the Shroud but then no word was forthcoming and the professor worried about Fanning's safety. However, the ability to start on the real work of the Project overrode all his other concerns and he threw himself into the job with a new passion.

The paralysis made everything he did more difficult and time consuming. He had to have his automobile rigged up for hand controls. He'd cooperated at first with the rehab routine at the physical therapy center but soon chafed at the slowness of the program, and signed himself out against medical advice to get on with his work. He learned to transfer from the wheelchair to his car by painstaking practice. He worked out a routine in which he wheeled himself up to the driver's door, locked the wheelchair's brakes, reached over and opened the door of his car and then used a plywood board to slide into the driver's seat with much grunting and effort. Then he had to slide the board out from underneath him, lifting the weight of his body with his hands and place it alongside him for the opposite struggle out of the car. He next had to turn and with a gargantuan effort drag the wheelchair into the back seat of the car after collapsing it and fix it in place behind his seat back. He'd been able to keep his old auto since it was a two door vehicle and he needed such a car so he could fold the seatback forward to facilitate this latter maneuver. When arriving at his destination he had to exit the car by the opposite procedure. This could be exhausting at the end of a hard day. He refused to encumber himself with leg braces. He could not stand upright on his own without braces so when he went anywhere, say to one of the many meetings he was obliged to attend, he had to catheterize his urinary bladder and strap a urine collection bag to his leg. In order not to develop a bladder infection he had to take antibiotics which sometimes gave him diarrhea.

He developed the hypertrophic muscular development that all paraplegics do as a result of the exclusive use of his upper extremity muscles and shoulder girdle. Of course, he also developed the recurrent urinary tract infections whenever he stopped the antibiotics. In fact, urinary tract infections, kidney stones, and renal failure are the most common cause of death in paraplegics and he knew it. He also had to be aware of developing decubiti or pressure sores on his buttocks and even the boney protuberances around the ankles. The ankles were susceptible to swelling from blood pooling and the dependent position. He had to inspect his feet laboriously every night and his own buttocks every few days using mirrors to catch any early skin redness that might presage a developing skin ulcer. At all costs he had to be alert to prevent these skin ulcerations from developing since he could not feel the irritation in his skin from an early pressure sore. Once established, he knew these lesions could become very deep, even eating down to the bone, and then infection could set in and make the ulcers difficult to cure requiring repeated extensive surgical debridements, intensive wound care, antibiotics, and even skin grafts to cover exposed bone. He remembered when he was an intern working in the ER he'd had to examine an elderly patient from a nursing home. As he completed his examination of the elderly, debilitated man he had to remove the bandages from the man's ankles. Removing the last folds of dressings he exposed a large, deep decubitus ulcer in which were a nest of wiggling, squirming maggots. At first exposure to the air the writhing, little, white, cigar-shaped creatures began crawling deep into the wound burying themselves in an attempt to avoid being picked off. Ironically, this type of maggot infestation produces a clean almost sterile wound since the little beasts feed on the dead tissue only leaving very little necrotic material for the bacteria to get at. He wanted to avoid any possibility of developing these sores on his own body.

In addition he had to do breathing exercises because his lower abdominal muscles were weakened and interfered somewhat with deep breathing, so that he had to develop and hypertrophy the remaining muscles to compensate. He had to try and stay otherwise healthy since flu or colds, or more seriously pneumonia could cause complications which could lead to his death. He did not fear death but first he had work to do. He had to use a device called an incentive spirometer, which required him to take deep breaths and blow it out in a closed-circuit apparatus, building up to a certain pressure by using his respiratory muscles as forcefully as possible.

All these extra concerns made his life a lot more complicated and a lesser man might have been tempted to give it all up. However, in his case these factors made him even more determined. He became like a man possessed and determined to succeed at all cost. He was determined to create and learn, or die in the process. He had to maintain himself thin enough so as to keep the necessary agility he now required but not so thin that his buttocks and lower extremities were devoid of padding, for this could quickly lead to the skin ulcers he feared.

For a man who was so fiercely independent, who had been so athletic and so private, these adjustments in his life were difficult. He made them partly through the work in which he was immersed, and partly because there was no one for him to complain to. But all this made him even more single-minded than ever.

He frequently went back over his data, repeating each measurement of the important protocol over and over to make sure nothing was amiss. He was fanatic in protecting the fragile sample that Fanning had sent him. He worked in secret at a feverish pace to isolate the small samples of what he believed was blood from the swatch of linen. He only wished Fanning were by his side to participate in the momentous beginning of it all at last. He used the techniques he had painstakingly learned by himself to remove and identify the samples he believed contained the precious DNA he'd waited so long for. He weighed, measured, examined, isolated, and recorded all the parameters of the small sample he was privy to, realizing he was probably the only scientist to have at his disposition a piece of the Shroud from a representative location. He stayed up all night again contemplating that which he'd coveted for so long, simply staring with awe at the container which held it, and even though he had planned his protocol in detail many times over he was fearful of making a mistake in its execution. He wheeled himself back and forth in the wheelchair past the prize he'd awaited for years. He laughed, planned, gloated, and anticipated the rosy future now, the future so filled with promise and optimism.

He vowed out loud to spare no effort, no pain, no inconvenience, and no deprivation to see this thing out to the end and astound the world with his genius. He promised the very Deity Himself that he would not stop until he was successful. He prayed, he meditated, exultant in the knowledge that it was now doable and he would be the one to do it. One day he received two visits, one pleasant and encouraging, the other disturbing and unwelcome. The first visit was from Dr. Anthony Mason, Chair of the Department of Paleontology. Dr. Mason offered condolences on the professor's recent accident and wished him well. He offered his assistance in any way possible. Before he left he inquired about Chris Fanning, the promising graduate student that Karahsha had stolen from his paleontology department. Dr. Mason wanted to know if Professor Karahsha's suggestion that he send Fanning out to dig for fossils in that specific location had had the desired result. The professor assured Mason that it did.

The other visitor was Detective Frank O'Hara. The policeman was cordial, respectful, and deferential, but his questions about Karahsha's association with Fanning and especially his relationship with Jake Hamilton were more than resented by the professor. O'Hara didn't mind telling the professor that he thought Fanning's trip out of the country was inappropriate in the middle of a murder investigation and did Karahsha have anything to do with that? The professor replied to each of O'Hara's queries with dignity and aplomb, revealing nothing of importance and avoiding the appearance of not wanting to cooperate. O'Hara was struck by the professor's lack of interest in the investigation of the assault that had paralyzed him. He thought, either this bird really doesn't care who put him in the wheelchair or he already knows. The most disturbing aspect of the interview to Karahsha however was the detective's passing remark about university funds being missing and whether the professor knew anything about that. The professor assured him that he did not.

O'Hara left the professor's office with a feeling of unease as if he was not seeing the whole picture. He was determined to find out more.

23

A closed system. Temperature controlled lactate bath laced with glucose. The pH critically adjusted to optimal. Light level down to near pitch black inside. Nutrients pumped in with a critical balance between sugar, proteins, fats, and substrates for optimization of environment. Broad spectrum antibiotics added and osmotic pressure adjusted. Scarce and expensive growth hormones, amino acids, vitamins, and elemental lipids in specific ratios. Oxygen pumped in gently to maintain PO_2 at 120 mm Hg. Nitrogen and carbon dioxide in smaller concentrations. Gentle recirculation pumps strategically placed to distribute needed growth hormones and dilute the waste materials. Entire construct fixed on a gently rocking platform with a low frequency continuous hum piped in to simulate the sounds of nature.

All this was the culmination of one man's brilliant conception, the design of a genius in imagination, in intellectual scope, in pushing back the envelope of the possible and trespassing on the impossible. This represented years of failure married to a mind receptive and willing to learn from that failure over years of single-mindedness of purpose to proceed in isolation, no, in secret lest wrongheaded people with their pseudo-ethical concerns snatch the independence of thought from him. Those who would transform his work from independent scientific effort to connective gridlock by bureaucracy. Already some would place limits on recombinant DNA research making the most innovative and productive in society go begging hat in hand for permission to advance mankind. They would force him to ask humbly for the right to his work from these meanspirited microbrains in suits who would dare to hobble him. No, he would have none of it. The only item remaining was the introduction of the appropriate DNA with its 46 chromosomes and 100,000 genes, the seed corn of the entire Project.

The Human Genome Project, occupying some of the most brilliant minds in this country and abroad, had been his secret passion for the past decade and a half. He had kept abreast of all the latest techniques of breaking down the macromolecules so that individual elements could be identified. He had made awesome contributions to this process himself but had kept them out of publication because of his penchant for secrecy and because he believed it suited his ultimate purpose.

The Project as he originally envisioned it was designed for the purpose of learning about and then treating, if not eliminating, disease caused by genetically transmitted abnormalities. But he quickly realized the ramifications were much more far-reaching. Already DNA typing was being used in some courts of law as a device to help in identifying paternity in disputed cases, for example. Its use in DNA identification of semen in cases of rape was becoming widespread. The specificity of DNA typing was said to rival in accuracy the older fingerprinting method and would someday supplant it. Genetic studies were being used to counsel prospective new parents on the likelihood of producing offspring with heritable disorders. Sometimes pregnancy was even terminated on the basis of genetic evidence. A technique was recently developed which allowed the removal of a single cell of a preimplantation fetus without harm to the developing embryo. Then the DNA from this one cell was examined to tell if it carried any lethal genes or genes for a specific disorder. The parents could then act on the information so obtained. There was even the possibility of injecting new genes into the fetal cell to allow an organism to produce a missing enzyme or hormone or protein in order to avert the disease or ease the severity of it.

Now at last the whole process was about to begin. The professor transferred the living human egg to the dissecting microscope. He jiggled it somewhat to allow it to settle in the dimple in the slide, secured the slide to the observation platform, focused in under high power, and began to dissect the ovum with great care in order to relieve it of its nuclear material. The microdissection equipment was operated through a sort of reverse lever system so as to minimize minor tremors in the operator's hands and to prevent major jerks and inappropriate muscle movements to be transmitted to the specimen on the slide. The result was a very damped and deliberate dissection apparatus designed to protect the precious living tissue from gross errors on the part of the operator.

He was oblivious to the rest of the world. Slowly, he made a tiny incision in the nuclear wall. Then he inserted a micropipette and applied a controlled suction, taking care to keep to a minimum the tear in the nuclear membrane. He suctioned out the DNA carefully. He had practiced this on mouse ova to make himself an expert. He got to the point where the nucleus was only a nutrient container ready to receive its new contents. With infinite patience, he brought the reconstituted Shroud DNA into the field in another micropipette into which he had previously placed it. He eased the tiny pointed end to the membrane defect which was already starting to seal over. With the most control he could gather he penetrated the self-sealing defect and brought the tip of the micropipette to the center of the nucleus. When he was satisfied as to its location he reversed the air flow in the micropipette, methodically depositing the precious material in the center of the nucleus.

When the job was accomplished, he slowly withdrew the instrument from the nucleus and then from the cell itself. He gazed at it intently for a moment then retrieved the slide from the microscope and prepared to place it into the carefully designed incubator. He transferred it to a special sterile, fluid filled glass funnel he had designed, and introduced the cell through a uniquely side vented spigot to the larger incubator chamber to maintain sterility. He watched it float about like a tiny cloud magnified in the viscous supportive broth he had so carefully concocted. Finally the blob was no longer visible to the naked eye.

Karahsha stared at the glass container for a long time before he left the room. He still hadn't heard from Fanning but he needed an assistant to help him and he hoped Chris would return soon. Otherwise he'd have to start searching for another assistant soon.

He'd resumed all his previous duties at the university including his research activities, that is, those that the university was aware of and those it was not. As much as he was a workaholic, these added duties, along with the advent of the Shroud material, as well as the difficulty created by his paraplegia, were starting to overtax his capabilities. He wondered what was keeping the lad but he could not wait for him to return in order to start the whole process. This was what had driven him for the last fifteen years and he intended to proceed forthwith with Fanning or without. He was able to set the controls, through his computer, to automatic pilot so to speak so that he would not have to be in attendance all of the time. There were, until Fanning returned, no other participants in the Project, and he deemed it safe to leave it alone for hours at a time. He had his own fellows and students from whom to choose to help him, but he preferred to wait for Fanning's return.

The laboratory chamber he used was in an unfrequented out of the way location in an unobtrusive corner of the main pathology laboratory facilities. The entrance, which was a locked door to which only he had the key, was hidden behind some plywood panels that he left leaning on the wall in a random way. In front of the panels he kept a bank of cabinets filled with his old laboratory specimens and strict orders for no one but himself to be allowed entry. The wheelchair hampered him to no end and made access to his private laboratory much more difficult than before.

At this point, he had no reason to believe that the Project would not go forward, but he had waited so long for this moment that he had trouble actually believing he was on his way. He was so excited he didn't know what to do. So he decided to examine the little slide creatures he had neglected for some time. He placed various specimens of what he referred to as his slide creatures in his microscope and began to apply different stimuli just to observe their reaction. He used heat on one end of the slide and watched the microscopic creatures swim to the other side of the slide. He applied various other stimuli and recorded the reaction produced. He slowly became mesmerized by the microscope and fell asleep right at the laboratory table.

24

Fanning heard the clank of metal and a noise like chains falling to the floor just outside his door. In fact the noise awakened him. Then he heard what sounded like muffled curses in a foreign language. He sat up in bed. He was now awake, sweaty, feeling vulnerable and somewhat scared. He did not see the door move slightly under the force of several bulky bodies pushing in on it. He did hear the sound of it and it frightened him to distraction. Who could these guys be? What did they want from him? Was it just a burglary or worse? He looked around in a panic assessing the window at the side of his bed. Too narrow for him to fit through. In any case the window was locked and he was up on the sixth floor. There was no ledge so even if he could get out the window there was nowhere to go. He picked up the bedside phone and dialed the front desk. The desk clerk took what seemed an eternity to answer. In the meantime, the pushing became more insistent at his door. He didn't know if they were the police or just some ruffians. The clerk answered, "Pronto?" he said sleepily.

"Look," Fanning said in desperation. "There are people at my door trying to break in. Someone is trying to get into my room."

"Mi dispiace, non parlo Inglese." The clerk indicated he could not communicate in English.

Fanning tried to remember enough Italian to ask the desk clerk for help, but in the panic of the moment he was unable to. He threw the phone across the room in frustration and in a frenzy of fear looked for somewhere to hide. At that moment the door gave way and four young men dressed as carabinieri bounded in. For a fraction of a second the four young men and the young man on the bed eyed each other like a snake gazing at a rabbit. Fanning was horrified more by the unknown than anything else. However, in that moment he couldn't help but notice how ill-fitting and wrinkled their uniforms appeared in contrast to the sharp, crisp ones he had seen on the men on the street. In an instant they were on him. He struggled mightily but it was no use. They simply overpowered him. He felt a sharp blow to the back of his head and sensed his wrists being snapped into handcuffs behind him. As he lost consciousness, he realized what he must have heard hit the ground before they broke in was handcuffs.

~~~

He recovered consciousness in the back seat of a small car which was speeding into the dark of the night on what must have been an autostrada or freeway judging by the high velocity. He found himself blindfolded and cramped face down. He felt what seemed like someone's shoe in the middle of his back. He did not let on that he was conscious and tried to take in the conversation as best as he could. He wondered why he was not being transported in one of the big blue vans he had seen the carabinieri use, and stranger still he wondered why he was not being transported to a nearby police station in Rome. Maybe they were taking him back to Turin to face charges. However, as he listened and made out snatches of the conversation he became more uneasy. He didn't like the things he was hearing or the way they were said. He became more suspicious that these goons were not really carabinieri but some other as yet unidentified thugs. And in that case he thought, I'm actually being abducted. Now he started to have some genuine fears for his life. Who would want him as a prisoner? Who were these guys and what did they intend to do with him? His physical discomfort was so great that he had trouble concentrating on the danger he faced. The foot resting on his back dug into his skin, but mercifully the foot's owner shifted position and relieved the pressure from time to time. The men in the vehicle spoke more like uneducated street denizens than the elite police he knew the carabinieri to be. Their speech was heavily accented with a dialect he didn't at all recognize. So he didn't understand most of what was said.

After what seemed an eternity he felt the car rise up a steep hill at a slow pace. The sound of the tires on the road suggested a gravel surface. They travelled at least an hour on this winding road then pulled onto a smaller, bumpier road like a remote country house driveway.

The vehicle came to an abrupt stop. The doors opened. He was grabbed by the hands and feet and roughly dumped on the ground. He felt gravel bite into his face and groaned involuntarily so that his captors knew he was awake. Three of them half dragged, half carried him into a small stone house which was cool and damp. Though the place was dark, he could see through the blindfold. Someone lit a candle and someone else threw him roughly into a chair. He began to have doubts as to whether he would get out of this alive. He was cuffed securely to the chair and his abductors began asking him questions in an Italian dialect he did not understand. He couldn't make out what they wanted. After a few punches to his face and stomach he was sure he would spill his guts on his own mother if that would get them to stop. They seemed to want him to tell them whom he worked for but he couldn't be sure. Then another man came in and spoke acceptable, even cultured English. He removed the blindfold and looked Fanning straight in the eye. Uh oh, Fanning thought, this means they don't care if I recognize them which means they are going to kill me. This new man was not so rough.

He started in a kind, grandfatherly voice. "My young friend, I apologize for the way you have been treated. Those cafoni, those brutes, they don't know any different. I do hope you will cooperate. If you do you can be sure that no further harm will come to you."

Fanning thought, this guy has some refinement, some education, maybe he could reason with him.

The older man continued, "Now I will ask you some questions and you will tell me the answers. When I am satisfied you have told me what I want to know, why then you are free to go."

"Just like that?" Chris wanted to know.

"Yes, just like that," was the reply.

"I'm afraid to ask, what do you want to know?"

"What I want to know, young American, is simply this, whom do you work for?"

"What? Whom do I work for? I work for Professor Karahsha at the University of Arizona."

"And what type of work do you do?"

Fanning looked around the room without appearing to look around the room in an effort to try and remember the details of the place. "I'm a graduate student in archeology and paleontology and I help Dr. Karahsha as his graduate assistant."

"Isn't that a bit out of your field, I mean this professor's specialty is pathology, no?"

"How do you know so much about the professor?"

"I'll ask the questions here if you don't mind, young American. I asked you, isn't your field and the professor's different? How does the fact that you are his graduate student help you in your chosen field?"

"Well, it's often done in the States. It is my way of broadening my horizons, so to speak."

"Don't trifle with me, Chris Fanning. I am not in the mood and I have no time for it."

Fanning stiffened at the sound of his name. He felt utterly alone in a foreign country and he was sure no one would even think about where to look for his body.

The older man continued, "Does the name Ali Agha Mehmet mean anything to you?"

"No," Fanning replied.

"How about the name, the Brotherhood of the Wolves, or the Grey Wolves?"

"No, no, I've never heard of those names before. I don't know what you are talking about."

"Let me remind you, Chris Fanning, you are in a country strange to you. There are only a few people who know you came to Rome and less who care. You could disappear forever and no one would know anything or be any the wiser. More to the point you could wind up being crucified, I mean actually nailed up on a cross to die if you don't cooperate. Have you ever seen what happens to an eyeball that has been stung by a wasp? I assure you we have no painkillers here. Do you think you pulled off your little burglary unobserved?"

Fanning was shocked by these last few sentences. "You mean you know about the Shroud, you saw me do it? But why did you let me get away with it? Why didn't you call the police?"

"I told you Mr. Fanning, I'll ask the questions here. Again I say, for whom do you work?"

"I told you, the University of Arizona, Professor Joseph Karahsha. I'm a graduate student in anthropology and paleontology."

"And why did you steal a piece of the holy relic, the Shroud of Turin?" Chris stared straight ahead. "Well, I'm waiting."

"We, ah wanted to do scientific tests on it."

"What kind of scientific tests?"

"Tests for blood pigments, iron residues, tests for porphyrins, hemoglobin, or any other residues. Tests that could verify if it is real or not." Chris hoped he was lying in a convincing manner.

"Then you are interested in proving whether it is authentic or not?"

"Yes."

"I happen to know you are not telling me the truth, Chris Fanning. I'll ask you again, have you ever heard of the Brotherhood of the Wolves, or the Grey Wolves?"

"No, no, no, I told you, I don't know who they are. I don't know what you are talking about."

"All right then, we'll go in a different direction. Are you aware of a plot to kill the pope?"

"What? The pope in Rome?"

"Are you aware that the pope had an assassination attempt made on his life?"

"Uh yeah, I guess so, but wasn't that a long time ago? I was only a kid then, 10 or 11."

"And yet you purport to be a serious Catholic? While you have been here in Italy you have not missed church on Sunday even once?"

"Yes that's true, but my wife's the devoted Catholic and I do it for her and the children." Again he hoped his lie was not transparent. He felt if these guys knew as much as they appeared to know about him they must also know about Margie and the children. Thank God they never made it to Italy.

During the questioning Fanning tried to study the layout of the house. If the opportunity came up for an escape attempt he wanted to be ready. He also wanted to be able to identify the place if it became necessary. There was a screened in porch in the front of the house. A long circular gravel driveway led up a hill from the road and looped around the house. The house itself was an old wooden frame building and Fanning found himself wondering if he was going to be just another body buried in an acid pit in the backyard someplace like Jimmy Hoffa. The room he was in was apparently the main room of the house. The room was roughly square with a small bedroom off each of the corners. A small corridor, directly in line with the front door but at the opposite end, contained a refrigerator and led to a rustic kitchen. He could smell a kerosene stove. Opposite the refrigerator was a rickety staircase that led to a second floor. He'd not seen it but he could hear people trooping up and down the stairs from time to time. He couldn't help but think how snug a little country house this would make with a little remodeling. He also couldn't help but reflect on the demeanor of his inquisitor. He was obviously educated, even learned. He had a very slight accent but Fanning couldn't place it. It was not Italian. He had the studied refinement of a professional man, not a gangster. He could even be a priest for all that Fanning knew. It was all so confusing and none of it made any sense.

"What other uses did you intend to put the portion of the Shroud that you took? Why not just take it all, the whole thing? How long have you been involved in this plot?"

"Plot? What plot? There is no plot."

Fanning sensed that in spite of the ominous drift of the conversation he really had nothing to fear from this questioner who acted so gentle and appeared as pained to ask the questions as he was in responding. He was not so sure of the others, those false policemen who had brought him here. He had the feeling that his interrogator was being careful not to reveal to Fanning any information he, Fanning, did not already know as if to hide his true identity.

Fanning continued, "I told you, we wanted to do scientific studies on the Shroud to verify its authenticity. There is no plot. And we didn't need more than a small, tiny, really tiny piece because the molecular studies we want to do just don't require a lot of sample."

"Molecular studies? What molecular studies?"

"I told you, heme, porphyrins, ferrous residues, that sort of thing."

"Could you also be interested in genetic studies, DNA identification, cloning?"

This took Fanning by surprise. "Uh, no, no. I don't know anything about that stuff. I'm not a biologist."

"Yet you only need a tiny piece of the Shroud, a scrap with dried blood on it? A scrap with old dried blood from which you can extract the DNA, study the DNA, replicate the DNA, reproduce the DNA and finally clone a new Jesus Christ? Do you think we are so ignorant as to not know what you are up to? Your attempt to kill the pope twelve years ago didn't work so now you are attempting to discredit the Vatican in another way, isn't that so?"

"No, no, that is just not true," Fanning half-lied. "I'm no molecular biologist. I don't know enough about genetics to even understand what you are describing. And anyway it sounds so outrageously nutso and far-fetched it couldn't work. Where did you come up with such a far out idea?"

"Nevertheless, that is what you and the professor are up to isn't it?"

"Well, just how do you know that Mr. ah, interrogator. Say, do you have a name?"

"Of course I have a name but believe me it's not in your best interest to know it. Another thing you don't need to know, Chris Fanning, is how I have arrived at this information."

Although the interrogator still had the upper hand, his tone appeared more and more tentative and defensive to Fanning. Even though he was handcuffed to the chair, his hands behind him, Chris felt less threatened as the questioning proceeded. Less threatened, that is, by this scholarly gentleman who seemed to have to force himself to appear menacing. He was still not sure about the ruffians who had brought him here in the first place. He thought there was nothing they were incapable of.

"I am warning you Mr. Fanning, in spite of your pious denials, you are meddling in affairs which you cannot understand. You are toying with questions that can destroy you and many others. There are some things better left undisturbed. Where do you and your professor get the chutzpah to even think of such a project? Who do you think you are? How do you justify the burglary of a house of God and the defamation of one of its holiest relics?"

"Oh come on now Mr. Nameless, you must know yourself that the church itself doesn't regard it as authentic."

"Yes, it is not formally recognized by the church as the official burial cloth of Christ but it is still looked upon by the church as a holy icon, one that should not be violated by every self-appointed scientist who wants to study it."

Fanning thought this was getting awfully close to the position the church took according to the professor. That is, for the church to say it was not the real thing as a way of disinforming the public, while it knew very well it was the real thing, but not admit it publicly. And the church could not verify its authenticity because to do so would inevitably put into motion the very type of project which had been initiated by the professor. Of course the church's official position was to deny the authenticity of the linen so as to deflect any possible experimentation along the lines that he and the professor were in fact now pursuing. Fanning suspected that the questioner's position and the church's official stance on the subject were too close to be accounted for by coincidence. But then this would mean that their nameless foes, those responsible for the death of his friend, Jake, and all the other dirty tricks including the threatening letter, the attack on the professor, and the scare that Margie had was the Catholic Church itself. My God, could this be true? The conclusion was inescapable if one followed the line of reasoning Fanning just went through. Now this guy thinks I'm involved in some way in the attempted assassination of the pope. Whoa baby, this is spinning out of control. Still, he could not admit he had taken the sample for DNA studies since the secrecy of the Project was essential to its success. He had to dope out how serious these guys were. Would they really kill him? What would they gain from that? Fanning was struck by the irony of the situation. He was on the one hand unable to admit to his real purpose in violating the Shroud and his inquisitor on the other hand was unable to admit his real reasons for trying to stop the Project, not that he felt compelled to do so.

"If you guys, whoever you are, were following me all the time then how come you let me break into the church and even worse how come you didn't stop me when I came out?"

"Wait a minute, Mr. Fanning. I am unfamiliar with this term 'how come'. Is that an Americanism? What exactly does it mean?"

Fanning almost laughed. "It just means why, or in what way or how."

"Oh," the older man's eyes sparked with understanding. "I see. Well, we depended on those ruffians and some of their comrades to follow you. But sometimes they are not the best or most reliable of undercover agents. They drink, they gamble, they chase women, they like to be with their children. They even like to visit their mothers. And we, ah, that is I, did not really have hard information, as you Americans say, that you were actually going to do it, let alone when."

Fanning couldn't help pushing his advantage.

"Sounds like awfully lax spying to me."

"Yes, well, we, I am not primarily in the business of spying."

Fanning sensed the situation becoming more benign. "Say look, why don't you let me out of these cuffs? I'm getting uncomfortable. I don't know where I am. It's dark out and you have half a dozen goons to catch me if I try to get away, which I won't."

"All right, I suppose it would be pretty impossible for you to escape from here."

Speaking in Italian, he told one of the five goons to remove the cuffs. The ruffians were reluctant to comply and only did so after some sharp words had passed between them. Relieved from having to wait with his hands behind him Fanning was filled with new hope that he would get out of the situation alive. He wanted to bring up the earlier allusion to torture and crucifixion just to satisfy his mind that the man was bluffing, but he thought better of it and kept quiet. With the obvious difficulty that the questioner was having in his new-found position, Fanning found that he almost felt sorry for him.

He thought it would be a good time to ask to be released but decided that would be premature. His interrogator did not appear to be through with him yet.

"Mr. Fanning, I have been very patient with you so far but now I mean to get some answers."

Uh oh, thought Fanning. Either he's going to get rough or we're going to be playing good cop, bad cop.

"What is the status of your knowledge in the field of DNA, polymerase chain reaction, cloning, and related disciplines?"

Fanning had difficulty in replying because of the sight he witnessed behind the questioner. The phony carabinieri were actually carrying a large wooden cross through the doorway. Fanning did not know whether they were trying to scare him, but it was working. Did they actually plan on crucifying him?

"Hey look here sir, this is not funny. What are those guys doing with that cross? It's one thing to threaten me but it's another to actually have a cross made for God's sake."

Adding to his panic now were the sounds of hammering on wood and several times he heard, "Dove sono i chiodi?" Fanning was not assured by those words either because he recognized the word "nails".

"You haven't answered my question, Chris Fanning."

"Look, I'm not going to answer any other questions if you don't tell me what all that hammering is about. What are you going to do with that cross?"

"Relax, Mr. Fanning, I certainly would not want something like that on my conscience. And besides I really don't see you as a Christ figure."

Fanning relaxed a little.

"But now, I cannot really speak for those ruffians can I?"

"Hey, will you stop that?" Fanning protested.

"All you have to do is answer my questions and you can go free."

"I told you and told you. I'm not a molecular biologist. I'm not a biologist at all. I don't know beans about genes, cloning, and that other stuff you mentioned like polymer chain reaction or recombinant DNA."

"But you know what your plans are Mr. Fanning, or at least you know what the madman professor's plans are. You may not know the technical means, the scientific details, but you know what he is up to."

"I swear I don't know." Fanning started to panic now.

The inquisitor said, "Mr. Fanning, you give me no choice but to turn you over to my, ah, colleagues."

"You mean the guys with the nails, the cross. Aw come on, have a heart. I'm not worthy of being crucified."

The nail pounding noise became more intense. Two of the hoodlums came in and indicated they were ready. The older man gave them an "OK" sign with a sigh of defeat.

Without warning, four of the hoods who had been lurking outside ran in and grabbed Fanning.

"Hey you guys, what the hell are you doing," Chris cried out in a sweaty panic. "My God, are you going through with it?"

The four men held him down while a fifth ripped his clothes off. They dragged him into the next room. Fanning was horrified by what he saw. A full sized wooden cross was leaning on the wall tilted at an angle because it was too tall for the ceiling. Four long evil looking spikes lay on the floor next to it. They held him for what seemed an interminable time while he stared aghast at the cross. This convinced him they were only trying to scare him. But then four of the ruffians carried the wooden construction outside. Fanning was momentarily relieved. But then half dragged, half carried, he was pulled outside to a deep hole in the ground. Now they dropped the longer limb of the vertical member into the hole as if testing it. There were also some heavy rocks to be used as anchors for the base of the cross.

Fanning was overcome by a horror so strong he could not find his voice. He still hoped against all the evidence that they were trying to scare him. He was not reassured when he saw the older man, his questioner, pull out of the driveway in his car. At that instant Fanning had a flashback to the dream he'd had the night before in Rome. He thought, my God that figure on the cross was me. But why? Struggling mightily and screaming at the top of his voice he produced no audible sound. He was forced supine onto the wooden deathbed. While overwhelming him, some of the men forced his hands to spread out, others made ready the nails. He still didn't really believe what was happening. When the first spike bit into his palm he knew they weren't kidding. He screamed without noise again as the nails were driven into his other hand and his feet. He was soaked with sweat in spite of the coolness of the evening. The searing pain in his extremities overwhelmed all other concerns, even the concern he had of dying. A new agony now!

The tormentors lifted the structure to the vertical position, placing unbelievable pressure on his hands and feet. He tried to struggle loose but each little move he made caused the pain to reach a higher plateau. Finally he hung from the erect cross which was anchored to the ground. The effort to breathe became intensely painful. Each respiration required him to forcefully expel the air from his lungs by pushing downward with his feet. But that movement was exceedingly painful since he had to push against the nails holding his feet to the wood. When he relaxed his body slumped and his chest filled up with air again passively necessitating another round of expiration.

The perpetrators of this beastly act were standing around not saying anything. They were somber and almost looked repentant.

"Why?" Fanning screamed at them, but his scream came silently from his lips. Exhausted with the effort, he slumped down and mumbled that even in Roman times the victim was given a potent mixture of alcohol and herbs to dull their senses. No one heard him. The crucifiers took their time as they made their way down the driveway. Occasionally, they turned and gazed at what they had done but there was no triumph in their faces, no smiles or grins, no joy. They piled into their cars and drove away leaving Fanning to himself.

A gentle warm rain began to fall. The rainwater intermingled with his blood and trickled down his body. He wondered how long it would take for him to die. He tried to rock the cross forward and backward, side to side, to dislodge the base. But the movement was so painful, and increased his need for oxygen, when he was already straining to breathe that he could not sustain the effort.

A feeling of resignation came over him. At least he had sent the scrap from the Shroud back to the professor before those gorillas could stop him. He regretted most that he would not see Margie and the children again. He thought of some of her little peculiarities of speech he'd always found so charming. For no reason at all he thought of the difficulty she had in pronouncing the word "pharmacist". He remembered how she always said how much did you give for that, instead of how much did you pay for that when referring to the price of some item or other. He closed tight his eyes and pictured her in her favorite leisure clothes of jeans and shirt. He tried to communicate with her by sheer force of his will, to tell her it would be OK. He'd see her again somewhere, somehow, some time in a better world. Then a strange peace overcame him and he heard the sounds of dogs baying in the distance as if mourning an impending death.

It was at this point that he lost consciousness.

25

In spite of his research and teaching duties, the professor continued to participate in the activities of the Department of Pathology carrying out autopsies, reading pathology slides, and supervising the blood bank, hematology and histology labs. One late night, he was reading pathology specimen slides like Pap smears, surgical specimens, biopsies and the like, he came across an interesting slide made from a needle biopsy of a lung. He was surprised to see the patient's name was Armstrong. Wasn't that the name of the man for whom he and Chris had cloned a new knee? As far as he knew up until now the old man had done well and he'd even received a call or two from him. Old man Armstrong wanted to know when the professor could clone another knee to replace the one remaining painful arthritic one. The professor was sorry to see that Mr. Armstrong had to have a biopsy and as he scanned the lung tissue on the slide he recognized another type of tissue which stained differently and represented a type of growth that had no business in the lung at all. The foreign tissue looked disorganized, uneven, without definite shape or boundaries. It had the appearance of bone, but an abnormal type of bone, a wildly growing, uncontrolled new growth that had no business in the lung and must have arrived there by blood borne metastasis. In other words this bone tissue in the lung represented aberrant and fast growing cells out of control, cancer.

He zoomed in on the slide with the high powered microscope and examined the cells at close view. They had the typical disorganized, wildly growing appearance of a particularly nasty and fatal bone cancer called osteogenic sarcoma. One thing, however, didn't fit. This tumor, although rare, is a tumor that strikes people mainly between ten and twenty years of age. He'd never seen osteogenic sarcoma in this elderly age group. A sinking feeling came over him. What if the new knee did it? What if certain bone cells in the man's new knee did not get the message to stop growing? What if he had gotten it wrong and did not program the end of growth correctly so that some of the bone cells just continued to grow? In theory it could be just one cell that went berserk and started on a rampage of uninhibited growth without end, growth without control, growth without limit. That after all is very near the definition of cancer. He'd have to go and see if Mr. Armstrong was hospitalized. He made a call to the hospital admissions office to inquire whether Mr. Armstrong was a patient. He was.

A feeling of impending disaster came over him. He called X-ray to ask the clerk to pull out Mr. Armstrong's recent X-ray films. Then he wheeled himself to the X-Ray Department to go over the films with whatever radiologist happened to be there. Sure enough there was a large cannonball-like lesion in the chest. Karahsha then asked to see the knee X-ray. Again the film revealed an enormously swollen, deformed knee with a tumor enlarging the joint to twice the normal size, bone destruction, and infiltration of tumor into healthy bone tissue. The radiologist commented on the unusual occurrence of this type of tumor in a man of such advanced years since unfortunately the disease is usually one of a much younger age group. The professor kept his previous experience with Mr. Armstrong quiet. He still wasn't totally sure. He was depressed by this disastrous turn of events and felt genuine sympathy for the victim, but he did not plan to allow this to deter him from his master plan. He wanted to see the old man before he died so he wheeled himself to an elevator and pulled himself off at the oncology ward.

At the nurse's station he asked for the chart and room number. He slowly rolled himself into the room. Mr. Armstrong was dozing, mouth open, tongue lolling out the side of his mouth moving in and out slightly with each breath. He noticed the IVs and the familiar urinary catheter. He couldn't help but think back to his internship many years ago when that particular posture of a sick patient, mouth drooping open, was called the "O" sign. Definitely not a good prognostic sign. With the tongue hanging out the side of the mouth, that was called the "Q" sign, an even more ominous portent. He wondered whether the younger generation of interns would even know what those signs were. He didn't know why, but he thought of an even more raunchy sign called the Throckmorton sign in which the shadow of the penis was supposed to point to the side of the pathology in a pelvic X-ray, say a broken hip or fractured femur. Surprisingly, that one seemed accurate more times than not. Oh well, he thought, that was a long time ago.

He gently rapped on the foot of the bed as if knocking on a door. He'd learned years ago that when awakening a sleeping patient this was the most gentle way to do it. He had shaken patients and talked them awake in the past but he found this tended to startle them sometimes, and he didn't want anyone with an unstable heart condition to awaken in a way that might precipitate a problem. He knocked again gently on the foot of the bed and the old man stirred, lifted his head from his pillow and searched the room with his eyes until they fell on the professor. After a few seconds, his recognition showed when his face lit up with pleasure.

"Ah, hello Professor, how are you? What's that? You in a wheelchair? What happened, did you fall and hurt yourself?"

"I had an accident," the professor said with no further explanation. "But let's talk about you. How do you feel? Are you in pain?"

"Yeah, prof, my knee hurts. It worked well for a few months, but then started to hurt me. My doctor took some X-rays that didn't show anything at first."

"Why didn't you come to see me Mr. Armstrong?"

"Oh, I didn't want to bother you. I know you are a busy man. Besides you did enough for me already."

The professor who was almost never at a loss for words did not know what to say. Was this some wild impossible coincidence or was the man's cancer a direct result of his genetic manipulations? A miscalculation on his part of the "P" proteins which command cells to slow down and stop growing, or a chance happening against all odds directly in conflict with the published statistics? In his heart he knew the answer.

"Your doctor knew about the new knee I put in you, Mr. Armstrong?"

"Call me Martin, professor. That's my first name. I'm not such a formal guy even though I'm an old man who's been around a long time. And now I know, I'm getting ready to check out. No, I didn't tell my doctor. If he's so smart why didn't he figure it out himself? What business was it of his anyway? I don't see why he has to know that. I don't see any connection between my new knee that took away my pain for three months and let me walk like a human being again. And anyway I know you did it for me in secret for no pay and I didn't want to get you in trouble."

Again the professor was at a loss for words. He asked to look at the knee. Uncovering the joint he exposed a swollen, erythematous, and ecchymotic mass twice the size of the other knee with engorged superficial veins and subcutaneous lesions threatening to rupture through the skin at any time. It was obvious that in order to prevent infection and generalized blood poisoning it would soon be necessary to amputate the extremity. This would in no way extend the patient's life because of the spread already to his lungs. Mr. Armstrong was a non-candidate for chemotherapy due to his advanced age and the multiple metastases in his lungs. The professor inquired about the pain again.

"Ah, it hurts me some to lie here, but it hurts me more to move it," he said with the stoicism of old age.

The professor felt defeated but he considered himself an honest man.

"Mr. Armstrong, I have to tell you there is a good possibility that something may have gone wrong with the new knee I put in you. The tissues may not have had enough of the correct proteins to tell the cells to stop growing. I may have made a mistake. I'm not sure."

Armstrong didn't reply for several minutes. "Look Doc. I'm an old man. Even if this hadn't happened how much longer would I have to live? A year, two, three? With my family gone, all of my friends dead, what do I have to look forward to anyway? I'm tired of living like this anyway. If you learned something and can help the next guy or the next 100 guys who come along with the same problem, well, just tell them you learned it from me. Just use my name. Don't forget my name. I know you did your best, Doc."

Once again the erudite professor was without words. He shook the old man's hand and wished him well. He could not help the moisture that came to his eyes. He wheeled himself out of the room and perused the chart. He came across notes made by the attending physician that indicated the patient's leg would have to be amputated as a purely palliative measure to prevent breakout of the tumor, fracture of the bone, infection, sepsis, and toxicity that would kill him sooner rather than later. There was no possibility of a cure as the professor understood from his years of experience. The lung "mets" meant that the tumor had already spread throughout the bloodstream and there was no telling where they would next find tumor. He thought he would do bone scan at this point, searching for other areas the tumor might have seeded. But he was not the attending physician and he would not interfere.

Back at his lab he went over the records seeking to detect any mistake in the program that might have caused this disaster. He made an exhaustive review of the protocol. A miscalculation of this nature in his main Project could cause an even more immense disaster. Search as he might he could not find a specific reason for what had happened. Then he went over all the various protocols for the Project checking every piece of software, every combination of parameters, every genetic program, every possible source of error, miscalculation, or faulty direction. He labored long into the night and could find none. He was, nevertheless, uneasy.

The next day he did it all over again with the same result. The following day he repeated the survey and still could not find a mistake. He wasn't surprised since he'd spent years in perfecting his plan which now was already in progress. He reconsidered his original concerns of whether to program for a fully formed adult or a newborn infant who would have to be raised, schooled, and guided into adulthood. He went with his original plan. To raise an infant from scratch, so to speak, would cause too many problems. How could he, an unmarried man, explain a child in his home for all the years it would take to raise him to adulthood? If he became sick and died what would happen to the baby? He had no wife to help him care for a child. He considered marriage just for this purpose but rejected it as too cynical. Besides, who would have him with his reputation as a crab? He worked all the time. He was hardly sociable. In fact, in these matters he was rather backward. He did not realize there was any number of women who would take him on as a husband just because of the prominent position he had attained in his field, his success, and his comfortable income although he did not live in a manner his income would allow. Many nights, even before he'd conceived of the Project, he'd work late into the night and then just curl up on a sofa in his office and go to sleep for a few hours. He almost always wore hospital scrubs because it was convenient, and he kept several changes of clean underwear around so he wouldn't have to go home. No. This was the best way. To have his creation emerge from his nutritious bath after nine months as a fully formed adult ready to take on the business of learning his place in the world of men teaching, preaching, and saving mankind from itself.

He thought of those arrogant physicists who thought it was given to them to find the ultimate secrets of the universe with their cyclotrons, their super-colliding superconductors, and their quantum, relativity physics. He almost gloated over how vastly superior his fundamental research was compared to their tinkering with the so-called building blocks of the universe. Their pathetic obsession with the big bang theory of creation was puny compared with what he was up to. If his experiment worked, and he didn't doubt for one minute that it would, he might have the answer to the creation for the asking. Of course, he was aware of the school of thought that held the human brain was not yet evolved enough to understand the creation, the big bang, the nature of space-time, and the ultimate fate of all contained therein. He chuckled to think that in a very short time those same physicists would beat a path to his door seeking the answers they were so keen on finding and which would reside with him alone. Surely this newborn Messiah would be favorably inclined to let him in on the eternal secrets of the universe, the secrets that puzzled the philosophers through the ages. He would be explaining to the physicists the lumpiness of the galaxies, the location of the dark matter, the unified field theory that would bring together the four forces these same physicists were always talking about. When he got to thinking in this way he could barely wait for the Project to come to fruition and he threw himself into his work with renewed vigor.

The absence of Chris Fanning still disturbed him. He was concerned that some harm might have come to Fanning, but he didn't know what to do or how to go about locating him. He considered consulting with the authorities but rejected that as too dangerous to his work. The fewer the number of people who knew why Fanning had gone to Italy the better. It was bad enough that the policeman, what was his name? Oh yes, it was Frank O'Hara. He had been nosing around looking to cause him trouble. He kept abreast of the foreign newspapers and could find no mention of the attack on the Shroud or of any word on what could have happened to Fanning. He also avoided talking to Fanning's wife, Margie, because he just didn't know what to tell her about Fanning's whereabouts and he didn't want to tell her any more than she already knew.

26

Day 1

The speck of life was not visible. It was not possible by merely looking at the apparatus to tell what might have happened here. No outward sign was given off by the extraordinary events set in motion by the professor. The large tank still glowed with an eerie bluish aura. But from the moment he had transferred the holy DNA to the enucleated ovum the professor knew he was in the presence of something special, something unusual, and something sacrosanct. Evidence of life was measurable by subtle increases in temperature and almost infinitesimal changes in nutrients. Oxygen tension changed by nanometers. Carbon dioxide and other products of respiration were detected by the tiny computer chips imbedded in the walls of the tank. These changes were continuously monitored, producing a voluminous record of data which would prove indisputable in the future. The data was stored in the memory discs of the attached computer. Needless to say the computer and all other paraphernalia were "appropriated" clandestinely by the professor over time.

Now in the magical reproductive environment devised by the professor the DNA strands organized themselves in response to the appropriate stimuli into templates which then caused the synthesis of messenger RNA, the so-called mRNA. This in turn mediated the next step in the growth of peptides into polypeptides, polymerization of the latter into proteins, and the subsequent incorporation of these proteins in the growing organism. At this stage the entire living form consisted of two cells only. Floating in the bath of 48 cubic feet in volume, unseen, unseeable and undetectable to the naked eye, the most powerful force in the history of man was taking shape, or so the professor thought and hoped with all his existence. As if to reassure himself he sometimes activated the computer functions that measured motion, electromotive force, micro voltage and the infinitesimal micro currents generated by the organism. Another measuring tool he had at his disposal was the magnetic field grid as used in magnetic resonance imaging. He just could not resist trying this parameter at such an early stage. After searching for a while and becoming almost despondent when he couldn't find anything he at last noticed the slowly rotating, transparent speck appear on the corner of the computer screen floating and tumbling in a faint greenish glow. With the proper amount of magnification and focus he could actually see the two cells and their nuclei. Using higher magnification he could begin to see the mitochondrion and other specialized organelles. He stood awed by the sight and confident of success. He could have used X-rays but after all these were human cells, albeit divine, and might have been injured by the radiation. The floating living mass was not even a blastula yet so it did not contain the hundreds of cells that would in turn be directed to divide itself into the various segments the body would ultimately contain.

Soon the Hedgehog genes would turn on the Hox genes to begin that very process which results in the segmented human body. The Hedgehog genes have recently been shown to act in the human embryo at the stage of 15 to 28 days of gestation. Their existence has been postulated by scientists for the last 20 or 30 years but they have only recently been found in chickens, mice and Drosophila, the fruit fly. The name Hedgehog genes were given to them by researchers because when these genes were manipulated in the fruit fly they gave the fly a bristly appearance reminiscent of a hedgehog's bristles. This effect in the fly is only seen under the microscope. These genes have recently been shown to trigger the elaboration of a protein, the function of which is to act as a growth stimulator at special sites in the young organism. The existence of this humoral growth stimulator has been suspected for fifty years but only recently has its existence been shown to be fact. It is a mechanism remarkably preserved and repeated throughout the animal kingdom from insect to anthropoid. Along the primitive body, whether it be dragon fly or raccoon, at certain strategic areas called zones of polarization exist cells which when given the proper stimulation are destined to become a right arm or a left arm, a tail, a knee, a nose, a hindbrain, a forebrain, a cortex, a cerebellum, an eye, an ear or a mouth. These polarization zones are now known to be stimulated by the Hedgehog genes which in turn are thought to stimulate the Hox genes to cause a specifically oriented development to begin a kind of cascading process.

The original work was done on fruit flies, or Drosophila. The use of Drosophila has facilitated genetic research for a long time. The little flies breed rapidly, producing many generations in a year. Their chromosome number is considerably smaller than that of vertebrates, making them much easier to study. They don't eat much, don't take a lot of space, don't smell, and are easily mutated using X-rays to scramble up their genes. The evidence also shows that the protein stimulated by the Hedgehog genes produces a concentration gradient related effect. That is, the instruction to the cells in the polarization zone is proportional to the concentration of the stimulating protein. For example, a higher concentration of the protein might stimulate cells in the leg bud region to develop into a fifth toe, while a lower concentration might stimulate the same cells to develop into a big toe. An intermediate concentration in the polarization zone might stimulate the development of the 2nd, 3rd, and 4th toes. Farther up toward the body, along the leg bud, the different concentration of protein, the growth stimulators, will induce the development of, say, a right knee. Seemingly trivial, there are distinctive anatomical and functional differences between a right knee and a left knee. This may be more easily understood when considering the hand since there is a fundamental difference in the orientation of the thumbs. The right hand is a mirror image of the left and it would be totally inappropriate and dysfunctional to have two right hands. The hands would be attached to the ends of the right and left forearms but if they were both right hands a basic functional deficiency would be present. The right palm and fingers would point to the middle of the front of the body but the hand on the left side would point away from the body, creating all kinds of difficulty in activities in which both hands are to be used. The fact that this does not occur is evidence that the system is so refined and works so well that although there are congenital anomalies aplenty this is not one of them. The analogy can be extended to any of the paired organs like the ears, the eyes, kidneys, teeth, gonads, and even to the two sides of a person's body since one side is a mirror image of the other, with some exceptions. The exceptions relate mainly to the viscera. The heart is a midline structure but it sort of points to the left. The liver and intestines are exceptions. The liver lying on the right side of the peritoneal cavity with its gall bladder is asymmetric. The appendix, except in very rare exceptions, lies on the right side of the peritoneal cavity. The point of this description is that the determinants of body symmetry are specifically set in motion by a knowable mechanism and that mechanism is now being elucidated. The long elusive controllers of the development of life itself are now falling under the grasp of scientists' understanding. The future of biological science is full of opportunity and promise as well as danger signs.

"Hox" is short for homeobox, or a nest of molecules in specific molecular sequence responsible, one at a time, for telling each cell whether it will be a component of the eye, brain, finger, skin, bone, muscle, and so forth. Human DNA contains precisely 39 of these Hox genes. Simpler animals have fewer Hox genes but recent discoveries by molecular biologists have uncovered a very interesting and significant set of facts. From toad to tapir, fruit fly to praying mantis, mouse to gorilla, lion to pelican, all these living things have the Hox genes in common. These genes sequentially and in a precisely timed fashion program the very earliest of organisms, developing forms into head tail, thorax, and abdomen, front and rear. The human body may not appear to be segmented like a common earthworm, but in taking a closer look, say by X-ray, it is quite apparent that the human body is indeed segmented. The segments start with the head, proceed to the 7th vertebrae of the neck, 12th thoracic vertebrae, 5th lumbar, and the sacral and coccygeal vertebrae, which are fused. These specific local differences were determined by the Hox genes which told the head segment it would be a head and programmed it to differentiate into eyes, ears, brain, mouth, and so on. The same is true of the segments which developed into those containing the arms, thorax, pelvis, legs, feet, etc. This differentiation by segmentation is true of all animal forms. When fruit flies are bombarded by X-rays the Hox gene mechanism is disrupted, causing head segments to develop legs where there should be antennae. Apparently nature has devised a good thing and has decided to stick with it throughout the animal kingdom. The tendency to preserve a mechanism and use it over again in many species is thus another indication of the similarity of all life.

27

Day 4

The multicellular blastocyst now measured 0.1 of a millimeter. In the slowly bubbling, agitated nutrient broth it was still impossible to see with the naked eye. The cell number approximated 60 and was already beginning to take on the characteristic spherical shape common to all early mammalian embryos. Using the sophisticated sensing computer chips imbedded in the walls of the tank it was possible, however, to see it on the modular display screen as it tumbled slowly about absorbing nutrients and respiring, metabolizing, growing, excreting, and slowly taking form. While he watched transfixed, Karahsha was occasionally able to catch a cell in the act of dividing, and the entire process could be observed from beginning to end just like in a high school biology textbook. If left to its own devices, the entire process was programmed to take the familiar 9 months of human gestation. But by the judicious addition of a growth hormone, and by sophisticated manipulation of the gene sequencing controlling the rate of growth and differentiation, Karahsha hoped to accelerate the process to take only a total of 6 weeks. To this end, the waste products of metabolism, respiration, and growth were removed almost immediately as they formed. This acted to promote faster propagation of the entire process, for it is a principle of physical chemistry that rapid removal of the products of a reaction forces the reaction to proceed more quickly. He had cleverly adapted this principle to the living, growing tissue of the organism.

The computer monitoring equipment was so precise and fine-tuned that it could produce a mountain of data just by punching the correct request buttons on the keyboard. The computer was able to provide information on the exact number of cells present in real time. Whether a particular cell was in the process of division or was preparing to divide was instantly available. The size of the aggregate, as well as the size of each individual cell, was also instantly available. The products of metabolism were measurable both in terms of type and quantity while still inside the cell. Thus any incipient problems could be immediately noted and corrected by the computer program or manually by the operator. These data were all continuously recorded and would, in the future, provide hard proof of the process. The existence and location of the recording discs were kept secret, because with them, and enough of the original DNA, one trained in the field and possessed of sufficient skill could reproduce the Project, and that is the last thing Karahsha wanted. He wanted to be the originator, the only one responsible for the coming miracle.

Repetitively, he studied the small image on the computer screen. He could hardly believe it was happening. The idea that had consumed him for the past 15 years, the single goal of his life, was beginning to take shape under his very eyes. He exulted in his apparent coming success. At last, the culmination of his lifelong ambition was about to take place and he would receive the acclaim which he knew in his heart he so richly deserved. Only one fly remained in the ointment. Where was Chris Fanning? What had happened to the lad? Karahsha wished he would turn up or at least send a message saying he was all right. Or even that he was not all right. That would be preferable to the awful suspense of not knowing. But in any case, he vowed to himself the Project would go on.

28

The Italian morning began with a faint greying of the eastern sky. A dog could be heard yowling mournfully in the distance. The weather was not cold but there was dampness in the air that penetrated the body. Angelo Abbato walked up the mountain path he was so familiar with. He loved taking these solitary walks as the night gave way to the daylight. He had started in the summer as a way of getting some exercise after retirement when he found that through habit he couldn't sleep past 5 in the morning. He found the exercise invigorating and appetite-suppressive and he continued the walks even after the summer was over reveling in the nearness with the outdoors and the solitude of the early morning hours.

This morning as he rounded a curve in the road he couldn't believe his eyes. Up ahead in the misty fog of the dawn he saw what appeared to be a human figure suspended in the air in the position of crucifixion. He approached warily, suspicious this might be a trick or a trap. The figure was silent and motionless and naked. As he came closer he noticed a slight respiratory effort in the body which looked more like a corpse than a living human being. An ominous thought struck him. Suppose the perpetrators of this crime were still around watching the results of their dirty work. Might he himself be putting his life in danger by trying to help this poor victim? What could he have done to bring this type of wrath upon himself? He watched in silence for a time. He heard no voices, no sound in the brush, and saw no suspicious movement that might lead him to believe someone might be watching. Overcome with guilt at the idea that if he did nothing he would be as culpable as the crucifiers, he determined to do what he could to save the poor wretch, freezing with exposure and dying of his predicament.

He came up close and was surprised to see a healthy young man near death. He tried to shake the base of the wooden cross loose from where it was buried but the base was too firmly planted in the ground. He noticed a small country house not far away and went there seeking tools. He found a shovel and used it to dig out the base of the upright. There was no way he could control the fall and the whole contraption fell uncontrollably down to the ground. Luckily the cross fell in such a way as to land Fanning on his back and the combination of falling and the change in position had a salutary effect on his consciousness, waking him up with a start. The next thing Angelo set about doing was to try and set Fanning free from the nails that fastened him to the wooden cross. This proved to be more difficult than he imagined because the nails were solidly placed in the wood through the wrists and feet and every attempt at removing them brought agonized screams from Fanning. What to do! Finally, he removed his coat, covered Fanning as best he could and went off to search for a power saw. He knew there was none at the little house in the woods since he had just been there looking for tools so he made for his own lodgings a mile or more away.

~~~

Fanning revived from the small warmth the man's coat afforded him and from the ease of breathing the change in position produced. He began to hope that he might actually be rescued from the fiends who had done this to him. He waited and waited. After a time, which seemed an eternity, he heard someone approaching from downhill. My God, he thought, suppose it is the hooligans who tried to kill him. Were they returning to see if the job was finished? He couldn't see who it was who approached until the very last moment. When he recognized the old man Angelo Abbato, he fairly wept with relief. He wondered what the fellow was up to when he saw the power saw he carried. Jesus, was he going to dismember him alive to finish the job? Fanning soon realized what Abbato was up to. He started using the power saw to cut the cross into more manageable, smaller sizes so as to handle it more easily. He was able to saw around the nails and free Fanning from the wood of the cross. Removing the nails from the wood produced a biting severe pain in Fanning's hands and feet but he was able to tolerate that.

When Abbato tried removing the nails from the impaled body parts, Fanning shrieked so pitifully that Abbato had to stop. He couldn't stand to inflict that kind of pain on anyone. Besides he was afraid of attracting any unwanted company such as the perpetrators of this foul deed. So he waited. When Abbato had gone back to his house to get the power saw he also did two other things. One was he made sure he brought with him a shotgun as well as the saw, and the other was to make a telephone call to the local rescue service. The latter arrived and gathered up Fanning after covering him up with blankets and starting an intravenous infusion.

Chris was taken to a hospital in Rome where his wounds were cleansed and he was brought back to his usual state of health except for the damage done to his hands and feet. His hands fared far worse than his feet since no major nerves were injured in the feet. The hands were another situation since he'd sustained major damage to the median nerves, the right worse than the left, and since he was right-handed he was severely handicapped.

He became the center of a media circus because of the way he had been injured. But somehow no one associated him with the Shroud burglary and he made plans to leave Italy as soon as possible to return to America. He was naturally concerned about how his nerve injuries would affect his activities: professional, academic and leisure. How could he write again? How could he pound at a computer keyboard, return to his beloved rock climbing, even lift the kids and roughhouse with them? How would this affect his relationship with Margie, with the professor? How would his in-laws feel about having a defective son in-law? Would they be supportive? Could he continue in the Project or would he be more of a hindrance then a help in his present condition? Well, he thought, if the professor could carry on with his handicap so could he.

His physical wounds healed fast. They were barely noticeable by the time he got back to Arizona. He was able to resume walking without issues since the nails had not broken any bones, but the injury to his hands was another matter. He suffered lancinating pains in the wrists, pains that ran into his fingers and up into his forearms that caused him to drop what he was holding and interfered with his ability to write.

Margie and the children welcomed him back unconditionally and with open arms. The professor was delighted to have him back at work but was concerned that he would not be able to function at full tilt on account of the residual nerve damage to his hands. Fanning, on his part, was anxious to return to the experiment and see what had been accomplished so far. He was amazed, astounded, and delighted when he was admitted to the professor's inner sanctum to witness the Project in process for the first time. He studied the tiny image on the computer screen and had difficulty believing that this was the culmination of their months of work and his near scrape with death. He didn't even remember the name of his rescuer in the Italian countryside, the old man who had cut him down from the cross. Now they must work even more feverishly and in more secrecy to accomplish their goal since he and the professor were now sure that their enemies knew all about their work, even possibly the location of their laboratory.

Margie, however, was devastated by what had happened to her husband. At first she had difficulty believing Fanning's account of the events had even transpired. She came to accept the story when faced with the wounds on Fanning's hands and feet. She did not, however, have a clue on how to inform the children. After discussing the matter with her husband they decided to keep the truth from them as long as possible. Jerry and Josie had been asking about their daddy for weeks and it was enough for them that he was back home with them. Fanning managed to hide his healed wounds from them.

Margie Fanning started to develop a capacity she'd never had before, one she thought she'd never be capable of or needed. She developed a deep hatred of the nameless, faceless people who had been responsible for this horrible, cowardly act of violence against her family. She found herself thinking about learning their identity and perpetrating the most unspeakable revenge against them. Why weren't the authorities in Italy more forthcoming in their reports to her? She'd only received a sketchy description of the circumstances of the tragedy from the local prefect of police in the country town where he was assaulted. Why couldn't the State Department or the FBI do something about finding the criminals? She was constrained by the fact that Fanning admitted the burglary but was not connected to it by any authorities. She didn't want to do anything that would bring trouble to Fanning. She found herself frustrated at every turn and became more embittered at the lack of interest on the part of those who should have cared. In her rage at her inability to find out more about the perpetrators she even contemplated traveling to Italy herself, on her own, to make waves over there. What were they going to do, crucify her too?

In the end the responsibility of caring for her children and the need to keep Fanning's identity far from the burglary made that option an impractical one. But she would still lay awake at night thinking of what she could do to identify the culprits. She was not above a desire for revenge and fantasized how fulfilling a vendetta would be if only she knew who was responsible. Then slowly she started to think of the who, how, and why of the situation. Over a period of days she began to have a realization of what the likely scenario had been and what her likely part in it was. After the return of Fanning she couldn't bring herself to face the daily chores of living for weeks. She remembered talking to her friends the nuns, and she remembered revealing more than she should have to those seemingly benign friends. Now, she thought, suppose the nuns had innocently transferred that information to the parish priest. Might he not have passed it on to the bishop and from him to the cardinal, thence to the pope himself? She felt responsible for Fanning's travails herself. Could she have been the one to put her husband's life in such danger?

She needed help from her mother to care for the children. She neglected her looks, ate next to nothing, and began to lose weight. She neglected her hair, her exercise routine, and stayed in bed all day at times. She was miserable, desperate, and guilt-ridden and she could not be consoled. She came to believe she must do something to strike back at the criminals. But what? And at whom? She sought solace among her church friends and the Sisters of the Order of the Nuns. She conveyed to them how she felt, how she ached for retribution, vindication, and vengeance. The nuns gave her sympathy and support. They tried to help her get on with her life and forget these wild ideas of revenge. They cajoled, pleaded and threatened her, telling her she would do irreparable harm to herself and the children if she persisted in this way. Their ministrations only cast her into a deeper depression than before. She could not bring herself to tell Chris her suspected involvement in the whole affair by way of the information she had let slip to the nuns those many months ago.

She began to fear the hours after midnight, for then, in the sleepless bowels of the night, she was tormented by demons visual and vague. Panic attacks gripped her as soon as she lay her head on her pillow, so she had to immediately rise, dress, and go into another room for relief. Sometimes this was not enough and she had to go outdoors for a walk to obtain any relief. She turned on her TV in the hours between midnight and 6 a.m. but found no help there. She took to dressing in the middle of the night to slip out of the house to walk in the dark around the sleeping neighborhood by herself. On such occasions she was careful not to wake Fanning, and he remained unaware of her nighttime excursions. He was always exhausted by his efforts on the Project and his attempts at renewing his graduate school activities, so he slept soundly. She took a few nasty spills tripping and falling in the black of the night, bruising her lip on one occasion so that she had to make up a lie as to what had happened. Chris and her mother believed her, Chris because he was too busy helping the professor and attending graduate school, and her mother, because it never entered her mind that Margie would lie to her. The only enjoyment she seemed to have was in the coming of morning and in dealing with her children, although the children exhausted her as they never did before. She thought she must be going mad, but when her parents and friends advised her to seek professional help she fiercely resisted, determined to fight it out by herself. If she could not do that she was determined to abandon herself to the madness that beckoned.

She slept more in the daytime than at night. Somehow it was less threatening that way. But during the day it was not a restful sleep or a refreshing sleep because she invariably dreamed of Chris, alone, 5,000 miles away, on that cross out in the open, that cross she was convinced she had helped to put him on. She continued in this state for weeks until Fanning and her parents could stand it no longer. She was forced against her will to seek counseling or face the possibility of losing her children. To her great surprise she found great relief in talking to the therapist. After a slow and painful process, she began to come out of her depression. She began to find some delight in her children again and she began to sleep a little better. She regained some of the weight she had lost and she began to find a reason to live again. That is not to say she was any less determined to find the perpetrators of the crime against her husband. She began again to talk with the soulmates of her youth, the nuns of the church in whom she found new solace. She was reminded of the long nights she and Chris would have in discussions with the nuns and these renewed discussions without Fanning were as therapy to her. Those previous carefree times seemed so remote to her now.

It took time, but she came to be able to face the most painful truth of her young life. Those who had motive for stopping the Project, those who had the most to lose should the Project succeed, were none other than the Vatican itself with the Holy Father at the top of the list. Her friends the nuns didn't come right out and say it but she deduced from their conversation that the entire hierarchy of the Catholic Church had been aware of the Project from the start. Not in the sense that they knew specifically of the professor's plans but they knew someone, somewhere would have the bright idea to do just what the professor had in mind and the word had come down in secret from the Vatican to all the vast reaches of the church, to the parish priest, to be on the lookout for just such a scheme so it could be thwarted.

She thus became aware of the most likely candidates who could have been responsible for the outrage perpetrated against her husband. After a hint from one of her nun friends she learned through research in the library of the murky past of a group of priest warriors called the Knights of the Temple or the Knights Templar for short. These dedicated zealots established their cult in the times of the Crusades to allow safe passage from Europe to the Holy City of Jerusalem when such travelers might be threatened by the Saracens, the Islamic hordes dedicated to the destruction of Christianity. The Knights Templar had taken an oath of celibacy, veracity, poverty, and 100 percent dedication to the protection of mother church against the forces arrayed against her. They established fortifications at various intervals between Europe and Jerusalem as places of solace for religious pilgrims and other travelers. In their role as a banking agency, they were gaining power, influence, and even considerable quantities of wealth.

They gained so much influence in France that the French king felt threatened by their ascendency and had them all arrested, tortured, and burned at the stake. However, a few who were not in France at the time escaped and kept the organization alive, although it was forced to go underground for survival. There have been hints and intimations that one or the other of the extant secret men's organizations have persisted to this day in different parts of Europe, the U.S., and other countries and are direct descendants of the Knights Templar. There is no viable proof of this, however.

When Margie Fanning learned of this group she began to research them in the library. It was largely through the sense of purpose these efforts gave her that she began the climb back toward sanity. As she learned more about the Knights she became resentful and thus determined to exact revenge. But how? What could she possibly do to have an effect on an organization she wasn't sure even existed? She felt used and abused by the Holy Mother Church to whom she had devoted a significant amount of her emotional energy not to mention cash support over the years. She felt helpless, foolish, and an increasing anger that this could happen just so some old men wouldn't have to lose their vast power and privilege. They had no right, she thought. If the Project worked, why those old goats ought to be tickled pink to welcome the Savior back to earth in their lifetimes. Even if it didn't work what right did they have to obstruct it in such a vicious way? They were only employees of the church. They had custody of its institutions while they held office. But they did not own the church. The institution did not exist solely for their benefit and profit.

Strangely, she did not harbor any ill will toward the nuns, her friends, nor against the parish priest who had likely passed the word of the Project on to the bishop. Her resentment started there, with the upper echelon of the hierarchy, the bishop, the cardinal, and the pope himself to whom she developed a burning animosity. She wanted to shake them by their ears and set their priorities straight for them. She wanted to bring them to their holy knees with their self-righteousness and their sinfulness exposed and to make them acknowledge how wrong they were. But she didn't know of any way to do that. She daydreamed about it. She night dreamed about it. She racked her brain to come up with some way to get even, some way to help the Project to succeed in spite of their interference. She did not know it at this time but the seeds of her revenge were already taking root.

On the more practical side of her life she began to assume more responsibility for her previously neglected duties such as the care of her children. She took more interest in her appearance and began to eat and exercise more regularly. As her determination grew her depression fell off her like so much dead skin. She even began to enjoy life again. She gained weight and started thinking long term about her future. Her clothes fit again. Her relationship with her parents improved in the sense that she became much more accessible and responsive to them than she was in the dark stages of what she now recognized to be a deep depression. She allowed her parents to pamper her and take her and the children out for restaurant meals and shopping trips. She had never been extravagant in her tastes, always taking satisfaction in the quiet knowledge that if she really wanted something expensive her parents were all too happy to give it to her. Now she allowed them to indulge her without going overboard. She asked her dad for a new minivan and all of them, except Chris, who was too busy, enjoyed the trips to the various dealers, test driving the vehicles, looking into the various payment plans and loans. Ever since she had graduated from high school these shopping trips for a new car at 4 or 5 year intervals were ways for her to stay close to her daddy. She always took his word for whatever safety features he wanted her to have especially since the children came. He generally wound up buying her a middle of the line vehicle she was always proud to drive. She never asked for Porsche, Mercedes, or BMW, and her daddy never bought her one.

After the ritual of repetitive trips to all the local dealers, Margie and her dad settled on a new Chevy van. She took delivery in a few days and the first thing she did was to take the kids out to the country home retracing the path where the two desperadoes had chased her and the children not too long ago. The trip was kept secret from her parents lest they go ballistic in concern for her safety. In fact the whole family was now living with her parents for security reasons. Daddy had a new state of the art security system installed and even hired a set of house guards for twenty-four protection. She drew the line at constant bodyguards to accompany her wherever she and the kids went.

The next day she left the kids in the care of her mom and told her mom a white lie. She aimed the van in the direction of the desert where Fanning had first found the skeleton and where he'd had his climbing mishap with the rattlesnake. It all seemed so remote in time now. She didn't know exactly why she wanted to drive out there where it had all begun but she wanted to go over the terrain, see where those bones of contention were found and maybe come closer to her injured husband in some way.

The buttes and varicolored cliffs seemed a living entity to her. The mottled sunlight alternated with shade and the shaded areas took on a nature of impenetrable darkness, forbidding and perilous on the rocky hillsides. The desert always gave her a vague feeling of unease but somehow she didn't mind it, even reveled in it. She had never been out here by herself. The 4x4 took the hills and curves with relish. Out here she had the same feeling of being watched as Fanning had.

She approached a circle of buzzards floating high above the desert floor. Their easy grace at that distance belied their ugliness up close with their red turkey necks and unseemly dowager's hump hidden by their flight posture. She hated the big, black birds but grudgingly admired their grace in flight. She especially liked the way they used their wing tip feathers like fingers to fine-tune their trajectory as they floated on the air currents.

She'd been scared by buzzards once when she was a child. She'd been walking alone on a country road near her parent's summer house in the country. As she came around a curve she was suddenly confronted by a half dozen of the crouching, squawking, humpbacked, long necked varmints perched in trees and fences greedily eying a young deer, not yet dead, lying by the side of the road. It had apparently been hit by a car. The animal worked its forelegs furiously but the hind legs were paralyzed. The beast's back was broken but Margie did not know that. The birds started to tear it open from the rear end. Whenever one took a bite or used its talons in an area where the animal still had feeling it would again furiously pump its forelegs in an effort to flee them. She had no intention of keeping them from their meal but she remembered wishing they would wait until the injured animal died. She felt menaced by the birds even though they did not make as if to attack her or threaten her in any way. She ran away back to the house as fast as she could. She dragged her daddy back to where the deer lay. It had had its back broken by a car and continued to make frantic running movements with its front legs while the rear legs lay there, incapable of motion. Her dad took her back to the house and a short while thereafter, she heard a muffled shotgun blast from the road. She never asked her daddy what he did and he never told her. But since that time she hated those big, black, ugly birds with their evil eyes and sharp beaks.

She parked the vehicle and walked off a short distance trying to see what it was the birds were circling but she was unable to see anything. She continued to feel as if she was being watched. Again she pondered what she might do to help the Project and thwart the evil men who had injured her husband and thus her and her family. She thought much more rationally now without the wild ideas of exacting a terrible revenge, but her thirst for retribution had not abated. She worried for Fanning's future with his crippled right hand. She had urged him to begin therapy to try and minimize the effects of the nerve injury but he was too busy to attend right now. Later, he said, after the Project was successfully completed. Then he'd have time for all the therapy in the world. Maybe, if the Project was successful, he might not need any therapy at all. Whenever the discussion took a turn in this direction Margie's common sense took over and she warned him about the fallacy of expecting anything in return for the ordeal he'd been through. On a rational level Fanning agreed with her, but on an emotional level he had it somewhere in the dark recesses of his mind that all would be made well by the successful completion of the Project.

His disability was inconvenient enough, but when the two of them discussed the professor's paralysis they both recognized it to be an order of magnitude more severe. The professor never discussed his paraplegia with anyone and discouraged any reference to it, even a casual one, by ignoring the statement, changing the subject, or leaving the room. Margie was even more circumspect on the possibility of Karahsha having his disability reversed by the being they were trying to recreate. She had the opinion that if it was meant to be that the professor become paralyzed as the price of his involvement in this process why then he would have to live with it. If he was meant to be whole and not suffer any permanent paralysis at all then it would never have happened in the first place. Fanning did not really disagree with her but deep down he still harbored the unspoken hope that all would be put right again.

These thoughts wandered through her consciousness while she ambled along enjoying the solitude and the beautiful countryside. She now thought she had been too hard on Fanning when he had returned late that first night from his rock climbing. She too felt the powerful attraction of these isolated hills, dunes, and buttes. She too felt she would introduce the children to this unspoiled paradise just as soon as she and Fanning had some spare time and after the Project was completed, one way or another. It would be good for the little ones to learn the vigors of climbing and the outdoor survivalist lifestyle.

As she drove home she thought about the professor and his total, no, his fanatical dedication to his work. She feared Chris would turn out to be such a workaholic and become neglectful of her and the children. She didn't know how to dissuade him from such a course but she was determined to try. Already she could see some of the signs in him which worried her. His single-minded determination to come home from Italy with the Shroud at any cost to himself was one good example. He had developed an almost awe-like reverence for Professor Karahsha and in her view never questioned his decisions or motives, even when it affected his family, namely the children and herself. She got the idea Fanning would follow him to hell and back if Karahsha asked it. It was at times like this that she needed and found the required solace in her deep-seated religious nature and in prayer. She resolved to stop at church before going home and communicate with her God. In these considerations the irony of the situation did not strike her, for Chris and his mentor, the professor, were engaged in the same type of activity. Only their methods differed.

29

Day 19

Now almost 1 mm in diameter and the color of a pale earthworm, the small living mass of cells was still transparent but visible in the bubbling, circulating brew. It could actually be seen with the naked eye if one's eye were lucky enough to fall on It. The component cells started to specialize now as to their location in space if not morphology. That would come later. Knowing no other way, the collection of cells formed Itself into the shape It would have taken had It been implanted in Its mother's uterus.

The implantation itself in a normally fertilized human ovum is responsible, to a large degree, for the orientation of the future embryo. The part that comes in contact with the maternal tissue will become ventral as in toward the belly-chest area. The opposite surface free from attachment will become the dorsal or back area. The directing mechanism here is the Hox gene system which is responsible for orientation front to back, head to tail, and the beginning of the segmentation system. Also, at this stage, the precursors of the great body cavities and major tissue divisions come to be established. A tissue sheet called ectoderm, the outer layer, was laid down now. This was to develop into the entire nervous system, brain, spinal system, and peripheral nerves. The mesoderm or middle germ layer also developed at this point and was the precursor to the musculoskeletal system. The third layer, called endoderm, the inner germ layer, would develop into the inner layer of the body cavities in the future adult form. Obviously this explanation is a simplified presentation for the non-technical general reader. The interested layman is invited to look into the current textbooks available on biology, embryology, and mammalian reproduction.

Already the organism was oriented as to head and tail ends, front and back, left and right. The first three segments were devoted to the formation of the head. In an embryo, as in a newborn, the head is the largest and most prominent part of the entire structure encompassing a full 1/3 of the bulk of the whole. The location and orientation of the heart was determined at this stage. The location of the primordial limb buds was also established at this time. Segmentation proceeded rearward to delineate the tail structure, for at this stage the human embryo has a tail, just as all mammals do, at the same stage of embryological development. Of course with further growth and development the tail was destined to become absorbed and disappear in the adult human.

The developing structure was exquisitely sensitive to small changes in the environment at this phase. The two scientists needed to be continuously attentive to all parameters of the fluid bath since it was acting as a substitute for a uterus, maternal blood supply, yolk sac, umbilical cord, and mother's body. The growing organism was particularly susceptible to ionizing radiation and could be easily damaged by X-rays. The effects of light on an infant were not very well known since under normal conditions the human fetus is hidden away in the darkness of its mother during gestation. The professor, however, was taking no chances, so that the level of illumination was held to a bare minimum, with glare-free, low energy, cold light from fluorescent lamps. When there was no need for light the entire room was bathed in darkness and quiet. In addition, at this point, they had to prepare for the time when the organism would grow too large to absorb all Its required nutrients and get rid of Its wastes by simple absorption and osmosis. They knew there would come a time when the organism would have to be outfitted with a sort of artificial umbilical cord to continue Its required nutrient and waste exchanges. This would have to be similar to the arteriovenous shunts used in modern kidney dialysis. The two practiced daily under the microscope their microsurgical techniques so that when the time came they would be ready. Of course, Fanning was only able to participate in a passive way due to the damage his hands had sustained. But he helped the professor to hone his skills by practicing repair of rat tail arteries to which they had produced various traumatic lesions. This was tedious but necessary if they were to do a competent job on the Project.

They had the same discussion over and over again, to wit: If they were really destined to resurrect Jesus Christ it shouldn't matter how many mistakes they made. If it was the will of God then the two of them were mere pawns in the process. It shouldn't matter if they were not so meticulous in their technique. But if this had nothing to do with the will of the Almighty then they had to do everything exactly correct or risk failure. Well, Karahsha was unwilling to do anything less than the maximum effort, and that is what he demanded from Fanning as well. Fanning for his part was willing to go all out as well considering what he had already been through.

30

Day 28

The embryo, now approximately 1 cm in crown to rump length, was visible to the unaided eye floating slowly, tumbling end over end, gently buffeted by the various currents of circulation in the nutrient bath maintained at constant conditions. Even though visible the structure was hardly identifiable as a living embryo with the naked eye. Nevertheless, multiple segmentation was already present all the way into the tail, which was destined to be absorbed over the next several weeks. At this stage, absorption of nutrition and the elimination of waste were still possible by simple osmosis. But as the organism grew and resistance to diffusion increased it would be necessary to add a mechanism to make the tissues more permeable without producing any damage. Karahsha planned to do this by adding hyaluronic acid to the bath. The effect of this acid is to increase the permeability of the tissues and facilitate diffusion into and out of the cells. The professor knew there were certain amphibians such as frogs which absorb oxygen through their skin while buried in mud for months at a time.

Another mechanism available to the professor was a simple increase in the concentration pressure of the gases necessary for the growing organism to absorb. It would be a simple matter to jack up the pressure of oxygen in the bath but Karahsha was reluctant to do this since high oxygen tension is known to be related to a condition called retrolental fibroplasia which causes blindness in infants. In premature babies, one of the main problems they face is respiratory insufficiency since the lungs are frequently immature. This has prompted neonatologists to use high concentrations of oxygen, which have been associated with blindness. The professor was unwilling to subject his Project to that possibility because he didn't know if it might cause blindness at this stage of early development. He just did not know if the little organism he was working on was subject to the same risks as a human being or immune to these dangers due to Its divine nature.

As the Project developed and the possibility of failure appeared less remote the two experimenters took more and more precautions to ensure secrecy. They still feared their efforts might fall into the hands of their enemies, who had shown a willingness to try and destroy it at any cost. They didn't know how far these unknown antagonists would go in trying to stop them.

The original, small amount of DNA was already expended in starting the Project and no way existed to obtain more, except another raid on the Shroud. They considered that not to be an option. The professor was not so reckless as to have missed the opportunity to replicate the original DNA at the start of the Project, but this replicated DNA was of untested efficacy being a derivative material and not the original. He also had the option of withdrawing blood samples from the organism when it grew big enough and retrieving DNA from the blood cells. That too represented a secondary derivative material but was still a viable option if it became necessary.

The replicated DNA was produced from the original by a process called polymerase chain reaction, or PCR. It is a method which has revolutionized the field of genetics. The process involves isolating the DNA from cells which have nuclei in any of the body's cells, called somatic cells, or even the blood cells, except red blood cells, which have no nuclei and therefore no DNA. Isolated DNA from a cell's nucleus is subjected to enzymatic breakage, splitting the double stranded helix into a single strand. This in turn is subjected to different enzymes which dismember the DNA along the chain producing shorter or longer fragments. These fragments can then be isolated on an agarose gel by an electric field which takes advantage of the inherent bipolarity of the molecules. When specific segments of the DNA are thus isolated, polymerase chain reaction (PCR) can be used to duplicate the same segments in very large numbers. Any or all of the segments of a gene's DNA can be reproduced. Now, it is one thing to reproduce isolated sections of DNA. It is quite another to use the entire DNA structure of all the genes (of which the human body has approximately 100,000) to rebuild a human from scratch. Even the cloning of amphibians, which has already been done in many research centers, involves using the ovum of the female and removing the nuclear material containing the chromosomes from it. Then the nuclear material from a somatic cell of a tadpole, say an intestinal cell, is placed into the emptied egg nucleus, and the appropriate conditions of temperature, salinity, pH, etc. are reproduced. This construct will then develop into a live, functional frog, which will be fully capable of reproduction. However, cloning by the use of DNA produced from PCR is something that no one has done before, until tackled by Professor Karahsha.

As far back as the 1950s experiments were carried out in which water, oxygen, nitrogen, and carbon were isolated in a closed chamber and electricity passed through to simulate lightning. These experiments produced certain amines, which are the building blocks of amino acids, the precursors of proteins. The technology has advanced spectacularly since those early beginnings.

With the organism showing evidence of normal growth, the level of tension elevated noticeably in all the participants. Karahsha, however, maintained a feigned air of confidence and nonchalance that irked Chris and Margie Fanning. After all, it now appeared that the Project had at least a fifty percent chance of successful completion, and by any measure this was no ordinary scientific experiment. They all agreed the scope of this work surpassed by orders of magnitude anything that had ever been done or even anything that had ever been conceived by others. If they were successful they should be entitled to the next ten years worth of Nobel Prizes in medicine, physics, chemistry, biology, and the Nobel Peace Prize. Wow! What a healthy chunk of cash that would represent! But the potential fame and recognition was far sweeter to contemplate as would be the expected offers of university professorships and department chairs all over the world.

31

Day 56

The crown to rump length was now 4 cm. The little Body was clearly visible in the slowly agitated fluid. Crown to rump length is widely used by obstetricians to describe the length of the in utero embryo because of the difficulty in estimating the leg lengths. At this stage, the position of the embryo is one of flexion of the spine and acute flexion at the hips and knees so that the legs come to lie curled up in front of the Body. The easiest most reproducible measurement is thus the crown to rump dimension.

Now the little living speck was clearly identifiable as a human embryo. The future ear location was marked by an "otic pit" near the top of the structure on either side of what was to become the head. The five branchial arches and clefts, which are analogous to the gill slits in fishes, were already present and visible to the naked eye with close scrutiny. These arches and clefts are forerunners of the mature pharynx, jaws, and neck in the adult. At this stage the head end is much enlarged compared to the rest of the body. The heart, already present, remarkably pulsates at around 130 beats per minute. The brain, in an early stage of growth, consists of the forebrain, the midbrain, and the hindbrain. The twelve cranial nerves are present in the earliest primordial stages of development.

Quickly running them down they are: I, the olfactory nerve, the nerve of smell; II, the optic nerve, the nerve of sight; III, the oculomotor nerve, a nerve which moves the eyeball; IV, the trochlear nerve which also helps to move the eye in its socket; V, the trigeminal nerve, the nerve of mastication; VI, the abducent nerve, another motor nerve of the eye; VII, the facial nerve, a nerve of facial expression; VIII, the acoustic nerve, the nerve of hearing: IX, the glossopharyngeal nerve, the nerve of taste and parotid gland stimulation; X, the vagus nerve with too many functions to enumerate here; XI, the spinal accessory nerve; and the XII, the hypoglossal nerve, which is the muscle of the tongue. Many medical students are familiar with the mnemonic used to remember these nerves: "On old Olympus towering top a Finn and German view a hop." Of course the first letters of each word stand for the corresponding cranial nerve.

The spinal cord and all of its branching spinal nerves were also present in rudimentary form at this stage. The precursors of the liver, pancreas, kidneys, stomach, intestines, lungs, trachea, esophagus, bronchi and adrenal glands were all in place. The rudimentary skeletal system, with the soft cartilaginous precursors of bone, was there as well as the early muscles, voluntary and involuntary. The thymus, spleen, thyroid gland, and reproductive organs were all in place. The beginnings of tendon, ligament, mucous membrane, and salivary glands were taking shape. The limb buds were already present and developing.

Karahsha studied the developing life form with a specific purpose, not idle curiosity. He looked for something crucial to the ultimate success of the Project. He was scrutinizing the living form for the first sign of visible arteries and veins. He knew that after a critical size the mere exchange of gases, nutrients, and waste products by osmosis would no longer be possible because of the sheer increase in the thickness of tissue. The problem he faced was that he did not know what that size was since he nor anyone else had done this before.

In order to prepare for the time when the arteries and veins would have to be catheterized for the necessary fluid exchange, they spent a large part of their time practicing on rat tail artery repair. The professor figured the embryo's vessels would have to be at least that large for him to be able to work with. Fanning, with his damaged hands, could only support the professor in this work since he now lacked the requisite fine control of his hands. This was tedious, meticulous, painstaking work made all the harder because the professor was confined to his wheelchair and couldn't move around as he wanted. At times they sat for hours while Karahsha practiced with the microvascular instruments. These sessions were just as hard on Fanning since he had to sit there and just watch for those long hours. During these sessions the professor was unable to drink coffee or caffeinated soft drinks since these produced too much of a tremor in the hands. The problem they faced was in being able to detect an artery and vein large enough to enable them to install a catheter, sort of an artificial umbilical cord. This would be used for gaseous exchange, removal of wastes, and nutrient supply. Many nights they worked long into the morning hours to perfect the technique since successful completion of this process was critical to the favorable outcome of the Project.

Another issue that was proving increasingly vexing to the professor was the harassment, as he saw it, of the university comptroller who was becoming more and more insistent on receiving an accounting of how Karahsha's grant money was being spent. Also, he wanted a much more detailed accounting of the Pathology Department's finances. The professor put him off as much as he could but there was a limit to how long he could delay the ultimate accounting. Karahsha had been diverting a significant percentage of his budget to his own secret research for many years and he was behind the eight ball on that account for many thousands of dollars.

Fanning happened to mention the professor's financial difficulty to Margie one day. Suddenly, she knew how she was going to get even with her husband's assailants. She would get her daddy to contribute to the professor's budget, bailing him out with the university, and thereby making her own contribution to the Project and helping to ensure its success. Fanning didn't mind since the money was not directly for him or to improve his family's financial prospects. The professor was on the point of desperation and was glad for the financial help at a time when he might have his beloved Project stopped and even have legal troubles due to his long term misappropriation of university money. Margie was easily able to get her dad to part with some of his many dollars by convincing him of the importance of the Project without revealing too many of the details.

The time came when the professor, under magnification, was able to make out the unmistakable throbbing of the little heart, the aorta, and all the tiny beating arteries sending their nutrient filled, oxygenated, bright red blood out to the periphery. The veins were more difficult to identify. Having a thin wall, the veins were distinguished by their smaller size and their slightly bluish tint given off by the deoxygenated blood they carried. In most areas of the body, the veins and arteries course alongside each other with arterial blood flowing one way and the deoxygenated venous blood flowing the other. The veins also distinguished by valves at specific intervals and were more variable in their course than the arteries. Little thickenings in the walls represented the outside manifestations of the valvular structures within.

The next procedure had to be carried out with the utmost skill. Infection had to be avoided at all cost because the survival of the Project could be at stake. Indeed, infection could kill the entire organism. It had to be done with precision and as little damage to the vessel walls as possible. And it had to be done right the first time. They might not have another chance. When all was in readiness, the professor delicately scooped the fragile creature into a small net similar to those used to capture goldfish in a bowl. The professor and Fanning were dressed in sterile surgical gowns, shoe covers, masks, and sterile gloves. The very air they breathed was first filtered and passed over infrared and ultraviolet light to kill any airborne pathogens. Gingerly, the professor scooped the precious little blob of life onto the dimple well of the operating microscope. Fanning dared not breathe for fear of he knew not what. The professor ever so gently attached the small polyethylene tubes to the slide for temporary nutrient flow and removal of waste materials. These would prevent interference of respiration and nutrition during the time of this necessary procedure. While Fanning manipulated the more gross aspects of the microscope to help make the professor's job easier, the professor took charge of the more intricate and finer aspects of the procedure. Fanning felt frustration, anger, and helplessness at not being able to participate more in the real microsurgical aspects of the operation, but Karahsha assured him that he had already done his part what with the assault on his person and the financial contribution his father-in-law had recently made.

While Fanning steadied the tiny arms of the micro dissector, the professor gently maneuvered the Body so that one arm bud could be dropped into a special grooved depression on the slide. With infinite patience he coaxed the tiny pre-limb into the small groove and covered the tiny hand bud with an exceedingly fine mesh netting to hold it in place. Then he did the same with the other arm bud. Once settled, he placed a tiny plastic cap on the Body like a miniature contact lens to keep the fluid currents from moving it around. It was not possible to extend the lower limb buds for immobilization since they were all curled up in front of the Body in the fetal position.

Now the operation began in earnest. Using microvascular forceps powered by hydraulics, he was able to translate a gross movement of 1/4 inch on a foot pedal to a fraction of a millimeter in his operating field. Peering through the microscope, while Fanning held the whole thing firmly in place, he located the little nub of the umbilical cord. He could see the tiny forceps jump rhythmically with the heartbeat. The pulsation in the artery was transmitted to his probe, then to a pulsometer. He made a tiny incision in the skin transversely oriented across the long axis of the artery. Immediately he could see the whole Body withdraw from his tiny microscope in response to the pain. Karahsha hadn't expected this. The tiny living being was capable of feeling pain and even responding to it! He looked at Fanning in confusion and awe. What latent memories of long ago torture might be evoked by this simple invasion of the skin of the umbilicus, by his sharp instrument? Was he going to be responsible for a new insult on this divine creature, a being who could not defend Himself, nor decide whether or not to cooperate with this new tormenter? Was the brain of this minuscule embryo capable of understanding what was happening?

He backed off. For the first time in his life, the professor was in doubt of how to proceed. After a few minutes of hesitation Fanning suggested rather meekly that he use a small amount of a local anesthetic. "Of course, why didn't I think of that?" the professor asked aloud, smacking his head with the palm of his hand. After the use of an exceedingly minute amount of Marcaine injected with a needle the diameter of a human hair, he was able to resume his work with no further sign of pain or withdrawal by his little patient.

By sharp dissection, he located the artery which was right below the skin. He passed a fine 11-0 suture underneath the artery and used it to tent up the artery for accessibility. He also applied a little traction to force the walls of the artery together and minimize bleeding. He used his mini micro scalpel to make a small longitudinal slit in the vessel. Then he threaded a very fine polyethylene tube into the artery and tied it in place. He next used a small dissecting tool to find the more delicate vein and similarly catheterized it, bringing the two small tubes out to be tied again in such a way as to prevent them from being pulled out by accident. He did not bother to suture the small incision in the skin knowing that it would heal in a matter of days at this young age. As It grew and Its needs outstripped the capacity of the small plastic tubing, the procedure would have to be repeated every so often until the Project was completed, sort of a man-made umbilical cord.

They, especially the professor, had to become expert in microvascular surgery and the fundamentals of dialysis. They had to teach themselves to be anatomists and neonatologists. They had to be expert in the use of hormones, enzymes, and antibiotics. Of course the professor had been preparing almost all his adult life for this Project, but as in all things scientific he could not possibly anticipate every snag, every problem that might come up. They had to be proficient in the new disciplines of gene manipulation and recombinant DNA or at least the rudiments thereof. All this had to be done in secret with an unknown enemy breathing down their necks, an enemy whose potential for malice had already been demonstrated.

After hooking up the tubing to their exchange machine, they carefully removed the little organism from the microscope slide and replaced It in the tank. From now on the nutrient bath would be supplemented by the tubes providing continuous hemodialysis. The little growing organism would be tethered from now on. It would have a regular supply of nutrients and all the other growth factors, a balanced electrolyte input, and the required antibiotics.

At an appropriate later stage in Its growth, the professor applied micro electrocardiogram leads to the chest for a rough monitor of heart function. At these early stages he was satisfied with the QRS complexes as well as the heart's rate and rhythm. However, he did notice on those occasions when the organism was subjected to some type of stress like cold or manipulation of the arterial tubing that there might be a quickening of the heartbeat or even a dropped beat. This was easily corrected by proceeding with gentleness and care, or stopping the procedure for a while.

As the organism grew, Karahsha noted more reaction on Its part to being handled. The little Body could be seen to squirm around and try to avoid noxious stimuli. If held very carefully in the palm of the hand, especially a warmly gloved sterile hand, It could be seen almost to cuddle as if to make a nest. At these times the professor could not wait until It would grow to the point where he could communicate with It. What conversations he could imagine having with this reincarnation, this re-embodiment of the Savior! What insights could He offer on the human condition today as compared to two thousand years ago? What would He do? Would He preach as in the ways of old? Would He establish a new ministry that would evolve into a new church or even a new religion? How dependent would He be on the creator, Professor Karahsha, if indeed he really was the Creator? Would He be inclined to shed any light on the age old mysteries of man? Would He have to be taught English or would He speak in the old Aramaic tongue? Would He dress in modern clothes or the simple robe of the ancients? Would He wear His hair long? Would He wear a beard? If so what color would it be? What color would His skin be? Would He be subject to disease having no built-in immunity to polio, measles, diphtheria, scarlet fever, smallpox, or bacterial infection? Would the State of Arizona give Him a birth certificate? A social security number? Would He have to pay taxes if He had any income? Where would He live? Would He be content to remain in the community of His rebirth or would He want to return to Jerusalem or travel the world? Would He learn to drive a car? Listen to the radio? Watch TV? What would be His reaction to the movies of today? Would He need an education? What if He became sick, say, needed an operation for appendicitis for instance? Who would pay for it? Would He need health insurance? Who would have the chutzpah to operate on Jesus Christ? Would He need a lawyer, a retirement account, a savings account? Would He have an appendectomy free given who He is? Would He go to Vatican City and meet the pope there or would the pope come to Arizona to meet Him? Would the pope even recognize Him for what He is or deny His identity?

Would He want to meet with the pope at all? Would He try to consolidate all Christian denominations?

In addition, what about all the other religions on Earth? Would He debunk them or would He try to come to some mutually respectful accommodation? The questions were endless. What light might He be able to shed on Mary, the disciples, the Romans of the biblical period, the Hebrews, the Last Supper, and all the mythic events that transpired afterward? Would He be willing to tell us what He has been doing for the last 2,000 years? Would He share any insights as to the ultimate fate of the human race? Could He really walk on water? Would He travel the land, cure the sick, heal the lame, and restore sight to the blind? Would He be on comfortable terms with the rich and powerful or would He find his counsel with the poor, the powerless, the disenfranchised? Would He prefer to spend most of His time in some third world country like Peru or Nigeria? All these questions swirled through his head in a tornado of doubt. He thought for now they must remain unanswered. But not for long.

As the tiny organism grew, he monitored the state of His health by drawing off minute blood samples during the arterial tube changes, necessitated by the increasing size of the vessels and the disparity between them and the plastic tubes. He monitored the hemoglobin, hematocrit, the white blood count, especially important in the early detection of infection. He measured serum proteins, electrolytes, glucose, glycerides, thyroid hormones, growth hormone, pH, and many more. The professor was even able to collect urine on occasion and analyze it for an insight into kidney function. He was delighted to find all tests indicated a completely normal gestation so to speak. He thought in a moment of levity this might give new meaning to the phrase Immaculate Conception, although he was aware that the Immaculate Conception referred to Mary's being born without original sin and not to the pregnancy that resulted in the birth of Christ.

At one stage he even attached tiny electroencephalographic leads to the head and was elated to find these to be completely normal. They even indicated the organism was having periods of brain alertness and other quiescent periods which could be interpreted as sleep. It was, however, too early to tell whether there was any sign of cognitive awareness as yet. At these moments the two scientists could not contain their excitement now that it appeared that success was almost at hand.

Fanning continued to be disturbed by the lingering nerve injury to his right median nerve. The damage produced a continuous numbness in the index finger and thumb. Occasionally he suffered sudden, sharp electric-like pains radiating up his arm all the way up to his shoulder. The median nerve is a structure that lies on the volar, or palmar, side of the wrist and is protected only by the skin, the fascia, and a small tendon of the palmaris longus muscle. After severe injury, as he had sustained, the recovery process can be long and drawn out, even to the extent of years. In fact there is no guarantee of complete recovery at all. He could only hope that the successful completion of the Project would offer him some hope of recovery, even if he had to ask the reborn Christ for a favor. Sort of a reward for his troubles. But even Fanning knew his disability was nothing compared to Karahsha's.

32

12 Weeks

The Infant was now 7 cm in crown-rump length. The external genitalia were clearly identifiable as being male, and the digits of the hands and feet were beginning to be recognizable as separate and discrete little structures with suggestions of fingernails on them. On one or two occasions the professor and Chris had observed the Baby momentarily sucking Its thumb. At this stage, some early fine hairs were just discernible on the scalp. The fetus, tethered as it was to the dialysis line, slowly floated in a warm bath, seemingly oblivious to its surroundings, contented, warm, and protected. Had they wanted to subject it to an X-ray they would have seen that in most bones the centers of ossification had already made their appearance. There were the very beginnings of the osseous structures that would form the bones of the skull, the spinal column, the ribs, pelvis and breastbone, the shoulder girdle bones, and the long bones of the upper and lower extremities.

The professor explained to Fanning how in his previous experiments he would lose control at this point. The osseous structures had somehow taken over the metabolism, had hogged the nutrition, and ultimately grown out of control at the expense of the other soft parts, sort of an explosion of benign osseous tissue that nevertheless by its behavior acted as a malignancy in that it resulted in the death of the organism. Karahsha was reminded of Mr. Armstrong's tumor and how it had killed him. He had not told Fanning about the unfortunate result suffered by Armstrong, and Fanning had not asked. However, he explained, by manipulating and fine-tuning the concentration of the various growth stimulating factors he had learned to solve that particular problem. He had also learned to fine-tune the cascading process by which the Hox genes set off the development of each of the specific tissues at just the correct juncture, producing a smooth transition from the original ovum into the multilayered, coherent, integrated, functioning organism developing right in front of their eyes.

The more Fanning saw and understood the scope of what the professor had done the more his admiration grew for the wiry self-taught genius who seemed to be about to carry to fruition one of the most daring, farsighted experiments in the history of science modern or ancient, bar none. Fanning found himself leaning faster than he could in any graduate program for he was privy to more cutting edge technology and information than he could possibly have seen anywhere else. He did not mind one bit playing second fiddle to the professor's genius.

The pertinent data was continuing to be recorded on a computer printout for storage, documentation, and study. The emerging Body was now large enough to measure, weigh, and photograph. The data were so voluminous now so as to necessitate storage on multiple computer discs. Karahsha wanted no element of the Project to be challenged in the future by anyone citing an absence of corroborating data. When he was ready, it would be there for all the world to see. He was even considering writing a book on the entire Project aside from the technical papers that would appear in the peer reviewed scientific journals. He would write it in simple terms for the non-scientist to comprehend. The professor chuckled to himself when he thought of the scrambling that would take place in the academic community to catch up with his achievement. All the standard reference works, textbooks, and graduate courses in the field would have to be completely revised and updated. They would all have to come to him to accomplish that. He surmised it would not be too far-fetched to think he could have his own research foundation for the study of genetics much as Dr. Jonas Salk had his own institute for viral research. He relished the thought of being able to lecture at the great universities and institutes such as Oxford, Cambridge, and the Pasteur Institute.

The telephone startled him out of his reverie. It was his secretary with the treasurer of the university on the line. "Wonder what the hell he wants," the professor growled. "He only wants to talk to me when he's trying to raise funds for the university or some other 'good' cause."

"Hello Professor Karahsha, how are you? Listen, I have to talk to you person to person, one on one, you understand? It doesn't have to be this minute but sometime in the next week. It's fairly urgent. I really can't get into the details on the phone, but there seems to be an irregularity in the budget and a rather important sum of money can't be accounted for. I'm sure it's just an accounting glitch and the figures will straighten out somewhere. We'll have to go over the books from all departments with a fine tooth comb. Just make an appointment with my secretary when it's convenient for you. Look, I know how busy you are, trying to do the jobs of two men from a wheelchair, and I'm sorry for the trouble. However, it just has to be done."

The professor covered the speaker with his hand and turned to Fanning with a look of annoyance on his face.

"What's wrong?" Fanning asked.

"Oh, in the big scheme of things it's not too important. Just another hurdle to have to deal with. Just one more reason for the bureaucrats to justify their existence."

He removed his hand from the speaker, told the treasurer he'd make the requested appointment and hung up.

"Let's not worry about finances right now, eh? Think of it Chris Fanning, we are on the verge of successfully restoring Jesus Christ Himself to life and thereby changing the history of the world. Or at least I think He will. Put it this way, He ought to change the world big time just like He did the first time. Are you prepared for fame and possibly fortune? Do you know what this could mean to your future, of which you have more than I do since you are younger? There is a possibility our names could go in the history books alongside Newton, Galileo, Copernicus, and Einstein to mention just a few. In fact, our situation is much like Galileo's. He was persecuted by the church for his beliefs which he could show to be true by careful observation. Did you ever wonder what possesses certain men to disbelieve the incontrovertible evidence right before their eyes? I mean, they are so blinded by their lugubrious faith in whatever happens to be the gospel of the day that they cannot, will not, allow the weight of evidence to sway them from their point of view. We are in such a similar situation. We face an establishment which is blind to the facts. We are on the verge of a new technology that is going to be implemented whether we want it or not. Resistance is useless. There are no instances in the past where new knowledge, new technology, new discoveries were bottled up and frustrated. Every new technique, new discovery, every advance in our knowledge has eventually been used for good or evil. Just look at gunpowder, chemical weapons, biological warfare, atomic energy, lasers. There was even a guy, a surgeon by trade, who went around the country freezing peoples' stomach ulcers to cure them. He did thousands before he was stopped because it didn't work. But in most cases the new whatever, if it has any merit at all, takes its place in the useful service of mankind. On the other hand, the value of our work may not be appreciated or realized until after we are dead and gone. That is the more likely scenario. But we must continue until we succeed or fail." He paused and relented.

"Forgive me my young friend. You have sacrificed much towards our goal. I didn't mean to aim my diatribe at you. I know you are already convinced. Otherwise you would not have gone this far."

Fanning felt like the parishioners in the Sunday morning Mass when the priest exhorted those who had strayed to return to the church. At such times he'd had to restrain himself from yelling, "Hey, we're the ones who are here. You don't need to tell us to come." But he didn't say anything. There was no point.

The professor went on. "Please stop me if I've raved about this before."

Fanning knew he didn't want to be stopped.

"If you think education, scholarly pursuits, and lofty positions are qualities that produce magnanimity and generosity, tolerance and forbearance, think again. Some of the worst monsters in history have been in exalted positions doing what they did out of ambition, greed, lust for power or just plain lust. If they didn't have formal education or training they made sure they acquired the tools that would serve their ambitions. On the other hand, I don't want to belong to the mass of men who live quietly and die uncelebrated. I want to be among that fraction of one tenth of one percent who make a difference, whose names are remembered after they are just so much dust, after they are just a memory. Only with me I won't be a memory for long, since I have no family and no heirs. I only have my work. Maybe I have spent money unwisely. Maybe I have been somewhat deceptive in the cost of my budget. But look what we are about to accomplish. Imagine what the world can look forward to through our efforts. Maybe it is salvation. Maybe it is an arrogance of the highest sort. Maybe we have been chosen. Perhaps I was put on Earth to be the agent of that salvation. I don't know. I won't pretend that some angel of God came to me and offered me the job. It did come to me though didn't it? You think I'm a madman? I know there was a time you did. But do you still think I'm mad? After all, I've shown you how possible, how within our grasp it really is. You can see for yourself the life we've created from scratch, so to speak. It floats before your very eyes. It is not as if I have any control of the situation. More like the situation has control of me. I only know I must do this. Do you understand? In spite of anything, in the face of any imaginable obstacle, I would risk the harshest opprobrium to succeed. And if not this time, then the next. But I believe it will be this time. I know it will be this time. I know it in my bones. Don't ask me how or why. I know it just as surely as we are standing here talking!"

Wow, Fanning thought, how can you argue with such determination? How can you question a man's purpose who has no fear, no reason to doubt himself, whose sole purpose in life is to succeed in the one goal he has set for himself?

33

20 Weeks

Crown-rump length is 12 cm. Weight is 115 grams. In the muted bluish light, the growing organism might be mistaken for a tropical fish or a seahorse from a distance. However, up close with the naked eye there was no mistaking the human form with Its oversized head compared to the Body. Slowly It floated end over end, sometimes gently bumping into the glass wall of the container, sometimes caught in a stream of bubbles from the oxygen source, and sometimes pushed by the invisible currents of various nutrients injected into the tank under a gentle pressure. Remote probes in the glass walls were already recording the electrical activity emanating from the organism. Potentiometers and ammeter readings recorded heart and brain activity. These were stored for future study and for verification of the experiment. The weight, dimensions, color, shape, and movements were all recorded. Measurements of lengths, of diameters of fingers, circumference of toes, torso, head, and abdomen were assessed and recorded. Videotape of the organism was taken at regular intervals, providing in that way an extra backup copy of the record of growth. At precisely determined intervals the Body outline, and all possible combinations of measurement parameters were measured and stored on computer discs. Changes in water temperature, pH, oxygen saturation, concentration of metabolites, electrolytes, hormones, vitamins, minerals, and enzymes among a myriad of other parameters were measured, recorded, adjusted, and fine-tuned. No possible element was left to chance.

But there were aspects of this new life that could not be measured. There were dimensions that could not be quantified, and the professor was keenly aware of these. Did the Baby's brain harbor any thought or images or ideas yet? If He were truly divinely related, did His heart contain the original's passion for humanity? And in a sense if It were truly a clone of the original then didn't It already have a sense of self-awareness? In charge of Its own destiny through these human agents chosen for their work even as the original parents were chosen before them? These questions Karahsha pondered as he lovingly incubated his treasure and wondered at times just who was in charge here. It intrigued him to imagine that the little Body taking shape before him might already be aware of His own existence even as the professor studied Him. In a few days, it must have been true that in some sense It was aware and more than aware, for even now it would be necessary to take a blood sample to obtain information he could gather in no other way.

The professor wondered if he could complete this experimental Project without the disaster that had stymied his other earlier efforts. Infection was still a possibility that could cause a catastrophe since this little organism lacked the protection of a mother's immune system and its ability to protect a growing infant. Broad spectrum antibiotics were introduced into the bath fluid on a continuous basis in small, discrete doses since antibiotics are known to have their own mutagenic effect in excessive doses. No one has exposed a growing fetus to direct contact with antibiotics before. It has always been through the mother's blood stream. A viral infection was another situation altogether. This organism had neither the protection of a mother's immune system nor the protection of any immunization from vaccination. No one had ever immunized an unborn fetus before, and the professor was unwilling to subject his Project to any of the currently available OPT, polio, or measles vaccines because he didn't know what the result would be. One of the parameters to be defined was the blood type of this young organism. The professor could not conceal his excitement, not even to himself. Imagine, determining the blood type of Jesus Christ himself! Another purpose for the test was to determine the integrity of the DNA. That is, to make sure no deterioration occurred, and to have surplus DNA for storage. One strand of intact DNA could be made into many by the process of PCR, polymerase chain reaction as already described.

The professor was also anxious to biopsy many other tissues for detailed study like liver, kidney, muscle, and skin, but these he considered too risky and was content to defer them until such time that the little Body could better tolerate it. The idea of quantifying parameters in what he considered the Deity was mind-boggling even to the professor.

Now he had in the back of his mind an additional issue which he didn't allow himself to think about in a conscious fashion. In the far recesses of his mind, he dared to hope that the Project would somehow restore him to his previously whole condition, reverse the paralysis that chained him to his wheelchair, and allow him to be a man again. He forced himself not to think of this though and kept his mind focused on the work at hand.

34

25 Weeks

Now the time came to accelerate the growth so that at the end of 40 weeks He would be fully grown, adult, and ready to be born, so to speak. By careful addition of the various growth factors, hormones, and other proteins and enzymes, Karahsha subtly adjusted the stimulus to rapid growth. Here, he had to use all of the knowledge he'd painstakingly gathered in the foregoing years. Over time, He responded to the professor's manipulations. He passed through the various stages of fetal life rapidly, achieving the size and shape of a newborn at term.

In due course, the professor was able to use the special arm coverings that he had built into the sides of the tank for a sterile examination. These allowed Karahsha to palpate the Body and use a sterile stethoscope attached electronically to his computer. He tested the startle reflex and the hearing. He checked on the neurological function of the 12 cranial nerves and the nerve supply to the upper and lower extremities. He examined the hips for congenital dysplasia and found none. He looked into the ears, the mouth, the eyes, and noted no abnormality. He attached the electroencephalogram leads and studied the rudimentary brain function. To his utter elation there was not one suggestion of abnormality. No reading was even marginally out of line. He weighed 7 1b 3 oz., measured 21 inches long, and could be observed on occasion to suck his thumb. From that point on, He was treated like a child already born. Progress was thereafter rapid in all senses. He gained weight rapidly, growing so fast that sometimes Karahsha swore he could see the growth take place.

Margie was duly attentive to the scientists' needs, because in doing so she felt she was doing her part to make the Project a success and thus get some measure of revenge on the perpetrators of her husband's ordeal. She still hadn't gotten over the guilt she felt in letting a hint of the Project be known to her friends, the Sisters of the Order. She was naturally more attentive to Fanning's needs but she could also see the anticipation build in Karahsha as the Project came closer to completion.

A fundamental change occurred in the Infant's behavior that took Professor Karahsha by surprise. It was a development he had not anticipated, and he wasn't sure how to deal with it. After handling the little Body in Its bath, he noticed a definite sense of unease in the child manifested by changes in Its facial expression. It almost appeared as if the little one was about to cry. He certainly had a pouty expression on His face at these times. Other times when Karahsha had been absent for a time, then approached the transparent glass tank, he could swear that the tiny eyes would open and focus on him, following him around the room and actually narrowing with pleasure if he came right up close to the glass wall. Karahsha was not prepared for this. However, Margie recognized this right away as the behavior of a newborn infant attaching itself to what it perceived as its mother.

The professor was dismayed. He didn't know how to handle this turn of events. He didn't want to handle this turn of events. He also began to notice signs of severe discomfort in Him whenever He was left alone. At these times He would kick His feet, thrash His arms about, and make crying faces although these latter were necessarily silent. He would even dart into the glass wall of the tank with an unnerving thud. Margie thought it cute. The professor thought it horrible.

There was another aspect to His behavior that Karahsha couldn't fathom. The Baby started to make sucking movements with His mouth but promptly spit out the fluid ingested apparently disapproving of the taste.

Again Margie's insight was valuable. She told Karahsha, "It's obvious, He's hungry."

The professor wouldn't believe it. What was he to do?

"Why, you'll have to feed him," Margie volunteered. The professor was totally confused and taken off guard. Fanning sat back in amusement and almost laughed out loud.

"Feed him? You mean a bottle?"

"Yes, of course a bottle. What else?" she demanded. "He has the size and development of a newborn and wants to eat like one."

This, of course, put the professor in a state. Another unanticipated development. What would he have to do now? Buy some Enfamil or Similac? What other complications would arise that he hadn't thought of? Now this really introduced an unplanned contingency. Other than the tactical problems of getting the milk into Him, if any kind of food went in surely some sort of waste product would come out. Renally produced waste product he could handle. These would become diluted as soon as they were produced by virtue of the large amount of fluid bath and the constant recirculation. But solid waste with its high concentration of coliform bacteria would be another problem. He'd have to use a diaper by God to keep the contamination to a minimum. He'd have to take cultures at more frequent intervals and then use more antibiotics with any added problems these could cause.

What other unexpected problems could come up? When the time came would He want to go on a date or to dances as He matured? Oh no, he thought, you are not getting out of your tank until fully grown. Then he realized whom he was dealing with. In a more respectful tone, he thought maybe the Father of the Son could render some help in this regard. He turned to prayer, something he hadn't done in many years. He'd not had this problem in the past because heretofore at about this stage in development the bones would take over and the Project would fail. He never had an intact human being to contend with. He worried, what if He became unmanageable, rebellious, and tried to break out of the tank when he was a bit older and stronger? Of course, given who He was He could probably break out any time He wanted anyway. This would put a whole new set of problems on the agenda. But the professor was determined to handle them no matter what they were. He wondered how long it would have taken him to figure out what had come to Margie easily. Maybe he should start to pipe in music to the tank, or maybe play tapes in different languages. Maybe the little rascal had an ability to learn already. He just didn't know. If only there was some precedent, some previous experience he could call on. But of course, no one had ever done this before.

He found himself asking Margie to help him negotiate his wheelchair into the Catholic Church where he searched for some sort of sign, some hint on how to proceed. He liked the church ambience, the solace. It made him feel good somehow and he resolved to come more often later when the Project was completed and he was not so busy. He was afraid to leave the Infant alone, but as He grew Karahsha learned to leave more of the babysitting chores to Fanning, who didn't mind at all. The professor learned how to cope with the growing creature's idiosyncrasies and juvenile demands so much that he thought of a curious side effect that might become possible because of his work. He'd often heard parents complain that they wished children could be brought into the world fully grown. He thought if the Project were a success then it would lie in the realm of possibility to do so and thus end the heartache for some parents going through the hellfire of child raising. A valuable side effect! Probably someone would go for it though, another unforeseen benefit of the Project.

Again, the professor could not shake the feeling that he was not sure of who was doing the experimenting and who was the subject of the experimentation. He had increasing doubts about who was really in charge here. What about the phase of His growth corresponding to the toddler stage? Would He suffer from lack of playmates? What about the more dangerous adolescent age? How aware of His surroundings would He be? Would He be deprived from a lack of peers to play with, interact with? Maybe he should clone a whole class of beings by means of the polymerase chain reaction . . . impractical. He didn't have the space, the time, or the money.

The professor considered a fundamental change in the Project by removing the growing Body from the complicated bath, disconnecting the IV lines, and raising the Baby as a normal child. He rejected that option because of the added problems it would bring in terms of dealing with a growing youngster in isolation. This method promised to present some rather interesting problems of its own. For example, if he kept the Body in the glass enclosed tank the entire time until the equivalent age of say the mid twenties, how would the bones react to the near weightlessness of floating around supported by fluid all Its life? It would be akin to the problems the astronauts have had in the weightlessness of space. If the problems of calcium loss and bone demineralization arise from just a few weeks or months in space, what effects would this weightlessness produce on his creation? When the time came to remove Him from His glass uterus will He crumple because the bones are so osteoporotic as to be unable to support His weight? Now he decided he had to institute a program of exercise in order to prevent just such an occurrence. But how to go about it?

As it happened, the problem solved itself because after the Body reached the size of a newborn at term He became much more active all on His own. When left to His own devices, the Infant could be seen to swim about the tank, turn somersaults, barrel rolls, and turn flips so much that He nearly twisted His lifeline to the point of strangulation several times. The professor became paranoid about leaving Him alone for fear He would choke off His oxygen supply. Therefore he made it a rule that the growing Infant could not be left alone for more than a few minutes at a time. Needless to say this presented a problem for all of them. Fanning had his graduate studies and was hampered by the injuries to his hands so that any writing or work at a computer took him twice as long as before. Margie had taken full charge of the children again and had to arrange for babysitters, although her mom was happy to do it any time she was in town. Therefore, it devolved upon the professor to spend as much time with the Baby as possible since he was loath to let anyone else in on the secret proceedings.

In spite of the time constraints placed on all of them the Infant flourished, grew rapidly, and didn't strangle Himself. But the strain of the secrecy, added to the uncertainty of whether their enemies would again try to stop them, built the tension up to the point where they were always on edge and the least little snag could potentially develop into a flat-out argument. On top of these concerns the university was becoming more insistent on an accounting of how all of Karahsha's grant money was being spent. Through it all the professor maintained his usual duties in the

Department of Pathology, Blood Banking, Clinical Histology, and Bacteriology. This schedule allowed him almost no sleep. Even though his constitution was equal to that of three men the strain began to show, especially since everything he did had to be carried out from his wheelchair. Therefore, he determined to accelerate growth maximally without damaging the growing creature and to this end used more and more of his growth stimulating hormones and gene manipulation techniques he'd learned throughout his long apprenticeship. He was determined to bring this Project to a successful conclusion as soon as possible.

Development proceeded at a rapid pace now. The little Body went from the infant stage to the pre-toddler, to the toddler stage, to preadolescent, and then began the adolescent growth spurt. The Body proportions remained appropriate. As far as any of them could tell the emotional development kept apace. Karahsha could now foresee the day when he would preside over the birth of the new Messiah. Oh, what a joyful time that would be! The culmination of his life's work, the conclusion and beginning of an experiment never before performed by humanity, this would be the triumph he'd been working for all his life.

As for Fanning and Margie, they could hardly believe their eyes. What was occurring under their very noses was no less than the reincarnation of the Son of God, the Creator, the original prime mover! And they were privy to it all. Indeed, the whole event would not have been possible save for Fanning's sacrifice and Margie's support.

35

At a rare family picnic with Margie's parents one weekend towards the later stages of the Project, Fanning was attempting to swing the smaller of the two children by the arms. In the excitement of being all together for a family outing Fanning completely forgot about the weakness in his hands. The child was spinning around at shoulder height while Fanning twirled her at arm's length. Suddenly his hands could no longer sustain the effort and she went careening through the air, landing some fifteen feet away flat on her belly and face. She sustained some minor abrasions to the face and upper chest, but was more frightened by the experience than anything else. After cleaning her up and ministering to her injuries, they left the children with the in-laws and Fanning went home alone with Margie, intending that Margie would pick up the children the next day.

On the way home in the car Margie was angry and didn't hesitate to let Fanning know it.

"What were you trying to prove, Mr. Genius? Were you trying to see how far you could throw her?"

Fanning replied, "No, of course not, I wouldn't hurt her for the world. You know that."

"Well, you sure did a good job of it. I wonder what could have happened if you meant to throw her."

"Margie, what the hell are you talking about? You know it is only because of the damage to my hands that it happened in the first place. I just forgot how weak they still were."

"Nevertheless, when it comes to the children, you should be more careful."

"Yeah, well, when it comes to keeping things in confidence that are asked of you, you too might be more careful." He regretted it as soon as he said it.

"And what the hell do you mean by that?" she demanded.

"Nothing, just skip it, forget about it."

"No, no, I want to hear it. I want to hear all about it."

"Look, all we are going to do is get into a fight and wind up mad at each other. Let's just drop it, all right?"

"No. It's not all right. I want to know what's eating you. Do you blame me for your hands? Is that it?"

"Well as long as you want to hear it, wasn't it through your blabbing that the nuns found out about the Project? Didn't I ask you not to say anything to anybody about it, to anyone?"

"Oh, you asked me to keep it in confidence all right, but you didn't tell me it was going to place our lives in jeopardy, especially the kids. How could you do anything that could put our kids in danger like that?"

"So if I ask you to keep something under your hat you first have to know what all the ramifications are before you go along? Let's stop talking about this right now before one of us says something we'll be sorry for."

"If you had enough confidence in me to tell me the whole story maybe I would not have said anything to anybody, maybe I would have insisted you stop helping that madman of a professor. And all this would never have happened, even Jake's killing."

"Oh, so now you blame me for Jake's murder too."

"I didn't say that Chris."

"Look Margie, I love you. I don't blame you for anything. Just in case, the next time, if I ask you not to mention anything to anyone, please just trust me and keep quiet. This experience has been unique, one that is not given to anyone lightly. I think we are better for it and I think the world will be a better place for it. Let's not blame each other. God, when I was in that predicament, when I thought I would never see you and the kids again, that was the worst time of my life. Having survived that, I can survive anything else. So don't let's lose sight of what we have together by playing this petty blame game."

Margie was silent for a time.

Fanning continued, "I believe that nothing that's worth anything comes without risk. I did not think I was putting you or the kids to any serious risk or I would not have done it. I was wrong. I admit it. We have been through some rough times and survived. We may be in for some more rough times but I'm sure we will survive them too. So please, let's not become vindictive with each other and allow that to destroy what we have together."

"Daddy's money helped too didn't it?" Margie couldn't resist reminding him about her father's contribution. They didn't discuss the subject any further.

36

Frank O'Hara sat at his desk in the police station mulling over the facts as he knew them. So far he had one unsolved murder, with no more information now than at the beginning of the investigation. He had four sets of bones, two adults, two children, and nothing to tie the murder of Jake Hamilton to the bones. At this point, he still did not know if the two had anything to do with each other. Forensics had not been able to identify the bones except to tell him they appeared to belong to four victims whose disappearance was also a mystery. As far as he could determine, there was no missing family in the area for miles around. In fact, O'Hara could not find any report of such a group of people missing even when he consulted the FBI for help.

Another aspect of the situation puzzled him but failed to shed any light on the unknowns. He was made aware of a financial discrepancy at the university by his interviews with the comptroller when he attempted to discover more about the professor and his relationship to Chris Fanning. He thought there was more than coincidence that connected Fanning, the professor, the dead Jake Hamilton, and the hint of fiduciary scandal in the making. He just could not put it all together.

Both Fanning and the professor were non-committal when he'd asked them what Fanning was doing in Italy. O'Hara was not entirely happy with the answer that Fanning had been doing research on the antiquities having to do with the beginnings of Christianity in Italy. But he had nothing to go on in that direction. The more he thought about it, the more he came to the inescapable conclusion that Fanning and the professor were involved in some kind of secret conspiracy and that it was likely the missing grant monies were a part of it. He didn't know how these disparate pieces fit together, but he was determined to find out.

He made a decision. The next day he would present these facts to his boss and then he planned to question Karahsha at length. He also planned to carry out a search of the professor's laboratory to see what he could see.

37

The Body was now full grown. All the organ systems were fully developed and capable of functioning on their own now. The glass tank was actually too small for the encased organism, hindering His efforts at movement and giving the professor a concern that He might twist His lifelines to the point where He might harm Himself. The professor's relationship to the Body in the tank was different than it had been. No more did the organism express displeasure at being left alone. No more did He frolic in the tank, partly because there was not enough room, but also Karahsha suspected because He had achieved a certain level of maturity. The professor noted a marked difference in the reaction to His presence. The bath fluid had become progressively murky with the continued growth so it was hard for Karahsha to be sure, but he thought the being's eyes followed him and he was sure He moved his head in response to the professor's presence and movement about the room.

Karahsha, therefore, resolved to bring this phase of the experiment to an end. He summoned Fanning and Margie to his office and made this known to them. He told them that early the next morning he planned to release the new Messiah from His cocoon and begin the second phase of the Project. An air of electricity filled the small office. They looked at each other with an expression of joy that could not be communicated verbally. They hugged each other as if they had been rescued from a concentration camp. They danced around the small space like children on a kindergarten playground. Their enthusiasm exploded and Karahsha did something he'd never done before nor would ever do again. He took them all out for drinks and dinner, celebrating the achievement soon to be realized.

Later that night, Karahsha wheeled himself into the kitchen of his modest one story house heading straight for the refrigerator. There was nothing like a mouthful or two of strawberry ice cream to top off a long day. In hindsight, it was a wise decision to have bought a one story house considering his new wheelchair bound life. Something in him always preferred to be close to the ground. As he reached for the freezer door he heard a strange tap. Now, refrigerators and especially freezers make noises that will drive you crazy if you let them. But he wasn't sure if this was a refrigerator noise or some other noise. It sounded like it came from elsewhere in the house but he was tired and wasn't sure what he heard. He stared at the refrigerator for a couple of minutes, hearing the same noise again but closer since he was next to the refrigerator. He wondered if he was beginning to lose his mind or if someone might be after him once again. He was so tired and ill-prepared to do anything about it he was almost willing to let whoever it was who might be stalking him do what they were going to do to him. But, for the sake of the Project, he thought he would check out the noise, whatever it was, even just to rule out spooks in the night. He felt responsible for the new life's well-being and wouldn't hesitate to put himself in harm's way to protect it. He didn't realize it, but he was thinking like a parent.

Karahsha wheeled into his study where he kept a loaded Colt .45 in an unlocked drawer. He had forgotten the gun was there many times over the years, never having been an avid shooter. He surprised himself many times upon opening the drawer. As he felt the weight of the gun in his hands he was reminded of why he left it in the study and not the bedroom, as do most people. He simply spent more time in the study, often drifting to sleep in the comfy leather chair. Some days he never even went into the bedroom except to change clothes and shower.

He rested the Colt .45 in his lap and moved into the main hallway of the house. He heard another refrigerator type noise, though he was nowhere near the refrigerator. He took the gun in his hand then felt a sharp pain in his neck. Damn, that hurt. Well, not for very long. Uh oh, I'm feeling lightheaded. He wished it was a powerful bee that just stung him but he knew that wasn't the case. He heard footsteps coming towards him from behind.

Feeling dizzy, he slumped down into the wheelchair, his revolver falling to the floor. He briefly had the thought, better unconscious than dead. Then he saw and heard nothing.

~~~

Fanning had a dream that night he was in the back of a van or a truck bouncing on the hard floor. The vehicle must have been driving at a steady speed on an open highway with little traffic as he didn't sense the vehicle making any turns or using its brakes. He thought his leg touched another object, perhaps a bag of clothing or another person, he wasn't sure. Though he was pretty sure his life was in danger all he wanted to do was go back to sleep, which he did.

The next thing Fanning knew he was staring at the Milky Way, the band of light from billions of stars stretching across the night sky. What an awesome sight, he thought, before he realized he was slightly cold. He was relieved to no longer be lying on a hard surface like the back of a van though he couldn't be sure if he dreamed the van, remembered it, or if his brain was confabulating that he was transported to this spot in a van. One side of the brain will try to provide explanations for a troublesome situation so that the other side of the brain doesn't panic. Fanning sat up on the ground, which was well lit by stars in a sky free of city lights. In fact, there were no human made lights anywhere to be seen.

His mind raced around the question of how he came to this place. His interlopers must have snuck past or disabled the bodyguard at the house, broke into the house, then snatched him out of his bed. Or they might have snagged him when he went to the bathroom in the middle of the night which he usually did. Boy, these guys must be professionals, like the ones who stole him out of his hotel room in Italy. He worried what might have been done to his family, but was strangely comforted by the fact that he didn't see Margie or the kids with him presently. He knew that he and the professor were the main targets of whomever was behind the effort to stop the Project and hopefully they left his family out of it this time around. His kidnapers must have dumped him somewhere in the desert, perhaps near Hang Man's

Gulch where this whole adventure started. There his brain went again, trying to find the familiar in an unfamiliar situation.

Fanning assessed himself. All his limbs were attached, no nails or other foreign substances were lodged in his hands or wrists, no pain except for a little soreness in his neck muscles from having slept on a hard surface without a pillow. He had a tender spot on the back of his neck, perhaps where he was shot with a dart filled with tranquilizer. That's how scientists take down big animals, and that's probably what they did to him. His eyes were already well adjusted to the darkness, or rather lack of sunlight. He surveyed his surroundings, nothing but cacti, sagebrush, and sand. And stars, lots of them. He saw the shape of another body lying in the sand just a few feet away. Fanning hoped it was the professor and not Margie or one of his children. He instantly felt guilty for wishing it was the professor, what with his paralysis and all. The thought of the professor being there actually gave him a bit of hope, as long as he wasn't dead. That wouldn't be very hopeful. He was glad not to be alone, as being alone in the desert and foreign countries had caused him nothing but trouble.

Fanning moved towards the other body, which indeed belonged to the professor. He felt a pulse and checked his breathing. All seemed okay. He debated whether to shake the professor awake or pour cold water on his face. But alas he had no water or any idea where they could get some. That was a problem. He figured whatever was used to tranquilize him and the professor was going to keep Karahsha out until it wore off. That could be hours, Fanning thought, as he assumed that he recovered faster since he was younger and more muscular than the professor. Youth has its advantages, but not for long if they don't find something to drink.

After a few minutes Karahsha stirred. He too went through the same process of waking up, checking out his surroundings, realizing what kind of situation he was in. Fanning let him figure these things out instead of assaulting the professor with a ton of questions. Fanning was actually glad no one was asking him how he was and checking his vitals upon waking up, as that might have made him more worried than he needed to be in that moment.

Karahsha seemed reassured to see Fanning sitting next to him. They both knew exactly what had happened. No sense in wasting their breath on what was beyond their control. What was weighing on Fanning's mind was what do they do now? Pick a direction and go there? Walk around a bit, try to spot a home or some semblance of civilization? Find the tracks of the vehicle that brought them there and follow them towards a road? How would they see tracks at night? He figured they couldn't be too far from a road since their kidnapers probably didn't stray too far out into the open desert as they carried them both by hand away from their vehicle. They must have been strong, young men like the ones who captured him in Italy. Fanning knew in his bones that he and the professor weren't meant to be killed, just inconvenienced so the kidnapers could invade the lab and see how far along they were in the Project. He assumed the order from on high was that there were to be no more acts of violence. If they were meant to be delayed then they had only to find their way home from here.

"What do you think they injected us with?" asked Fanning.

"Oh, probably just some general anesthesia. You recovered faster as you have more body mass than I do. We'll be fine," responded Karahsha. "Did you see who did this to us? Was it the same guys as in Italy?"

"I couldn't see them."

"Neither could I," lamented Karahsha.

"What do you think they're going to do with the Body?"

"Take it. Or worse."

Neither of them wanted to contemplate what that might possibly entail.

Karahsha stared straight up at the sky. "It's so beautiful."

"Yeah, that's nice, but how do we get out of here?"

"Well, there's Little Bear, what you would call the Little Dipper." Karahsha responded as he calmly considered the stars. "Polaris, the North Star, is the last star on the handle. It appears not to move because it's within a degree of Celestial North."

Fanning studied astronomy at one point in high school but never took it seriously enough to be able to navigate by star as Karahsha could. The city lights of New York prevented any real attempt at amateur astronomy. He admired the professor's grasp of star navigation, a skill he must have developed as a curious youngster growing up in the deserts of Arizona.

Karahsha stretched his arm out towards the horizon and made a fist. Then he placed one fist on top of the other working his way up to Polaris. "Each fist is about ten degrees from the horizon. So that's about 30 degrees latitude from the horizon, or 30 degrees north of the equator. If we were at the North Pole it would be 90 degrees as Polaris would be directly above us. So for longitude, we have to calculate how many time zones we are from Greenwich Mean Time. Each time zone corresponds to 15 degrees of longitude." The professor consulted his wristwatch. "It's now 1:20AM."

"I was out for about three hours, that means they drove us about two hours or 120 miles outside of Tempe. That's a lot of places," said Fanning.

"Yes, but they're not all desert. If they drove west on the 10 we're either north or south of the freeway, and if they drove down the 10 we'd be somewhere east of the freeway near Casa Grande. Of course they could have gone down the 85 as well. I doubt they'd drop me on a reservation as I would never get lost. We know where north is, so we need to go either due east or northwest. If we pick wrong, we're toast."

"What's our longitude?" Fanning interjected.

"Well, we need to find the difference between the current time and Greenwich Mean Time. We're how many time zones from them, seven? Eight? I think it's eight. So that's eight time zones times 15 degrees per time zone. What's 15 times 8?"

Fanning, not expecting his math skills to be tested, struggled for a moment. He saw the professor calculating the time in his head and Fanning raced to beat him to it. "120," he blurted out.

"120!" Karahsha said excitedly. "So we're 120 degrees west and 30 degrees latitude north. Roughly."

"So . . . where are we?"

"Well, I grew up around 36 north by 109 west so I'd say we're west of Phoenix, north of the 10, maybe around Tonopah or Centennial."

"Are you sure?"

"Pretty sure. You learn a thing or two when you spend your youth in the desert alone."

Fanning studied the professor's face, realizing how lonely he must have been as a child, how isolated, unlike his peers with his interest in animals, biology, stars, the outdoors, the bigger questions of life. He saw how familiar Karahsha was with the desert, how at home he seemed even in his paralyzed condition, how the hospital, the university, the laboratory, and all they had done together was the fulfillment of a lifelong dream of a young, ambitious boy who had only himself to rely on in this hostile territory. In that moment Fanning determined to carry the professor all the way back to Tempe if necessary.

"All right. Let's do this," Fanning said.

Chris reached down and lifted the professor onto his shoulders in a fireman's carry.

"Remember, as long as Polaris is to our left we'll be going east," said Karahsha.

"Shouldn't we head south towards the 10?"

"What if I'm wrong and we're south of the 10? Then we'll just head further into desert."

Fanning thought it over, then headed east.

"And don't step on any snakes."

Fanning didn't need reminding of that.

After a couple of hours Fanning needed to rest. He gently laid the professor on the ground where he was pretty sure there weren't any nasty critters. After lying down for a bit himself, Fanning resumed carrying the professor. After a few more hours of walking and resting they noticed the first rays of sunlight on the eastern horizon ahead. If they were able to consult a map they would have seen they were actually heading in a southeasterly direction. By avoiding the hills in front of them and angling to their right they put themselves in the path of Interstate 10, where they saw headlights of a semi-truck passing by. Neither of them had the energy to climb onto the curb and wave down a passing car. But they did eventually find a rest stop with a payphone. After drinking their fill at a water fountain

Fanning placed a collect call to his wife. Margie and the kids were okay. She figured he left the house early in the morning while everyone else was still asleep. She wanted to call an ambulance for them but Fanning said that would take too much time. He instead asked her to call a taxi to pick them up and take them directly to the lab, and for her to meet them there. And bring a wheelchair.

38

Margie met them at the entrance to the Department of Pathology with a wheelchair. As soon as Karahsha was in the chair they dashed for the elevator and waited for what seemed like an eternity before the old rickety car reached his floor. Karahsha sped out of the elevator car at top speed, the anticipation almost killing him. As always, he wanted to be the first on the scene, which he was. He turned the key to his office, pushed the door open, and drove his wheelchair at top speed to the hidden rear corridor leading to the private inner sanctum of his secret laboratory. He fumbled slightly for the key, drove it home, and turned it over in the lock. He flung the door open and they could not believe what they saw inside.

There on the floor was the glass tank shattered into a million pieces. Water was all over the floor, his neatly arranged shelves with their aberrant microscopic life forms strewn all over, their contents spread on the floor like so much used garbage. The Body, the Messiah he'd devoted his life's work to reincarnating, was gone, nowhere to be seen.

Karahsha was not able to absorb the enormity of the disaster all at once. He opened his mouth to scream but no sound came. He pushed violently on his chair arms, propelling himself to the erect position. His voice came, a deep gurgling rasp from somewhere in his guts that crescendoed in a roar like that of an enraged elephant. He struggled to move from where he was but his paralyzed legs would not support him anymore. He collapsed onto the floor in a tangled mass of defeat, humiliation, and despair. He didn't even notice the glass shards biting into his skin. He wasn't aware of the lacerations, the bleeding, or the microscopic creatures entering his body and his bloodstream from the flood on the floor. He fell into a deep coma from the crack he'd taken on the head when he fell. Fanning and Margie lifted the professor off the floor and rushed him to the Emergency Department.

The professor recovered quickly after an overnight stay in hospital. His lacerations were sutured and a CAT scan showed no brain damage, so physically he appeared to be no worse off than before. Fanning and Margie visited him in the hospital, but as in his previous hospitalization he demanded to be released when he was ready the next morning, not when his attending physician said he could go. On the way home in Margie's car they discussed the possibilities of what might have happened. It was the professor's opinion that the Body was stolen by the same culprits who had attacked Fanning in Italy and abandoned them in the desert. There was no word, no suggestion as to what had happened. The three were against reporting the incident to the authorities. What would they be able to tell the police that wouldn't make them the butt of ridicule? How could they go about searching for their missing Messiah without being taken for some sort of collective nut cases? But what could have happened? Surely the Body didn't just lift Itself out of the tank and walk away. Or did it?

Frank O'Hara went to the professor's lab, but all he could find was a damp place on the floor which marked the site of the flooded room. Further questioning of the three involved in the Project revealed nothing to him since Karahsha, true to his word, stonewalled the detective, and Fanning followed his lead, giving nothing new to the police that they didn't already have. This proved extremely frustrating to O'Hara because he just knew in his heart of hearts that something had gone down, something unethical and maybe illegal. The financial difficulties the university was having were so tangled up in layers of bookkeeping obfuscation that it was going to take an accounting genius to untangle them, not a policeman.

39

The three were thrown into a fit of deep depression. The professor had been careful to generate an extra supply of DNA by the process of polymerase chain reaction, but to start all over, and then maybe have the same thing happen! The professor couldn't bring himself around to even consider the notion at this time. The three of them went on about their business in a state of shock, going through the motions of their relative duties without enthusiasm or interest. It was as if a member of their family had been kidnapped or disappeared without a trace. Fanning felt a grief as deep as when he had lost Jake Hamilton. And during their ordeal of not knowing there was absolutely nothing for them to do to locate the new Christ figure. They didn't even know if He was alive or if the Project had been a total failure. Fanning went through his graduate school activities numbly as if he were in a trance.

Margie tended to the children in her usual way, finding strength in herself from somewhere deep down. The recent disaster affected her the least, perhaps because she had the least invested emotionally in the Project, or perhaps she realized how important it was to be a full time mother to her children now and how Fanning needed her support. Visions of revenge were starting to fade from her priorities.

But the professor, he was almost as a dead man. He carried out his usual duties of teaching and functions in the pathology lab but his heart wasn't in it. He was scheming in his own mind, trying to react to this new catastrophe while being bothered by a new vexing symptom that intruded on his consciousness. He began to suffer from headaches and a troublesome difficulty with his memory. He had always been sharp and his mind was always the best part of him, but now he found himself succumbing to uncharacteristic lapses of memory and purpose. He'd wheel himself up to a closet door then forget why he'd done so. He found himself getting up in the middle of the night driving to his lab and remembering only when he reached the lab that the Project was over for all intents and purposes. He would hear his phone ring. When he went to answer it, he would only hear a dial tone. He started to question his sanity. For the first time in his life he began to have floaters, those ghostly remnants of cellular debris and breakdown that become trapped in the eyeball and float into and out of one's field of vision unexpectedly and uninvited. He made a tentative decision to give it all up, to retire into the wild land he still loved and just disappear into the countryside to live the native life close to Mother Earth by himself. He was prepared to simply ignore the university's more insistent demands for accountability and tell them to take their grant money and go straight to hell. He was sorry for what had happened to Fanning, but he was more devastated by the way things had turned out. The headaches worsened and now his balance was beginning to be affected. He thought, one good aspect about being in a wheelchair, he wouldn't fall to the floor and hurt himself.

He went to bed and closed his eyes. The floaters returned to his vision even with his eyes closed. He swore they were not amorphous blobs without shape any more, he could see some of them more clearly now. Some of them reminded him of corkscrews and little fish. Was he dreaming? Where would it end? How could he fall to his present condition from the pinnacle of success as he had so recently enjoyed? He slept in intermittent fits that brought no respite, no renewal, and no relief.

Karahsha considered his life and regarded himself a failure. He had worked all his life for recognition, vindication, and success. And he considered he had failed. He did not regard his many accomplishments aside from the Project as anything worthwhile. He felt totally defeated and confused. And now these vague symptoms added to his discomfort.

The floaters became worse so that they even started to interfere with his vision, at times making driving hazardous. The wafting shapes became more definite so that he could sometimes make out discrete features of the little beasts. The resemblance to his microscopic slide creatures did not provide him any reassurance. They seemed to be mocking him, cavorting in his eyeballs like they used to do on his slides. He was sure he was losing his mind. He could get no relief or escape from these little swimming devils. He considered suicide, but that was contrary to all he knew. He thought he might go to a physician or a psychiatrist but rejected that idea as not useful. He lost weight, and began to lose his hair. He found himself at certain locations without knowing how he got there. He became easily disoriented and lost in his own neighborhood, the area in which he'd spent the last twenty years. Strange joint pains tormented his knees, and his fingers sometimes jerked spasmodically, completely out of his control. After three days of this he received a strange and urgent phone call from Chris Fanning.

40

Fanning woke him in the middle of the night with a frantic phone call. The gist of it was that Margie had received a telephone call herself from the priest, Father McBride, at the Catholic Church. He had gone into the church for some midnight prayers and was astounded at what he'd discovered. Father was in a state of panic. Fanning was about to leave for the church and wanted the professor to meet him there. Unfortunately Margie wouldn't be able to find a babysitter at this time, so she was stuck home with the kids. Fanning offered to pick the professor up and in his state of exhaustion Karahsha was in no position to argue. He dressed quickly and waited for Fanning to come. They quickly maneuvered Karahsha in his wheelchair to the car Fanning was driving and on the short ride over to the church speculated on what could be so important to prompt Father McBride himself to call Margie and get them all roused in the middle of the night. When they arrived at the church neither of them were prepared for what they would next encounter.

Fanning had to push the professor's wheelchair up the church stairs or rather pull it up backwards. As they wheeled down the aisle, they could see Father McBride lying supine on the floor. A small trickle of blood came from the back of his head, but he was breathing. No one else was in the church. Fanning felt for a pulse and confirmed the priest had a viable circulation.

"Make sure his airway is clear," the professor commanded.

"I know a little first aid," Fanning growled back. "He seems to be alive, but comatose. I'll go call for an ambulance."

"No, no," the professor yelled. "Here, use my cellular phone." And he struggled to get it out of his shirt pocket. "No, I'll make the call. You make sure he continues to breathe. You know cardiopulmonary resuscitation?"

Fanning simply looked at the professor.

"He's breathing, he's breathing," Fanning yelled back. Fanning arose to go for help by seeking one of the Nuns of the Order, who were strangely absent. As he turned, he faced the altar which had been in the dark. Suddenly, a shaft of moonlight shone through a window bathing the altar in an eerie white light. Fanning was transfixed by the sight he witnessed. Karahsha could not believe his eyes. He stopped in his tracks, his hands clutching the rails of his wheelchair. He too was riveted by a sight no one had seen for two thousand years. There, on the altar, bathed in ethereal moonlight, was the Body of the living Christ, naked except for a loin cloth, blood actively trickling from the pierced hands and feet. There was a stab wound in the right side which oozed blood. The hands and feet were firmly fastened to the wooden cross which replaced the usual plaster one on the altar. The spikes were only slightly smaller than railroad spikes. They reminded Fanning of his own recent experience with spikes. The head slumped loosely on the chest. The eyes were closed. The long brown hair tumbled on each side of the face almost femininely. The small reddish beard was matted with dried blood. The skin bore evidence of a recent scourging. The forehead contained multiple puncture wounds and some blood weakly oozed from these as well. The Body bore evidence of dehydration and exhaustion, appreciated by the professor, only.

The two mortals were paralyzed, as if in the grip of a giant invisible hand holding them fast and mute. The still living Body on the cross showed no sign of pain or anguish. Rather It reflected the white light with a glow of Its own as if the light came from deep within, but it was no ordinary light either of them had ever seen. At that moment a wind of terrific force blew through the church, all the more remarkable because all the doors and windows were shut. Then something totally unexpected happened. The eyes on the cross flickered open, and for the most fleeting instant, regarded the both of them. The vaguest shadow of a suggestion of a smile passed over the lips and the chest heaved ever so slightly as if taking the final breath. The whole Body relaxed and drooped slightly. The flow of blood went from a trickle to a standstill right under their very eyes. The respiratory movements stopped, the head sagged onto the chest again, and all was quiet. It took an eternity before the two witnesses were released from their trancelike state. They looked at each other, both drained of any facial color.

"What does this mean?" they both wanted to cry out.

Then it was obvious what they must do. Fanning sprang to the altar and forced the cross' upright member out of its anchor, lifting it with a superhuman strength. With a power born of panic, he slowly eased the wooden cross down to the ground, with its load, until the Body lay supine on the floor. He felt for any breath or pulse, or any other sign of life. There was none.

Karahsha pushed himself out of his wheelchair for the second time in three days and threw himself onto the Body, starting cardiopulmonary resuscitation as best as he could. He had no IVs, no drugs, no endotracheal tubes, or even oxygen. After several minutes of this there was no response. Fanning looked around for some means to help the professor, totally forgetting about the unconscious priest. As he did, he noticed the priest lying on the ground, who now started to stir.

"Omigosh, I forgot about Father McBride."

He turned to see to the fallen priest while Karahsha continued with his vain efforts to revive the product of his years of labor. The professor now tried to pull out the nails that held Him fast to the cross but could not budge them with his bare hands. He had the use of only his upper extremities and trunk, and he nearly burst with frustration at not being able to do more.

By this time Father McBride had roused himself up. He sat up on the floor of the church in a bit of a daze wondering what had happened. Fanning, still incredulous, helped him to his feet, and the priest's legs shakily held him up. As he became more alert, it dawned on Father McBride what had happened to cause him to lose consciousness in the first place. He strode to the altar, Fanning supporting him. When he beheld the sight of the supine Body nailed to the cross and the paralyzed professor trying to pry him loose, he nearly fainted again. The blood drained from his face and he cried out, "Oh my God, what have I done? What have I done?" he said over and over.

"Wait a minute Father, I have to go call an ambulance."

The priest directed him to the nearest pay phone.

"Damn it, I said use my cell phone," Karahsha spat out violently.

While Fanning made the call, the two men eyed each other in a hostile fashion. "What did you mean, just a moment ago, when you said what have I done?" the professor demanded.

The priest collapsed on the first pew, consumed by guilt and by the impression he was responsible for this awful turn of events. He began to explain his small part in the difficulties the two researchers had been having. He explained how it was Margie who had told her two friends, the Nuns of the Order, about the Project in all innocence. He told how the nuns had passed the information on to him and how he in turn had given the information to the bishop. He assumed the bishop had informed the cardinal and that is how the details of the Project had become known to the highest levels of the church authorities. He did not want this, however, to be the final result. Now the professor became agitated.

"You," he screamed. "You and your church hierarchy are responsible for the problems we've been having. The murder of Jake Hamilton, the attempted assault on Margie and the kids, the kidnapping of Fanning here and his near death by crucifixion, my own attack and paralysis, and now you are admitting to responsibility for this latest outrage, the destruction of something I have been working on for years? Did you know your goons were responsible for paralyzing me? Do you even care?"

"No, no, I did not know that. And yes, of course I care. What kind of monster do you take me for? But my God that pales before this," he gestured toward the dead figure on the cross.

Fanning could only stare wide eyed, as he made his call to 911.

Finally the priest went to his rectory and returned with a claw hammer to pull out the nails. With difficulty, they freed the arms and feet from their cruel fastenings. They removed the Body from the cross, placed it on a bench, and commenced to wash away the blood from the wounds with moistened handkerchiefs. They washed the hair and beard which were matted with dried blood. They lit candles and sat around the slim Body, each absorbed in his own thoughts, while awaiting the rescue ambulance. From time to time Fanning went to feel the bruised wrists for a pulse and checked for any sign of life, however small. There was none. If they had had much experience with cardiopulmonary resuscitation, they would have continued the cardiac massage while waiting, but none of them were expert in this type of emergency treatment.

Soon, some of the nuns came in to see if they could help, and were aghast at what they saw before them. The nuns, like the priest, were confused and frightened and would not be consoled. One of them went out and returned with a long linen cloth with which to wrap the Body. The others lit candles and prayed. By the time an ambulance responded to the 911 call and arrived to take the Body to hospital, a small crowd had gathered outside the church. Somehow, a rumor had started that a Christ-like figure had been found nailed to a cross on the altar of the Holy Trinity Catholic Church in place of the usual ceramic statue of the crucifixion. As the paramedics started to load the Body on their gurney, a shout went up from the crowd to leave the Christ figure where It lay. A significant crowd had formed by that time. The paramedics became concerned at the threatening attitude of the mob, and decided to back off to see what would happen. The mob grew and became more threatening, so that the paramedics decided to leave while they still could.

When they left they called the police, who were likewise faced by a hostile mob of religious enthusiasts. The initial squad car had to call in for a backup. By the time the backup arrived a full scale riot was in progress and the police who were present were no match for it. The faithful were determined to have a say in the disposition of the Body because they were convinced a major miracle had taken place and they were determined to keep it in the church. Finally, the police were dispatched in enough numbers to deal with the crowd. The Body was at last taken, over Karahsha's protests, to the hospital for identification and examination, including autopsy. Unfortunately, the paramedics did not take the Body to the university hospital but rather to the local county hospital so that the jurisdiction was not under that of Professor Karahsha. The professor was by this time dispirited and disoriented.

The Nuns of the Order were left in a state of semi-shock as was Father McBride. It appeared that the work of years had gone up in smoke. The grandiose dreams of a spiritual reawakening were quenched for now. But

Chris Fanning was the only one who did not feel defeated. In fact, he felt vindicated, and on the threshold of a new adventure of his own.

Karahsha had to be hospitalized. He appeared to suffer from an unknown illness characterized by the presence in his bloodstream of an unidentified multifarious type of parasite which had never been seen before and for which no treatment existed. No known therapy seemed to have an effect on his condition. He shortly went into a coma from which he did not recover. After his death, Fanning revealed the entire unbelievable story to the university authorities. They, of course, did not give it any credence, while insisting on finding out what Fanning knew of the misspent funds. The computer records of the Project were confiscated by university officials. But even the secret laboratory records could not convince them of the veracity of Fanning's story.

Fanning retreated to the anonymity of his graduate studies, and gave up trying to convince the authorities of what had happened. In fact, he was regarded as a bit of an eccentric by those in whom he tried to confide.

41

The results of the autopsy report were made public to anyone who wanted to read it because of the great public interest in the so-called miracle. The county medical examiner had the autopsy conducted by a prominent forensic pathologist who released the final report as follows:

AUTOPSY REPORT: John Doe . . . No further identification available.

GROSS DESCRIPTION: This is a white male (Caucasian), bearded, with long shoulder length brown hair, found hanging from a cross at the Holy Trinity Catholic Church. The body was determined to have been deceased for approximately 12 hours before being autopsied. There were no distinguishing marks or scars save puncture holes in the wrists and feet where he had been nailed to the cross. The body shows signs of dehydration and what appears to be a stab wound from some type of sharp instrument in the right inferior costal region. The body measures 5 feet 11 inches (180 cm) and 150 lbs. (68 kg). There were multiple small puncture wounds around the forehead extending to the occipital area. There were multiple indentations of the skin of the buttocks and back of the legs bilaterally which appear to have been produced by some sort of flagellation. The body exhibited evidence of having died in the vertical position since there was pooling of blood around the lower extremities (livor mortis), relative blanching of the head, upper extremities, and upper torso. There was no sign of recent weight gain or loss except for the rather marked dehydration. There was no subcutaneous emphysema. There was no sign of gangrene, cellulitis, or infection. There were no obvious fractures of the long bones, the facial bones, or the pelvis. The teeth were all present and in a good state of preservation with none broken or abscessed. Post mortem X-rays of the head, cervical spine, and thoracic spine showed no signs of skull fracture, cervical fracture or dislocation, and no sign of thoracic trauma. Cultures of various body fluids, blood cerebrospinal fluid, bladder urine failed to grow any organisms. The blood and urine were negative for drugs, alcohol, and toxins. There were no puncture wounds of the arms, and no tracts to indicate drug abuse. The skin was dry as one would expect in dehydration. The distribution of the hair was male.

VITAL ORGANS: Gross and microscopic examination of the brain showed no particular pathologic changes that could be correlated with the cause of death. The brain weighed 1050 gm. Color was yellow-white with a minimum of edema. The heart weighed 300 gm and was colored dark maroon-red. The ventricles were distended, but not hypertrophic. There was no fatty degeneration. There was a puncture wound in the right atrium 1 mm long. The liver was edematous, that is to say, engorged with ascitic fluids but contained no evidence of cirrhosis of fatty infiltration. There was no sign of hepatitis, tumor, or cystic formation. There were no signs of infection or parasites. The bone marrow showed red cell hyperplasia, increased formation of red cells, presumably in response to hypoxia, (a deficiency of oxygen in the circulating blood), an attempt by the bone marrow to compensate for the low concentration of oxygen in the blood. The spikes used to impale the wrists and feet were seen to have passed through spaces between the bones and not to have produced injuries to the bones per se. The gastrointestinal tract was normal. The stomach contained no evidence of a meal within the twenty-four hours prior to death. The kidneys, ureters, adrenals, and urinary bladder were essentially normal in appearance. The lungs showed evidence of excessive fluid accumulation as in heart failure, but no underlying pathological condition. There was no sign of pneumonia or emphysema. The lungs had the appearance of belonging to a non-smoker who had not lived in an area of pollution. The vascular system showed no evidence of atherosclerosis or narrowing of the vessels. The coronary arteries were patent and without plaques. The vena cava was open and clean. The pulmonary arteries and veins showed no narrowing, no evidence of pulmonary hypertension, and contained no sign of pulmonary or fat embolus.

CONCLUSION AND DISCUSSION

This appears to have been a healthy male, about 33 or 34 years old, who died of asphyxia due to crucifixion. There has been no success in identifying him. There has been no family to come forward and claim the body. The fingerprints do not show up on any law enforcement computer banks. In view of the obvious superficial similarity to the most famous victim of crucifixion, mitochondrial DNA, or m-DNA, studies were performed. These studies seem to suggest that this present victim was related to such m-DNA to a group of Middle Eastern Semites who lived in Jerusalem some two thousand years ago. The mitochondrial DNA, in contrast to the vast majority of nuclear DNA, resides in the mitochondria. The mitochondria are extranuclear, located in the cytoplasm of the cells. They are responsible for using oxygen and the cell's food supply to produce the energy needed for cellular physiology and all other energy requirements of the cell. The very unique feature of the mitochondrial DNA, which constitute only a tiny percentage of total DNA, is the fact that they are transmitted to the embryo by the maternal parent only. This fact provides a valuable tracer of the maternal ancestry of any population and has been used to trace the migration of distinct groups of people from their places of origin to those areas which they now occupy.

END OF DOCUMENT

42

Professor Karahsha died in a coma never having regained consciousness. Attempts at making a diagnosis failed and his death was ascribed to an infection of unknown origin. An autopsy failed to elucidate the cause of death. The university carried out an investigation as to the professor's activities and his misuse of grant monies. His Project was condemned as unethical, immoral, and having been carried out in direct opposition to the policies and procedures of the institution. Fanning's role in the Project was also condemned and he was forced to take a leave of absence from his graduate school studies, although he was given the choice of re-matriculation in a year or two if he demonstrated the proper degree of remorse and apologized to the Catholic Church and the Italian government for his misdeeds. He was not criminally prosecuted for his crime of defacing the Shroud since it was determined he had suffered enough from the murder attempt on his life and the lingering effects on his hands.

As for the Body collected by the authorities and autopsied by the county coroner, a dispute arose about the jurisdiction of possession of the remains by various interested parties such as the Catholic Church, the Mormons, the local parishioners who wanted to make a shrine for It, and the county itself. The question was made moot because the Body disappeared on the third day from Its descent from the cross. It disappeared without a trace and no evidence of Its existence could be found by any law enforcement organization although an extensive search was launched. However, a strange phenomenon was reported from all over the world. During the three days from the discovery of the Body on the cross to the disappearance of the Body exactly three days later, no one was reported killed in a war, or in a crime or in any violent way. Further, there were no deaths of children from the serious illnesses that plagued them during that period. No leukemia deaths, no child abuse deaths, no trauma deaths were noted all over the world. There were no deaths attributed to famine or any natural disasters during that period either. No one had a rational explanation.

Chris Fanning was determined to finish his graduate studies in molecular biology. He decided to wait out the time during which he was supposed to repent and instead set out to learn all he could about genetics, recombinant DNA, and the Human Genome Project. By day he hounded the libraries and studied all that he could on the subjects mentioned. By night he could be seen working in a makeshift laboratory he had built in a small room off his garage. He had a long way to go to achieve the sophistication of the professor, his mentor in these manners, but he was hard at work with DNA samples of his own, obtained, shall we say, by not the most ethical means. He was at a distinct disadvantage, working as he was, without the facilities of a university laboratory. But he was determined to carry out the work of the late professor in one way or another. Margie's fears of losing him to constant work were unfortunately coming to pass.

The samples he worked on were labeled Smilodon DNA, obtained from the teeth of museum specimens which had been preserved in prehistoric ice. In reserve, he had blood samples labeled Jake Hamilton and Joseph Karahsha.

Made in the USA
Monee, IL
23 July 2021